BOOKS BY B.K. BORISON

LOVELIGHT

Lovelight Farms
In the Weeds
Mixed Signals
Business Casual

HEARTSTRINGS

First-Time Caller
And Now, Back to You

PRAISE FOR B.K. BORISON'S *FIRST-TIME CALLER*

'It will thaw even the hardest hearts'

People

'Bursting with humour and heart. . . . Borison gives readers a laugh-out-loud romp grounded by the hard knocks life has dealt her two protagonists. Readers looking for a love story that will touch both their hearts and their funny bone[s] need look no further'

Entertainment Weekly

'*First-Time Caller* is a beautiful, steamy, effervescent romance that pours hope and love right into your soul! Absolute magic lives inside these pages'

Sarah Adams, *New York Times* bestselling author of *In Your Dreams*

'*First-Time Caller* made me feel like I was reading my favourite story for the first time – because I was. Bright, effervescent and painfully relatable, B.K. Borison's writing is a masterclass in tender care. I was kicking my heels and smiling through my tears – what a joyful ode to happily ever after!'

Ashley Poston, *New York Times* bestselling author of *Sounds Like Love*

'*First-Time Caller* is everything: tender, sexy, stuffed with flirty banter that had me screaming into my pillow. Full of characters who feel real, like family. A beautiful love letter to love and the movie that made me believe in it. Infused with the kind of magic I can't properly put into words, because B.K. Borison took all the prettiest ones for this book. It's B.K. at her very best, a reminder that it's her world and we're the lucky readers who get to live in it. Hang this one in the Louvre'

Jessica Joyce, *USA Today* bestselling author of *The Ex Vows*

'Sharp, swoon-worthy and profoundly romantic – *First-Time Caller* is brimming with heart, vulnerability and humour. B.K. Borison handles her characters and their stories with such care that you can't help but clutch at your chest as you cheer them towards their happy ending. Aiden and Lucie remind us what a truly courageous thing it is to both be loved and give love in return'

Lyla Sage, *New York Times* bestselling author of *Soul Searching*

'*First-Time Caller* is going to blow fans of Borison away. It is filled to the brim with brilliant prose, delicious banter and enough flirting to make any reader blush. While still feeling fresh, new and current, *First-Time Caller* somehow also manages to evoke feelings of nostalgia that brought me to tears on multiple occasions. This was a heart-clutching, giddy-grinning and sexy-steamy read from beginning to end and I truly could not love it more'

Hannah Bonam-Young, *USA Today* bestselling author of *People Watching*

'A perfect romance in every way – off-the-charts chemistry, banter for days and an emotional connection that I'll be thinking about for a long time. *First-Time Caller* is a total charmer'

Annabel Monaghan, *New York Times* bestselling author of *It's a Love Story*

'Chemistry that sizzles across airwaves! *First-Time Caller* effortlessly draws you in and keeps you hooked until the very last chapter. With dynamic characters, sharp wit and laugh-out-loud moments, you'll fall in love with every turn of the page'

Bal Khabra, *USA Today* bestselling author of *Revolve*

'B.K. Borison's *First-Time Caller* is an unmissable modern romance – B.K. manages to be classic and incredibly fresh at the same time. Lucie and Aiden's blistering chemistry and heart-melting connection will leave you swooning. A fresh, funny and unforgettable love story filled with banter, emotion and all of Baltimore's charm'

Nikki Payne, author of *The Princess and the P.I.*

'A wonderfully tender and sexy story full of swoon-worthy lines and perfect moments that will elicit smiles, sighs and tears and keep readers thoroughly invested in the happily ever after'

Library Journal (starred review)

'Lucie and Aiden are perfectly imperfect together and will have eager readers rooting for their romance. Quirky supporting characters . . . add depth, while Borison's skilful plotting keeps the pages flying. This first-rate tale will resonate with true romantics'

Publishers Weekly

'Warm-hearted and thoroughly delightful, Borison's winning latest will likely expand the fan base that fell for her Lovelight series'

Booklist

PRAISE FOR THE LOVELIGHT SERIES

'I'll never pass up an opportunity to head back to Lovelight Farms. Charlie and Nova are the perfect mix of sweet, funny and sexy . . . I remain enchanted by everything [B.K. Borison] writes'

Hannah Grace, *New York Times* bestselling author of *Daydream*

'B.K. Borison just gets better and better! *Business Casual* is a magical combination of cosy and heartwarming yet irresistibly tender and sexy. The result is a soul-satisfying romance that will burrow itself deep into your heart and stay there'

Amy Lea, international bestselling author of *The Bodyguard Affair*

'Sparkling, immersive and cosy AF. The chemistry between grumpy, guarded Nova and sweet, golden-retriever Charlie is positively electric. I love spending time in Inglewild. It's as much fun as watching an episode of *Gilmore Girls*, except no one is an asshole. *Business Casual* is B.K. Borison at her best'

Rosie Danan, *USA Today* bestselling author of *Fan Service*

'The butterflies started right from the beginning with these two [in *Business Casual*], but I didn't expect anything less from B.K. Borison. She's a magician with those butterflies'

Penny Reid, *New York Times* bestselling author of the Winston Brothers series

'Charlie and Nova's story was everything I'd hoped for and so much more. This is B.K. Borison's best writing yet and I cannot wait for her many fans to fall in love with Charlie and Nova too'

Chloe Liese, *USA Today* bestselling author of *Once Smitten, Twice Shy*

'Oh, how I love spending time with B.K. Borison's lovable characters in the beyond-charming small town of Inglewild! *Business Casual* is cosy yet high heat and so, so sweet – like toasting marshmallows over an autumn bonfire. This is the comfort read my grumpy/sunshine-adoring heart needed'

Sarah Adler, *USA Today* bestselling author of *Finders Keepers*

AND NOW, BACK TO YOU

B.K. BORISON

PAN BOOKS

First published in the US 2026 by Berkley

This paperback edition first published in the UK 2026 by Pan Books
an imprint of Pan Macmillan
The Smithson, 6 Briset Street, London EC1M 5NR
EU representative: Macmillan Publishers Ireland Ltd, 1st Floor,
The Liffey Trust Centre, 117–126 Sheriff Street Upper,
Dublin 1 D01 YC43
Associated companies throughout the world

ISBN 978-1-0350-7391-7

Copyright © B.K. Borison 2025
Excerpt from *Lovelight Farms* © B.K. Borison 2021

The right of B.K. Borison to be identified as the
author of this work has been asserted in accordance with
the Copyright, Designs and Patents Act 1988.

Published by arrangement with Berkley,
an imprint of Penguin Publishing Group, a division of
Penguin Random House LLC.

All rights reserved. No part of this publication may be reproduced, stored in a retrieval system, or transmitted, in any form, or by any means (including, without limitation, electronic, mechanical, photocopying, recording or otherwise) without the prior written permission of the publisher. No part of this book may be used or reproduced in any manner for the purpose of training artificial intelligence technologies or systems. This work is reserved from text and data mining (Article 4(3) Directive (EU) 2019/790).

Pan Macmillan does not have any control over, or any responsibility for,
any author or third-party websites (including, without limitation, URLS,
emails and QR codes) referred to in or on this book.

3 5 7 9 8 6 4 2

A CIP catalogue record for this book is available from the British Library.

Printed and bound in the UK using 100% Renewable Electricity by CPI Group (UK) Ltd

Book design by Daniel Brount

This book is sold subject to the condition that it shall not, by way of trade or otherwise, be lent, hired out, or otherwise circulated without the publisher's prior consent in any form of binding or cover other than that in which it is published and without a similar condition including this condition being imposed on the subsequent purchaser. The publisher does not authorize the use or reproduction of any part of this book in any manner for the purpose of training artificial intelligence technologies or systems. The publisher expressly reserves this book from the Text and Data Mining exception in accordance with Article 4(3) of the European Union Digital Single Market Directive 2019/790.

Visit **www.panmacmillan.com** to read more about
all our books and to buy them.

For the sunshine optimists.
And the cloudy skies they brighten.

AND NOW, BACK TO YOU

CHAPTER 1

JACKSON

"Do you believe in fate?"

"I believe that you should put your shoes on," I answer without looking up from the toaster oven.

"Answer the question first."

"I don't think I will, thanks."

I slept like garbage last night. There's an unidentified substance on one of my glasses lenses from packing lunches. I had to switch my Tuesday shirt with my Thursday shirt after an unfortunate incident with the peanut butter jar, and the only thing holding me together is the hope and glory of the emergency cruffin that's currently in the toaster oven. I refuse to burn it.

Adeline huffs. "This is a serious question, Jackson."

"A serious question at half past seven on a Tuesday morning is not a serious question, Addie."

She is undeterred next to me, starry-eyed and shoveling Lucky Charms into her mouth. A horseshoe marshmallow flies into the sink.

"Do you believe in fate?" she asks again.

"Do I believe in cosmic forces that guide our decision-making and lead us on a predestined path to an already decided end?" I twist the toaster oven knob hard to the right. "Absolutely not."

Her eyes widen. "*Really?* After everything we've been through?" Adeline hip-checks me on the way to return the cereal box she's been eating directly out of, her face a teenage mask of outrage. "Don't you think fate brought me, you, and Penelope together?"

I snort. "No. I believe Child Protective Services brought us together. Custody hearings. Our mother's inability to be a responsible parent." I nod toward the front hallway. "Shoes, please. We're running late."

"I need my bonus cereal first." Adeline exchanges the Lucky Charms for the Froot Loops and pours them into a rogue coffee mug, exactly one piece of cereal at a time. I stand at the toaster oven and try not to have a mental breakdown.

"Are you doing this on purpose?"

She slants me a look only a fifteen-year-old can. "What?"

"The thing with the cereal."

Another three loops hit the sides of her container. *Plop. Plop. Plop.* She stares at me with a smirk. "What thing with the cereal?"

"Never mind." I don't have time for this. I pop open the front of the toaster oven and slide out the tiny tray holding my sanity. "Where's your sister?"

"Why is she *my* sister when she's late, but *your* sister when she's ordering that weird hippie pizza you like?"

I carefully wrap the cruffin in a paper towel and cradle it close to my chest. Like a newborn.

Adeline frowns. "Did you sleep last night?"

"I did." Four hours, give or take, but I was definitely unconscious at some point.

"Don't lie to me. You're eating your emergency cruffin and you're being more snippy than usual."

"I'm never snippy." I grab the cereal box out of her hand and put it back in the pantry behind us, ignoring her pout. "And I'm not that predictable."

"Jackson," Adeline says. "You're the most predictable person I know."

She hikes her backpack higher over her shoulder, her dark blond hair swinging in the ponytail she tugged it into. For all the things my mother did lack—common sense, the concept of a schedule, the ability to remember to feed her children—she didn't miss when it came to passing on her genetics.

Honey blond hair with just a hint of curl. Pale blue eyes. The way our bottom lip dips on one side when we smile. Adeline, Penelope, and I might as well be carbon copies of one another, different fathers be damned.

"Why do we have to leave so early?" Adeline whines.

"Because I have a meeting at the station."

Adeline's eyes narrow. "About what?"

"I have no idea." My role at the radio station doesn't usually require one-on-one meetings with the boss. I occupy a solid thirty-six seconds of airtime every hour. I report the weather and traffic, and then I disappear into the background. Exactly how I like it.

The rest of my time is spent managing the finances for our local station. The spreadsheets calm me. Maybe Maggie, the station manager in charge of 101.6 LITE FM, wants to talk about my new color-coding strategy.

"Is Maggie going to give you your own show?"

I don't like the thread of excitement I hear in her voice. Or the sheer panic that immediately grips me by the throat.

"No, I don't think she wants to do that."

"Why not?"

"Because I'd have nothing to talk about."

"Or maybe you'd have *too much* to talk about," Adeline says, shuffling forward to pluck off the corner of my cruffin. I try to slap her hand away, but she manages a piece, popping it into her mouth with a grin of victory. "Last time you covered for Aiden, you ranted for, like, twenty-three minutes about snow lightning."

For someone who voluntarily works in radio, I don't have a great relationship with ad-libbing. Whenever I'm asked to fill in for one of the other hosts, I tend to go off the rails. It's not so much stage fright as it is . . . a complete and total break from reality. Without my script, my brain goes blank. I lose command of the English language. I'm pretty sure I black out. I never remember a thing about it, either, except a lingering sense of humiliation.

I sigh. "You shouldn't be listening to me on the radio. You should be sleeping."

"Ms. Singh doesn't mind."

Our eighty-six-year-old neighbor stays with the girls on the nights I work late. She sits in the living room and works on her never-ending cross-stitch and makes passive-aggressive comments about the lack of sweets in the pantry. "Oh, good. I'm glad Ms. Singh doesn't mind."

"Penelope and I like to listen sometimes when we're falling asleep. Do you remember when we were little, and you used to read us the forecast instead of bedtime stories?"

"Yeah, I remember." I remember their little heads tucked together on a shared pillow, looking up at me with wide, unblinking blue eyes. *Mostly cloudy with a low around fifty-nine. Monday. A chance of showers. Partly sunny with a high near seventy-three.* I had no idea what I was doing with them, but I knew I wanted to give them something better than they had. Something better than *I* had. "You can always text me when I'm at the station. Or if you don't want me gone at night anymore, I can restructure my hours. I don't need to do the weather report."

Adeline shakes her head. "Absolutely not. You love doing the weather report, and we're fine here. Ms. Singh has been working on matching scarves for us. Can't burst her bubble." She sneaks over and steals another bite of my cruffin. I allow it. "Plus, I kind of like the idea of you putting the entire city of Baltimore to sleep."

I consider that. "I can't tell if that's a compliment or not."

"It's a compliment." She collects her coffee mug of cereal from the counter. "I'll let you know if we're unhappy with your work situation."

"Promise?"

"When have we ever had an issue with letting you know we're unhappy?" She flicks me in the middle of my glasses. "I promise, Jackie."

"Good."

When I officially took custody of the girls, I told them I might not always do the right thing with them, but I promised to try. All they had to do was talk to me. I was only twenty and they were only eight, but we figured out how to be a family.

Which is why I hope I'm not being fired from my job this morning. This meeting with Maggie appeared on my calendar late last night without any context. Just a blank invitation, a block of time shaded in blue, and the foreboding subject line PLANNING.

My attention ping-pongs between the clock, the stairs, and the front door.

"Penelope!" I bellow. Adeline flinches. "We need to go!"

"I'm coming!" she screeches back.

"You said that ten minutes ago!"

"Yes, well, I'm working on it!"

"Why don't I believe you?"

"Because you have trust issues!" immediately floats down the stairs. "Something to discuss with your therapist!" she adds.

"I have! At length!" Another number ticks forward on the

glowing neon clock beneath the microwave. "If you're not down here in thirty seconds—"

"I'm coming, I'm coming," she manages, breathless, her feet pounding down the stairs. A head of blond hair appears, cropped to just above her shoulders. When she was ten, she decided she wanted to be *different* from her twin. That manifested with a self-administered haircut in her bedroom closet that had them both crying for two weeks afterward.

She blindly picks up her backpack off the floor, her nose glued to her phone.

"Penelope. You know the rules. No phones before school."

She holds up her hand. "There's a reason."

I grab my messenger bag and loop it over my shoulder. "If I have to listen to another podcast about whether you're Team Conrad or Team Jeremiah, I'm going to lose my mind."

She spares me a quick disgusted look. "That's because you can't handle being wrong."

"The *only* reason you're Team Jeremiah is because of their on-screen chemistry," I say, fired up all over again. Listening to that podcast in the car on the way to Ocean City was the worst decision I've ever made. Neither of us talked to each other for a full day. "If you paid attention to the damned books, you'd be Team Conrad."

Penelope quickly shushes me as Adeline tips over to get a look at the screen. Her eyes widen.

"Oh, shit," Adeline says. "I didn't realize that was today."

I begrudgingly try to look over both of their shoulders, but the phone is angled down and two heads of blond hair block my view. "What are you talking about? What's happening?"

"The turtle," they say in unison.

"What turtle?"

Adeline reaches over and turns up the volume on the side of Penelope's phone. A familiar feminine voice fills the kitchen.

"Welcome back, Baltimore. We're having a shell of a time down at the National Aquarium as we await the arrival of Domino, a green sea turtle who is ready to make a splash in Charm City."

I'd know that voice anywhere. In the dark. In the startling light of day. In my very limited sleep. In my *nightmares*. Clear and bright and infused with an unflagging sense of optimism, it is my own personal harbinger of doom.

I try to grab the phone, hell-bent on tossing it out the window, but Penelope shifts to the left without bothering to look up. Adeline moves with her, plucking the phone out of her hand and giving me her back, neither of them turning away from the broadcast on the screen.

I sigh in defeat. "Why are you watching Delilah Stewart?"

"Because of the turtle," Penelope says. "And because I like Delilah Stewart."

"You do *not* like Delilah Stewart," I say, irritation making my throat feel tight. It's one thing for all of Baltimore to be in love with the reporter from YBAL News. It's another thing entirely for my *sisters* to fall under her spell.

Adeline fixes me with a look. "You're still on that kick, huh?"

"It's not a kick." A kick implies something fleeting. My stance on Delilah Stewart has been long-standing and consistent. I scarf down the rest of my cruffin and chew aggressively. "She has no respect for the weather."

"What does *respect for the weather* look like?"

"She uses too many puns," I say. "And props. No self-respecting weather reporter uses props."

Delilah Stewart approaches the weather report like a kid in a candy shop. Everything is wonderful. Nothing is an inconvenience.

Unexpected thunderstorms? Not a problem. Humidity so thick it feels like you're walking through Jell-O? Delightful.

She appears on the six o'clock news with her pretty, chestnut-colored hair and sunny smile and no one even cares if she's right or wrong. I bet she doesn't get six-page-long emails from Cathy over in Dundalk about how a misguided weather report caused her Buick to flood because she didn't close the sunroof.

Never mind that Cathy in Dundalk never should have left her sunroof open in the first place.

I have a perfectly justified, professional dislike of Delilah Stewart and her methods.

"I think you're still mad Delilah spilled pudding all over your favorite shirt," Penelope offers, not looking up from the phone. "And because she scratched your car door."

"Yes, she did do both of those things."

In addition to her slapstick weather coverage, Delilah Stewart is an absolute disaster of a human being.

The television broadcast studio is right across the street from the radio station. We share a parking lot on what the city affectionately calls Broadcast Hill. I tend to see Delilah three to five times a week, and it almost always ends with the destruction of something in my possession. A scarf. My favorite green shirt. The passenger-side door of my car.

"Is that why you hate her?" Penelope asks.

"I don't hate her," I grumble.

I don't understand her. I find her irritating. Abrasive. *Chaotic.* I've never done well with messy, and Delilah Stewart is a hurricane wrapped in delusion draped in mismatched pastels with a stain from whatever she had for lunch smack-dab in the middle of her chest.

"She's a lot," I add.

Penelope and Adeline exchange a look.

"What?"

"Are you still leaving Post-it notes on the window of her car?"

I hesitate. "Only when she parks over the line." Which is Tuesdays and Wednesdays and—oddly enough—every other Friday. Her chaos *does* seem to follow a pattern. If you squint. "I'm nice about it," I defend.

"You leave passive-aggressive Post-it notes on the window of her car, Jackson. How is that nice?"

"I could leave aggressive-*aggressive* notes on the window of her car."

Adeline gives me another unamused look. "I think you're just jealous *she* doesn't turn into a rambling encyclopedia of weather whenever she's in front of a camera."

I drag my hand over my face. This morning has completely deteriorated.

"Yeah, that's probably a fair point." I grab the phone out of Adeline's hand. "Why is she wearing a turtle costume?"

"Haven't you been paying attention? There's a new turtle at the aquarium."

On the tiny phone screen, Delilah beams at the camera, ignoring the people behind her who stop, stare, and point at the oversized shell she has strapped to her back. It reminds me of the broadcast she did for Orioles opening day, where she was dressed like a giant jar of relish. Where does she manage to find these outfits? *Ridiculous.*

"That doesn't explain why Delilah is reporting on it." I bring the phone closer to my face. "She's supposed to do the weather."

Penelope snatches her phone back. "She's been branching out. Last week she did a story on how they're trying to make the Inner Harbor swimmable by the spring."

A laugh coughs out of me. The last time I was down by the harbor, there was an entire shopping cart floating off the edge of the Bond Street dock. "That's a real thing? I thought it was a joke."

They both ignore me. "And the week before that, she did a cool story about the arboretum. She's more than the weather, Jackson."

Yes, apparently, she's got a soft spot for turtles named Domino and thematic costumes.

"Okay, well, we are going to be more than late if we don't get in the car right now." I check my watch and sigh. I'm barely going to make school drop-off. I'm almost certainly going to be late for Maggie's last-minute meeting.

Maggie's last-minute, panic-inducing meeting.

An uncomfortable itch settles at the back of my neck. "Give me your phone, please."

I'm hit with the full force of two matching pouts, but they relinquish the phone without any additional commentary. They wander down the hallway away from me, collecting the things they need for school, probably grumbling under their breath about what an overbearing asshole their brother is.

I go to darken the screen, but I'm distracted by Delilah Stewart instead.

She waves one finned hand at the camera, a crooked smile so wide it makes her eyes squint shut. She looks absurd standing there at the edge of the pier, her curled hair falling in loose waves over her shoulders and her round cheeks pink from the cold. Her turtle shell keeps slipping off her left shoulder, and there's a group of teenagers taking turns sprinting through the frame about ten feet behind her.

But she smiles in the face of all of it. Perhaps in spite of it.

"Domino could have ended up anywhere, and yet he's here with us. Set to arrive at one of the top rehabilitation facilities for marine life in the country. All because he was somewhere he wasn't supposed to be. It looks like fate took

a hand in delivering this new shell-ebrity"—I roll my eyes—*"to his forever home."*

I blink at the screen. Fate. A ridiculous concept meant for ridiculous people. Teenage girls and whimsical weather women, hell-bent on turning science into a circus. I snort and finally darken the phone.

What a bizarre woman.

DELILAH STEWART: Delilah Stewart, reporting live from the National Aquarium. And now, back to you.

CHAPTER 2

DELILAH

Just keep smiling, I say to myself as I stare at the tiny red light on the camera. *You're almost there. A few more minutes. Just keep smiling.*

Mark, our beleaguered and bearded cameraman, holds up his hand and counts down from five. When his thumb finally tucks in, the little light goes dark and I release my pent-up sigh, pushing my turtle helmet off my forehead.

"You got it?"

He grunts, which is Mark for *Yes, well done. Your finest broadcast yet. I'm so proud of you.* He communicates mainly in monosyllabic sounds, hand signals, and vaguely apathetic looks. I have to fill in a lot of the blanks with Mark, but it works for us. After three years of partnership, I've almost cracked that hard exterior.

Almost.

"Great." I try to shimmy out of the shell strapped to my back. It's February in Baltimore, but the turtle costume is hot and the shell is heavy. I'm sweating bullets underneath this thing. I have no idea where Keith—my boss, and apparent turtle aficionado—even found it.

The University of Maryland? Did he steal it from Testudo himself?

I unclip my helmet and glance at Mark. "Are we heading back to the station or does Keith want me to interview the turtle?"

I'm only half joking. My assignments have been steadily increasing in absurdity. Two weeks ago, Keith had me attend the Toilet Races at Hampdenfest. Usually, I wouldn't bat an eye at reporting on the Baltimore-beloved tradition—especially in my own neighborhood—but he had me sit on an actual toilet for the duration of the broadcast.

It was hard to smile that day.

I want to be taken seriously. It's hard to be taken seriously when you're sitting on toilets and wearing turtle shells.

Mark doesn't look up from his phone, flicking across the screen with his thumb. I'm pretty sure I could be hit by a city bus and he wouldn't notice. For a cameraman, his attention span is very limited.

"Mark," I try again. "Are we done?"

He nods, not bothering with eye contact. "Yeah. You're due back at the station."

I try to shimmy my other arm out of the turtle shell strap, but it's twisted. I turn, around and around, like a dog chasing her tail. "I know. The weather report is in, like, thirty minutes."

"Not for that," he says. "Leon is doing the weather this morning. Keith wants you in a meeting."

I stop trying to chase my strap, my heart sinking like a stone. "But I always do the morning report."

The weather is what I *want* to be reporting on. But somehow, I've landed in quirky feature hell instead. Toilets and turtles and an empty warehouse Keith said was a historical renovation but really turned out to just be a dumping site.

Mark finally looks up from his phone, his face twisted into something vaguely sympathetic. "Not today. Today I'm supposed to drop you off at Keith's office as soon as we're back. No excuses."

I bristle. "What? Are you my chaperone? Am I a flight risk?"

"I'm not your chaperone, although—" Mark's mouth turns up at the corners. "You did fail to show up to the staff meeting where we reviewed your Pimlico coverage."

I sniff and avert my attention to the glistening water of the harbor. The sun is bright today, not a cloud in the sky.

"Yes, well, my car wouldn't start." I also didn't feel the need to watch the footage of me slipping and face-planting in the mud at the racetrack thirteen times over. We rarely review footage of past features, but for some reason Keith demanded that the entire station gather to take a look at that specific coverage. He probably had the moment I slipped and fell live on air recalibrated in slow motion and set to some ridiculous song. I bet it's the screen saver on his computer. Me, at the racetrack in my sunshine yellow derby hat, covered in mud from my chin to my shins.

I don't know when Keith started explicitly taking joy in watching me humiliate myself, but it's been a slow slog through hell. I'm tired. I'm so tired of him scraping the bottom of the barrel and assigning me whatever he dregs up. I've reported while standing in the harbor next to a half-submerged shopping cart. I've reported live from Fort McHenry while wearing a colonial dress, two sizes too big. I've reported with an actual monkey on my head.

And while I've never had a problem looking ridiculous on camera, it's starting to feel a little mean-spirited.

This was supposed to be my dream job, not my living nightmare.

"I'm really not doing the weather today?" I ask Mark again.

"Not today." He pauses in his collection of camera equipment and squints up at me. "Sorry."

God, it must be bad if Mark is saying sorry. He once whacked me in the head with a mic boom and told me it was *good for my overall constitution*.

"It's fine." I slip the fins off my hands and shove them under my arm. "Hey, did Luna try that recipe I gave you?"

Mark's whole face brightens at the mention of his daughter. "Yeah, you really saved the day with that, thanks. It worked great for her science experiment." He scratches at his jaw. "Why did you have a recipe for slime lying around anyway?"

Because I was a nerd of a kid who turned into a nerd of an adult. "Do you not have slime recipes lying around?" Mark blinks. "Okay, well, your loss." I push my sleeve up and glance at my watch with a sigh. "We should probably get going, huh?"

Mark's eyes narrow in suspicion. "Yeah, we should."

"Back to the station."

"Back to the station," he agrees, his entire being basically the dictionary definitions of *confused* and *alarmed*.

I bet he was prepared to toss me in the van and hightail it back, me kicking and screaming the entire time. But I don't have the energy. I could fight Keith on the whole bullshit assignment thing, but I've never been much of a fighter.

I always thought if I just did a good job with the tasks assigned to me, then I'd be able to climb the corporate ladder. But the corporate ladder has turned out to be a bottomless pit from which there is no escape, lorded over by a man with a severe superiority complex.

"Where did you park the van?" I ask.

Mark loops our stash of wires over his shoulder. "Down by the dolphin fountain."

He's watching me like I'm about to make a break for it. Like I'm going to sprint down a Baltimore side street in full turtle costume.

"Great. I'll meet you there."

"You better."

The threat is unnecessary. The walk to the van is as uneventful as a walk through a busy downtown area in a turtle costume can be. Cars slow down and honk. A guy on a bicycle yells, "Fins up, bro!" as he speeds past. Someone bellows, *"AND NOW, BACK TO YOUUUUUU,"* from one pier over, his hands cupped around his mouth. I laugh and wave cheerfully at the attention, a bit of my Keith-inspired dread slipping away.

I love this part. I love connecting with my community. I love making people smile. I love knowing that somewhere on the other side of the city, my grandpa is sitting in his favorite spot on his favorite couch, watching me on his television. No matter how silly the story, there's always a part of me that hopes I'm brightening someone's day.

I grew up in Baltimore, watching the news on a staticky television in my grandpa's cramped living room. The live, local, and late-breaking has been the backdrop to every major event in my life. I've always wanted to be a part of that magic.

I just never thought it would be dressed as a turtle.

The news van is right where we left it, tucked between an out-of-service ice-cream truck and a dumpster. I finally manage to get the shell off my back and fling it inside, grabbing for the duffel I left just behind the passenger seat. I unzip it while muttering under my breath about slime recipes and Keith and turtles named Domino, all while wishing desperately that the ice-cream truck would slide open its doors and deliver me a strawberry sundae.

I rummage around in my bag. Two empty water bottles. A police scanner. A flyer from a Christmas tree farm on the Eastern Shore and a postcard from some antiques shop in Annapolis. A compact, my favorite ruby red lipstick, and a brush with a broken handle.

Not a single sweater to be found. Or the navy blue slacks I could have sworn I packed last night.

"No," I breathe, digging through the bag like a secret compartment might open up and reveal a wardrobe decision that isn't a turtle suit. "No."

Mark tosses his cord collection in next to my shell, then his camera case. "Ready to go?"

"No."

"Why not?"

"I can't find my clothes."

His eyes flick down and up again. "Are you not . . . wearing clothes?"

I stop trying to turn my bag inside out. "This is a turtle suit, Mark."

"And yet, there are pants."

I stare down at my feet. My flipper-covered feet. "These are turtle pants."

"I don't see the difference, to be honest."

"I don't—" I huff, rolling my lips together. "You know what? Never mind. I need a change of clothes. Can we swing by my house on the way to the station?"

Mark gently pinches my bicep between his thumb and forefinger and guides me around to the front of the news van. He deposits me at the passenger-side door and pats the top of my head. Of course, my side is the dumpster side. "We don't have time. You need to go to your meeting."

"I am not going to this meeting dressed as a turtle, Mark!"

He rounds the front of the van. "I'm telling you, they don't look like turtle pants."

"They have fins!"

"Is that what those are?" He jams his key into the ignition. The van rattles to life beneath us. "Huh."

I cross my arms over my chest. "You can drop me off at the station, but I am *not* going inside dressed like a turtle."

Thirty minutes later, I am standing in the front lobby of YBAL News, dressed like a turtle.

"Woah," Gianna says, stumbling to a stop halfway across the

lobby, backing up with a mug of coffee in each hand. I know they're both for her. When she's in research mode, she's powered by caffeine and those little packages of fruit snacks from Costco. The only time she leaves her desk is when she runs out. I must have caught her during a refresh cycle.

She tilts her head and squints at me, the pencil shoved through the middle of her enormous bun wobbling. Glossy auburn hair, gemstone eyes. Even going on what I'm sure is day three of not showering, she's a stunner.

"Delilah?" she calls.

"Yeah, it's me."

She blinks furiously. "I thought I was hallucinating," she mutters. "Why are you dressed like a turtle?"

"Not a hallucination." Just a Keith-induced waking nightmare. "Please tell me you have something in the break room for me to change into."

"Uh." She glances down at her legs, then at mine. Where Gianna is petite and waiflike, I have a size fourteen set of hips and curvy legs. She drags her eyes back to mine with a wince. "I think I have an extra shirt in there. From the station-sponsored marathon a couple years ago?"

"Did you run that marathon?"

"No, but I like free T-shirts." She brings one of the mugs to her mouth and takes a loud slurp. "What's going on? You weren't dressed like that when I saw you this morning."

"You didn't see me this morning."

Her forehead scrunches. "Yes, I did? We talked about the new happy hour spot you want to try. The one with the Tater Tots?"

"That was yesterday."

Gianna blinks, surprised. "Really?"

I lean closer and sniff at her hair. She smells like the very bottom of a coffeepot. "When was the last time you showered?"

"Um . . ." She pauses, mentally calculating.

"And that answers my question." I sigh. "Gianna, you need to take care of yourself."

She lifts her shoulders and her two mugs with the same weak shrug. "I'm in the middle of this embezzlement thing and I want to get further along before I take a break."

As the primary researcher for the news department, Gianna is usually in the middle of *something*. Last year when there was a mayoral scandal, she didn't leave her cubicle for six straight days. I had to practically force-feed her chicken noodle soup and wrestle her into a change of clothes.

Working with Gianna is what I imagine having a toddler is like. A toddler with a caffeine addiction and an absolutely foul mouth.

"All right." I study her critically. "But consume something other than coffee. I have those—"

"Protein bars in the bottom drawer of your desk. I know." Her hands occupied, she affectionately butts her forehead against my shoulder. "Thanks for making sure I eat."

Behind us, someone clears their throat. I turn halfway to find Mark staring at me expectantly, both of his dark eyebrows furrowed in a heavy line. He holds out his wrist and taps the face of his watch.

Gianna snorts. "Why is camera boy acting like your keeper?"

I sigh. "I have a meeting with Keith."

Gianna's attention snaps away from Mark and her face darkens. "Fuck that guy."

"Gi—"

"No, seriously. Fuck that guy. Is he why you're wearing the turtle suit? Do I need to key his car again?"

I wave my hands wildly and shush her. Thankfully, Mark has moved his intimidation routine to the other side of the lobby, standing and waiting by the door that leads to the back of the studio. I duck my head closer to Gianna. "Again?" I whisper.

An absolutely devious look twists her delicate features. "Yes," she whispers back, her mouth hidden behind the rim of her mug. "Again."

"Gianna."

"I'll tell you all the gory details as soon as this embezzlement case is done. I also shit in his—"

I clap my hand over her mouth. "We cannot discuss this in the lobby of our office, Gianna."

She nods solemnly. "I'll send you a memo."

"Please don't send me a memo. Go back to your desk. I'm going to pretend this conversation never happened."

She starts to meander in the general direction of the door where Mark is stationed before turning around and creeping right back. "You need to talk to HR," she says quietly, her eyes serious this time.

"I did, remember?"

It got me exactly nowhere. I worked up my courage to file a formal report only to be told by the head of HR that Keith's behavior was typical *newsroom bluster*, whatever the hell that means. I was told, more or less, to suck it up or find another job. That there was a long line of excited candidates behind me if I wanted to find a station that might be a better fit.

I suppose that's the worst of it. I don't want another station. I want this one. Working here has always been my dream. Ever since I was a little girl, watching my grandpa watch the local news every day at 7 a.m. and 4 p.m. I wanted to be the one the world woke up to. The one kids saw when they got home from school. I have always wanted to be the meteorologist for YBAL, Baltimore's News Station. My grandpa's favorite news program.

So I've sucked it up. And I've made the best of it. But I'm starting to crumble beneath the pressure of Keith's malicious attention.

Maybe I *should* start looking for another job.

I squeeze her arm. "We'll talk later. Go back to embezzlement."

"What about Ava Monroe?"

"What about her?"

"Have you thought about approaching her with what's going on?"

I snort. "I'm not going to approach the president of Emory Communications, Gianna."

"Why not?"

"Because she has bigger things to deal with than newsroom squabbling. I don't need to tattle. I'm fine." I refuse to go over Keith's head with this. What would I even say? That he's being mean to me? No. The potential blowback far outweighs the possible improvement. I don't need things with Keith getting worse.

"Okay, but we're coming back to this. I'm not going to forget," she warns.

"I know you won't." Her mind is like a neatly organized file cabinet, armed with explosives. She gives me one last heavy look before she wanders back across the lobby. Mark's attention sticks to her like glue, his hand moving to prop the door open above her head. She slides past him, tipping her face up toward his. For a second it almost looks like she's going to smile, but then she bares all her teeth, hissing a loud sound from between them.

Mark jumps, flinching back into the doorframe as she glides past with a cackle.

I snort as I follow, rushing to make it through the door.

"How can one so small be so terrifying?" he asks, his eyes distant, color high on his cheeks.

"We may never know." I pat his shoulder. "Listen, you don't have to march me to Keith's office. I can manage my way there just fine."

He arches an eyebrow. "I don't like being on babysitting duty, you know. This isn't fun for me either."

"I get it," I agree. "We both have better things to do with our time."

"Yeah. We do." He watches me, considering. I'm so close I can *taste it*. "You'll go to his office? Straight there? I don't want to hear about it later."

"Did he threaten your favorite camera or something?" I make a tiny cross over my heart. "I'll go straight there."

"Good. I'll see you later, then."

"See you—"

He's already gone, buried in the labyrinth of the newsroom. I watch his dark hair disappear behind the sports desk.

"Later," I finish with a sigh.

I bite my bottom lip and eyeball the distance between Keith's office and the supply closet. There are some extra fundraiser T-shirts in there. I'd much rather be in one of those than in a poorly ventilated costume. I make it two steps in that direction before a hand stacked with shiny gold rings loops around my elbow.

"Delilah." Simone Leeds, one of the anchors, gives me a tight smile. Shiny hair with a shiny personality to match, Simone always looks like she stepped off the runway and landed in the newsroom. She flicks her hair over her shoulder. "Keith is looking for you."

God, this man. Has he told everyone in the newsroom that I need to report to his office like some wayward school student?

I glare at the closed door of his office. "On a scale from one to ten—"

"What's his level of obnoxious today?" Simone smirks. "A solid eight." Her eyes flick down my body, then back up. "This is a new look for you."

"Yeah, no kidding." Standing next to tall, pretty Simone, I feel even more like an idiot.

"It's not a *bad* look," she rushes to add.

I tip my head back and groan at the ceiling.

"It's just an *interesting* one." She drags me forward, closer to Keith's door. "C'mon. You know if you keep him waiting, it'll only be worse for you."

That's the thing, though. It's only ever worse for me. It seems like Keith hoards all his animosity and personality issues for me specifically. I'm the one paying the price, and I don't even know the crime I committed.

"You know we're all rooting for you," Simone whispers. "Don't let him push you around."

Yes, well, it would be nice if everyone rooted for me a little more publicly. I usually have to bear my humiliations alone. Everyone is too scared of Keith—or maybe too scared of becoming the new punching bag—to say anything.

Simone squeezes my shoulder and leaves me in front of Keith's door. I stare at the shiny wood, wishing the floor would swallow me whole. Keith is the only one in the entire office granted the privilege of a *door*. I raise my hand to knock, wincing at the sleeve of my turtle suit.

"Enter," a voice calls from inside.

I crack open the door and poke my head in. "You wanted to see me?"

Keith frowns at me from behind his desk, his face pinched. He always manages to look like he has a lemon stuck in his mouth, his ruddy cheeks sucked slightly in, his bottom lip pouted slightly out.

"We have a meeting," he says. "And you're late."

"I didn't see anything on my calendar," I offer. "Mark let me know about it after our shoot."

His bushy eyebrows are two angry caterpillars on his forehead. "Oh? Do I need to put things on your calendar now? Run it by your secretary?" He snorts. "You've wasted enough of our time. Let's get started."

"Maybe an introduction first," suggests another voice. A

woman with sleek dark hair stands gracefully from the meeting table in the middle of Keith's office. She offers me a kind, if not slightly strained, smile.

"It's a pleasure to meet you, Delilah. My name is Maggie Lin. I oversee the radio station across the street."

If Keith looks like the remnants of a science experiment gone wrong, this woman looks like one gone right. Everything about her screams: *put together.*

She extends her hand.

I stare at it, my fin-less fingers gripping the edge of the door. I think I'm starting to get hives from the turtle suit.

"Um," I say. "Hi."

She slowly lowers her hand, her smile faltering.

"Delilah," Keith bites out.

"Sorry, I just—" I hike my thumb over my shoulder, laughing nervously. "I was hoping to stop by the break room before we get started. I think I have an extra change of clothes in my locker."

"We don't have time for another one of your catastrophes, Delilah. Get in here."

My cheeks burn hot. I try to find the backbone Gianna is always encouraging me to have, but it's hard when my past mistakes are continuously trotted out like a prized show pony.

I'm more than a little accident-prone. I'm clumsy on my best day. My grandpa liked to joke when I was growing up that I must have angered a particularly vengeful spirit. My luck is atrocious. Whatever is worse than atrocious. Maybe I stepped on every crack in the sidewalk as a child. Or walked under a thousand ladders. Because if something can go wrong, it's almost a guarantee it will.

The turtle suit. The mud pit at the Preakness. During a potluck last year, I made chocolate pudding for one of the crime desk guys only to slip in the parking lot and dump half of it on myself.

So, no. I don't want to step into this room with this perfect woman and my impertinent boss for a meeting I'm not prepared for while I'm dressed in a turtle suit. I *don't*. There's only so much humiliation a person can withstand, and I'd like to be taken seriously. *For once.*

I take a bracing breath. "I'm going to go to the break room," I say, slowly and clearly. "I'll be back in just a few minutes and we can get started."

I turn quickly, hoping to make my escape before Keith can launch any more cutting remarks my way, hell-bent on standing my ground. But I don't account for the person quickly rushing toward me in the opposite direction, equally determined to get to wherever *they're* going.

It happens in slow motion. I get a glimpse of a blue checkered shirt and try to jerk left, but he does too. Our bodies slam together and we tip sideways, my hip slamming into a meticulously polished case of awards. Keith's second-place television station softball tournament trophy wedges itself against my rib cage and I squeak, reaching for something to steady myself. Except the only thing I have to steady myself with is a surprisingly strong, blue-check-clad arm.

Coffee spills, something snaps, and then I'm on my back against cold linoleum, gasping for breath, pinned to the floor.

A low groan rumbles against my neck and a puff of warm air brushes over my throat. The man currently plastered to my front bites out a low sigh that sounds suspiciously like my name.

Coffee spreads around us in a slow bleed. It seeps through my suit and warms my skin. I try to breathe around the hot, pricking sensation.

The man above me pushes up on his elbows.

He looks different without his glasses, but I'd recognize that stubborn set of his jaw anywhere. Jackson Clark. The tight-ass from the radio station across the street. He's flattened me bodily to the floor outside Keith's office. The same guy who has been leaving me weird notes on the window of my car for almost two years has decided to resort to violence.

Recognition makes his blue eyes flash darker.

"Of course," he says, his mouth in a flat line and his hand tangled in my hair. "It's you."

AIDEN VALENTINE: You're listening to Baltimore's home for easy listening, 101.6 LITE FM.

AIDEN VALENTINE: Now with traffic and weather together, here's Jackson Clark.

[pause]

AIDEN VALENTINE: [clears throat] Here is Jackson Clark.

JACKSON CLARK: Oh, right.

JACKSON CLARK: [nervous laughter] Here I am.

AIDEN VALENTINE: With traffic and weather together.

JACKSON CLARK: Yes. I am here to report the weather. And the traffic. Both of them. Together.

CHAPTER 3

JACKSON

I lie face down in the middle of the hallway on top of Delilah Stewart, my pride somewhere on the floor with my coffee.

"Hello, Delilah." I sigh, trying to figure out if anything is broken or just badly bruised. My glasses are nowhere to be found. Everything is blurry smudges of color.

"Hello, Jackson."

She sounds defeated.

"Always a pleasure."

Beneath me, Delilah snickers. "Something like that," she says, her voice low and sweet. A laugh, caught somewhere behind her teeth.

Well, I'm glad one of us finds this funny.

Delilah squirms, somehow managing to knock me in the groin and the solar plexus at the same time.

"Please," I groan, directly into her ear. She smells like my light roast coffee and something sweeter. Strawberry jam, maybe. "Please stop moving," I beg.

She immediately stills and I drop my forehead to her shoulder. I can't breathe, and I can't stand up if I can't breathe.

"What are you doing?" she whispers.

"Trying not to die," I wheeze.

She huffs and wiggles again. One hand pats at my rib cage. "There, there," she says awkwardly. "Easy does it."

I snort a laugh and some of her hair flutters around my face. Delilah Stewart, Human Disaster, strikes again. Somehow we've found ourselves stuck in a loop with each other. Every time I see her, something inevitably goes wrong. We're the opposite of magnets, blasting away as soon as we enter each other's force field.

She gives me another pat, then drops her hands to her side.

"I would appreciate it," she says, her voice muffled, "if you removed yourself from my person now."

I press up on my knees with no small amount of effort, a heavy grunt at the base of my throat as I steady myself with my hands planted over her shoulders. Without my glasses, I can only see her vague outline. Smudges of color against a pale white floor.

Chestnut brown. Ruby red. Deep emerald green. She must still be wearing her turtle suit.

"Why are you looking at me like that?" she whispers.

"Like what?"

A hand flutters in front of my face. "Squinting."

"I can't see without my glasses," I grind out, grunting when her knee hits the inside of my thigh. I almost go down again. "You know. Those things that are always on my face."

"Oh." One arm presses above her head, her elbow glancing along my side. My shirt is wet and sticking to my chest but all I can focus on is the places we're touching. My knees, pressed between hers. The inside of my left wrist, brushing against her hair. This is the closest I've been to a woman in six months and naturally, it's Delilah Stewart. In the middle of the newsroom floor at the local television station. In the world's most uncomfortable game of Twister.

Breaking News. Local Man Makes Fool of Himself with Woman Dressed as Turtle.

I'm my worst self with Delilah, and it's entirely her fault.

"Here," she says, fingers easing the frames over my nose. She holds them there with her thumb between my eyes, then gives me a bright smile. Now I can see every detail of her face beneath mine. The collection of freckles on either side of her nose. The slight gap between her two front teeth. Her long hair, spilling out beneath her on the floor.

"There," she says. "Good as new."

I blink at her. "These are my favorite glasses."

"And they look great."

She removes her hand and they tilt crooked. One half of her is blurry, the other in focus. Her hand snaps back into place, holding them steady.

"I can fix them," she whispers.

"Please don't." I'm not interested in whatever that nightmare brain cooks up next. I replace her hand with mine, holding the glasses against my face.

I shift to the side and leverage myself up, extending a hand to help her. She ignores it, crawling up slowly after me instead, using the wall for leverage. She has a giant coffee stain in the middle of her turtle-clad chest, one side of her hair wet at the ends. I have a stain, too, slowly spreading across my abdomen.

We stand there in the corner of the bustling newsroom, staring at each other. No one pays us any attention, and I have to wonder: How often is Delilah tackling people to the ground?

"So," she says. "What are you doing over here?"

When I stare at her blankly from behind my broken glasses, her cheeks flush pink. "I usually see you in the parking lot," she explains. "Not in the middle of the station."

"I have a meeting."

She stops trying to wring the coffee out of her hair. "Here?"

"Not in the hallway, no, but at this station. Yes."

She frowns. "With who?"

"I'm not exactly sure." I reach into my wet pocket and pull out the half-crumpled note that was left on my desk at the radio station. Delilah plucks it out of my hand. "Help yourself," I mumble.

"*YBAL offices*," she reads. "*Ask for Keith.*" Her eyes close in defeat as she slaps the note against the middle of my wet chest. "I think I know where your meeting is."

"Where?"

She points wordlessly at the half-ajar door no more than two feet away. I glance at it.

"Great," I say slowly. "Thanks."

I move toward it and Delilah follows. I stop abruptly at the threshold and she bumps into my back.

"Is there something I can help you with?" I'm still holding my glasses to the side of my face. "Want one more shot before we go our separate ways?"

"Fun as that sounds"—resignation firms the corners of her mouth—"I have a meeting too."

I point at the door. "In this room?"

She nods. "Yup."

"With me?"

"It would seem so."

A prickling sense of awareness creeps up my spine, itching between my shoulders.

I'm not going to like whatever happens in this office. I know it.

"If you have a meeting, why were you walking in the opposite direction?"

"Because I wanted to spare myself the humiliation of sitting in a business meeting dressed as a tortoise." She gestures at her coffee-stained chest. "Clearly, that's no longer a concern."

We linger at the doorway playing the world's most awkward game of chicken.

"Are you going to go inside?"

"I'm really not sure," I answer. "I'm considering climbing out the window, actually."

She snickers. "I think it's too late for that. Our fate is sealed."

Fate. It rattles around my skull and plunks down to land somewhere in the middle of my chest. A marble in an empty soda can. A tuning fork, vibrating at a frequency I can't hear.

A silly thing, for silly people. I control what happens. Not some mystical force.

"Says who?" I ask.

"Says me." Maggie appears in the doorway. Her eyes flick briefly to where I'm holding my glasses together. "You're late."

"I thought our meeting was at the station." *Our station.* "I'm here now."

"Yes, and with quite the stunning entrance." Her face remains impassive, but delight shines in her catlike eyes. They cut in Delilah's direction, softening slightly. "Do you need a minute before we get started?"

Delilah shrugs. "It can't get much worse, can it?"

It can, in fact, get worse.

The four of us sit in silence in Keith's spacious office. Keith, who didn't so much as grunt a greeting when we all finally settled around the meeting table. Keith, who looks more enamored with his extra-large Dunkin' frozen coffee than whatever it is we're here to discuss. Keith, who seems determined to make this a power play between himself and Maggie by remaining frustratingly disinterested and silent.

I try to grab Maggie's attention with a look that appropriately conveys *What is happening?* and *Why am I here for it?* but she's busy trying to disintegrate Keith's skull with her stare.

This could have, by every definition, been an email.

If it were, maybe my glasses would have survived the morning.

Delilah sits in a corner of the room on a too-small folding chair that looks like it might collapse at any second. Either Keith couldn't move his chair to make room for her, or he refused to.

Given how this meeting is going, I have my suspicions.

She pinches her turtle top and pulls it away from her chest with a grimace.

I clear my throat and three sets of eyes snap to mine.

"I, uh—" I nod at Delilah, trying to force my face into something polite. If no one wants to start this meeting, the least I can do is make small talk. I can *try*. "I like your suit."

She blinks at me. "What?"

"The . . . turtle thing. You look nice."

Maggie immediately stomps on my foot—hard—beneath the table. I suck in a sharp breath through my teeth.

"*Be nice*," she whispers under her breath.

What would have been *nice* is if Maggie didn't ambush me with a surprise meeting with Delilah Stewart, of all people.

"Oh, um." Delilah glances down at herself, like she's forgotten she's dressed as a reptile. "Thank you?"

"Do you like turtles?" I ask.

A crease appears in the middle of her forehead. "Turtles are fine."

"I've heard female sea turtles use the earth's magnetic field to return to the same beach where they were born to lay their eggs."

Delilah looks at me like I'm the one about to lay eggs. She scratches her temple and adjusts her position on the uncomfortable metal chair. "That's, um. That's great?"

My enthusiasm for the conversation, limited as it was, slowly ebbs. Of course Delilah doesn't know anything about turtles. She probably tossed on her little costume and headed out the door for her *turtle feature* without a care in the world for preparation. The same way she approaches the weather.

Suddenly, I feel the need to quote even more turtle facts. It's *imperative* that I know more about turtles than she does.

"Did you know that turtles—"

"Keith," Maggie interrupts, cutting me off with a withering look. "Maybe we should get started."

"You could have let me finish," I mumble under my breath.

Maggie shakes her head. "Absolutely no one in this room wanted you to finish," she whispers. She tips her chin up to Keith. "Shall we?"

"Sure," he says with all the enthusiasm of a cloud of dust. He swivels back and forth in his chair, one hand perched under his chin, the other curled around his frozen drink. He brings it to his mouth and takes a loud slurp from the orange straw, his bloated cheeks wobbling.

Delilah exhales a short, frustrated sound from the corner.

I know Keith. Everyone in Baltimore knows Keith. He had a successful broadcast career in the early nineties before taking on a senior administrative role with the station. They used to call him the Face of Baltimore, but I've always found his face to be largely insufferable. His personality too. He's arrogant, self-centered, and he uses way too much hair product on far too little hair. Two years ago, he led a one-man campaign to rename the road that leads into the station after himself. The city denied him, and when he tried to petition the public for grassroots support, *they* denied him as well. He seems determined to hold on to his glory days, despite being almost three decades past.

I have no idea why we're giving this guy our time. It's not like Maggie to entertain the antics of an asshole.

"Keith," Maggie says again, some of her endless patience beginning to slip. "If you don't mind, we have a broadcast of our own to get back to."

"Ah, yes." His smile is condescending, his too-white teeth glinting under the fluorescents. "Your little radio show. Wouldn't want to be late for that."

Maggie's answering smile is as sharp as her response. "Our little radio show has almost three times the organic reach as your little news station. It is the reason, as you recall, we are having this conversation."

Keith's eyes flash. He sets his coffee to the side.

"Too right," he snaps. "Jackson. Delilah. You're here as part of a new proposed partnership between 101.6 LITE FM and YBAL News."

"What?" I ask at the same time Delilah blurts, "Why?"

Keith finally turns his head to look at Delilah, his lip curling. "To report the weather."

"Like . . . together?" She glances at me and points one fin in my direction. She's been tugging them on and off her hands since we sat down at this meeting. "As in, the both of us?"

"Yes, that is the plan." Maggie clasps her hands in front of her on the table. She's in negotiation mode while I'm playing catch-up in the seat next to her. My brain is stuck on the word *partnership*—as in *two people working together toward a common goal*.

The only thing Delilah and I have ever been aligned on is chaos. The only thing we've ever worked toward together is mutual destruction.

"Jackson," Maggie says. "What does the *Farmers' Almanac* say about February?"

"Um." I blink away from Delilah and press my glasses up my nose. "It says we'll see colder than usual temperatures this winter, which has held true."

"And the storms?" Maggie asks, not looking away from Keith. "What does it say about the storms?"

"It says we should expect historic snow conditions." I frown. "Though the storms Maryland has seen this winter have been right on par with previous seasons."

"You just . . . have the *Farmers' Almanac* memorized?" Delilah asks.

Her tone makes it clear that rote memorization of the almanac is not something to be proud of. I cross my arms over my chest. "It's helpful information."

"For all those . . . crops you have at home?"

"Farmers aren't the only ones who use that almanac," I defend. "It has plenty of helpful applications."

"Sure."

"I get a copy every year. It's—" I huff. "I don't have to explain myself to you."

"Do you get a copy of the Yellow Pages too?" Her lips lift at the corners. "Do you have a Rolodex?"

I do have a Rolodex that sits on the corner of my desk at the radio station where I keep all my contacts. I like writing things down on paper. It makes it easier for me to find them. But over my dead body am I going to admit that to Delilah.

Apparently, I don't have to. She studies my face for the span of three seconds, then descends into a bright, cackling laugh.

"Oh my god, you do. You have a Rolodex."

I turn and look at Maggie. "This isn't going to work."

Any partnership I have with Delilah will result in us at each other's throats. I can't work with someone so fundamentally different from myself. She probably uses a map and a set of crystals to predict the weather. A Magic 8 Ball.

Maggie pats my forearm gently. "It'll be fine. Just listen, and we'll talk through the rest of the details later, okay?"

"What details?" I bite out. "What, exactly, are you suggesting?"

"Is it alphabetized?" Delilah volleys from her side of the room.

I slant my eyes in her direction. She's practically vibrating in her metal folding chair. "Is what alphabetized?"

"Your Rolodex. Do you keep it alphabetized?"

"How else do you suggest I keep my Rolodex?" I'm not a goddamned monster.

She presses her lips together. "I really can't tell if you're joking right now," she whispers.

I pointedly turn my attention to my boss, who is gazing at the tabletop as if she'd like nothing more than to be absorbed within the wood grain. "What, exactly, are you suggesting?"

"We've pulled together some weather projections and run them by the folks down at the National Weather Service," Keith offers, somehow managing to sound both smug and stupid in the same breath. "We'll obviously know more in the coming days, but there's a snowstorm heading our way that could bring record-breaking snowfall."

I've seen similar markers in the models I've been watching, but it's far too early to tell if it's a passing low-pressure system, or the start of a massive storm barreling down over the mountains.

Delilah's amusement evaporates. "You sent in those projections? The ones I gave you last week?"

"By the looks of it, Western Maryland is about to get walloped," Keith says, not bothering to acknowledge Delilah or her question. She might as well be a pretty picture on the wall for the amount of attention he's given her in this meeting. "It's too early to issue any warnings, of course, but all the ingredients are there. It's a once-in-a-lifetime storm."

"When I brought you those projections, you told me they were garbage," Delilah says. The legs of her chair screech across the floor as she tries to keep their conversation private. "You said they weren't usable."

Keith flicks his fingers. "Because they weren't. Megan at the National Weather Service gave us usable data."

"But it was my report you used. I laid everything out. I collected the data and I drew out the projections. I—" She pauses and swallows heavily. "That was my work, Keith."

"That was the station's work. I was the one who coordinated everything with the NWS."

"But it was my analysis. The low-pressure system over the Rockies and the precipitation coming up from the Gulf. I—"

"Used station resources aggregating it," Keith says, his voice sharpening. "Have you been waiting for your shiny gold star, Delilah? Congratulations. You did your job." He rolls his eyes and shifts so his back is to her, wedged in the corner of the room. Something twists in my gut, even as I try to come to terms with the fact that Delilah apparently *doesn't* use a cup of sticks to predict the weather.

"What model did you use?" I ask.

Delilah reluctantly lifts her eyes to mine. "The European model."

"Ah," I say, satisfied that I didn't miss something. "Okay."

Her mouth pinches and pink brushes across the tops of her cheeks. "Is there something wrong with the European model, Jackson?"

"The Global Forecast System model is better."

"Not in the winter, it isn't."

"When you're looking at a lead of longer than five days, your best bet is—"

"The point remains," Keith interrupts, sounding like he'd rather drown himself in the harbor than listen to us talk about weather models for another second, "a storm is coming and if we hope to maximize engagement for both of our stations, we need to coordinate our efforts now."

"Coordinate? Why would we coordinate?" I ask. I turn halfway toward Maggie. "Do you see this impacting the radio station's weather updates?"

"This will be all the region is talking about, Jackson," Maggie says. "It's going to be bigger than the weather update. We hope to dedicate a whole segment to it for the duration of the storm."

"Oh, that's fine." I try to catch Delilah's eye. "Feel free to double broadcast, or whatever it is you intend to do. No hard feelings from me."

She blinks at me, the corners of her mouth turned down. "Even though I use an inferior model?" she snipes.

I crack a smile. I like her rattled. "Even then."

"We had something else in mind, actually," Maggie hedges. I stare and wait. This entire meeting is twenty questions, apparently. I wish everyone would stop talking in riddles and just explain what the hell is going on.

Maggie must be able to sense my growing frustration because she straightens her shoulders. Fixes me with a severe, unrelenting look.

"The two of you are going to cover the storm with joint broadcasts for the duration of the snowfall. We're sending you to Garrett County, Jackson. You're going to cover the storm live, right where it's supposed to hit the hardest." She gestures across the table at Delilah. "And you're going to do it together."

DELILAH STEWART: Now, if you look way out west, you can see the whispers of a winter storm beginning to form. The westernmost part of Maryland, Garrett County, will likely be hit the hardest as it's completely within the shelter of the Appalachians. But if everything comes together over the next couple of days and the storm picks up power in the mountains, the effects could be felt all the way in Baltimore. Stay tuned.

CHAPTER 4
JACKSON

Once when Penelope was six, she decided to take a vow of silence until I bought her the Polly Pocket Groom and Glam Poodle Compact she wanted. Unfortunately for her, I've always enjoyed silence. She caved before I did and had to settle for a secondhand barrel of Legos instead.

I've been channeling that same energy since I left the YBAL News studio two days ago. I didn't agree to a partnership with Delilah and Delilah didn't agree to a partnership with me. Maggie has been trying to get me to commit, but I feel fundamentally unable to comment on the situation.

"Hey, buddy." Aiden Valentine, host of the late-night romance hotline and my supposed best friend, edges his way into my office. "I brought you some cookies."

I grunt in acknowledgment of his presence, not looking up from the weather model on my screen. I've been running dual projections every day with the European model and the Global Forecast System model. The differences aren't huge, but they're there. And one thing is glaringly obvious.

Delilah was right about the European model. It is more accurate for this type of storm prediction. I dismissed her because I thought I knew better, but—

Delilah was right.

I minimize the forecast screen. "Did Maggie send you?"

"Yep."

"Because she wants an answer about the broadcast?"

"Correct."

"Great." I click around some more, trying to pretend I'm doing something productive. "I still don't have an answer for her. You can leave now."

"Don't be like that." Aiden holds out his peace offering and shakes it. "Have a cookie, at least. I brought you your favorite."

I eye them speculatively, then turn back to my computer screen.

"One is missing," I say woodenly.

"What?" He looks down at the box. "How do you know?"

"Because Berger Cookies don't come with the plastic wrap torn open and you have chocolate on your chin." Aiden immediately lifts his hand to wipe at the spot that doesn't exist. I snicker. "Guilty, asshole."

Aiden rolls his eyes and tosses the box of cookies at me, collapsing in the one small chair I have wedged up against the wall. When Maggie said I could have an office at the station, she neglected to tell me it used to be the cleaning supply closet.

"What's going on with you?"

"You mean besides being guilted into accepting an absolute disaster of an assignment that sends me to the wilderness of Western Maryland three hours away from Baltimore to report on a historic snowstorm that will probably leave me stranded with a woman who thinks chocolate pudding is an acceptable dish at a potluck?"

"You and this pudding," Aiden mutters.

"It was my favorite shirt," I defend. "She spilled pudding all over my favorite shirt. And I lost my second-favorite shirt to the coffee incident on Tuesday. I now have a collection of shirts ruined by Delilah Stewart. How many more shirts need to sacrifice themselves before enough is enough?"

"All right, bud." Aiden tries to hide his smile and does a poor job of it. "I get it. Anything else holding you back?"

"I have a lot on my plate right now," I deflect, dragging the projections up on my screen again, staring at them like I can change them by sheer force of will. They've only solidified in the two days since our meeting at YBAL News, both of them aligning in agreement on one thing.

There is a storm coming and it's a big one. Some of the heaviest snowfall Maryland has ever seen.

And Maggie wants me to get in a car, drive two hundred miles west, and place myself smack-dab in the middle of it . . . with *Delilah*.

The rest of the meeting at YBAL was an out-of-body experience. Everyone's voices faded into low, droning *womp womp womps* as I stared a hole into the carpet, my hands clenched so tight against the armrests I had marks on my palms for the rest of the day.

Joint broadcasts.

Covering the storm live.

You're going to do it together.

Together.

Together.

At the end of the meeting, I stood up and left without a word. I walked straight out the front door of the television station to my car, where I sat unmoving until it was time for my radio shift to start.

Aiden creeps forward and reaches for the box of cookies. I swat it out of his reach.

"What did Maggie say?" I ask.

"She demanded I get an answer out of you by whatever means necessary." He nods at the box. "Cookies were the first step."

"And the next?"

"Haven't figured that out yet." He kicks his long legs out. "Why haven't you given her an answer?"

"Because I don't want to give her an answer," I grumble, picking at the edge of the cookie box.

"Well, you have to. You can't just pretend it doesn't exist." Aiden tilts his head to the side, considering me. "You know, this is a real role-reversal situation. Usually, I'm the one being surly and difficult."

"I preferred you when you were surly and difficult. Now you're optimistic and irritating."

Aiden grins. "That's the power of love, my friend." His head tips to the side. "And biweekly therapy sessions."

I snort. A year ago, Aiden would have punched this version of himself in the face. He was busy trying to pretend all his emotions were inconvenient impulses he could bury under a terrible attitude and denial. But then a kid called into the station looking for relationship advice for her mom, and their phone call went viral. Aiden was roped into helping Baltimore's favorite single mom find her match. When Lucie made her 101.6 LITE FM debut, she bowled Aiden over. It was delightful watching him try to keep his head above water, but now that he and Lucie have been together for a while, his attitude has officially lost its shine.

Now he's in tune with his *feelings*.

It's the worst.

"Let's talk it out, buddy." I give him a dark look and he chuckles, sprawling himself in my spare chair like he has no intention of leaving anytime soon. "Bit by bit. What's your biggest holdup?"

"Delilah," I bite out immediately.

Aiden grins. "Ah, yes. The weather woman you love to hate."

"I don't *love* to hate her." I don't even hate her, but no one believes me when I say it. Maybe it's because I descend into a grunting, groaning asshole whenever her name is mentioned. Maybe it's because we argued about weather models for half our meeting on Tuesday. Maybe it's because the prospect of working with her sent me into a catatonic tailspin, and I sat silently in my car for close to three hours. "I just find her irritating."

"Because she doesn't like spreadsheets? Because she does things differently than you? I think she's fun."

"Fun," I repeat.

Aiden nods. "She does a good job with the weather, when they actually let her report on it. The two of you are actually more alike than you think." I take an oversized bite of cookie. "You're both massive nerds."

"You've been watching her reports?"

"Why did you say that like I'm cheating on you?"

"Because you should come to *me* for your weather reports. Not Delilah." I grab up a half-crumpled piece of paper wedged under my pencil cup and thrust it at Aiden. "Look at this. I found it taped to my car window this morning. She wants me to pay for the turtle suit."

I thought it was a parking ticket. But then I saw it was stuck to my window with a wad of chewed gum and knew immediately who it was from.

Aiden's forehead crinkles in confusion. "The what?"

"Her turtle suit. She wants me to pay to have it dry-cleaned, even though she was the one who ruined it when she ran into me."

Aiden looks delighted. "Is she leaving you notes on your car now?" He reaches for it. "Good for her."

"No." I yank the note away, thrusting it in the top drawer of my desk. "Not good for her."

"Jackson," he sighs. "You have got to relax."

"I am relaxed."

"You are hunched over your desk and shoveling cookies into your mouth like a troll. When I came in here, you were muttering under your breath about low-pressure systems. You are not relaxed."

I tug off my glasses and toss them on the desk, digging my palms against my eyes until I see spots. I hear the creak of leather as Aiden shifts in his chair. The slow slide of the cookie box against the desk as he seizes my moment of weakness for his own advantage.

"Do you want me to coddle you, or be honest?"

"You've never coddled me a day in your life," I grumble.

Aiden snickers. "You don't have to do this if you don't want to. Maggie won't force you. It's a good opportunity for the station, but we'll have better. Our numbers are strong. This isn't the same situation as last year."

Last year, when we were so close to having to shut down completely. We're better than we were, but not by much. I'm the one who runs the numbers. I know exactly how thin of a line it is between us staying on the air, and everyone looking for new jobs.

I feel the press of that truth like a weight in the middle of my chest. I struggle with choosing my own comfort when other people are depending on me. If this arrangement will benefit the station, I'm not sure how I'll be able to say no. Which is exactly the issue I've been wrestling with for the past forty-eight hours.

"But if the only reason you have for not doing it is *Delilah*, well—are you really going to let someone who infuriates you dictate your behavior?"

I clench my jaw so tight my teeth grind together. "No."

"You sure? Because that's what it looks like." He plucks another cookie from the box with a smug look on his stupid face. "It looks like you're afraid of a five-foot-nothing woman who dresses in amphibian costumes."

"Turtles are reptiles, you idiot." I scrub my hand against the back of my head. "And I meant *no*, that's not the only reason I have for not agreeing to Maggie's plan." I swallow heavily, my mouth going dry just thinking about it. "I don't want to be on television."

"Why?"

"You know why."

"Because you get a little tongue-tied?"

"I wouldn't call the departure of my soul from my body every time I have to talk about something other than the forecast getting *tongue-tied*." I pause. "Maggie said we're going to be broadcasting live."

Aiden shrugs. "Maybe television will be easier than radio."

I stare at him. "It'll probably be worse."

"It can get worse?" At my dark look, Aiden cracks another smile, holding up his hands. "I'm just giving you a hard time. You won't know until you try, yeah?"

I mutter a string of obscenities under my breath.

"What else? C'mon. I know you like your lists."

I drag my hand down my face. This is my heaviest burden. The thing that keeps me staring at the ceiling of my bedroom long into the night. There are so many things that can go wrong, and I'd be so far away. "Who will look after the girls if I'm not here?"

"I told you. They can stay with me, Lucie, and Maya. We've got the space." Aiden moved in with Lucie and her daughter after they expanded Lucie's Fells Point row home into the house next door. "Maya is excited about the prospect of an extended sleepover."

"With this storm, we'll likely be stuck out there for a week. Maybe two. It's a lot to ask."

"You didn't ask. I offered. And you raised those two to be scary-good houseguests. Last time they stayed with Maya, my entire record collection was organized *and* dusted."

"By color?"

"By genre and artist last name, as god intended. You did good with them, Jackie." He leans forward, his face earnest. The teasing is over now, and Aiden means business. "You can trust me with this. I'm not going to let you down."

"I know you won't. I trust you." And I do. I know the girls will be in good hands if they stay with Lucie and Aiden. "I just—I haven't been away from them since I got full custody. I like our routine."

"I know you do." There's no judgment in Aiden's voice. Just quiet understanding. He knows how much I rely on having things neatly laid out in predictable sequences. "But I think it might be good for you to break out of it every once in a while. Try something new. Have a little fun." He stands from his chair and brushes the crumbs off his lap. "Look at me. I tried something new and I found Lucie."

"Your *something new* was emotions."

He shrugs. "Yeah, well. It worked out all right in the end." He raps his knuckles against the doorframe. "Maggie isn't going to let you think on it for too much longer," he warns. "I'll buy you some time, but you'll need to give her an answer sooner rather than later. I'll see you in an hour?"

"Yeah," I agree. "I'll meet you in the booth."

Aiden leaves and I try to break it down logically, but my brain follows the tried-and-true route instead. I think about the girls, and how excited they were at the prospect of something different. I think about giving in, saying yes, and the long drive I'll have to take to the doldrums of Western Maryland. I think about standing in the middle of a field—a street, a sidewalk—holding a microphone in my hand and staring at the blinking red light of a camera. I think about Delilah Stewart standing right next to me, watching as I fumble. I think about the smug delight that would light up her eyes.

I think about stepping outside of my routine, and the way everything could crumble because of it. I think about falling short and making an ass of myself. I think of the crushing disappointment, not just for me, but for the girls too. The station. I think about letting everyone down, letting everyone *see*. The cracks in the foundation that reach up. The things that make me *wrong*.

My phone buzzes across my desk and I reach for my glasses. I tried to fix them last night using one of Penelope's bracelet-making pliers, but I think I just made them worse.

Maybe tomorrow I'll tape an eyeglass repair bill to Delilah's car window.

My phone stops vibrating, then immediately starts up again. I glance at the screen.

"Fuck," I whisper.

This is another one of my routines, though I don't particularly care for the predictability of it. I hesitate, then swipe my thumb across the screen.

"Camille." I clear my throat. "Hello."

Cars rush in the background. A horn honks, someone yells, and it's another fifteen seconds of panting and ambient noise before she remembers she's dialed the phone.

Or, in other words, a typical conversation with my mother.

"Jackson," she says, sounding out of breath. "I really wish you'd call me Mom."

"Okay," I deflect without agreeing, a skill I've honed to perfection after years of wild demands. I stare at the weather model open on my computer screen and watch the massive low-pressure system that's forming at the base of the Rockies. The map cycles through the forward projection and the pressure grows and grows. A giant blob of red that shifts and morphs. I can relate.

"What do you need?"

"Don't you mean, *How are you doing?*"

I don't need to ask. I know exactly how she's doing. She's in an exciting new place with an exciting new job and exciting new friends, and everything is sunshine and rainbows and chocolate-frosted cake.

Still, I cave. "How is the essential oil business these days?"

"That was two cities ago, Jack. I've told you, haven't I? I work in music management now."

The background noise abruptly cuts out and a car door slams. Music management. Coffee shop supply. Antique broker. It's always something. Once during one of these little check-ins, she was sitting in a truck full of livestock exploring her options in restorative goat yoga.

"That's great," I answer, unable to rally any enthusiasm. This is not what I need today. It's another brick on top of my otherwise impossible load. I'm buckling beneath the pressure. "What can I do for you?"

She laughs and my skin pulls tight. "Maybe I just wanted to say hello."

She never wants to say hello. "Hello. What else?"

"Jackson," she sighs. "You really do think the worst of me."

"It's a prediction based on previous behavior."

My mother doesn't do check-ins. She prefers whimsical appearances and sporadic phone calls whenever she needs something for her bright and shiny new adventure, usually with dollar signs attached.

"You make me sound like a monster."

No, not a monster. Just absent and self-absorbed.

"Camille." I find the clock at the bottom right of my computer screen. I have about twenty minutes before I need to go on the air. "What is this call about?"

She sighs, put-upon that I'm not indulging her. "I wanted to ask about the girls."

"Why?" I ask, my hackles immediately up.

"Because they're mine," she says simply. "And it's been too long since I've seen them."

They're not yours, I immediately want to say. They're mine. I've changed diapers and cooked dinners and done seventy-three thousand loads of laundry. I've been at every back-to-school night and fixed every ponytail. I've done every sleepless night and every early morning. You gave them to me. They're mine.

"The girls are fine," I bite out.

"That's it?" She laughs. "That's all you have for me?"

"That's it."

She pauses, waiting for me to fill in the gaps. I refuse to.

"Well, what are they involved in? They're twelve now, right? Almost high school."

Something in the middle of my chest bends and buckles. She doesn't even know how old they are.

Suddenly, I'm seven years old again, sitting at a kitchen table with a hollow, aching stomach and clothes that are two sizes too small, watching my mother bake a cake and wondering if she will remember to take it out of the oven before it burns. Ten years old and sitting on the curb outside of my elementary school, watching the sun sink over the parking lot, painting the asphalt in golds while I wait and wait and *wait*.

Where's your mom, Jackson?

She's probably working late. She'll be here soon.

Always wondering. Always waiting.

"They're fifteen," I grind out. "They're in their sophomore year."

They skipped seventh grade because they were both reading at an advanced level and got bored in their classes. They're smart and kind, and wildly funny. They both made the volleyball team, though I think Adeline is more interested in hiding in the library. But she didn't want Penelope to be alone at tryouts so they did it together. They still do everything together.

You would know this if you really did care, I almost say. *You would know this if you stuck around.*

But I don't, because she doesn't deserve to know.

"Fifteen," my mother repeats.

"Yes."

"That's . . ." Her voice drifts. "That's incredible. I bet they're fun. Are they fun?"

I stay quiet.

"Don't tell me they're little pencil pushers like you." She laughs and it slithers beneath my rib cage. Twists into something harsh and ugly that pinches and prods. "I swear, Jackson. You were the most serious little boy. You would write your schedule down in your school notebook and tape it to the refrigerator. Do you remember that?"

"Yeah, I remember." I glance at the file cabinet in the corner of my office and the habit I never figured out how to kick. The days of the week are labeled in neat, color-coded dry-erase maker.

I feel a hot flush of embarrassment.

"You've gotta make sure you're giving those girls fun, Jackson. Teenage girls need fun."

"Okay."

"I'm serious, Jack. Don't be a stuffed shirt. You've got to *live* every once in a while. You don't want your sisters to end up like you, do you?" A laugh bursts out of her, prickling at my skin. "All work and no play makes Jack a dull boy."

I am this way because of you, I want to snap. I want to twist my words like knives until they hurt. *You made me this way. Utterly reliant on systems and routines and habits so I can fucking breathe.*

Instead, I say, "Thanks for the advice. I'll take it under consideration. I'm hanging up now."

And then I do. I hang up on my mother and place my phone carefully to the left of my keyboard, breathing in through my nose and out through my mouth. Again. *Again.*

My phone buzzes with an incoming call and I pick it up.

"What is it now?"

Silence fills the line. Then, "Is that how you always answer the phone?"

I pinch the bridge of my nose. This fucking day.

"Not usually, no." I dig a knuckle into my eye, then adjust my glasses. "I'm sorry. I thought you were someone else."

"A jilted lover? A loan shark? Who inspires that level of venom from Jackson Clark?"

I slump back in my chair. "How did you get this number?"

"Your loan shark," Delilah answers, light and breezy.

"Is this loan shark named Maggie?"

She snickers. "This loan shark is named Aiden Valentine, and he left your phone number taped to my car window."

"Of course he did," I sigh. *Asshole.*

"I thought the note thing was your move."

"Apparently, not just mine." I pick up the dry-cleaning bill I found stuck to my window this morning and a reluctant smile tugs at my mouth. Some of the tight feeling in my chest disappears. If nothing else, Delilah is an excellent distraction. "What can I do for you, Delilah?"

"You and I . . . we need to talk."

JACKSON CLARK: Storms typically develop out of low-pressure systems. In a low-pressure system, air from higher-pressure areas moves down toward the low, and as air rises and cools, any moisture in it condenses, forming clouds. The greater the difference in pressures, often, you know, the bigger the storms. And other factors can obviously exacerbate this as well, but pressure plays a huge part. Lots of pressure. Tons of pressure just—moving around.

AIDEN VALENTINE: What do you—

JACKSON CLARK: There's this thing called an atmospheric lift where rising air can cause significant cooling and condensation. An orographic lift is when air is forced to rise over a topographic feature like a mountain. All of it driven by immense pressure.

AIDEN VALENTINE: Are we . . . experiencing one of those?

JACKSON CLARK: One of what?

AIDEN VALENTINE: Whatever that lift thing is you just described.

JACKSON CLARK: Oh. No. I'm just talking about pressure.

JACKSON CLARK: So much pressure.

AIDEN VALENTINE: I think you need another cookie.

CHAPTER 5

DELILAH

I set the time, but Jackson decides the place. I'd pat myself on the back for how well we're already working together if it didn't take fifteen minutes of bickering back and forth to come to such a simple conclusion.

The café where Jackson demanded we meet is nestled on a narrow side street of Fells Point, tucked between an antiques mall and a sneaker store. SKULLDUGGERY is written in large, looping letters on the wooden sign that hangs over the door, creaking as it swings in the late-February wind.

The few times I've managed to come here are during the busiest parts of the day, so it feels like a treat to walk in without getting smacked in the face with a rogue handbag. Today the only people here are a guy typing furiously on his laptop, a beleaguered medical professional in wrinkled scrubs, a woman taking a picture of her croissant, and . . . Jackson sitting at the high-top bar in the back, a newspaper folded at his elbow and one foot propped up on the bottom rung of his stool. His other leg stretches out beneath the seat next to him, his coat folded neatly on top.

Jackson Clark. Always so *neat*. Always so *organized*. I wonder if he sleeps in his pressed chino pants.

The bell above the door jingles as it shuts and he turns halfway, light glancing along his clean-shaven jaw. A pair of thick, dark-framed glasses slip down his nose and he pushes them back up with his thumb. They're practical frames, like something Gregory Peck used to wear. When they fell off his face in the hallway, there was an indent in the side, likely from where he's run his fingers along the metal.

He does that now as I watch, dragging his pointer finger along the edge before adjusting them with a frown. My stomach gives a low swoop, something about that easy, practiced motion feeling indecent. Then he pushes his dark blond hair back over his forehead, forearm flexing beneath the rolled sleeve of his sweater, and I have to avert my eyes to the chalkboard menu just behind his head.

Objectively speaking, he's a very handsome man. I think I'd be able to appreciate it more if he didn't have the personality of a wet piece of cardboard.

As it stands, he probably dreams about alphabetization. I bet his darkest fantasy involves a pocket protector. He's probably never given a woman an orgasm in his *life*.

I'm still snickering to myself as he clears the stool next to him, draping his coat over the counter instead. I slide onto the seat, fighting my way out of my parka.

"What's so funny?" he asks, watching as I struggle with one of my sleeves.

"Nothing." I bite my bottom lip and try to contain myself, but I've always been terrible at hiding what I'm feeling. "Do you have any pocket protectors?"

Jackson blinks at me. "What?"

"Never mind." I shove my jacket in between the bottom legs of the stool, then reach over him for the menu. I'm two inches short, and I grunt as I try to close the distance. "Can you hand me that?"

He's busy staring at my coat on the floor like I've just personally offended him *and* his grandmother. "Don't you want to hang up your jacket?"

"It's fine where it is."

"It's on the floor."

"I found it at the station's lost and found two years ago. I'm not worried about it." Jackson keeps staring at the heap of my jacket while I press up on the bottom rung of the stool and lean across him, my shoulder digging into the middle of his surprisingly hard chest. He smells like maple syrup and fresh air. Perfectly sharpened number two pencils.

I pluck the menu from the tiny brass pirate ship holding it in place. "What's good here?"

He grabs the menu and places it back in the ship. "I already ordered you something."

"You did?"

"I did."

"How do you know what I like?"

The barest hint of amusement crinkles the corners of his eyes, and my stomach flips over itself. I bet he's devastating when he smiles. "I ordered whatever had the most sprinkles," he deadpans.

Okay, fair enough.

I cross my arms over my chest. "I don't even like sprinkles."

He rolls his eyes. "Sure."

"What did you order?" I poke at his arm. "Oat Bran? Fruitcake? Steel-cut oatmeal mixed with water?"

His mouth twitches. "I ordered a cruffin."

"That's a surprisingly whimsical decision, Jackson."

"I can be whimsical."

"Yeah, okay," I snort, trying to situate myself on the stool so I don't flip right off. With my luck, I probably will and I'll take him down with me. Break off the other side of his glasses so they're even.

"I was trying to be nice, Delilah. Not insult you."

"You've left mean Post-it notes on my car window for almost two years, Jackson. Forgive me if I'm a little suspicious."

He looks confused. "They weren't mean."

I shrug. "A little bit."

He frowns. "I never meant to be mean, Delilah."

"Could have fooled me."

The most delicious shade of pink climbs either side of his neck, right above the collar of his sweater. "Well, I wouldn't have to leave you notes if you just parked within the lines."

"I *do* park within the lines."

"Crooked. You park *crooked*, and I can't park in the space next to you with your bumper hanging out."

"I drive a Volkswagen Beetle. It's physically impossible for the bumper to hang out." I tilt my head to the side. "There are always a ton of spots. Why do you need to park in the space next to mine?"

"This isn't—" Jackson pinches his nose, then gives me a long-suffering look. "Can we start over, please? Talk about something that isn't a parking space?"

"Fine," I sniff. I don't know what it is about Jackson that immediately gets me riled up and ready to brawl. It's out of character for me, arguing over something as trivial as a parking space. I decide to extend a peace offering. "Thank you for ordering me the sprinkles."

"You're welcome." He rubs two fingers across his forehead. "I'm sorry about the notes. You're right. They were mean. I think you caught me at a bad time."

I stare at him. "For two years?"

His smile is subdued. "I'll do better." He seems to brace himself. "In the spirit of that . . . you were right about the European model."

"What?"

His eyes cut in my direction. "You were right about the European model," he repeats, his voice stronger. "It was a more accurate representation of the data."

A loud laugh bursts out of me.

"Wow." I press the back of my hand to his cheek, the same way my grandpa used to do when I was nine and trying to weasel my way out of going to school. "Are you coming down with something? Was that painful for you?"

He reaches up and grips my wrist, pulling my hand away from his face. "I regret saying anything."

I laugh. "No, you don't."

He squeezes my wrist. "I do. I think I like it better when we're arguing."

"Well, the day is young. I'm sure we'll find something else to disagree on."

I tap my hands on the counter and study our surroundings. A cozy dining space fills the bottom floor of the café. Booths against the wall and a long counter along the back. Heavy wooden beams stretch across the ceiling and an empty fireplace anchors one wall. There's no fire, the grate filled instead with stacked books and empty mugs, the ceramic handles scribbled with handwritten names of the regulars. Mismatched love seats slot together in front of it, paired with upcycled coffee tables. A narrow staircase on the left leads to a loft up above, overflowing with used books. Little pirate flags peek out above the shelves, labeled with genres. *Fantasy. Mystery. Romance.* A surprisingly robust *Self-Help* section and two entire shelves dedicated to *Baltimore Lore*.

"I didn't realize they had an upstairs."

Jackson nods. "It's usually too crowded to get up there. If you come on a weekday around eleven, you can get a good spot. The owner, Patty, is usually taking fresh stuff out of the oven to restock from the morning, and the lunch rush hasn't hit yet."

I was wondering why he chose such a specific time. Incredible, how he approaches every aspect of his life with such detail. "So you're always this fun, then."

His back goes rigid. "I guess so," he says, defensive again.

I exhale a deep sigh. I didn't come here to fight with Jackson. I came to figure out how in the hell we're going to work together to cover this snowstorm. After our nightmare of a meeting the other day, Keith made it clear that Jackson's agreement to the plan is now my responsibility. If I can't get him to agree, I've got a feeling there will be more turtle coverage in my future.

"All right, I've got two cinnamon bun lattes. One with oat milk just a hair short of scalding, brown sugar instead of white, and the cinnamon crumble on the side." Our server gives Jackson a stern look as she slides the drinks on the counter in front of us. "The other as god intended."

"Thanks, Patty."

She sets her hands on her hips. "You're lucky I like you, Jackson. I don't do special orders."

"I've seen you do three special orders just this morning," he says with a quirk of his brow.

"Well, I don't *like* doing special orders."

"Noted." He drops his spoon into his mug and stirs. "It's appreciated as always, Patty."

Patty's eyes slant in my direction. Her mouth pops open in delight. It's a look I'm familiar with, and the warm burst that comes with being recognized by my community pops like a champagne bubble in the middle of my chest.

"Delilah Stewart!"

"That's me!" I beam at her. "Hi!"

"What are you doing here?" She drops one elbow on the counter, immediately leaning into my space like we're old friends. It's my very favorite thing. I love when people feel like they know me. I put so much of myself into my job, it's a treat to have those pieces held safe in the hands of the people watching. To be seen. To be known. To be welcomed into their worlds, even if it's just for ten minutes every morning and every night.

Patty drops her chin into her hand. "I watched your segment the other day. The one with—what was it? Oh! It was the one about Mr. Trash Wheel. I can't believe you actually got in there and poked through some of the trash. You're a brave woman."

I flinch. Mr. Trash Wheel is a semiautonomous trash interceptor in the harbor that's been humanized by the city of Baltimore. Keith thought it would be fun if I tried to find the most interesting thing Mr. Trash Wheel scooped out of the harbor that day. I had genuine concerns for the first six minutes of that segment that I was about to discover a python while picking through the trash. Luckily, all I found in the rubble was one of those portable scooters that have been terrorizing the city. And a cardboard cutout of Pedro Pascal.

I gave it to Gianna.

"I learned a lot about the people of Baltimore that day."

Patty barks out a laugh. Her honey blond hair is tied back with a bandana, and she has a cute little pale pink nose ring. "I bet you did." She pushes off the counter. "What are you doing here with my favorite radio man?"

"Oh, um." I glance at Jackson, hoping for an assist. But he's busy staring at his latte like it holds the answers to life's great mysteries. "Jackson and I might be collaborating on a work project."

"Oh?"

"I'm still trying to wrestle him into a commitment," I say, bright and cheery. Like his continued lack of enthusiasm about working with me doesn't feel like another wobbly brick on my half-leaning tower of self-consciousness. "Maybe your coffee will loosen him up."

Jackson finally deigns to join the conversation. "I'm loose," he defends.

Another loud laugh tumbles out of Patty. She pats the top of his head gently. "Sure you are, honey." The bell rings at the register and Patty glances over her shoulder. "The people beckon. Give me a holler if you two need anything."

Patty leaves and a heavy silence descends. Jackson stares thoughtfully down at his coffee while I stir mine. For all our awkward encounters over the years, I don't think we've ever spent more than a handful of minutes in each other's company. Despite our proximity, we don't know each other at all.

"So," I start. My brain wants to fill in the empty space. Learn as much as possible, as quickly as I can. "What do you think—"

"Why did you stop reporting the weather?" he interrupts.

My mouth snaps shut. "What do you mean?"

He curls one big hand around his mug and gives me a *Don't be stupid* look. I'm used to seeing that look from across a parking lot. Up close, it's a lot more impactful.

"Why are you reporting on Mr. Trash Wheel," he asks, "instead of the five-day forecast?"

"Mr. Trash Wheel is a very important part of the Baltimore community," I defend.

"I'm aware," Jackson says lightly. "I have the limited-edition sticker to prove it."

I perk up on my stool. "Did you see they started making shirts too? They've got his little cartoon body printed all over it."

"Don't change the subject, Delilah." He brings his mug to his mouth, staring at me over the rim. "Why aren't you reporting on the weather anymore?"

I shrug and decide to play dumb. It's easier than explaining. The truth just makes me feel like an idiot. Or a pushover. Or an idiot who also happens to be a pushover. I keep my mouth lifted in an easy smile. "Keith wanted me on different projects."

Jackson's eyes are hidden behind the glare of his glasses. "Keith doesn't seem to like you very much," he says.

"Well, don't beat around the bush about it," I laugh. Embarrassment pricks at the back of my neck, but I push through it, busying myself with a sugar packet. It's one thing for me to notice, but Jackson? The guy who thought I couldn't interpret a weather model? I blow out a gusting breath. "Maybe the two of you can form a club. Get a new commemorative sticker for your water bottle that says 'I Hate Delilah Stewart.'"

"Delilah." Jackson's voice sharpens around the consonants of my name, his teeth biting down with a clench of his jaw. "I don't hate you."

"You once left a note that was just a frowning face."

He drags his hand over his mouth, trying to hide a . . . smile?

"I don't hate you," he repeats. "I'm just . . . confused by you."

A laugh sputters out of me. "Oh, that's much better."

"It is," he insists, blue eyes earnest.

I roll mine. "Sure."

"I'm serious. You don't—you don't even realize, do you?"

"What?"

He studies me, choosing his words carefully. My heart picks up the pace under his attention, my throat suddenly dry.

"You are utterly unpredictable," he finally says. Beneath the counter, his knee bumps into mine. "Most of the time, I'm just trying to figure you out."

"And correct my parking," I try to joke.

The barest hint of a smile teases the corner of his mouth. "Also that."

My eyes search his, looking for the hidden insult. But all I see is an honest sort of apprehension, a deep groove between his brows. "Okay," I say slowly. "I believe you."

His mouth lifts. "Yeah?"

I nod. "Yeah."

"Good," he says. His shoulders curl forward with relief. He props one elbow against the counter and slips his spoon back into his coffee.

Ultimately, it doesn't matter what Jackson thinks of me. I've gotten very good at ignoring the opinions of others. "I suppose I do have a habit of making your life more difficult," I concede.

He smiles down at his mug. "More colorful, certainly."

I snort a laugh. That's a nice way of looking at it. I think I'll hold on to that.

Not difficult.

More colorful.

I've always loved a little color.

Jackson fixes me with a look. "You going to tell me the truth now?"

Why not? Jackson already has his preconceived notions of me. There's not much further I can slip. I abandon my sugar packets. "I haven't been reporting on the weather because Keith is trying to sabotage my job."

His spoon clinks against his mug, but his face remains impassive. "Why do you think?"

I like that he's asked *Why?* and not *Are you sure?* He didn't ask me to defend myself, and the knot of pressure that sits heavy over my heart loosens, just a bit. It's nice to be believed. Right from the very start.

"A couple of months ago, we had this marketing company come in. He wanted to do an analysis of all of the on-air personalities. I think he was hoping—I don't know. I think he was hoping to embarrass me. There was a roundtable with regular viewers where they shared their opinions. We got to watch the live video feedback." I trace my finger across a bit of foam on the top of my latte. "Despite some leading questions, everyone had really positive things to say about me. I scored the highest out of the broadcast team."

"Shouldn't Keith be happy about that?"

I thought he would be. I remember sitting in the meeting when we discussed the results, not understanding why he was delivering good news with such an ugly look on his face. "I'm not entirely sure what his problem with me is. I just know I've been paying for it ever since. He hardly ever lets me report on the weather anymore, even though he knows it's what I like doing best."

It's what I went to school for. It's why I was hired at the station. It's what I dreamed of, spread out on the floor of my grandfather's living room, watching Bob Turk on the boxy television with a static-filled picture.

"That's why I wanted to meet with you before you agree to this snowstorm coverage," I say slowly. "I think it's another setup from Keith."

"You think he's sending you to the middle of nowhere to make you look like an idiot?"

"It would certainly fit his recent pattern of behavior, yeah. And it's the first time he's given me a weather feature since that dumb marketing meeting. I think he's hedging his bets that he can put me in at least seven different ridiculous scenarios during this coverage." I offer him a tight smile. "You don't need to be a part of it."

"But you're going through with it," Jackson says. "Even though you think Keith has ulterior motives. Why?"

I debate sharing the truth. Can I trust Jackson? Will he understand?

Or will he use this against me later?

"I don't really care why Keith is giving me this opportunity," I say. "I want to use it to show him that I'm not the disaster he keeps trying to turn me into. I love this job. I'm good at it. And I think if I go out there and deliver on this coverage without the whole circus act, Keith might actually let me do it." I sneak a peek at Jackson, but there's no judgment or amusement there. Just a rapt sort of attention that I've rarely felt the glow of. "I want to do my job without becoming a punch line, you know?"

Patty arrives with a tray in her hand, unloading the small plates on the counter in front of us. Two cruffins, and a doughnut roughly the size of my head, covered completely with rainbow sprinkles. Jackson slides the latter in front of me without a word and I'm grateful for the distraction. It feels like I just opened up my chest and showed him some of my stickiest parts.

"What about you?" I ask, picking the sprinkles off one by one and popping them into my mouth. "What do you want out of this assignment?"

He rubs his thumb over the handwriting across the handle of his mug. His name is written in bubbly letters, a heart instead of an *O* at the end of *JACKSON*. I'm familiar enough with his notes to know what his handwriting looks like. Someone else doodled his name across the ceramic.

"I have guardianship over my sisters," he says quietly. My eyes snap up to his. "They're fifteen and they're—" He huffs out a short laugh. "They're really excited about this. About the idea of me trying something different. Apparently"—he drags out the word—"I'm more boring than I thought. Or maybe, I guess, I'm just as boring as I thought. I don't want to disappoint them. And—"

He stops and swallows, the long line of his throat tensing and relaxing.

"And?" I prompt.

"And I think I need to try something different. Something new. I think I need to step out of my comfort zone. I think I need to know that I can."

Neat and orderly Jackson. Breaking his mold.

I smile. "Can I have a Post-it note?"

Jackson's eyes flick down to my mouth, then dart quickly back up. "Who says I have Post-its?"

I roll my eyes. "Please, I know you keep them on your person." I hold open my hand, palm up, fingers wiggling. "Gimme."

He grumbles something under his breath then reaches for his neatly folded jacket, withdrawing a square stack of yellow Post-its. He slaps them into my hand.

I grab a stray pen and immediately start to write. Jackson leans over, trying to get a look, but I pull the paper closer to my chest, shielding it with my hand.

Jackson huffs, hovering. "What are you writing?"

"A contract," I tell him without looking up. "So we're both on our best behavior. If we do this, we need to be a real team."

I hand him the finished Post-it. His blue eyes scan what I wrote, then the corner of his mouth lifts into a smirk.

I, Delilah Stewart, promise to be on my best behavior for the duration of this trip.* No picking fights, no making fun, and no parking sabotage.

*mishaps and mistakes, notwithstanding

"So you admit the parking is on purpose," he says.

"I said no such thing."

He laughs. A low, rough rumble. "I like the asterisk."

"I figured if I made an absolute guarantee, you'd have your doubts."

"Fair point." He holds out his hand. "My turn."

I hand over the pen and he scribbles something on the tiny notepad.

"There," he says. I flip the pad around and read. A laugh bursts out of me.

I, Jackson Clark, promise to be on my best behavior for the duration of this trip.* No picking fights, no making fun, and no sad-face notes left on car windows.

*and will allow for mishaps and mistakes, without complaint

I laugh. Jackson smiles, pleased with himself. I set the notepad down next to my sprinkle plate and extend my hand. "Deal?" I ask.

His eyes are right on me. Shining and bright, bright blue.

His hand slips into mine. I ignore the flip in my belly and squeeze tight.

"It's a deal."

DELILAH STEWART: How binding is a Post-it note contract?

DELILAH STEWART: If I were to, I don't know, somehow destroy the document . . . would the contents within still be valid?

JACKSON CLARK: What happened to the Post-it note, Delilah?

DELILAH STEWART: I spilled my coffee on it.

DELILAH STEWART: But it's okay! I dried it off with a blow-dryer.

DELILAH STEWART: Only burned off a corner of it when it caught fire!

DELILAH STEWART: It's still together. Mostly.

DELILAH STEWART: Jackson?

DELILAH STEWART: You haven't answered.

JACKSON CLARK: Yes, the contents within are still valid.

DELILAH STEWART: Great.

CHAPTER 6

JACKSON

"I can't believe you're going to be on TV." Adeline bounces her way across my bed, one of my dress shirts around her neck like a cape. She launches herself in the air on her third bounce and extends her legs, then lands flat on her back. My shirt flutters over her face while I have a silent heart attack. "This is so cool," she adds, her voice muffled.

Cool. I can't believe I've gotten to the place where a teenager's opinion on my professional life makes me feel like I've swallowed a helium balloon, but here we are.

I fold another sweater and place it in the open suitcase. "You really think so?"

"It's super cool." Penelope flops down next to Adeline on the bed. "You're going to be on the news, Jackie. Isn't this what you've always wanted?"

"No." Pretty sure I've had nightmares that start this way. "I wanted to work at the National Weather Service, not be on television."

Penelope and Adeline give me matching unimpressed looks. "C'mon. Not even a *teensy-tiny* part of you is excited about this?" Adeline asks.

I fiddle with a folded pair of socks. "Maybe a little bit," I admit.

While I'm not thrilled about the broadcast piece of it, I am excited to cover a storm in real time. Fifteen-year-old me who used to fall asleep with his face buried in his science textbook is absolutely losing his mind.

"I knew it." Penelope points at my face. "Look at you. You're smiling."

"I'm not smiling."

"You are." She shifts so her head is resting on her sister's lap. "Gosh, just think of it. You could have been doing cool stuff like this for years if you never got saddled with us."

"Stop acting like I didn't actively pursue custody of you guys." I poke her in the forehead, then do the same to Adeline. "I wanted you with me."

I wanted them so bad, I spent months working every odd job I could to pad my bank account. I put together a presentation for my mother with timelines and data sets and graphs, trying to convince her it was the best for everyone. I went to Bed Bath & Beyond and stood in front of the comforters, debating if they'd want lilac or sky blue. I got a house with enough room for all of us. I built a bunk bed.

And in the end, my mother didn't even fight me on it. She simply said, *I love that idea!* Like granting me custody of the girls was the same as dropping off dry cleaning or picking up pizza for dinner.

I refold my socks and nestle them into the proper spot next to my sweaters, then do it again with the next pair. The debilitating doubt creeps out of the corner I've shoved it into. Am I doing enough for them? Are they happy here, with me?

My mother's voice coils around my apprehension and tugs. *You've gotta make sure you're giving those girls fun. Teenage girls need fun.*

Am I fun? Am I what they need?

I try to think of the last fun thing we did, but come up blank. We went ice-skating at the harbor over the holidays. They loved that when they were little.

But they're not eight anymore. They need something different. They're changing and growing and expanding and I need to change with them. I've spent so much time focusing on the practical, the rest of me feels like a garden gate with vines growing over the hinges.

I'm hoping this trip fixes that for me. I'm hoping I can figure out how to be someone they want to be around.

"Why do you look like you're mad at the socks?" Adeline asks, eyes narrowing.

"Yeah. What did the socks ever do to you?"

"The socks did nothing," I mumble. I drag my fingers through my hair, tugging at it in frustration. I don't usually tell the girls when Camille calls, but it's been the devil on my shoulder since she reached out a few days ago. It's not unusual for her to call out of the blue after months of radio silence, but it *is* unusual for her to ask about anyone other than herself.

"Jackson," Adeline sighs. "You look like you're about to explode."

"Fine. Camille called," I say, reluctant. The smiles slip from their faces, and I almost wish I could snatch the words out from the space between us. I sigh, committed now. Annoyed with myself as much as the situation. "She wanted to know how you're doing."

Adeline's face settles into a stony mask. "Why?"

"I don't know. You know there's rarely a rhyme or a reason." Just vibes and planetary alignments. Hastily scribbled horoscopes and prescriptions left unfilled.

I flip my suitcase closed, then sit down on the edge of the bed.

I choose my words carefully, trying to hedge the delicate balance that comes with all their interactions with Camille. Honesty, with a touch of protective caution. "She was interested in how school is going for you both."

Adeline rolls her eyes. "Interested," she repeats. She plucks at the top of my comforter. "That's not the word I'd use."

Penelope and I exchange a loaded look.

"What word would you use?" I ask.

"I don't know," she says, crossing her arms over her chest. Her gaze goes somewhere behind me. Penelope and I wait. Adeline's nosedive into a sullen attitude is unusual for her. She's my sunshine girl. The one who used Crayola markers to doodle seventy-three rainbows on my bedroom wall when she was five.

She hides her face behind a curtain of hair. "I don't want to talk about this anymore," she mumbles.

I nod. "We don't have to talk about it."

"Fine."

Silence blankets the room. The ancient heater cranks on downstairs and the floorboards groan. Adeline makes a small sound under her breath then rolls off the bed, the shirt that was tied around her neck fluttering to the floor. She shuffles out of the room. A second later, a door clicks shut quietly down the hallway.

"I shouldn't have said anything," I sigh.

"No, it's good to know when Mom is sniffing around. Remember when she showed up at Easter that one year? With the skateboards?"

"Yeah, I remember." She said she wanted to take the girls to the skate park and teach them how to shred. The girls had been eleven with approximately no interest in shredding. Camille left two hours later, despite promising the girls she'd make a new ravioli recipe for dinner. She left to get ricotta, and we didn't see her again for close to a year.

Another time, she stayed in town for two weeks, only to disappear the night of the girls' dance recital with a hastily written note left on the kitchen counter.

Opportunity came up, it said. *I'll catch the next one.*

She didn't make the next one. Or the one after that. Or . . . any of the recitals before the girls decided they didn't want to dance anymore.

"It's hard for Addie," Penelope continues, "when Mom pretends that she's interested in knowing us, only to vanish for another eleven-month stretch." She sits up on the bed and tucks her long legs under her. "There's this luncheon coming up at school. I think Addie is more sensitive than usual."

We have a calendar taped to the middle of the fridge downstairs. I try to remember what I've penciled in recently. "What luncheon?"

"There's a brunch thing coming up for the sophomores. Our school is great about making it inclusive, but most of the other girls are bringing their moms. Addie has been having a tough time."

"She hasn't said anything."

"Duh." Penelope gives me a bemused look. "You haven't exactly made it a secret you're not Mom's biggest fan. Adeline doesn't want to disappoint you by wanting her there."

Guilt loops around my heart. "Shit."

"I mean, totally warranted given the history of behavior. But I think between the three of us, Addie is the hopeful one. She wants things to be different."

I make a mental note to check in with her over cereal tomorrow morning. To be *better* at this too. "What about you? Are you having a hard time?"

"No." She gives me a small, sad smile. "Like I said, Addie is the hopeful one."

They should both be the hopeful ones, but Camille has a bad

habit of taking good things and twisting them until they're broken. I study Penelope, looking for the lie. She keeps her face impassive, letting me look.

"All right." Satisfied she's not suppressing any major emotions, I zip my suitcase shut. "You should have said something."

"I'm saying something now, aren't I?"

I pull my luggage off the bed and set it to the side. "Maybe I should stay home," I say. "This doesn't feel like the right time to leave you guys."

"Noooo," Penelope whines, throwing her body dramatically across my bed. "Jackson. I love you, but *please* go on this trip. We have big plans for movie marathons and unhealthy dinners and braiding Aiden's hair. We're going to make popcorn and play *Stardew Valley* and talk about boys. It's going to be great. We won't think about Mom at all."

That feels like a convenient excuse with suspicious timing, but I allow it. "Do you plan on going to school at any point?"

She waves her hand over her head. "If the storm really is as big as you say it is, then we won't have school. The city of Baltimore has, like, two snowplows." She lifts herself off the bed, grabs my suitcase, and tosses it into the hall. It skids across the floor before it tips over down the staircase, descending one dull thud at a time.

"Go on the trip, Jackie," Penelope says. "Be nice to Delilah Stewart. Get your weather kicks in. Talk to someone who understands what you're saying."

"Are you sure?"

She nods. "*Oh my god*, yes. Consider it a favor to us at this point." She grabs onto my arm with both hands and tries to shake me back and forth. "Fly the nest, big brother. Spread those wings and soar."

I frown. "What have you been watching on TV?"

"I've been listening to inspirational podcasts. Very helpful."

She gives me one last shake, then skips toward my door. "Oh, and if you could become best friends with Delilah, that would be great. Adeline and I want to invite her to dinner."

Friendship is the furthest thing from my mind when I pull up into the station's parking lot the next afternoon, Delilah's car parked in its usual spot.

Meaning it's parked halfway in *my* usual spot, the pale pink Volkswagen Beetle so far over the line I can barely wedge my car door open.

A half-torn sandwich wrapper catches my attention as I attempt to untangle my messenger bag from the front bumper of my car. I squint at it, then realize it's a note. Taped to the passenger-side window of her car.

Try parking somewhere else next time, it says.

She even drew a smiley face at the bottom.

"I don't know why you do this to yourself." Aiden appears at my bumper and claps a heavy hand over my shoulder, dragging me forward from between the two cars. "You could park in a different spot."

"I'm aware." I crumple the sandwich wrapper in my hand. There's something vaguely sticky on it. "But this one is mine."

It's the principle of the matter. Or something.

"Were you hoping to get stuck between the cars so you didn't have to come inside?"

I keep my face carefully blank. "Maybe."

The embarrassment of being pinned to my Honda Accord by *Herbie: Fully Loaded* might pale in comparison to whatever is about to happen in that booth.

Today we're introducing the partnership between 101.6 LITE FM and YBAL News on *Heartstrings*. I had my hesitations about

Delilah and me appearing on the romance hotline for the announcement, but Maggie insisted. *It's our most popular show, Jackson. We're more likely to get a higher reach, Jackson. Don't be absurd, Jackson. It's not open for debate, Jackson.*

I stare at the entrance of the station like I'm approaching the guillotine.

"It's just a little case of stage fright," Aiden assures me. "Once you get started, you'll settle right in. You're going to be fine."

"Better than fine," another voice adds. Aiden's better half pops up behind him, the three of us forming the most unenthusiastic conga line this parking lot has ever seen. Lucie grins at me. "You're going to be amazing, Jackson. This is exactly what you need."

I readjust my bag. "Public humiliation?"

She laughs and I watch as the sound makes its impact against Aiden. He leans toward her, his eyes going soft. Tiny bluebirds start to circle around his head. Hearts float out of his temples.

I try to turn around and head back to my car, but Aiden loops one arm around my midsection and starts forcibly dragging me toward the station.

"Time to rip off the Band-Aid, bud."

"Are we ripping Band-Aids?" Delilah appears at the edge of the sidewalk, slightly out of breath, her monstrosity of a jacket wrapped over her shoulders. She looks even smaller than usual bundled up in the thick material, twin patches of pink on her cheeks. Her eyes land on me and her smile twists into something mischievous. "I call first dibs, if we're ripping stuff."

Maybe a coffee spill *does* invalidate a Post-it note contract.

And here I thought we had a breakthrough at the café the other day.

"Delilah," I greet.

"Jackson," she replies with a laugh. "I was thinking. We should come up with a name."

"A name?"

"For our segment."

"It needs a name?"

She shrugs. "It would be nice, don't you think?"

"Why don't we just call it *Jackson and Delilah Report on the Weather*?"

"Oh wow," she deadpans. "Did you come up with that on your own?"

I scratch at the back of my neck. I'm not going to be embarrassed about a perfectly reasonable suggestion. "What's your idea?"

"Well, we have options." She reaches into her pocket and pulls out a narrow, crumpled piece of paper. It's at least two feet long, so I assume she's been to CVS in the past week. "*Snow Much Fun with Jackson and Delilah, Say It Ain't Snow with Jackson and Delilah, We're Off to See the Blizzard, Jackson and Delilah, Weather Together—*"

"That one," I say quickly. "That's the one I want."

"Great." Her eyes cut to my side and her grin seems to double in size. "You must be Lucie." She shuffles forward in her ridiculous coat. I also forgot Aiden and Lucie were standing next to us. "I'm such a fan. I listened to all your broadcasts last winter."

Lucie presses her palms to her cheeks. "Are you kidding? *I'm* such a fan. I loved that piece you did on the Papermoon Diner."

Delilah's eyes brighten as she wiggles in excitement. "Oh, I loved that segment. That's one of my favorite places in the city."

"Mine too. My daughter loves the figurines. And the pancakes."

And just like that they're off. Lucie and Delilah descend into a rapid-fire conversation about local Baltimore oddities while Aiden and I stand stupefied at their side. Aiden, I assume, awash with affection for the love of his life. Me, drowning in trepidation at the nightmare that awaits me inside.

I might be looking forward to covering a major weather event, but I haven't figured out how to pack away my anxieties on the *how*. I'm a radio meteorologist who loves data but hates talking for longer than fifteen seconds. It's why reporting on the forecast has always suited me best. I aggregate the data, I prepare my script, and I read from my notes. There's not a lot you can screw up with "chance of showers, don't forget to bring your umbrella." I've found comfort in the predictable.

I tend to lose the plot when I need to speak on the fly.

I try to breathe through the inevitable panic, but it's like fighting gravity. The voices around me slowly slip into something monotone and fuzzy. My ears fill with cotton balls. My throat grows thick. I'm aware that I'm panicking over something trivial, but I can't control my reaction. There's so much that can go wrong. I don't know how to hold myself steady.

The group shifts. Aiden and Lucie twist their fingers together and head into the station. Delilah trails after them. I catch her bicep with my palm before she can get too far, more of an impulse than a conscious thought. I gently guide her back to me.

She looks up at me with wide brown eyes, the remnants of her amusement still caught around the edges of her mouth. It evaporates as her face softens with concern.

"What is it?" she asks. Her eyes narrow. "Is this about the sandwich wrapper?"

I shake my head. "I don't care about the sandwich wrapper."

She arches one delicate eyebrow.

"Okay. I care a little bit about the sandwich wrapper." I pause. "But I need to talk to you about something. Before we head in."

"Why do you sound so ominous?"

I swallow and it feels like I have an entire shovel wedged in my throat. "I should have told you when we were at Skullduggery, but I didn't know how."

She blinks. "Are you dying?"

"No."

"It sounds like you're dying."

"I'm not dying." It sort of feels like I might be dying.

Her eyes brighten. "Have you killed a man?"

My mouth is so dry, I'm unable to summon the appropriate words.

"Oh god," she says, her smile slipping off her face. She leans closer. "Have you killed a man?"

"No, nothing like that." I glance at the door to the station, the cracked pavement beneath our feet, the sky. I wish for one of these things to swallow me whole. "I have a problem."

"Okay."

"I have a problem, specifically, with speaking."

Delilah's nose scrunches in her confusion. "You're speaking right now."

"No, I mean, on the radio."

She stares at me. "I'm not really following what's happening right now. You're a radio weatherman, Jackson. Speaking on the radio is your job."

"I know." I pull in a deep breath through my nose, then release it in a cloud of white. Like an emotionally destitute dragon. "I have trouble with stuff that's not the weather."

"Ah. Are you talking about that cute thing you do where you ramble?"

I frown. "It's not cute."

"You did it the last time you had to cover *Heartstrings*. You went on about snow lightning for, like, twenty minutes."

I did and then I emerged from the booth on wobbly legs, sweating like I just ran back-to-back Ultraman marathons.

"You're very passionate about weather phenomena, Jackson. That's nothing to be ashamed of."

She tries to move past me toward the door, but I hook her arm again and reel her back. She tilts her head to look at me. "You're serious about this."

"I am. I think we should consider the possibility that Keith's big setup was asking you to do this with me."

Maybe Keith partnered Delilah with me because he knows *I'm* the disaster. Maybe he's counting on me to mess up the broadcast and drag Delilah down with me.

Delilah pauses, turning the idea over. I flex my fingers and roll my wrists, trying to get the prickly, uncomfortable sensation vibrating just beneath my skin to disappear.

"No, I don't think so," she finally says. "Keith isn't that observant. Or clever. To be honest, I doubt he's ever noticed your weather rambles. Or listened to your station."

"Weather rambles?"

Her head tips to the side. Some chocolate-colored waves slip over her shoulder. "What would you like to call it?"

"What's it called when someone drives their car directly into a ravine?"

Delilah laughs and some of my cotton-ball-feeling clears. "*Thelma and Louise*? Are you going to *Louise* us into a canyon, Jackson?"

"It was Thelma's idea to drive off that cliff."

Delilah snorts. "Remind me not to let you drive during our road trip." She curls her fingers around my wrist and tugs. "Come on. Inside we go."

I resist. "I'm not sure I want to."

Like I summoned her with my reluctance, Maggie appears, banging through the door of the station. She sticks her head out and bellows across the parking lot, "Jackson! Delilah! You're on in twenty minutes!"

Delilah waves in acknowledgment and yanks on my wrist again. I continue to pretend my feet are planted in the cement.

"It's okay," she says. She turns back to look at me, hair whipping across her face, her brown eyes lit up gold. I wonder what it's like to feel that easy. That comfortable.

"You have nothing to worry about," she says. Her hand is still around my wrist. "I'll be with you the entire time."

JACKSON CLARK: Evening, everybody. I'm—um. Filling in for a second while Aiden—while Aiden does something. He's getting water? I think? Either way, he asked me to sit in, so. Here I am.

[awkward laughter]

JACKSON CLARK: What should we talk about?

[pause]

JACKSON CLARK: Has anyone ever told you about the difference between snow and sleet? Snow forms directly from water vapor as ice crystals, but sleet starts as snow, then partially melts in a warmer layer of air before refreezing into small ice pellets as it falls through a colder layer. It's sort of like—sort of like the meatloaf leftovers of the meteorological world, if you can believe that.

[pause]

JACKSON CLARK: I'm not sure when Aiden will be back? But I could tell you about snow lightning, too, if you wanted? It's—

CHAPTER 7

DELILAH

Jackson was not exaggerating.

As soon as we enter the building, it's like his soul departs his body. He stares unseeingly at some mysterious spot in front of him, only offering one-word answers to the questions I continuously lob in his direction in an attempt to distract him.

Did you notice where my sandwich wrapper was from? The one I wrote your note on? Silence. *It was from Chaps Pit Beef. Have you ever had Chaps?* More silence. *My grandpa took me to the one that's in the parking lot of the Gold Club when I was six and I've been hooked ever since. I don't think he even realized it was a strip club until like 1998 when they put up that giant billboard for the Golden Rods. Have you been?*

That had finally garnered a reaction. Jackson turned halfway toward me. "Are you asking if I've been to the strip club?"

"No. I'm asking if you've been to Chaps. That specific Chaps. The one in the parking lot of the strip club."

"Ah," he said, reaching up to squeeze at the back of his neck as he led us through the radio station hallways. "No."

"You should go sometime."

That was seven minutes ago and the very last thing we said to each other before a pretty woman with dip-dyed box braids handed us each a pair of headphones and ushered us into a window-lined booth.

Now, Aiden is at the long table in the middle of the room, hastily trying to clear various cookie boxes, chocolate mint wrappers, and half-empty mugs of coffee. Lucie spins herself around in Aiden's chair, tossing tiny paper airplanes in the middle of the mess, her feet tucked up underneath her and one of Aiden's sweatshirts draped around her shoulders. He stops her mid-spin with his hand against the armrest and ducks down for a firm kiss against her smiling mouth.

My chest squeezes.

They're happy here, at the radio station. Everyone I've seen. People greet each other by name and ask about weekend plans and talk about kids' birthdays. At the news station, I'm constantly walking on eggshells, trying not to anger Keith, trying not to be a nuisance.

But here, everyone revolves around one another in a perfectly choreographed dance of productivity. It's a humming hive of activity as everyone sets up for the show, laughing and shouting and tossing boxes and cables back and forth.

And Jackson floats through the middle of it, straight into the booth where he sits down in a beanbag chair in the corner, his knees practically to his chest. He scoops up a heart-shaped pillow and holds it in his arms.

I'm not entirely confident he's breathing.

"Delilah. Hey. Thank you again for doing this."

Maggie appears at my side, her phone in her hand and a white earbud wedged in one ear. She's just as sleek and professional as she was at the news station, while I'm wearing a purple sparkly parka I dug out of a lost-and-found bin.

A short man wearing suspenders appears at her side, his chin tucked to his chest as he runs his finger down a list on his clipboard. He has a headpiece that looks like a Britney Spears concert replica and a cellophane-wrapped box of chocolate mints. He startles when he looks up, then grins so wide his earpiece jostles.

I like him immediately.

"This is Hughie," Maggie offers, grabbing his clipboard and jotting a note down in the margin. "He helps out around the station."

"I take care of what needs taking care of," he says with a nod.

"You can start by taking her jacket, Hughie. Thank you."

The small, strange man takes my coat and disappears without another word. Maggie heaves a long-suffering sigh. "He asked to do a college rotation credit here and I haven't been able to get rid of him since." She bends and picks up the box of mints. "Though I suppose he does serve his purpose well." She angles her chin toward the booth. "How's Jackson doing?"

"He's, um. Well." I scratch at my neck. "He's not doing great."

Maggie's mouth twists.

"Is it always this bad?" I ask.

Through the glass, Aiden tosses a small foam football at Jackson. It hits him in the middle of his forehead. He doesn't react. Aiden and Lucie exchange a concerned look.

"Not this bad, usually, no. When he has to do something outside of his forecasting, he rambles a bit, but he doesn't usually shut down," Maggie says. "I didn't give him much time to adjust, which is my fault. I know Jackson is a creature of habit."

I rub my lips together. "He thinks Keith agreed to this assignment to embarrass us both. That his anxiety is being . . . weaponized, I guess."

"Keith isn't that diabolical," Maggie says with a snort. "You have to possess at least two brain cells to be diabolical." She cuts a look in my direction. "Sorry."

"Please," I laugh. "I'm not loyal to Keith. Speak freely."

"Oh, thank god. I thought I was going to have to launch a side quest to convince you that he sucks." Maggie shifts her body, dropping one shoulder against the glass wall of the booth and crossing her legs at the ankles. Her hazel eyes are penetrating. "It's why I suggested the partnership. You're better than what he has you doing."

"What? You're like my . . . broadcast fairy godmother?"

A sharp smile curls the corners of her mouth. "I'd look ridiculous in tulle. My main goal is, and always will be, the station." She eases a lock of dark hair behind her ear. "This is an opportunity to give the station serious exposure, and Jackson is brilliant." We turn in unison and look at him through the glass. He's gripping his headphones to his chest like they are an emotional support teddy bear. Maggie frowns. "When he's not having an existential crisis."

"You think he can pull it together in time?"

Maggie's phone rings and she glances down at the ID. "I know he can," she says, distracted. She silences her phone and regards me with cool, assessing eyes. "What about you? Can you hold it together?"

"I can. I will."

"Good."

Her phone rings again. She rolls her eyes to the ceiling and taps the green answer button. "How did you get this number?" she snaps.

I'm close enough to hear the low rumble of a man's voice in response.

Maggie huffs. "Stop bothering me. I have work to do."

She taps End Call. Another immediately rolls in. She scrolls up with her thumb and blocks it without hesitation, but another rolls in. And then another.

Maggie's fist clenches around the edge of her phone, knuckles white.

"I need to deal with this," she says.

"Don't let me stop you."

"You're on in seven minutes," she offers. Her phone is still ringing in her hand. An angry buzz that's somehow picking up speed and intensity. "The bathrooms are down the hall. There's a vending machine stocked with snacks. Aiden keeps the good coffee hidden, but feel free to bribe him with these." She hands me the box of chocolates that came from Hughie and taps the headphone in her ear. "I'll be listening. Good luck."

She's off without another word, raising her phone to her ear and hissing out a string of what I can only assume are creative and spectacular threats. Maggie seems the sort to wield her words as weapons, and I have no doubt they're deadly.

I'm just turning toward the booth when my phone starts to ring, a picture of my grandpa flashing across the screen.

I remember the day I took the picture. A baseball game. The first truly warm day of spring. The sky so blue it made my eyes hurt to look at and Grandpa's wide and toothy smile, the seats of Camden Yards stretching out behind him like an ocean of green.

That had been a good day. We haven't had a lot of good days lately.

I answer his call with a quick swipe of my thumb.

"Grandpa, hi." I turn toward the wall. Tuck myself against it and make myself as small as possible. "Everything okay?"

There's a pause and then a rough, agitated sound and my heart knows before my head does.

"It's four thirty," he says and his voice sounds wrong. Short and tired and confused.

I glance at the clock right above the door of the booth. "A few minutes until, yes."

"You were supposed to be home from school an hour ago. You know I don't like it when you go over to your friends' houses without asking."

I saw my teeth over my bottom lip and suck in a deep breath through my nose. It doesn't matter how many times it happens, it feels like a punch to the gut every time.

"I know," I rasp, rubbing at the bridge of my nose, trying to press that burning, aching feeling away. The doctors say I shouldn't argue with him when he's like this. That it'll only make him more agitated. More confused. "I'm sorry. I got a new assignment that I'm excited about. Time got away from me." There. A bit of the truth, without disrupting wherever he's slipped off to. For me the hardest part of these episodes has always been the lies I have to tell. It feels wrong, when Grandpa has always asked for the truth. When he's always given it to me in return.

I glance at the clock again. Three minutes until we're on. "I'll be home soon, okay? We can have lemon cookies and tea and watch *General Hospital*. Just like always."

Comfort. Routines. All the things that make his Alzheimer's more manageable. He grumbles some more, but it lacks the low hum of frustration he had when I answered the phone. "I suppose that's okay," he finally says.

"Okay. Good." I force a smile I don't feel. "I'll see you soon."

"You will," he agrees. "I love you, darling."

"Love you too," I manage, my voice pitched slightly too high. I drop my forehead against the cold wall and wait until I hear him hang up the phone, then close my eyes and breathe deep.

It's okay, I tell myself. *He's okay.*

You said the right things.

You didn't make it worse.

I allow myself another minute and then pack it all away. I'll deal with this later, with lemon cookies and tea, just as I promised.

But when I turn toward the booth, I feel my resolve buckle.

Jackson isn't staring at the wall anymore. He's looking right at me.

DELILAH STEWART: Say it.

JACKSON CLARK: No.

DELILAH STEWART: Come on. Say it. The people need to know.

JACKSON CLARK: You say it, then.

DELILAH STEWART: We're a team, Jackson.

[sigh]

JACKSON CLARK: Jackson and Delilah, Weather Together.

DELILAH STEWART: Weather Together!

CHAPTER 8

JACKSON

Delilah waits until the last possible second to slip into the booth, dropping herself into the chair next to me without meeting my eye. I stare at her, watching the way she twists her fingers around the cord of her headphones.

"Everything okay?" I ask.

She didn't look okay in the hallway. She looked sad. Like whatever light source shines out from the middle of her was set to dim. She took a phone call, then wilted like a flower.

She forces herself to smile, looking at the desk in front of me instead of anywhere close to my face. "Why do you have three pages of handwritten notes?"

I cover them with my palm. "Delilah," I say, ignoring the question. "Are you okay?"

Her sigh is small. Quiet. A fraction of her usual energy, dulled down into too-small pieces. "I'm fine. Though now I'm concerned I don't have three pages of handwritten notes."

"You don't seem fine."

She rolls her eyes up to the ceiling, tugging her headphones over her ears. Some of her hair tangles around the band. "Thanks for that," she says, but there's no bite to it. Not like there was a week ago.

"No, I mean—" I reach forward and gently straighten the hair that's stuck, smoothing it back behind her headphones. I have to shift closer to do it, my chair bumping against hers. "It's okay if you're not fine. I can wait."

Her eyes snap to mine, curious.

"I mean," I correct myself again, cheeks heating, "the show can wait. We don't have to start until you're ready."

I don't let go of the hair that's twisted around my finger. I rub my thumb over it, unconscious. It's so soft, and she smells like cherries. I angle my body in front of hers so she has some privacy if she needs it, my shoulders blocking her out from the people who are still moving around the room.

"I'm fine," she says again, softer this time, her eyes dancing back and forth between mine. "Thank you, Jackson. I'm okay."

"Okay." I let go of her hair and drop my hands to my lap beneath the desk. I curl them into fists.

A throat clears on the other end of the table. Aiden is staring at me, his eyes narrowed in thought. "You ready?" he asks.

I turn toward Delilah. "Are you?" I ask.

She nods. This booth was barely made for one person, let alone three. We're so close I can count every freckle across the bridge of her nose.

It only takes three minutes into the broadcast to realize this might be my own personal hellscape. Delilah wiggles every ten seconds, and with the way we're smashed together, I can't get away. Our bodies are pressed together knee to thigh. Maybe my anxiety is manifesting with hyperfixation, because every time she even thinks about moving, I swear to god it shaves five years off my life.

Delilah tries to shift but it only ends up pressing more of her against more of me. In a fit of desperation, I reach under the desk and grab her thigh, fingers tightening in a silent plea to *stop wiggling*. She sucks in a sharp breath and I abruptly move my hand away.

No more touching.

"Welcome to *Heartstrings*, Baltimore. I'm your host, Aiden Valentine, and we have two guests in the booth with us tonight. You know them both, but you're about to know them better. Say hello, Jackson and Delilah."

Delilah wiggles in her seat, excited. I clench my jaw so tight I fear something might snap.

"Hello, Baltimore." Her full mouth quirks and her eyes find mine. "Hello, Jackson."

I lean forward so fast I slam my face into the microphone. Static explodes in our headphones. "Hello," I say around a wince.

One word and I'm already sweating, a tingling sensation in the back of my throat and in the palms of my hands. I stare hard at my notes and try to collect myself, but the urge to start spewing random facts about the weather is *strong*.

At least I haven't blacked out yet, I guess.

I kind of wish I would. Because being hyperaware of how dramatically I'm spiraling isn't exactly a good time.

"I hear there's a storm headed our way," Aiden says. The words piece together slowly, swimming like soup through my brain.

Storm. Headed. Our way.

I'm three seconds behind this broadcast, on a time delay while I watch Aiden and Delilah interact from behind a thick piece of glass.

"Yes," Delilah says. "That's the rumor. A winter storm is set to hit sometime next week. A little late in the season, which gives it the potential to smash some snowfall records."

Both of them shift their attention to me. I make a wheezing sound directly into the microphone.

Delilah's forehead creases in concern. "We've been talking about it on the air for the past couple of days as a possibility, but it seems like all the major factors have locked into place now. While the weather system will stretch the length of the coast, Maryland is smack-dab in the worst of it."

Beneath the desk, Delilah's hand grabs mine. She squeezes tight, and some of the fog clears.

"Sounds serious," Aiden says, fiddling with the wrapper of a chocolate mint. "Is there anything people should do to prepare?"

"I don't want to cause panic, but you should start stocking up on nonperishable goods. Not, like, end-of-days stocking up, but maybe an extra can of soup or two. Check on your neighbors, especially the elderly. Make sure they have a plan to keep warm and safe if the power goes out. And make sure your home is equipped with flashlights, batteries, and portable heaters." She grins. "You should also definitely break out the sleds. Fed Hill is going to be amazing with the snow."

She's so good at this. Comfortable. Confident. She tucks her legs up beneath her in the half-crooked rolling chair someone found wedged in a closet at the end of the hall and scoots herself closer to the desk. Like she wants to climb directly into the microphone. Like she can't hold on to her own enthusiasm.

Whatever happened in the hallway, she's back to herself now, her brightness all the way up.

Aiden laughs. "Oh yeah? Got big sledding plans?"

He picks up a pen and lobs it at my head. I yank my attention away from Delilah.

Participate, he mouths.

"I don't have a sled," I say dumbly. My voice sounds like I

smoked six packs of cigarettes before stepping into this room. Like I've pressed my mouth directly to an exhaust pipe.

Delilah bumps against my shoulder. "You can borrow mine."

My answer is immediate. "No, thank you."

She slowly swivels in her chair, facing me fully. "What? Is my sled not good enough for you?"

"More than twenty thousand people visit the emergency department each year with sledding-related incidents." I press my finger to the side of my glasses, adjusting them. "And there's a road at the bottom of Federal Hill."

"Obviously, I'd sled the other way. Away from the road. I'm not advocating for anyone to sled directly into the road, Jackson."

"I know that."

"Where did you find that statistic? Do you keep them in a little notebook?" She glances at the paper in front of me. "Is that why you have those notes?"

"No. These are weather notes." Heat climbs the back of my neck. "What about you? You just have a sled at your house? Ready for Federal Hill?"

"Of course I do. Why wouldn't I?"

She drives a pale pink Volkswagen Beetle and her jacket makes her look like a sparkly purple doughnut, so I guess owning a sled is not outside the realm of possibility for Delilah Stewart. "Because we live in Maryland where the average annual snowfall is twenty-one inches," I say. "Last year it didn't even snow at all."

"Yes, and I was devastated. My doughnut sled sat sadly in the corner of my dining room from November to March."

"Doughnut sled?"

"Yes. My sled is in the shape of a doughnut. It has strawberry sprinkles."

And she told me she doesn't like sprinkles.

"So it's an inner tube."

"An inner tube snow sled, yes."

"Inner tubes are not sleds, Delilah."

A devastating smile starts somewhere around her eyes and slips down to play at her mouth. "You're getting tied up in semantics, *Jackson*."

I don't even know what we're talking about anymore. Just that there's a fire in my belly the longer I look at her, welling up and over like a tide. Frustration, maybe. Confusion, likely. Bewilderment, potentially. Probably an odd and distracting combination of all three.

Our knees knock together beneath the desk as I turn fully toward her and that heavy, hot feeling grips me by the throat. When Aiden said *participate*, I'm not sure he meant like this.

"Are you bringing the doughnut on the trip?"

"I wasn't planning on it, but now I might. Now, maybe all of my reporting will be done from inside the doughnut."

"Good segue, guys." Aiden throws another pen at my head, but this one goes sailing two inches past my temple. "Jackson and Delilah will be covering the storm from Garrett County. You can expect live broadcasts on conditions and any relevant, up-to-date information including how the snowfall is looking for those doughnut sleds." Aiden grins. "Our boy is leaving us for the big leagues, Baltimore."

"I wouldn't say that. We're just—" I nudge my glasses with my knuckles. "We're taking a trip. For the—for the snow. We're going to tell you everything you need to know about . . ." My voice drifts. Delilah stares at me.

"Snow," she finishes for me when my mouth continues to move soundlessly. "We're going to tell you everything you need to know about the snow. That's right. But for now, Baltimore, back to you."

She shoots me a subtle thumbs-up and I want to hurl myself through the glass wall of this soundproof booth.

"Excellent. On that note, we're going to cut to our first song. Stay tuned, everyone." "Winter Wonderland" by Harry Connick Jr. starts to trickle through the headphones as Aiden taps his way across his keyboard. He wrenches his off and tosses them on top of an empty cookie box he forgot to clear. "That was good, you guys."

I drop my forehead to the middle of the desk and keep it there. "Which part? The part where I couldn't remember the word for snow?"

"It's an improvement over you yelling about the snow."

I roll my head to the side against my notes, squinting blearily at Delilah. I feel like I've just gone seven rounds and lost every one. "Do you really have a doughnut inner tube in your house?"

"Of course I do. I don't lie about doughnut sleds." She offers me a tentative smile. "Should I bring it on our trip?"

"No." I think about it. "Actually, maybe. I can use it to sled directly into Deep Creek Lake when the broadcast starts going south."

"While I'd pay good money to see that, I think you're going to do just fine. Apparently, all I need to do is find something to antagonize you about during each broadcast until you forget about your weather rambles. That seemed to work, didn't it?"

"I guess," I grumble. I was so distracted by Delilah, I forgot to be nervous. I frown and the paper beneath my cheek crinkles. "I really don't know why Maggie wants me to do this."

"Because no one knows weather systems better than you, with the exception of the woman sitting to your right," says a voice from the doorway. Maggie is wedged in the half-open door of the booth, tapping at her phone with a weary look on her face. "And because I need the win."

"What is it?" I ask.

She slips her phone back into her pocket. "Orion," she says.

"They're still interested in our programming." She pauses and presses two fingers to the middle of her forehead. "They've upped the price again."

The satellite giant has been after our station for two years now, and they've only gotten more aggressive after the runaway success of *Heartstrings* last February. For some reason, they want our programming, and they're not inclined to take no for an answer. Maggie has been doing her part to push back against their advances, determined to keep our little station local. But Orion has been throwing Hail Marys to the tune of six-figure acquisition deals. Our ownership team has started paying attention.

"If Orion gets their hands on us, we'll turn into segmented programming. They'd bleed everything local out of us until we're just another husk of Top 40 hits. But if I can make the case to ownership that local content still performs well, then—"

"Then maybe they'll finally tell Orion to shove it," Aiden summarizes.

"You got it." Maggie's eyes find mine. "And there's nothing more local than a freakishly strong snowstorm, barreling straight toward us. If we can prove that we can keep the lights on ourselves *without* whatever snake oil Orion is selling, we should be able to shut them up once and for all. But we've gotta back it up with strong numbers."

My hands flex on the headphones until the plastic creaks. Out of the corner of my eye, I see Delilah shift. "No pressure, then."

Maggie's face softens. "You're brilliant, Jackson. I wouldn't put you in this position if I didn't have full confidence in you. Try to enjoy it, yeah? Try to have some fun."

There's that word again. *Fun.* It scratches at the inside of my skull until my shoulders pull tight. I've never had much use for fun. I've relied on practical, predictable, probable, and logical.

The best path forward has always been the one I can clearly see laid out in front of me in perfectly manageable steps.

But that hasn't exactly served me well. I think somewhere along the way, I got so settled in my routines and habits and plans that now I'm trapped by them. They twist around me like vines, holding me in place. Keeping me from moving forward.

The damned garden gate, sealed shut.

I don't want to be like this.

"We can do that," Delilah says. She offers me another careful smile. "We can pull it off. Right, Jackson?"

"Yeah," I agree, hoping I sound like I mean it. "Absolutely."

AIDEN VALENTINE: A quick note from one of our sponsors. Eddie's in Roland Park now has doughnut snow sleds in stock.

AIDEN VALENTINE: Mention AND NOW, BACK TO YOU for twenty-five percent off.

CHAPTER 9
DELILAH

"This is so much fun," Jackson deadpans from the driver's side of the news van, his hands flexing on the wheel. "This is the most fun I've ever had in my life."

I launch a peach ring at his head, smirking when it bounces off his temple and lands somewhere in between the armrest and the center console. He slowly turns, giving me the most haughty, offended look I've ever seen.

I immediately descend into giggles.

"You're just mad I disregarded the timetable."

"What timetable?" he grumbles.

"The one you think I didn't see."

Jackson picked me up in front of my tiny Hampden row home this morning just as the sun was edging its way over the horizon. He stood at the curb, two cups of coffee in his hands, and one of those sleek, efficient winter coats hugging the strong lines of his body. He didn't let me haul my suitcase down the steps. He just wordlessly held out the coffees until I gave in, then slotted my roller board with the broken wheel and my doughnut sled neatly in the back of the van. He was surprisingly quiet about the sled, only sparing the doughnut a quick, scathing glance.

Then we bickered in the narrow street for seven minutes about who was going to drive. I only relented when Jackson pointed out that as passenger, I could control the radio and snack distribution.

"You're going to let me eat in the van?"

He had placed his hands on his hips and leveled me with a stern look from behind his glasses. "I'm not a monster, Delilah."

Unfortunately for me, radio control turned out to be a bust. The only two stations the van gets are NPR and a static-filled salsa mix. I vetoed the conga drums right away, but maybe I shouldn't have.

"Not to be dramatic, but if I have to listen to one more second of BBC World Service Newshour, I am going to fling myself from this vehicle."

Jackson snorts. "You don't like NPR?"

"I love public radio, but I don't like whatever medieval-medicine episode we've been listening to for the past one hour and twenty-three minutes." I burrow down further in my seat, shivering. "It's depressing."

I don't want to hear about holes in skulls and rare fungal diseases and whatever implements they used to use to crack people open. I want to eat peach rings off my fingers and sing along to Whitney Houston.

But this van is not outfitted with any sort of modern equipment. I can't plug my phone into the audio system, and I don't have any cassettes on hand to feed into the player. So it's just us and the spotty radio, an utterly demoralizing NPR broadcast and bursts of static.

I curl my arms around my middle, shivering again. This van is also not equipped with proper heating. I'm about to dig out one of the silver thermal emergency blankets in the back and wrap myself like a burrito. "How much longer do we have?"

"If only we had some sort of timetable," Jackson says.

I snicker. "Like you don't have it memorized."

He rolls his eyes and I turn my body toward the window, trying to imagine myself someplace warmer. But everything is cast in heavy grays today, the sun's weak rays barely managing to peek out from behind the cloud cover. It's only going to get colder as we head into the mountains, the storm's icy fingers starting to reach toward the foothills.

Something heavy and warm lands on my lap. I glance down at Jackson's coat spread across my thighs.

"Your lips are turning blue," he says in explanation.

While I've been shivering in the passenger seat, Jackson has been pushing up the sleeves of his slate gray crewneck. There's a tear at the collar I can't stop looking at. A nick in his shiny armor. He balances one watch-clad wrist over the steering wheel and glances at me again from over the top of his thick-framed glasses. Sitting over there like that, he looks like some sort of hot calculator ad.

"What's that about?" he asks.

"What?"

"You're giving me a look."

"What sort of look?"

He swallows and my eyes drop to the strong line of his throat. He's all dips and lines and curves. Shadowed skin in the thin light that streams in through the windshield.

It is my professional opinion that no one should look so good while driving a news van.

"Like you're thinking of new and creative ways to assault me with peach rings," he says, his voice a low rumble.

"Breaking news, Jackson." I drop my chin to my chest and do my best broadcast voice. "Woman considers new and creative ways to assault weather partner with peach rings."

Another shiver twists my shoulders.

"Delilah," he says, concern quickly overshadowing his amusement. "Put the jacket on."

"Or what?" I ask.

The barest hint of a smile deepens the lines by his eyes. "Or I'll put it on for you," he says.

The traffic in front of us finally starts to break and he turns his attention back to the road. I unfold the jacket and carefully spread it across my lap, tucking the collar to my chin and slipping my arms through the sleeves. They fold over my hands and I curl my fingers in the buttery soft material, a happy sigh pressing out of me when I'm instantly wrapped in coffee-scented warmth.

"Better?" he asks.

I nod, nosing down further in the material and tucking my legs beneath me on the seat. Only my eyes are visible, like some sort of North Face gremlin. "Much," I say, my voice muffled. "Thank you."

He hums. "Look at us. The picture of teamwork."

I snort and wiggle in my coat blanket. "Does that mean you're ready to talk about it?"

His face instantly shutters. "No," he snaps. "I'm not."

I let my forehead fall against the window and give in to the laughter that's been burning a hole through the center of my chest since 6:03 a.m. We decided to introduce Jackson with the morning weather report at YBAL before we got on the road. Unfortunately, that didn't proceed much better than the radio broadcast.

"What possessed you to wear *green*?" I say with another peal of laughter, my voice high and breathy. I try to wrangle control of myself but I *can't*. I will be holding on to the mental image of Jackson's floating head in front of the weather map until my dying day. "You wore a green shirt in front of a *green screen*, Jackson."

Jackson drags one hand through his hair and anchors it against the back of his neck, his arm straining beneath the material of his sweater. His face is a delightful combination of bemused and bewildered and it only makes me laugh harder.

"My Friday shirt is green," he says faintly.

"You didn't think to change it?"

"I haven't done a television broadcast before, Delilah. I forgot about the green screen. Radio doesn't have a green screen." He drops his arm with a heavy exhale. "Why didn't you say anything to me before we started?"

"I tried to. I would have, if you didn't wait in your car until the last possible second."

"I was meditating," he says, eyes squinting with the lie.

"You were stress-eating a hash brown."

I could see him from the front window of the studio while I waited for him to come inside. He sat in the driver's seat of his car staring at the building like he'd rather toss himself off the top of it, shoveling a greasy hash brown into his mouth.

"Listen," I say, taking a deep breath, trying to push down on the laughter that keeps bubbling up. "If I'm forcing you to do this—"

"You're not forcing me to do anything," he cuts me off quickly. His features relax, that little line between his brows disappearing. "I'm fine, I'm just processing. I'm trying to figure out how to do this."

"This?"

"The broadcasts. The . . . partnership. I want to be good at it." He pauses for a second, then, quieter, "I don't want to let anyone down."

My laughter finally settles, a silly smile still stretched across my face. It's the most honest Jackson has ever been with me, and I know it cost him. I can tell by the way he's holding himself. How he's firmed his shoulders, waiting for me to rib him some more.

"Well, you don't need to figure it out alone," I tell him gently. "We're a team now, remember?"

Jackson glances over at me, a smile quirking his lips. Behind his head, rich, full evergreens blur past. Frost-tipped fence posts and open fields. A kaleidoscope of winter colors.

"Yeah," he agrees. "A team."

"Yeah." My lips twitch. "And while your news debut didn't go the way you wanted, you certainly made an impression."

He winces. "Great."

"Very Wizard of Oz."

He palms his hand along his jaw. "I was too afraid to look at the screen. Was it just my head? Floating around?"

Another laugh rockets out of me. I clap my hand over my mouth, then spread my fingers to whisper, "You could see some of your shoulders too."

"Oh, good. Glad my shoulders could make it." His hands flex on the steering wheel, the lines of his body tensing and then relaxing.

"All of Baltimore now understands why you've stuck to radio."

His eyebrows pop up. "Are you saying I'm too ugly for television?"

"That's not what I'm saying."

"It sounds like what you're saying."

I eyeball him, holding himself still on the other side of the van. Glancing over at me every so often out of the corner of his eye.

"Jackson," I hedge. "Are you fishing for compliments?"

"Maybe." He pauses and clears his throat. "What would you say if I was?"

My attention drifts along the contours of his face and snags on his mouth. He has a faint scar, right below his bottom lip. I've never noticed it because I'm not sure he's ever given me these smiles before. Scowls? Sure. Vague grunts in my general direction? Obviously. But this easy, playful grin? Never.

"Is this another team-building exercise?"

"It could be." He shrugs. "I could even pull over, if you wanted. One of us could climb up to the top of the van and we could do trust falls."

I snicker. "You would never."

"Yeah, you're right. I would never." Another easy grin lights him up, transforming his face. All those severe lines, melting into something warmer. Is this how everyone else gets to see him? Does he save all his hard edges for me? "C'mon, Delilah. Tell me the truth. I can handle it."

"What do you want to know?" I laugh.

"Do I have a face for TV?" His half smile tumbles into a full one. "The first time we met, what did you think of me?"

"I think the first time I saw you, you were climbing out from the trunk of your car."

Pink touches the base of his throat. "That's because you always park too close to my car door. Sometimes I can't open it."

"Sure."

He mutters something under his breath. "All right, fine. How about later, then? At the start of this whole thing. What did you think?"

I remember his blue checkered shirt. The press of his body against mine. Too-sweet coffee and no air in my lungs. "I thought, *Where did this man come from and why is he on top of me in this hallway?*"

"When you found out you had to work with me," he clarifies with a huff. "In Keith's office. Or at the café, I don't know." He scratches roughly at the back of his head, some of the longer strands of his blond hair sticking up at odd angles. My fingers itch with the insane urge to smooth them back down.

I press my palms to my thighs and clear my throat, feeling flustered. This news van has never felt so small.

"Never mind," he says gruffly, his eyes intent on the road. He digs his knuckle into his cheek, jostling his glasses and then straightening them again. "I didn't mean—"

"When I saw you sitting at the counter at the café," I interrupt, "I thought it was a shame you're so handsome because you have the personality of a wet piece of cardboard."

There. In for a penny, in for a pound.

Jackson takes several seconds to process. His mouth opens, closes, then opens again. "You think I'm handsome?"

I snort. "I think you're focused on the wrong part of that statement."

"I don't think so." He grins, so sudden and uncharacteristic that it takes *me* several seconds to process. "I thought your smile was weird," he offers.

"What?"

"Your smile," he says again. "I thought it was odd."

"In what way?" I ask, offended.

"You're always smiling," he answers. "Even when you don't want to be." His fingertips tap their way across the top of the steering wheel. "It's weird," he adds as an afterthought, that little line appearing between his eyebrows again. Thoughtful.

"I don't like this game anymore." I burrow back down into his jacket. "I say you're handsome, and I get *Your smile is weird*."

"Would you rather I lie?"

"No. I never want you to lie to me." Maybe that's the best part about working with Jackson. He'll never tell me something untrue. He won't tell me one thing, but mean another. I'll always get the truth.

Still. He could use a little finesse.

"What's wrong with being happy?" I begrudgingly ask.

"Nothing," he says. "Not if you actually feel it."

I draw a tiny snowflake in the condensation on the bottom-right corner of the window, my eyes suddenly tight. "I feel it."

"Do you?"

"Yes." Usually. Most of the time. When it matters, I guess.

"Hmm," Jackson offers, and something about the short, knowing sound has frustration pulling tight across my shoulders. I sit up straighter, his jacket slipping down to pool in my lap.

"Well, I'm certainly not feeling it right now," I snap.

Jackson rolls his lips against a grin and my stare turns narrow-eyed. I imagine the satisfaction of a spitball, right to his temple. A crumpled up Post-it note to the middle of his forehead.

"You're infuriating, do you know that?"

"I've been told a time or two." He hits the blinker, shifting over lanes while checking the mirrors. "Do you want to know another thing? Something I thought when I saw your broadcast outside of the aquarium?"

I didn't realize he's been watching my broadcasts. I pick at a stray piece of thread poking out at the bottom of his jacket, twisting it around and around until it snaps. Curiosity is a terrible thing.

"What?"

"I was . . . irritated . . . by the turtle costume." The blush on his neck creeps up, along the line of his throat. "So do with that what you will."

"I have no idea what that means."

"Yes," he sighs. "You do."

The realization is a slow-moving thing, slowly bouncing from synapse to synapse until the connection is a tenuous thread.

"Jackson," I gasp. "Were you *attracted* to the turtle suit?"

He shifts, uncomfortable. "Let's not get carried away."

"Was it the shell?" I ask with a wobbling voice. There's a laugh caught in the middle of my chest that I'm frankly afraid to let out. "Or was it the finned hands that did it for you?"

"I think it was your enthusiasm, actually, and your ability to make everything look easy," he answers lightly, smacking the turn signal off. That shuts me up. My laughter sputters and dies, that tight feeling spreading from behind my eyes to the bridge of my nose.

"Oh," I say. "I see."

Jackson grunts in vague agreement, then merges over again. I glance out the window at the trees speeding past, my eyes tracking the billboards. One in particular catches my attention, and I make a split-second decision.

"Take the next exit," I tell Jackson.

"What? Why?"

"Because I want to see something."

He takes the ramp without further explanation. The news van slows considerably as we rumble around a sharp turn.

"Delilah?" he asks.

I need to get out of this van. I can't be this close to him—wrapped in a jacket that smells like his coffee and cologne—when he's being sincere.

Plus, my stomach has been grumbling for the past hour, and the peach rings aren't doing it for me anymore.

"Time for a little spontaneity," I say. Up the road there's a large rotating sign creaking above a parking lot proudly boasting BREAKFAST ALL DAY. Except *ALL DAY* is spelled with two upside-down sevens, and the *A* is another color entirely. Below the sign, handwritten in spray paint, is:

**ASK US ABOUT OUR FAMOUS
HOT TURKEY SANDWICHES**

"Oh no," Jackson says. "I have no desire for food poisoning, thanks."

"You said you wanted to try different things, right? Disrupt your routine?" I gesture out the window with wide eyes.

"I didn't say I wanted to die in Appalachia from salmonella."

"*Hot* turkey sandwiches," I emphasize. "Presumably, it's cooked through. You'll be fine." I wiggle happily in my seat. I hope they have French fries. And milkshakes. "It's a sign."

Jackson ducks his head and peers out the windshield. "I'm pretty sure that's a piece of plywood, Delilah."

The van slows to a creep as Jackson reluctantly enters the parking lot. He picks a spot near the back, though there's not exactly a shortage of choice. There are only two other cars in the lot. He cuts the ignition, but otherwise remains motionless in the front seat.

"Great, let's go." I unclick my seat belt, then reach over and do the same to his. I push my arms through the sleeves of his jacket and wedge open the passenger door. I hop out without waiting for him. "Turkey sandwiches await!"

For a second, I don't think he'll follow. Then I hear a car door slam and boots against the pavement.

Somewhere behind me, Jackson sighs, weary. "This wasn't in the timetable."

I smile into the collar of my stolen coat.

COMMENT FROM MORETHANRATSHERE:

Excuse me, but is that what Jackson Clark LOOKS LIKE?

COMMENT FROM ORIOLESMAGIC28:

It's what his head looks like, at least.

CHAPTER 10

JACKSON

"I'll have the turkey sandwich on whole wheat, not white. And fries instead of mashed potatoes, but not if they're breaded. If they're breaded, I'll do the mashed potatoes. Oh, and the salad with the Caesar dressing. But not if it's dressing from the bottle. Homemade only, please."

I hand over the menu to the unimpressed waitress. She smacks her gum and stares at me. "Of course the dressing is homemade. This is a diner, sweetheart, not a McDonald's."

I fold my hands together, not exactly inspired by how her pen hasn't taken a single note. This place is exactly as expected. Chipped vinyl flooring. An octogenarian with bright blue hair and ten thousand pounds of mascara manning the cash register. Leather booth seats that squeak when you move and miniature jukeboxes at the end of every table.

"We make everything in-house," our waitress continues. "Including the Caesar."

"Excellent, thank you."

"Mashed potatoes got skins," she adds, like she expects me to change my mind and list out another five to ten contingencies. But

I've exhausted the lot of them, and I don't like French fries that much anyway.

"That's fine," I say.

Our waitress turns wordlessly to Delilah, arching one penciled-on eyebrow. "Well," she says. Another snap of her gum. "What about you?"

Delilah hands over her menu without looking away from me. She's been doing that for most of this trip. Studying me like she wants to peel back my layers and poke around underneath.

"I'll have the turkey sandwich with fries. No additions or modifications, thank you." The waitress disappears back into the kitchen and Delilah scrunches her nose. She's still wearing my jacket, draped over her shoulders like a cape. I know she's been teasing me about my timetable, but if she reached into the left pocket, she'd find exactly that, folded into neat squares and highlighted to within an inch of its life.

"Really stepped outside your comfort zone with that order, huh."

I reach for the sugar packets, slowly arranging them by height and color. "I know what I like."

"You order food like a serial killer."

I swap a Sweet'N Low with a Sugar in the Raw, then change my mind and switch them back.

"I'm particular," I explain. "I like things done a certain way. And the sign said the turkey sandwich was famous."

I'm particularly particular when it feels like I'm losing control of everything else. I am currently hurtling toward a massive winter storm in the mountains with my polar opposite as company. I'm supposed to go on live television and explain—in clear and concise terms—what's happening. I left my sisters behind for the first time since I assumed custody, and my mother won't stop sending me text messages from random, unknown numbers, asking the most asinine questions.

My head is in shambles, and so I ordered the mashed potatoes. With skins.

Delilah drops her chin into her hand. "I'll accept that answer." She takes a noisy slurp of her chocolate milkshake. The one she politely inquired about as soon as we walked through the front door ("You don't happen to have chocolate milkshakes, do you?") and was somehow waiting for her at our table, like a foreign dignitary sitting down to a state dinner. I'll never understand how she draws people in and makes them love her, all with a sunny smile and a flick of her long hair.

She smacks her lips. "For now," she adds, a thin undercurrent of warning in her voice.

"Noted," I answer.

So far, this trip is both exactly what I expected and nothing like I planned. I thought Delilah would babble incessantly for the duration of our time in the car, some vapid, sugary-sweet commentary on the passing pine trees or gas station snacks. And while she did deliver a fifteen-minute monologue about the underrated power of a good peach ring, she's otherwise largely kept to herself.

"Tell me about your sisters," she demands from the other side of the table, reaching up to toy with the button at the base of her throat.

"Um," I say, distracted. She's wearing a soft-looking V-neck sweater that clings to all her curves, so different from her structured broadcast dresses. My eyes dipped once when she was climbing into the van and I pinched myself so hard, I still have the mark on my wrist. The last thing I need is to start *looking* at Delilah Stewart.

But holding that line is borderline impossible with the way she keeps dancing her fingers along the top of her chest. She closes the snap then undoes it again. Open. Closed.

My jaw clenches tight.

"How old are they?" she asks.

I have to forcibly drag my brain back into the conversation. "What?"

"Your sisters," Delilah says, amused. "How old are they?"

"Oh, they're fifteen." I push the sugar container away. "Twins," I explain.

"That's quite the age gap."

I shrug. I thought the same thing when my mom came back to our tiny apartment after being gone on a two-week bender, clutching a sonogram with tears in her eyes.

Our family just got bigger, Jack, she had said with a tremulous smile. *How lucky are we?*

I didn't feel lucky at all. I felt horrified that she'd bring two more children into the world when she was already doing such a shit job raising the first one.

"My mother is . . ." I try to think of a word that fully encompasses Camille Clark. "Unconventional," I finally settle on. "It's why I have full custody of the girls now."

I know what to expect at this point in the conversation. Pity will soften her features and she'll struggle to find something to say. She won't bring it up again, and she'll make her own assumptions about me, the girls, and the family we've stitched together. I've seen it happen a thousand times. The discomfort that people distort themselves into, just so they don't need to feel the edges of mine.

I brace myself for it, but when I lift my eyes, Delilah is toying with the cherry from the top of her milkshake, chewing on the stem thoughtfully.

"That's cool," she says, without a trace of . . . anything. "You must be close."

I blink, stupefied. "Yeah. We are."

"Are they excited to see you on TV?"

I think about the family text thread and how it's filled to the brim with a string of incomprehensible emojis and requests for updates. Penelope's last message of, Should I get a life-sized cardboard cutout of you for our viewing party? And Adeline's immediate response of, YES, WE ARE DOING IT I DON'T CARE WHAT YOU SAY.

A picture twenty-five minutes later of Aiden standing next to a cobbled-together cardboard cutout of me, his arm slung over its shoulders.

"Yeah, they're excited." I pick at a tiny chip in the side of the sugar container. "They're big fans of yours."

Her face lights up and she sits straighter in the cracked leather booth seat, the jacket slipping off one shoulder, taking the collar of her sweater with it. I get a glimpse of pale, creamy skin. The delicate line of her throat. She has a thin gold necklace on, anchored with some sort of rabbit charm.

Do not look below her chin, you asshole. Do not.

I'm acting like a Regency era viscount. Two inches of collarbone, and I'm gripping the edge of the table so hard it's biting into my palms.

"That's so nice," Delilah exclaims, like all of Baltimore isn't already in love with her and the loyalty of two teenagers is something awe-inspiring. It would be annoying if it wasn't also completely genuine. She pops the cherry into her mouth. "Honestly, the only reason I started doing broadcasts is because my grandpa was obsessed with seeing me on television. He said it was my destiny. Big horoscope guy, Gus Stewart."

"Yeah?"

She nods with a little hum. "Yeah. He's always believed in me best. I think if he could rewrite the stars for me, he would." She takes another long slurp of milkshake. "He raised me, you know. My mom was also . . . unconventional."

My breath backs up in my lungs. "Oh," is all I can think to say.

"She was a violin prodigy," Delilah continues, undeterred. "I've seen some videos of when she was little and she was incredible, even then, when the bow was bigger than her. My grandpa took her to the Peabody three times a week. Worked multiple jobs so she could have the very best of the best when it came to lessons, equipment. Eventually, she won a chair with the Royal Concertgebouw Orchestra in Amsterdam. Coincidentally around that time, she also got pregnant with me." Delilah shoots me a small, tight-lipped smile. "I guess she thought she could have both, but I was . . . too much, and she chose what she'd invested the most time in. She was going to put me up for adoption, but my grandpa begged her to reconsider. She signed over custody to him instead." She takes a noisy slurp of her drink. "He gets a kick out of seeing me on TV, and I like showing him he didn't make all those sacrifices for nothing." She frowns at her milkshake glass. "Hey, hand me that extra straw. This one is zapped."

I hand her my straw without looking away from her face. How can she do that? Open a vein and let all her barbed truths spill free without stumbling over a single word. Without being broken or burdened by it.

She taps the straw on the table to clear the wrapper, then drops it into her milkshake. "So. We have more in common than you think. Or, me and your sisters, I guess." She hits an empty spot with her straw and shifts it around, trying to find another pocket of chocolate while I navigate the brand-new, tipsy-topsy feeling tightening like a band around my chest.

"What do they think of your unmitigated hatred for me?"

I shift in the squeaky booth seat and decide I'm not going to dignify that with an answer. "They're excited for a weeklong sleepover with their friend."

"Probably longer if the snow does what we say it's going to do," Delilah muses. She wiggles her fingers and does something ridiculous with her face. "We hold all the power."

She adjusts the collar of the jacket so it's back at the base of her throat. Like the world's stupidest moth to the world's prettiest flame, my eyes follow. I wonder if my jacket will smell like her when she gives it back. Something fruity and light with a sharp bite. Dark cherries. Summer peaches dipped in wine.

I drag my eyes up to the ceiling of the diner. I don't know when this burgeoning attraction to Delilah went from a passing awareness to a fire poker in my side, but it couldn't have worse timing. It's the last thing I want when we're going to be more or less handcuffed together for the duration of this storm.

I'm so goddamned irritated. With myself. With the situation. With how easy some of this feels when I thought it would be anything but.

"I think we should talk about work now," I choke out, about as subtle as a kick to the face. Delilah stops trying to noisily suck up the remnants of her chocolate shake and flicks her gaze up to mine, bemused.

"Okay," she says slowly. She catches her straw between her teeth. "What *work thing* would you like to discuss?"

"We have a call with the radio station in an hour. I think they've got us coming on during the afternoon news block."

Delilah nods. I wait for her to say something. She doesn't.

"What do you want to talk about?" I ask.

Delilah's smile edges wider, that damned red straw still caught between her teeth. "Well, Jackson. We should probably talk about the weather."

"I thought maybe we could write a script during lunch. Something for us to stick to so we don't get side—"

"No," Delilah interrupts.

The rest of my planned speech crumbles to dust. "No? Why not?"

"Because then we'll sound wooden and weird. It's—what? A twenty-second spot? Thirty? Let's just do it and see how it goes."

"See how it goes," I repeat.

"Yup!" She slurps the very last of her milkshake noisily. "I know that's outside your normal operating sphere, but as we've discussed, it might be nice to try something new."

"I'm not great at that."

Her face softens. "I know. But you can talk to me and I'll talk to you and everything will be fine. Just . . . pretend it's the two of us. Having a conversation. We're pretty good at that, aren't we?"

Two turkey sandwiches appear on the table between us. One with French fries, the other with mashed potatoes. I stare blankly down at them, an uncomfortable pulling sensation in the middle of my chest. A thread unspooled. A crack in a stone-hewn wall, formed long ago.

"Everything the way you wanted it?" our waitress asks, still snapping that gum.

No. Nothing is the way I wanted it.

"Yeah," I answer instead, my tongue thick in my mouth. I clear my throat and manage a smile. "Everything looks great."

"Should I pull over?"

"I don't know," Delilah answers, her voice muffled. "Do you feel like you need to pull over?"

I reach over and curl one hand around her ankle, holding her steady while she does . . . whatever the hell it is she's doing in the back seat. Bent over the center console, she rummages around in her backpack, the curve of her ass a distracting six inches from my face while we hurtle down the highway at seventy miles per hour.

"Delilah," I grind out, tightening my grip on her when she wobbles precariously to the left. "Get up here and put your seat belt on."

"One second. I want to get the Wi-Fi connector thing for the call. I thought it was here, but I— Oh!" She shimmies back to the front seat, her hair in her face. She holds up a small black box the size of her fist. "Found it."

"Great." I let go of her ankle. "Put your seat belt on."

She chatters happily about spotty phone connections in the middle of the mountains, pulling the seat belt over her lap while balancing her phone on her knee. She taps at the screen and connects everything that needs to be connected while I keep my eyes on the road and try to deep breathe through the worst of my showtime jitters.

It was Delilah's idea to do this while driving. At first I balked, but it's turned out to be a good idea, back-seat traversing notwithstanding. It helps, I think, to have something to do. With my focus on the road while Delilah dials into the station, I have less mental space to catastrophize.

That is until a familiar voice fills the cab of the van. One I wasn't expecting to hear. "Hey, you two. How's the road trip?"

"Aiden?" I ask, glancing quickly at the phone like it'll summon his corporeal form into the middle seat of the news van. "What are you doing at the station? Are the girls okay? Did something happen?"

Delilah pats my knee lightly.

"Everything's fine. I came into the station because I thought you could use a friend on the other end. Relax." Someone murmurs something in the background and Aiden snorts. "Benny is none too pleased to be sharing his airtime, though."

"This is a serious segment, pretty boy," a rough voice crackles over the line. Benny, the host of the afternoon news hour program, must have just gotten into the booth. "I don't like you trying to commandeer my ship."

"No one is commandeering anything," Aiden says easily. "I'm here for moral support."

"I don't need moral support," Benny grouches back.

"Not for you, Ben."

A heavy burst of static explodes over the line and both Delilah and I wince. She lowers the volume, then cradles the phone in her hands.

"Thanks for giving us some of your time, Benny. We'll keep it short and sweet for you."

There's a long pause. "Is that Delilah?" he finally asks.

Delilah grins. "Sure is!"

"I suppose that will be fine, then."

Aiden snickers into the phone. "I've never seen someone over seventy blush before."

"You're about to see someone over seventy kick your ass," Benny snaps, sharp as a whip. Delilah covers her mouth with her palm, her eyes squinting at the corners as she tries not to laugh. I grin at her.

"Watch yourself, Aiden," I warn.

"Yeah, no kidding," he mutters. "Okay, are you guys ready? I kind of want to get out of this booth as soon as possible."

I look at Delilah's smiling face. Flushed cheeks. Red lips. She's looking at me like she believes I can do this, and it makes me think that maybe I can. Maybe I can flatten the curled-up edges of myself. Maybe old wounds don't have to hurt so bad. Maybe I can move past them into something new, better, different.

"Yeah," I say. "We're ready."

BENNY BARLOW: I'm told there is an update?

DELILAH STEWART: Yes, Benny. Thank you for having us. Jackson and I are currently heading out to Garrett County where the storm is set to arrive within the next forty-eight hours. We're expecting high winds, plummeting temperatures, and snowfall upwards of several feet. Baltimore should expect a milder version of the same storm, but we'll know more once we get up in the mountains.

DELILAH STEWART: Also, we stopped for turkey sandwiches.

BENNY BARLOW: Jackson. You're quiet. Anything to add?

JACKSON CLARK: Delilah has it covered.

[pause]

[indistinct arguing]

JACKSON CLARK: Uh, the turkey sandwiches were good?

BENNY BARLOW: Is that a question or a statement?

JACKSON CLARK: Statement. The turkey sandwiches were good.

BENNY BARLOW: So glad I made time for this riveting update.

DELILAH STEWART: [laughter] And now, back to you, Benny.

CHAPTER 11

DELILAH

"Mark says he'll be here tomorrow," Jackson says, his face turned down toward his phone and one arm propped against the open door of the trunk. I try to edge around his broad body at the back of the van, fighting to reach for the suitcase he won't let me grab.

"His daughter had a dance recital he didn't want to miss," I explain, biting the inside of my cheek as Jackson moves to block my reach for the twelfth time. I don't usually feel our size difference, but I'm feeling it right now. I feel like a baby rabbit, trying to paw at an overgrown oak tree. Is this how he feels every time he has to climb through the window of his car? Unbelievable. "He's heading out first thing. Should be here before the snow starts to fall."

"Great." He maneuvers my doughnut sled to the far side of the van, then grabs my bag, setting it neatly on the curb next to his. I huff, but he ignores me, closing the back and turning toward the sign that says LOBBY, both suitcases trailing behind him. Mine bumps along with its broken wheel.

"I can carry that."

He spares me a brief glance. "I know."

I have to take two hopping steps for every one of his. "Hand it over, then."

A smirk curls his lips. "No."

I stubbornly try to get it back anyway, trailing behind Jackson while trying to pull the handle out of his grip. I probably look like a fly on the back of a buffalo. Jackson pays me no mind, continuing along, tipping his head back and squinting into the muted sunlight to take in the rustic lodge we'll be staying at for the duration of the coverage.

I begrudgingly do the same. It's gorgeous. An old cabin that's been converted into a string of connected suites. Wide glass and warm wood and towering pines, anchored on either side of the front walkway. The front is low, built into the side of the foothill, but the back is nothing but wide-open space. The elevation drops without warning, the balconies from the cabins jutting out over a descent that cuts all the way down to the lake, spilling inky black in every direction. Everything is still and quiet in the way it only gets before a storm. The whole world holding its breath.

We push through the wide-set glass doors to a fire in the hearth, Jackson *still* holding on to my bag. A woman with long gray hair and an apron tied around her waist welcomes us in.

"You must be the newspeople. I'm Lottie, the owner of Wolf's Lodge. We're so happy to have you with us for the storm." She folds her hands in front of her. "I hope the trip out wasn't too much trouble?"

"No trouble at all." Jackson's eyes cut to me briefly. *Well*, that look says, *maybe some trouble*. I stick my tongue out and a gruff laugh rolls out of him. He shifts his attention back to Lottie. "Are you all right with us checking in early, or do you want us to kill some time at the arcade across the street?"

Lottie waves her hand. "That arcade hasn't been operational since 1983. A theme, I think you'll find, here at Deep Creek." She strides behind a long desk situated in front of the fireplace. There's no one else in the small lobby. "Now is a fine time to check in. We operate with a skeleton crew during storms like these." She pulls out a sheet of paper listing the hotel's amenities, several of them either crossed out or with handwritten notes next to them. "Most of the amenities will be closed for the duration of your stay, and there won't be any room service. But we will serve three hot meals a day and have a rotating tea service with coffee, pastries, and the like. Those will be family style for the guests and on-site staff."

Jackson nods. "That's no problem. We're here to work."

I wander to the back windows while Jackson and Lottie continue chatting through logistics, pressing my palm to the cold glass and staring out at the lake below. I came here a few times with my grandpa growing up, always in the summer when the water sparkled so bright I could never look at it directly. We'd wander down to the docks on the east side before the sun poked its way over the horizon, slowly shedding our layers as the sky turned purple, then pink, then bright, shining gold. We'd fish until our necks burned red, then sit in the backyard of the cabin we rented and roast the day's catch on an open fire. He'd tell me stories he made up and I'd pretend to believe them.

Does he remember it the same way I do? Cicadas in the grass and aloe on my fingertips. Ice cream melting over my knuckles, loose pebbles beneath my feet. Laughing so hard it hurt, the sky so bright above our heads I felt like I could put the stars in my pocket.

He went into assisted care two years ago when he started forgetting things. At first it was just small stuff, but it quickly escalated. He'd call me confused from the grocery store, not knowing how he got there. Not knowing how to get back. He started telling the same stories over and over. He'd call me by my mother's name.

When he was diagnosed with Alzheimer's, we started putting care routines in place.

Some days I wonder how much of him I'll get to keep and how much I'll have to watch slip away.

"Delilah?"

I turn to look at Jackson, shaking off the cobwebs. I don't need to worry about it now, when I'm on assignment. I made a promise to my grandpa that he'd only ever see me smiling and that's what he's going to get. Bright and shiny Delilah, every night on the evening news.

Jackson beckons me over, his glasses reflecting the glare from the back window so I can't read his eyes.

"What is it?" I ask.

"You made three reservations, right?"

"Yup." I reach for the phone in my back pocket, pulling up my email. I flagged it this morning so I'd have it when we got here. "Three of the junior one-bedroom suites."

Lottie's face collapses in dismay. "You didn't cancel one?"

"No," I say slowly. "I didn't." I look over at Jackson. He's watching me with a heavy, concerned look. "I didn't," I say again.

"I believe you," he assures me. He hands me back my phone and looks to Lottie. "Is it possible there was some sort of clerical error?"

She shakes her head, raising one trembling hand to her chin. "I got an early-morning cancellation via email. I'm sorry, but you only have two rooms booked, see?" Lottie turns the monitor on the desk so it's facing us. Three reservations in a line, one bolded and underlined in red. CANCELED.

I force a smile. "That's okay. We'll just book another room. No problem."

Lottie fills her cheeks with air, then blows it out noisily.

"What?" I ask. "What is it?"

"There are no other rooms," she says with a wince. "When we received your cancellation, we immediately offered it to the waiting list." She threads her fingers together and squeezes until her knuckles are white. "When storms this big roll in, the truckers that pass through town usually hunker down. We have an agreement with one of the dispatchers. We've got a pretty good waiting list going as we get everyone squared away."

I rub at my forehead. "All right. I'll just—it was my room?"

I'd call it bad luck, but I think this particular black cat is six-foot-nothing with a receding hairline and a mean streak.

Lottie turns the monitor back toward her and clicks around. "Just your room," she confirms. "In the email I received, it said you found alternate lodgings at"—she squints at the computer, mouth moving soundlessly as she reads—"oh, at, um, Liberty Hall across the street."

"Oh, well, that's good!" I nudge Jackson with my elbow. "I still have somewhere to sleep tonight."

Jackson is busy glowering at the computer monitor. "In this email you received," he says, "did it say who wanted to cancel Delilah's reservation?"

"There wasn't a name listed. Just a generic email with a signature line from the station. I thought it was—I'm so sorry, I thought it was legit."

I wave her off and wrestle my bag out of Jackson's grip. "It's no problem. Liberty Hall, you said?"

Lottie hesitates, then nods. Warning bells start to chime, but optimism is a choice, and I'm not letting this trip go to waste because Keith wants to play games. I'm going to kill this coverage, and I'm going to shut him up once and for all. Hopefully, this will be the last time I ever have to jump through these hoops.

"I'll go check in across the street, and then we'll meet back here for coffee. Oh." I glance at Lottie. "Can I still have coffee here? If I don't have a room?"

"Of course you can. Scones too." Lottie's face eases into something sympathetic. "Whatever you need. I'm so sorry this happened."

I manage a wobbly smile. The look on her face is like I've just announced a death in the family. The warning bells turn into an air siren. I don't have a great feeling about Liberty Hall. "Thank you. I appreciate your help. I'm sure I'll see you—wait." I'm distracted by Jackson, turning and wheeling both of our suitcases toward the front door. "What are you doing?"

Mine bumps along unsteadily next to his, that damned wheel still broken.

"Jackson." I rush to catch up. "I can do this myself."

He shakes his head. "We'll come back together, after you've checked in at your new place."

A hot flare of indignation settles between my shoulder blades. "You don't think I can walk across the street by myself? I can manage crossing the road."

"I just want to see," Jackson says, his voice free of argument. I'm throwing a temper tantrum, and he's out for an afternoon stroll. He pauses at the curb and gives me a long, considering look. Then he rolls my suitcase in front of me. A peace offering. I grip the handle and stare up at him. "I want to make sure you're okay over there. That you have everything you need."

The anger leaves me in a rush and I nod. Maybe it wouldn't be so horrible to have someone on my side for once. "Okay," I agree.

"Good," he says, that one word a rough sound in the back of his throat. I shiver, then immediately decide to blame it on the strong northeast wind whipping it's way over the mountains. Jackson shifts, then holds out his hand, palm up, between us.

I stare at it.

"What's that about?" I ask.

He glances down at his hand like it's operating independent of the rest of his body. He clenches it into a fist, then drops it. "Oh. Never mind."

"Did you want to . . . hold my hand?"

"No," he says immediately. "I was—" He swallows, staring off at some unidentified point in the distance, his eyes squinting. "I was measuring the wind direction."

He half-heartedly lifts his hand again, palm facing out.

"What direction is the wind blowing?" I ask.

He hesitates, then lets out a long-suffering sigh. "North," he mutters.

The winds are definitely moving counterclockwise as the storm approaches. We both know that. I snort a laugh, and he cuts a look in my direction. A man found out. A man defeated.

The giggles start, like champagne bubbles in my chest.

Jackson grunts. "Let's go."

It takes me four minutes to get myself together enough to follow him. I'm laughing too hard.

"No," he says, as soon as the door to the room swings open. "No. Absolutely not."

It's the fifth time he's repeated that word since we've made our way up from what could loosely be described as check-in. There wasn't anyone physically at the desk, but there was an envelope with my name on it, a cracked plastic key card held together with masking tape and mediocre vibes.

Liberty Hall is the antithesis of Wolf's Lodge across the street. While the lodge is warm wood and arched ceilings, Liberty Hall is stained carpets and doors with boot-shaped dents. Old popcorn strewn across the hallway floor and a discarded pile of clothes, shoved in the corner. The elevator isn't operational, so we trudge our way up the stairs with our suitcases, the single light bulb in the stairwell flickering ominously over our heads.

"Is it weird we haven't seen another person?" I glance down the length of the hallway, half expecting to see a set of Victorian twins holding hands at the very end. "It's kind of weird, right?"

Jackson is still staring into the depths of my new home for the next week. It smells vaguely like fried onions and something metallic. Pennies, wedged under a diesel truck car seat.

I lean my head in, careful to keep my feet in the hallway. Just in case. "Oh, look. There's a bed. See? I'll be fine."

There's also an unexplained crowbar, leaning up against the TV stand that does *not* feature a TV. Just some miscellaneous wires and a hole in the wall. "I bet I can use that crowbar as a doorstop."

Fortifying myself to make the most of it, I pick up my suitcase and step into the room. Or I would, anyway, if Jackson didn't immediately grab the back of my jacket and pull me into his chest.

"No," he repeats, and I feel the puff of his breath across the top of my head.

"Jackson," I sigh.

"Delilah," he echoes back. "This is insane."

It's certainly not ideal, that's for sure. "I need somewhere to stay, Jackson. And you heard Lottie. There are no other rooms."

"Mark and I will bunk together. You can take my room."

I'm already shaking my head. "Mark has sleep apnea. He wears this crazy machine to bed. Rooming with him is like sleeping next to a backfiring car." I pause. "He also has pretty wild sleep terrors. When we roomed together on the Eastern Shore for the White Marlin Open, he threw all of my clothes into the hallway because he thought they were on fire."

Mark has gotten his own room ever since.

"Then Mark can stay over here," Jackson says, agitated.

"I'll be fine," I insist. "I don't want to inconvenience anyone. I won't be spending much time in my room anyway."

Jackson gives me a dubious look. "You're really going to sleep in that bed?"

I glance at it. There's an unidentified lump on the left side. Only one pillow. No duvet as far as I can tell.

It requires a significant amount of effort to keep a smile on my face.

"It'll be an adventure," I say.

Jackson opens his mouth to respond, but something rustles in the closet. Our attention snaps toward the door.

Now the crowbar makes sense.

"Did you hear—"

"Yeah," Jackson says, his voice dark. "Yeah, I did."

The door suddenly bucks against the hinges and I shriek, already halfway down the hallway. Jackson is right behind me, the door to the hotel room slamming shut behind him.

"You are not staying here, Delilah."

"No," I agree, rushing down the stairs, Jackson hot on my heels. I don't even care that he's carrying my suitcase. I just need to get the hell out of this *Shining*-wannabe hotel. I shiver. "No, you're right. I'm not staying here."

I'm so spooked I don't even realize. It's the first time we've agreed on something.

PENELOPE CLARK: I've changed my mind. I don't want you on television.

ADELINE CLARK: Agreed.

ADELINE CLARK: It's not cool.

ADELINE CLARK: It's the worst.

JACKSON CLARK: ????

[unanswered call]

[unanswered call]

PENELOPE CLARK: I can't say it.

ADELINE CLARK: I WON'T say it.

JACKSON CLARK: What the hell is going on with you two?

JACKSON CLARK: Answer your damned phones.

PENELOPE CLARK: Calm down, Jackie. We're fine.

JACKSON CLARK: Then tell me what's going on.

PENELOPE CLARK: It's not a big deal.

ADELINE CLARK: It is a big deal.

PENELOPE CLARK: The entire school just thinks you're hot and now our lives are ruined.

ADELINE CLARK: I WILL NEVER RECOVER.

JACKSON CLARK: If this is a joke, it's a bad one.

ADELINE CLARK: I wish.

ADELINE CLARK: God, do I wish.

CHAPTER 12

JACKSON

"Keith is a jackass."

"We don't know that it was Keith," Delilah replies easily, a mug of hot chocolate at her elbow and her thumbs working furiously across the screen of her phone. She's been looking for alternative accommodations for the past twenty-three minutes, and so far her best bet is a shack two miles away, right at the water's edge.

"That could be fun," she said. "I've always wanted to stay in a yurt."

I don't look up from the weather projections on my laptop. I have both the Global Forecast System *and* the European model running. "That yurt doesn't have a toilet."

"Oh. Well." Her teeth drag over her bottom lip. I get a flash of that cute little gap. "I don't—"

"You need a toilet, Delilah."

She sighs. "Yeah, okay."

She takes a noisy slurp from her hot chocolate and goes back to scanning whatever website she's using to try to find a place to stay. I wouldn't be surprised if she made her own listing on some random social media platform:

WEATHER WOMAN STRANDED, LOOKING
FOR ACCOMMODATIONS.
WILL WORK FOR SUGAR-INFUSED DRINKS.

It's enough to have me punching the keys of my laptop aggressively.

She's staying with me tonight. I won't have her in a yurt without a toilet or on some knitting club's pullout couch. I don't know how I'm going to handle her in a bed three feet from me, but it's certainly better than the alternative: a slow slide into mental instability because I don't know where she is.

"Oh, this one looks promising." She turns her phone to show me the screen. It's a sideways picture of a beanbag chair in the corner of a basement with wood-paneled walls. God help me. "Look, they have a cat!"

"Great. I love cats." I reach into my pocket and pull out the extra key card I asked Lottie to program. I slide it across the table. "Anyway, here's your key."

She stares at it. "My key for what?"

"Your room. Here. At this lodge. Without cats." Or any questionable stains on the carpet in front of the door. Or suspicious sounds coming from the closet. Or weapons leaning up against an empty TV stand.

I'm going to have nightmares for weeks.

She picks it up like she expects it to bite, dangling it by the very corner between thumb and forefinger. "Lottie said there weren't any rooms."

"That's right. This is a key to my room."

Delilah snickers. "How very presumptuous of you." When I don't laugh, she sobers.

"Jackson," Delilah sighs. She slides the key back across the table. "I'm not taking your room."

"Of course not. You're sharing it." I poke around some more on my computer screen, trying to ignore the electricity that zings up my spine. It doesn't have to mean anything. I shared the cab of a van with her for six hours. I can share a hotel room with her for a week.

I'm sure this uncomfortable attraction and borderline affection I'm nursing will evaporate as soon as I see the way she brushes her teeth. Or how she's packed her suitcase. I glance at her across the length of the small table we've tucked ourselves into, right up against one of the glass windows. "I know this might be a deal-breaker for you, but there's a toilet and everything."

I watch her face move through the seven stages of grief, settling somewhere between bargaining and depression.

"No," she says. "I can't."

I pluck the key card out of her hand, then reach across the table and slip it into the tiny pocket on the front of her shirt. My knuckles brush against her collarbone. "Yes. You can."

I swear if I hear about one more accommodation that is *only probably, like, twenty percent haunted*, I'm going to lose my actual shit.

"Jackson, I—"

"This is the best possible solution." I steamroll right over her. "When there's two feet of snow on the ground with winds upwards of sixty miles per hour, how do you intend on walking from your *yurt* to wherever we're broadcasting?" Her mouth snaps closed. *God.* That probably shouldn't feel as good as it does. "You know as well as I do that this storm will likely knock out the power. You need to be somewhere that has a generator."

You need to be somewhere I won't worry about you, my brain tacks on.

An inconvenient truth, all the way around.

Delilah stares down at the key card in her pocket. "Are you sure?" she asks, her voice uncharacteristically hesitant. She trails her fingernail along the edge of the card and my body has an instant, visceral reaction.

"I insist." My voice sounds like I've swallowed ten pounds of gravel.

Her eyes hold mine. "You're not going to be weird about this, are you?"

I'm probably going to be at least a little weird about it.

"I won't," I promise instead, hoping that somewhere between here and there, I can figure out how to occupy the same space as her without making a total ass of myself. I won't throw all her clothes into the hallway in a fit of night terrors, I guess. That's a good start.

"I do want to point out, however, that Keith was likely behind the cancellation, and he is an asshole."

Delilah blows out a deep breath. "Yeah, you're probably right." She picks up her phone and starts tapping with her thumbs.

"I thought we agreed. No yurt."

"No yurt," she says. "But I've got a friend who works in research at the station. I'm going to have her do some digging."

"Into Keith?"

She nods, types some more, then sets her phone to the side. "I'm going to see if she can find any evidence he's deliberately trying to sabotage me at work." Some of the steel in her eyes melts away, her shoulders slumping. "I don't know what I'll do with it if I have it, though."

"You won't report him?"

She shakes her head. "Don't know who I'd report him to. I've gone to HR before about his behavior, and he wiggled his way out of repercussions. I think he has some sort of deal with management. He's cashing in on his early nineties' celebrity, I guess. Or maybe blackmail. I don't know." She rubs her thumb over her eyebrow. "Can we talk about the weather now? I don't want Keith to distract me from the reason I'm actually here."

It's a fair enough point. I tilt my computer screen so she can see it, pointing out the frankly terrifying red blob in the top left corner. The one that's slowly inching in our direction.

"Winds are picking up. Snowfall estimates too. It'll hit the hardest at the higher elevations, but everywhere is going to feel it."

Delilah leans closer, her body pressing against mine. An accident, I'm sure. "I've never covered a storm this big. It feels like a lot of responsibility, doesn't it?"

I blink away from the top of her head. Back to the screen.

"Yeah," I agree. "It does."

"Does it make you nervous?"

I shut my laptop and scratch roughly at the back of my head. Take off my glasses and dig my knuckles against my eyes. I feel like one giant, exposed nerve. "Yeah," I sigh. "It does."

When I push my glasses back over my face, Delilah is watching me. Her eyes turn mischievous.

"What makes you more nervous? The broadcast, or sharing your room with me?"

"Depends," I answer slowly. "Do you put your clothes away in the drawers, or leave them in your suitcase?"

She presses her lips together, fighting her laugh. "I think you already know the answer to that question, Jackson."

GIANNA: How's weather boy?

DELILAH STEWART: Good!

DELILAH STEWART: Nicer than I expected?

DELILAH STEWART: But very committed to his rules and regulations.

DELILAH STEWART: So.

DELILAH STEWART: The duality of man, I guess.

DELILAH STEWART: We might be friends now.

DELILAH STEWART: He has these flashes of kindness. Like I'm getting to see who he really is. But then it's gone again. Bundled up. In one of his very utilitarian but cozy-looking sweaters.

DELILAH STEWART: I don't know.

DELILAH STEWART: Did I tell you we're sharing a room?

GIANNA: You did not.

GIANNA: Maybe start with that next time.

CHAPTER 13

DELILAH

We stand together in the small entryway of the room, unmoving, staring at the bed smack-dab in the center of it. It's massive, with a plush velvet headboard and hand-carved posts, layered with pillows and blankets and a thick plaid comforter. It's indulgent. Cozy. It's so far from the bed across the street, it's laughable.

There is, however, an issue.

There's only one.

"It could be worse," Jackson says, wandering to the foot of the bed and dropping the duffel slung over his shoulder. He stretches his neck, one side and then the other. "It could be bunk beds."

"Joke's on you. I always wanted bunk beds." I place my bag next to his. "You're being surprisingly calm about this."

He shrugs. "I figured there'd only be one bed in the junior one-bedroom suite." He drags his hand through his hair, then leans up against the foot of the bed, his long legs extended. Crossed at the ankles. "I asked Lottie to bring up a cot."

I scan his six-foot-three frame and imagine him trying to wedge himself on a cot that probably folds up and is kept in a closet somewhere.

"Or—" I raise both eyebrows, staring at him.

He blinks once, slow and heavy. His glasses are the slightest bit crooked, and it makes him look younger. Boyish.

"Or?" he asks.

I glance at the bed. We could fit roughly seventeen Delilahs on this bed, stacked in a row.

"Or we could share."

"Share," he repeats.

"Mm-hmm." I hop up so I'm sitting on the edge and toe off my boots. I let out a happy sigh and flop backward, the blankets rising around me like a cloud. I have to bite my tongue against a moan.

"Jackson, I cannot in good conscience allow you to sleep on a cot when this bed feels like this." I reach out, one arm extended, and pat the space next to me. "Try it."

"I don't need—"

I sit up, grip his arm, and pull. "Try it," I say again.

He allows me to tug him down onto the bed, falling gracelessly next to me with a huff. He's a tangle of limbs, his head tipped against my shoulder and his hip pressed to mine. He moves around with a grumble, adjusting his long legs, but then he settles, sinking into the bed with an utterly indecent sound. Something deep and rough and delicious.

I grin at the top of his head. "Right?"

"Oh my *god*," he moans, and my belly flips. A sharp twist, right in the middle of me. "Okay, yeah. No cot."

"You're not going to argue with me?"

"Delilah, I *can't*." He rocks his head back and forth against the blankets, letting his body go heavy and limp. I hear two thumps as he toes off his boots and then he tilts his head back, peering up at me, his hair rustling against the fabric. He smiles and it's so soft, so *sweet*, that I have to curl my hand into the blankets to keep myself from reaching for him. From tracing that little groove between his eyebrows.

Finally, I think. *This is who you are beneath everything else. This is who you are when you let go of all that weight.*

Heavy blue eyes. A gentle curve of his mouth that feels like something just for me.

"Maybe we can find something to argue about tomorrow," he murmurs. "To make up for it."

I smile. "Maybe."

It should be more awkward than it is, sitting with our backs against the headboard, our shoulders pressed together, staring at the weather projection open on his laptop. But either we reached a new level of understanding, or Lottie spikes her hot chocolate, because it's been distractingly *easy* since we decided we can be two adults who share a bed.

"You see this?" Jackson trails one finger along the edge of the giant red blob slowly moving across his screen. That's distracting, too, and I thrust my hand into my bag of Swedish Fish. I am demolishing my stash of emotional support candy, and it's only day one. "It's slowing down," he explains.

I blink and lean closer, my chin hovering over his shoulder. "I thought you hit a slower speed on the playback."

He shakes his head. "No. The storm is slowing to a crawl as it creeps over the mountains. And see this?" He points to another part of the map, a graceful sweep of his pointer finger down and then up again. "The winds are—"

"Changing," I finish for him with a little laugh. He minimizes the map he was on (the European model, thank you very much) and pulls up another. The projections are almost in perfect sync.

"Holy crap. We're about to get dumped on. What do you think? Did we just upgrade from a winter storm to a blizzard?"

Jackson nods, dragging the palm of his hand along his jaw. "We'll have to confirm with the National Weather Service, but I wouldn't be surprised. I'll text Maggie and let her know. We can mention it when we do our call-in tomorrow."

I stare hard at his jaw. He has a brand-new layer of scruff, a darker blond than the hair on his head. His hand makes a delicious scraping sound as he drags it down his face.

I grab another handful of Swedish Fish.

It's not that I wasn't attracted to Jackson before. It was just outweighed by everything else. But now I *know* what he's really like. He's kind. Funny in a dry, droll sort of way. Sweet. Caring.

And we're sharing a room together for the next week with only one large, obscenely comfortable bed for the both of us. It's like my brain has found the section where I've been harboring a stealthy appreciation for his bone structure and decided to throw a firework right in the middle of it. I can't stop *looking* at him.

Be professional, Delilah, I remind myself. *This is your chance to have everyone take you seriously. You don't have to be a joke anymore.*

It's the reminder I need. I'm not going to fumble this assignment because I'm distracted by a mussed-looking Jackson, showing me weather diagrams.

I firm my resolve.

"Is it weird I'm sort of excited about all of this?" I gesture at the map on the computer. "This is the biggest weather event I've ever gotten to cover." I laugh a little bit. "We're going to be right in the middle of it."

"My guess is it'll be on top of us in a day or two." His blue eyes are bright, framed with a thick fringe of honey blond lashes. "Being here, where we can actually see the cloud formations starting over the mountains, it's—" He shakes his head, in awe. "I never thought I'd get to do something like this."

"I'm buzzing. I feel like I could run down to the lake and back."

"That's probably the sugar talking." He snaps his laptop shut and sets it to the side. "You've consumed a metric ton today."

I reach into my gas station gallon-sized bag for another cherry red fish, popping it into my mouth. "Nuh-uh. The candy keeps me sweet."

"Oh yeah?" He's so close I can see the red indents on his nose from his glasses. The slight smudge on the left lens from his thumb. I extend the bag toward him and my hand bumps against his chest. He steadies it, his fingers looped around my wrist.

"Want one?" I rasp.

His gaze drags down my face and lingers on my mouth. My hand clenches the bag with a loud crinkle.

"No, thank you."

"Okay," I whisper back. "You're missing out, but fine."

He doesn't move. "I'm sure I am."

"More for me," I say airily, feeling like I've just dropped down an elevator shaft. Or maybe had one of those dreams where I'm falling only to wake up abruptly with my heart in my throat.

We sit there against the headboard, staring at each other. It would be so easy to close the space between us. See how our mouths fit together. Suck at his full bottom lip until he made another rough sound, deep in his throat. Feel the scrape of his scruff against my cheek. My jaw. The soft, delicate place between my breasts.

But those are not colleague-friendly thoughts. They're not even *friend*-friendly thoughts. I've launched myself right over the neat little lines Jackson painted for us, into dangerous territory.

And we're sharing a *bed*.

At *my* insistence.

I crawl off the bed, putting space between us. These *feelings* are probably just due to the proximity and having been saved from the alternative, atrocious sleeping arrangement. I'm feeling grateful and tired and wildly overwhelmed. And Jackson is nice to look at and knows about cloud formations. Delilah catnip, basically.

"Okay, well, I'm feeling a little tired, so—" I hitch a thumb over my shoulder at my suitcase, lying in the exact place I dropped it. I am absolutely not tired. I'm riding an intense sugar high and I can't be trusted. These . . . horny feelings cannot be trusted. I back up a step. "I think I'm going to get ready for bed. To—to sleep."

Jackson nods, a bemused look on his stupid, handsome face. "Okay."

I suck in a deep breath through my nose and let it out slowly. I need to get it together.

"All right," I say. I take another step back, clutching my candy to my chest. "I'm just going to—"

My foot catches against the broken wheel of my suitcase. I lose my balance, slip slightly, and lurch forward, the hand with the candy flying out. Swedish Fish pelt the wall like gummy raindrops while my knee buckles and I hit the carpet. I'm all twisted up, kneeling on the floor and my face—

My face smack-dab in the middle of Jackson's thigh.

He sighs somewhere above me. "You really do have a gift for this sort of thing."

I groan, my eyes clenched shut. At least I didn't land with my face in his lap. This could have been so much worse.

"I lost my fish," I whine.

He hesitates, then eases his palm over the back of my head. "I'll buy you some more."

"I got them from a gas station, like, one thousand miles away."

He exhales a short laugh. "I'm sure we'll find something." His hand sifts under my hair and squeezes at the back of my neck. I shiver. "Do you need help getting up?"

"No, I'm fine."

I don't move. Another laugh shakes his chest. "You sure?"

I finally pull back, smiling ruefully. My knee is throbbing, but my ego hurts more. Jackson's hand moves from the back of my neck to the place just between my shoulders, fingers spread wide. The way he's hovering over me is really not helping things.

"Good?" he asks again, ducking his head closer to mine.

"M'fine," I mumble. I tug myself out of his grip and—very carefully—pick my way back to my side of the room. My poor Swedish Fish. They're littered over the carpet like tiny red land mines.

I flip open my suitcase and pull out my flannel pajamas. They're oversized and well loved, with a hole in the thigh. I thought I'd be wearing them in a room by myself, not in the minuscule space I'll be sharing with Jackson for the foreseeable future.

I grab my toiletry bag too. "Do you mind if I go first? I won't be long."

He shakes his head. "I'm going to call my sisters. I'll be out on the balcony. Give you some privacy."

"It's ten degrees out there."

"I'll be fine." He gives me a half smile. "I'll turn on the fireplace when I come back in."

That's right. The best feature of this room. A gas fireplace that takes up the length of one of the walls, two cozy armchairs on either side of it. I can't wait until snow is falling outside the massive window that anchors the other side of the room. Sitting in that armchair in front of the fire while I tap away on my computer sounds like an actual dream.

I glance at it, sighing happily. "Based on the room alone, I think this might be my favorite assignment ever."

When I turn back to him, he's still looking right at me. "Yeah. Me too."

Despite what I told Jackson, I take my time once I'm in the bathroom. I spend an obnoxious thirty-eight minutes underneath the rainfall showerhead. I shampoo and condition. I wrap myself in a fluffy towel and unpack my toiletries, careful to keep to my side of the sink, trying not to be nosy and pick through Jackson's stuff that he's already set up and organized. But the bad voices win.

I peer inside the leather pouch sitting next to an electric toothbrush. He's got a tin of breath mints in there. A travel-sized bottle of aftershave. A utilitarian razor and a small, worn, folded-up piece of paper. I squint at it and bend closer, trying to see what's written on it.

Something in crayon? Maybe?

I brush my teeth and rinse my face, eyeballing his case the entire time. It wouldn't hurt to take a little peek. Not if he never knows.

Except I've never been stealthy a day in my life, and when I'm reaching for the bag, I knock it off the side of the sink. The contents spill across the floor, a kaleidoscope of tiny blue mints and razor heads. The small piece of folded-up paper taunts me, and I reach for it last after I collect the rest of his things.

It's a small greeting card with one of the edges missing, the other folded and creased so many times it looks like it's an intentional part of the design.

BEST ~~DAD~~ BIG BROTHER EVER, the front says. It's a repurposed Father's Day card with three stick figures drawn at the bottom, right above a date from almost a decade ago. I slide it carefully back into place, my heart in my throat.

Jackson knocks at the door and I almost fumble the bag again.

"Everything okay in there? I heard something fall."

I toss his toiletry bag on the counter like it's on fire. "Everything is fine!" I make sure my shirt is buttoned, then crack open the door. "Everything is fine," I repeat.

Jackson is propped up against the doorframe, his forearm just above my head, his body one long slouch. He studies my face in the muted light, then raises his eyes to look behind me. I wait for him to say something about the half-open leather bag, but he doesn't.

"All right." He pushes off the door, still watching me carefully. He shakes his head, a little rueful smile. "I got distracted with work emails, but I'm going to give the girls a call now. Need anything?"

"I'm okay."

He taps the frame and a second later, I hear the balcony door slide open. A burst of cold wind swirls around the room before it snicks shut again, the heavy floor-to-ceiling drapes in front of the windows rustling.

Relieved I wasn't caught snooping, I finish up in the bathroom and slip out.

The room is mostly dark, nothing but the glow of the fire behind the grate and the dimmed nightstand light on Jackson's side. Everything is soft and glowing orange, a hazy warmth that curls around me like a blanket. I notice the candy has been picked up off the floor.

I climb under the heavy quilt and reach for the massive stack of pillows at the top of the bed, arranging a divide down the center of the mattress. I don't want to assume Jackson's comfort, and I don't want to wake up splayed over the top of him like a starfish. Satisfied with my pillow stack, I sink into the mattress and curl up in a ball, watching Jackson's shadow pace back and forth through the frost-edged window, his phone at his ear.

His laugh sinks through the thick glass and I smile, letting my eyes fall closed. The fire cracks and pops in the hearth. The wind whistles at the window. Jackson's low, muted voice weaves between it all and I let myself be wrapped in the comfort of it.

When I was a kid, my grandpa used to have poker nights every other week. He and his buddies would sit in the living room at an old card table that listed to the left, drinking cheap whiskey and telling the same stories over and over. I'd lie curled up in my bed and watch the light under my door and hear the clinking of glass and the low sound of voices and feel so safe. It was like being tucked in with their happiness. I never felt alone.

I feel that way now, listening to Jackson talk on the phone, his voice so low his words are indecipherable. But his presence is there. The heavy fall of his boots. The *swish swish* of his coat. I let it ease me into sleep like a lullaby, my mind caught somewhere between sleeping and awake when he finally comes back inside.

The balcony door opens and closes quickly, a whispered *shit* under his breath when he fumbles with the handle. I smile into the pillow but don't open my eyes.

I listen to these new sounds instead. His jacket sliding off his shoulders. The click of the hanger as he puts it back in the narrow wardrobe. His boots on the plush carpet and then the softer sound as he toes them off, down to his socks.

The snick of the bathroom door. The zip of his leather pouch. The rustle of something soft that tells me he's changing out of his clothes.

All of it intimate in a way I've never experienced before. It feels important, a whispering thought just out of reach. It feels *special*, though that might be the exhaustion talking.

His nightstand light clicks off and then it's just our breathing in the dark. I slip a little bit farther, my body heavy beneath the blankets.

"Delilah?" he asks sometime later, and I'm not sure if I'm dreaming or awake.

"Mmph," I answer back.

I hear the rustle of bedsheets and imagine Jackson turning over on his side. One arm under the pillow, his glasses folded neatly on the nightstand.

Neat, neat, neat.

Always so neat.

"I know you were looking through my stuff," he whispers.

I snicker into my pillow, sleep drunk and unashamed. "Do you want me to apologize?" I whisper back.

"No," he says, and I can hear the smile in his voice. Sheets rustle again, his long body stretching out. "Find anything interesting?"

"Just pieces of you," I answer lazily.

He laughs. "Not interesting at all, then."

I shake my head, frustrated with that. Frustrated that he keeps putting himself down. Frustrated he's only letting me see this side of him now, when it could have been like this the entire time.

I could have had a friend.

"I think you hide all of your best parts in tiny, little pouches, Jackson Clark."

And then I finally slip into unconsciousness.

SIMONE LEEDS: And tomorrow, we'll have an update from Delilah Stewart on the winter storm heading our way.

DAVID GARCIA: I'm looking forward to that. It's nice to see Delilah reporting on the weather.

SIMONE LEEDS: It is, isn't it?

DAVID GARCIA: She should do it more often.

SIMONE LEEDS: She certainly should.

CHAPTER 14

JACKSON

Delilah looks like a fuzzy little bear coming out of hibernation when she first wakes up. Heavy eyes. Wild hair. A bewildered, soft expression. They're details I'm not quite sure what to do with, so I file them away with her preferred brand of road trip snacks and her hate of medieval medicine.

She sits in the middle of the bed in a flannel shirt that's two sizes too big, one fist digging into her eye, a yawn so wide it cracks her jaw.

I'm drinking my second cup of coffee, trying not to stare.

"You're already dressed," she says around a yawn, lifting her arms above her head, giving in to an ambling, stretching groan. I put my cup back in the saucer noisily, the ceramic clinking together. She drops her hands. "How long have you been awake?"

"About an hour or two."

More like I woke up around two in the morning curled on my side with Delilah's fingers twisted through mine, our hands buried beneath the pillow wall she made. I liked it so much I couldn't fall back to sleep. I lay there with my thumb tracing the dips and valleys of her knuckles, my breathing slow and even, while my brain spun like a top. The cyclone of thoughts is always the worst at night, and I did my best to categorize everything into a list:

1. This assignment and what it means for the station. How I need to do a good job, so everyone else can keep theirs.
2. The girls and their self-proclaimed "best time ever, ever, ever" with Aiden, Lucie, and Maya. Their wild laughter and how it felt like they couldn't get off the phone fast enough. How it felt good to know they're happy, but bad too. Like pressing at the tender edge of a bruise. That damned insistent voice in the back of my head that sounds suspiciously like my mother, whispering that maybe they need someone who can be more fun without making a damned list.
3. The text message I received late last night from Camille that said, thinking about hopping on a flight to surprise the girls!!! and my immediate response of, please don't do that.

And, finally, the biggest distraction of them all:

4. Delilah, curled on her side beneath the blankets on the other side of a shoddily constructed pillow wall, a soft little snore on every third exhale that I accidentally set my breathing to.

That's when I finally let go of her hand, sliding quietly out of the bed to stumble into the bathroom. I took a shower to clear my mind, but just stared at the tiny hot pink loofah hanging from the neck of the showerhead instead. I've been sitting at the table by the fireplace ever since, distracting myself with projections.

"Your hair is wet," Delilah says groggily from the bed. She's heavy-eyed and sleep-rumpled in an old set of threadbare pajamas and the combination is more devastating than if she were naked beneath those sheets.

I drag my hand over my face. Somehow manage *not* to scream into my palm. "Took a shower," I grunt.

"Oh." She flips back the comforter and shuffles her way to the edge of the bed, swinging her legs over the side. "Did I sleep too late?"

"No." *I just feel like I'm standing at the very edge of a slippery slope. It's been one night and I have no idea how I'm going to survive seven more. I'm supposed to be annoyed by you, not whatever this is.* I blow out a breath. "Just wanted to shower."

Delilah's eyes narrow. "You're being weird."

"I'm not. I'm just—" I search for an explanation. "I'm not a morning person."

She hums. "Is that why you're showered, dressed, drinking coffee, and pulling together the weather report before"—she glances at the heavy old-fashioned clock sitting in the middle of the mantel—"eight in the morning? Because you're not a morning person?"

I don't answer. I am trying *very* hard not to look at the place where she missed the top button of her shirt. Frankly, I feel like I deserve a medal.

"Whatever," she grumbles, and she slides the rest of the way off the bed. She pads closer to the table where I've set up all our work stuff, planting one hand by the side of my laptop and leaning over me to get a look at the screen. She smells like warm skin and flannel. That tart cherry smell again that might be her shampoo or might just be her.

"Projections holding strong?" she asks.

I grumble something in the affirmative. I haven't retained a single thing happening on this computer screen.

She turns her head and her nose is half an inch from my cheek. I can feel it when she smiles.

"Such a weirdo," she whispers.

Then she steals my coffee mug and disappears to the bathroom. I glance in her direction briefly, then avert my eyes to the ceiling when I notice the hole in her loose pants, right beneath the curve of her ass.

I let out a sigh of relief as soon as the door shuts, only to feel every muscle in my body tense as soon as I hear the water turn on.

"Fuck," I bite out under my breath. For some reason it never occurred to me that Delilah would be taking *showers*.

I imagine her slipping out of that flannel shirt, the smooth arch of her bare shoulder, the heavy flare of her waist. Her pajama bottoms, a puddle on the floor. Heavy steam and her hair curlier than usual because of it. Clinging to her shoulders, the back of her neck. That soft, delicate place where my hand fit so good. Fingers squeezing, tracing down, down, down. To the curve of her ass and that spot right where her thigh meets her—

The door swings open and Delilah's head appears. I drive my knee into the bottom of the table.

"Hey. Can you throw me my makeup bag from the top of my suitcase?"

I feel like I'm moving through syrup while I do it. I flip open her suitcase and am immediately greeted by chaos. Not a single article of clothing is folded, everything shoved in haphazardly like she had ten seconds to pack under the threat of violence before coming on this trip.

I find her pale pink cosmetics bag wrapped halfway in a sweater and wedge it carefully out.

"Your suitcase is a disaster," I tell her as I hand it over.

She rolls her eyes. "Glad we've returned to our equilibrium this morning."

Then she shuts the door in my face.

Fantasies appropriately sidelined, I pour myself a new cup of coffee from the small dinette at the edge of the dresser and reclaim my seat at the table. The light coming in from the window is shallow and murky, a dense fog sitting low over the lake.

My phone rings with an incoming call, a picture of Penelope at the Peabody Library, her head tipped back as she gaped at the massive shelves lined with books.

I swipe it open and her smiling face appears, approximately half an inch from the camera.

"Woah," I say, propping her up on the side of my computer. "Jump scare."

"Hello, big brother," she singsongs.

"What's up?"

She's practically vibrating in her seat, an excited little wiggle she's been doing since she was five years old and couldn't quite keep still. "How much snow are we getting today?" she asks.

I smile. "You? None. Me? Probably a lot."

Adeline joins her in the frame, their cheeks squished together, and that tight, panicky feeling eases. I needed this after our rushed, distracted call last night. Aiden could barely pull them away from their movie with Maya to say good night, and it lit up every one of my insecurities.

But this is better. This is familiar.

"It's coming our way, right?" Addie asks, just as excited as Pen. "We're gonna get a lot of snow?"

"Haven't you been watching the forecasts?" I ask.

"Just the one," Penelope responds, "and you mainly did a lot of blank staring into the camera."

"It was also just your floating head, so." Adeline makes a poorly restrained gleeful face. "We were distracted."

I sigh. "Fair enough."

Delilah and I haven't had a live broadcast since that first one at the studio, but we're supposed to hit the air today. Twice.

I'm trying not to think too much about it.

"So? Tell us. How many days of school are we going to miss? We have a bet going."

Pots clank in the background. Maya darts by with a box of pancake mix above her head and Aiden's hand reaches out, snagging it without turning from the stove.

"Who bet what?" I ask.

"That's cheating," Penelope says, chin tilted up. "Just tell us what you know and let the chips fall as they may."

"Have you finalized those bets?" I ask. "This feels like insider trading."

Adeline and Penelope immediately descend into a spirited argument about what constitutes cheating and how this is just like that summer three years ago, when we were at the beach, and Adeline thought that the ice-cream place would take ten minutes, but Penelope thought it would take fifteen and—

I zone out a bit. I let their happy chatter fill the space around me and drink the rest of my coffee. I'm content. Relaxed. It's why I don't notice my critical mistake until it's too late.

With the way my phone is propped up, there's a clear shot of the bathroom door in the background. The door creaks open and Delilah shuffles out, wrapped in a thick white towel, her hair wet and loose around her shoulders. Her pajamas are bundled in a ball against her chest, and she tucks some of her hair behind her ear, kicking her suitcase back open.

"I used your shampoo," Delilah declares, her back to me as she pokes around in her suitcase. I can see the smooth column of her spine where she's bent over. Pale, pale skin. The stretch of her thighs beneath the terry cloth of the towel.

"It smelled good and I think I forgot mine. Is it sandalwood?"

she babbles on as I sit unmoving, my coffee mug raised to my mouth. "Never mind. I don't know what sandalwood smells like. It was more—oh." She turns halfway. "Are you on the phone?"

She's lowered her voice to a whisper, but it's already too late. On the screen, both of my sisters are open-mouthed. They remain motionless for a beat, and then matching delighted smiles light up their faces.

"Is that a woman?" Penelope asks.

"Is that *Delilah Stewart*?" Adeline's question is approximately sixteen octaves higher, shrieked at a volume that is earsplitting.

Delilah cuts a sharp look at me, waiting for instruction. I am frozen, immobile. Entirely unhelpful.

She rolls her eyes and straightens, clinging to her towel so hard her knuckles are white. Her wet hair paints rivers down her skin, tiny droplets of water tracing along her collarbones.

Delilah gives a wobbly smile. "I am both a woman and Delilah Stewart, yes. Um . . . hello."

I flinch. Aiden's stupid, smug face immediately fills the screen. "Something you want to share with the class, bud?"

A hand pushes his forehead out of the way and it's Lucie, smiling like a maniac. "Hi, Delilah! Good to see you again."

Delilah gives me a faintly pleading look. We have a brief conversation with our eyes.

What's happening right now?
I don't know.
What should we do?
I don't know.
Are you going to say anything?
I don't know.

Delilah huffs and moves closer so she's fully in the screen. She stands behind my chair in her towel, smelling like my soap and warm skin. *Fuck.*

"There was something in the closet," she explains. "At the other hotel."

Lucie blinks. "Okay?"

"That's why I'm here. In Jackson's room. He's letting me bunk with him." Delilah gives me a *good buddy* pat on the shoulder. "So I don't get killed by a raccoon and we can do our broadcasts."

I nod in encouragement. "It's a work thing," I add. "A raccoon thing."

There's a flurry of activity on the other side of the phone as everyone jostles for position. A whispered argument and words like *move* and *let me see* and *Delilah Stewart* float through the speaker. Someone screeches, something heavy hits the ground, and someone that sounds like Aiden mutters a heartfelt *fuck*. Adeline is the one who emerges victorious during the skirmish, securing the phone and flipping it around as she readjusts the angle.

She's breathing heavily into the speaker, eyes wide. "I have so many questions, I don't know where to start." Maya lets out an excited squeal somewhere close by. "What are the sleeping arrangements like? I tried to zoom in on the background and it looks like you're sharing a be—"

Heat climbs my cheeks. "I'm hanging up the phone now."

"No," she whines. "You can't do this to us, Jackie. Why didn't you say anything last night?"

The top of Penelope's forehead appears. "Yeah. All you did was ask us boring questions." She lowers her voice. *"Did you do your homework? Have you taken your vitamins? Have you thought about life insurance and have you started saving in your 401(k)?"*

Delilah snickers. "That's actually a pretty good impression of you."

I ignore her.

"You don't have a 401(k). I'm hanging up now," I repeat.

They scream in unison.

"What?" I sigh.

Penelope beams at me. "Love you."

I roll my eyes. "Love you too."

"What about me?" Adeline grumps.

"Yes, you as well." I give her my full attention so she knows I mean it. My softhearted girl. A reluctant smile brightens her face.

"And me?" Aiden calls from somewhere in the background. "Do you love me, Jackson?"

"You are questionable."

"You are also taken," Lucie adds. Behind the girls, I see her slip her arms around Aiden's waist. He presses a quick kiss to the side of her head. "Bye, Jackson. Bye, Delilah. Stay safe out there. We'll be watching this afternoon."

There's a chorus of goodbyes and one last foreboding *We'll talk about this later* from Adeline and then the screen goes dark. I flip it face down on the desk and pinch my nose.

"Well," I say. "That went well."

"I'm sensing some sarcasm, but I think it was fine. You weren't the one in a towel." Delilah returns to her suitcase and starts to root around inside. Like some sort of burrow-dwelling creature. "I like your sisters," she says. "They seem like they're having a good time with Aiden."

Summoned by the chant of his name like an excessively demented version of Beetlejuice, my phone lights up next to my laptop with a text message from Aiden. You sly motherfucker.

What, I type back.

You said you didn't like Delilah.

It's a work situation, Aiden. And I never said I didn't like her.

Me thinks you doth protest a whole hell of a lot.

I sigh and flip my phone over, my fingers itching with the urge to correct him. Explain. Justify my absolutely unhinged behavior.

Because the truth is I could have found Delilah another hotel room. I just didn't want to.

"Jackson," Delilah says, still hovering over her damned suitcase, her wet hair hanging on either side of her face. I'm going to organize it for her. Just so I don't have to endure her in a towel for longer than thirty seconds. So much skin. All of it, wet.

Delilah's mouth twitches. "I asked you a question."

"Could you repeat it?"

"It doesn't matter." She gives me a bemused look. "Give me a bit to get all of this under control." She gestures to her wet hair, then her towel-clad body. I have to bite the inside of my cheek. "And then we can go meet Mark downstairs. I want to plan out our shots, then review the talking points for our broadcast."

I blink at her. Hearing her talk about preparation and organization is almost worse than seeing her in a towel.

"What?" she asks.

I blow out a heavy breath. "I think I like you," I say with a sigh. That's what this off-balance feeling is, isn't it? The way I can still feel her hand in mine. The way I want to feel it again. I scratch at my eyebrow. "I don't really understand what's going on with me."

Delilah laughs. "You don't have to sound so mad about it. I like you too, if that helps."

My shoulders relax. "It does."

The look on her face is tender. Understanding. "This wasn't part of your plan, was it? Actually enjoying your time with me?"

I hesitate, then nod.

She bites her bottom lip. "You and your plans."

She disappears into the bathroom, only to poke her head out again a second later.

"It was the thing about the talking points that did it for you, wasn't it?"

I drag my hand over my mouth, watching her. Immediately, I think of her smiling on the other side of a dingy diner booth, a cherry red straw caught between her teeth.

"Among other things," I admit.

"Such a weirdo," she says again, but I see her face before she shuts the door to the bathroom.

She's smiling.

AIDEN VALENTINE: It sounds like our friends out west are settling in for the storm. More updates to come.

[pause]

AIDEN VALENTINE: I, personally, am *very* interested in what happens next.

CHAPTER 15

DELILAH

There's a pattern to Jackson's on-air anxiety.

He spends the morning taking meticulous notes on the forecast, rubbing his eyes every so often beneath his glasses, nudging them up with his knuckles. Rubbing his thumb over the bridge of his nose. A flurry of anxious activity and then . . . stillness. He grows more and more quiet as we approach our broadcast time until he eventually turns completely silent. He sets up our shot on the small deck that loops around the back of the property, his movements jerky and agitated. I chatter away, but it's like he's slipped beneath the surface, sinking down to a depth I can no longer reach.

Eventually, I stop trying, coordinating with Mark while Jackson gazes out at the view. He looks like something from a conservation catalog, standing there at the edge of the deck. Hands braced against the red-paint-flecked railing, his shoulders one sharp line. Blond hair a smudge of gold against the dark forest that spills out beneath our feet, all the way to the wide expanse of the lake, stretching out, out, out to the horizon.

It's beautiful.

It's also incredibly sad.

I hate that Jackson doesn't trust himself enough to do it right. That he's stuck in his own head, likely caught in a loop.

That he doesn't trust me enough to help.

Mark pulls me to the side, doing a half-assed job of pretending to fix my earpiece while Jackson does his best impression of a baroque statue six feet away from us.

I slap Mark's hand away when it gets caught in my hair, pulling. "What are you doing?" I hiss.

"I'm trying to have a discreet conversation with you, not that it matters much. Weather boy over there is in full meltdown mode." He frowns. "And I thought you were a handful," he mutters under his breath.

We turn in unison to look at Jackson, pacing now, right outside the double doors that lead back into the lobby of the hotel. Both of his hands work a circuit through his hair, the crisp lines of his white button-down clinging to his biceps. I asked him in the room if it was his Saturday shirt, but he ignored me completely, straightening the cuffs and smoothing down his tie.

Jackson stops on a dime when he notices us staring, looking like a bespectacled deer caught in headlights.

I give him a thumbs-up. He grimaces back.

"He's going to be fine."

"He better be," Mark sighs.

There's something in his tone that sounds like a warning. "What's that supposed to mean?"

His severe expression falters, eyes darting away to scan the view. He fixates on one of the oak trees closest to the hotel, its long branches reaching out over the roof.

"Nothing."

"No, no. It was something. What's going on?"

Mark sniffs, propping both of his hands on his hips. "I just want you to put your best foot forward, is all," he says slowly and carefully. "You're a talented broadcaster. I'd hate for someone to . . . find a reason to detract from that."

My mouth hinges open, my jaw somewhere on the weathered deck we're standing on.

"Mark," I say faintly. "How long have we been working together?"

His mouth twitches down into a frown. That, at least, is familiar. "Three years, more or less."

"And in those three years, you've barely remembered my birthday."

He glances at me, offended. "I've gotten you cards."

"You've written *It's your birthday* on the back of 7-Eleven receipts."

"Those receipts had coupons on them," he mutters, defensive. "Thought you'd like a Slurpee. Sue me."

"I do like Slurpees!"

"I know!" he shouts back, throwing his hands up. "That's why I got you one for your birthday!"

On the other side of the deck, Jackson stops his pacing and stares. His blue eyes flick back and forth between Mark and me, growing sharp when he sees whatever my face is doing.

"Everything okay?" he calls.

So he *can* communicate. That's good.

I manage a thin smile. "Everything is fine."

He holds my gaze for another moment, assessing, then resumes his loop around the deck, slower this time. I notice he's changed his path. Now he's swinging back around the opposite way, keeping me in clear view.

Mark thrusts my microphone battery pack against my chest, then one of the aux cords. I fumble to grab them both before they drop, matching one of Mark's scowls with my own.

"I didn't realize you cared."

He huffs. "Of course I do, Delilah."

I think of all the times I've wiggled my way into costumes. The absolutely ridiculous shots I've had to maintain. One time, specifically, where Keith decided right before our broadcast that it would be better if I was standing in waist-deep harbor water, and I had to wade my way in. I had smelled like old crab pots for *days*. Mark never said a word about any of it.

"You've had an interesting way of showing it," I say, some of my frustration welling up and over. "This sudden concern for my well-being would have been nice during that report on the monkeys at the Baltimore Zoo, or at the Preakness, or the literal hundreds of other times I've been forced to look like an idiot."

Mark stops fussing with his camera. "I thought Keith was just messing around."

"Yeah, well. I seem to be the only person he bestows that particular honor upon." I press two fingers between my eyebrows, then drop my hand. I don't have time for this right now. "Thank you for your concern. But I can manage this broadcast just fine."

Mark looks conflicted, but he doesn't say anything else on the subject. He seems to understand that I might try to strangle him with an aux cord if he does.

"Delilah—" he starts.

All right, maybe not. "What?" I snap.

He's staring at his camera in earnest now, turning the contrast dial up and then down again. "I have another question for you."

I stare at him. "Which is?"

He clears his throat, then clears it again. "It's about—it's about Gianna."

"Okay?"

He seems to war with himself down there in his hunched position, scratching roughly at the back of his head beneath the fabric of his beanie. Then he stands, plants his hands on his hips, and levels me with a look. "Is she seeing anyone?"

I blink, then blink again. Even if I had a road map for this conversation, I'd be surprised by every turn. "Like . . . romantically?"

Mark's eyes drag skyward, his mouth moving soundlessly. "Yes," he agrees reluctantly, clearly hating whatever it was inside of himself that insisted he should ask this question.

My frustration shifts to amusement at the absolute agony carved across his features. "I don't think she is, but she's always been a bit of a wild card in that department. Why do you ask?"

"That's not your business."

I huff, slingshotting right back to frustrated. "You asked me."

"No one said you had to answer."

I roll my eyes. "Whatever. I'm going to grab Jackson. We'll be at our marks in five minutes."

I slip my battery pack in the front pocket of my jacket and intercept Jackson on his next turn around the deck. I grab him by the wrist and start hauling him over to an alcove tucked around the bend of the porch. It's a small, private spot—likely used by catering teams in the summers—sheltered by the bare branches of the oak tree.

I push Jackson in first, then quickly follow. It's a tight fit for the both of us, and I have to tip my head back to meet his eyes.

His alarmed, frantic eyes, bright and focused on me.

"Uh." He tries to rearrange himself so he's not pressing me against the wall, but all he does is nudge his knee between my thighs. He abruptly stops moving, exhaling a harsh breath in an explosion of misty white. He props his hand somewhere above me, his body stretched out in one long line. "What's going on?"

"I wanted to talk to you."

"Yeah. I got that. When you hauled me bodily across the porch."

My mouth twitches. It's not like he put up a fight. "Are you doing okay?"

He nods, then releases a delayed breath. He sounds like a balloon losing air. "I'm fine."

He is not fine. He looks like he's being held at knifepoint. This broadcast is going to be a disaster if he goes on like this. He'll be made into a meme that's circulated no less than twenty-six thousand times. The thing with the floating head is already making the rounds.

I grab his arms. "Why did you want to work in weather?" I ask. On the other side of the deck, there's a heavy thud as Mark sets up the tripod for the camera. From this angle, we can just barely make out his legs and the tiny pieces of white tape I put on the deck to note our spots. Jackson turns his head, but I grip his chin, turning his face back to mine. "Jackson," I say, firm. Direct. "Why did you want to work in weather?"

Some of the fog clears. "I don't know, I guess I—"

I shake my head. "No. You know. What was it?"

"I guess I like how reliable it is," he confesses quietly. "I like reading the data and figuring out what's going to happen next."

I grin. Of course that's it. That's so delightfully in line with every single thing I know about this man.

"And when the girls were young . . . did you ever talk to them about the weather?"

He nods. "All of the time. I couldn't remember any good stories when they first came to live with me, and we didn't have children's books, so I used to read them weather reports to put them to sleep." He swallows hard and a shaky, trembling smile curls the corners of his mouth. "It worked every time."

I laugh. "Yeah, I bet it did." I squeeze his arms through the thick material of his coat. "Here's what we're going to do. We're going to go on the air in a handful of minutes. You're going to stand next to me and look into that camera and pretend you're talking to your sisters. Easy as that, okay?"

He doesn't look so sure. "All right," he agrees. "I think I can manage that."

"Good. Practice."

He blinks at me. "Practice?"

"Pretend I'm the camera. What are you going to say?"

I watch as his confidence flags. "I don't know, Delilah. Can't we just go out there and get this over with?"

"Definitely not. No offense, but I don't think you're up to winging it right now." I try to shake him back and forth, but he's an immovable object, pressed up against me in this tiny, hidden corner. "C'mon. This will help."

His jaw clenches. Then, very reluctantly he says, "Hello, Baltimore."

I nod, waiting for more. He remains stubbornly silent.

"Great. What's next?"

A short huff of frustration. "It's about to snow," he grinds out.

My god. This is about to be the longest broadcast of my life. "How much snow?" I ask.

"I don't know."

"Jackson, you took like forty-seven pages of notes this morning. Tell me about the shifting winds. What is it about this storm that's different? What can the people in Baltimore expect? How do *you* feel about it and why are you—"

"Snowstorms happen when cold air, moisture, and lift combine," he interrupts in a rush. "We know that. We've talked about it before. But this storm is different because the two air masses set to collide are wildly contrasting in temperature."

His eyes are bright, his words slightly too fast. I don't think he took a single breath during that entire bit.

I nod. We've managed to go from one end of the spectrum to the other. "Okay, and—"

"It's weird that the front coming in from the north is as cold as it is. We don't usually see such drastic temperatures so late in the year. With global warming forcing overall warmer temperatures, our climate has slowly been shifting away from snow to more rain. So it's weird to see this level of snowfall at this time of year and— did you hear about the corn sweat?"

I can feel my face pinch in confusion. "Corn sweat?"

He nods. "It's called evapotranspiration."

Oh, boy.

"In the Midwest," he continues, words somehow coming even faster, "millions of acres of corn have started simultaneously releasing water vapor into the atmosphere. Because of the high temperatures, you know?"

"Okay, yeah. But, Jackson—"

"This phenomenon can increase already elevated humidity levels, especially during peak growing season."

"Jackson."

"A single acre of corn can release approximately three thousand to four thousand gallons of water per day through evapotranspiration. That's about the size of two concrete trucks. And that's just in one day. Think about hundreds of acres, every day during the warm season."

"Jackson," I say again.

He doesn't hear me. "Thousands of concrete trucks every day of additional humidity leaking into the atmosphere. Global warming is slowly killing the planet. Sea levels are rising and temperatures are more volatile and corn is sweating somewhere in the middle of nowhere, Iowa, and—"

I can't take it anymore. He has completely lost the thread of his practice broadcast, in over his head in one of his weather rambles.

It's cute, but we're set to be at our marks in approximately thirty seconds. We don't have time for corn sweat, or whatever the hell else is bouncing around in that brain of his.

It's not so much a conscious decision as it is a bone-deep urgency. I grip the front of his jacket as he rambles on and on, then I press up on my toes and drag his mouth to mine.

It's quick—less than a handful of seconds—and chaste—my lips pressed firmly to his—but Jackson grows quiet and still against me. I linger for another heartbeat and then drop back to the flats of my feet. I stare up at him, my hands still fisted in the material of his jacket.

Pink cheeks. Crooked glasses.

Silence.

"Uh." He clears his throat. Reaches up and touches his fingertips to his bottom lip. He looks dazed and confused. "What was—what?"

I try to look more confident than I feel. I just *kissed* my coworker. To get him to shut up. I have long jumped over any and all professional boundaries.

"You were spiraling," I defend. "I was trying to distract you."

I am painfully aware of every single place our bodies touch in this tiny alcove.

"Well," he says. He drops his hand from his mouth. "Mission accomplished."

I flinch. "I shouldn't have done that," I whisper.

It was impulsive. *Stupid.* Jackson and I finally figured out how to work together and I threw a land mine in the middle of it.

"It's fine," he says, but he won't meet my eye and he's shifted backward, shoulders pressed to the wall at his back. He lifts his hand again but drops it abruptly, the long line of his throat working in a swallow. "It's . . . fine."

I have no idea what we're doing. Sometimes it feels like we

could almost be friends, and other times it feels like we're still two people standing on opposite sides of the parking lot, scribbling passive-aggressive notes on the back of old receipts.

And then there's times like right now, when it feels like all the oxygen has been sucked out of the space between us.

"Twenty seconds!" Mark barks from somewhere behind us and I flinch again. I could not have had worse timing if I tried.

"You ready?" I ask Jackson, but he's staring somewhere above my head, forehead creased in thought. I sigh and slip out of our hiding space, hoping Jackson follows. Hoping I didn't just make everything worse.

I grab my mic. I put in my earpiece. I distill myself down to a series of actions so I don't have to think beyond this moment. I find my spot and Jackson reluctantly fills the space next to me. I force a smile on my face and feel it wobble.

Mark counts us down. Jackson shifts and for one aching heartbeat, I think he's going to pull away. Leave me here alone in front of the camera.

But he doesn't. The hand hanging at his side lifts, his knuckles brushing up against mine. My fingers twitch, wondering if it's an accident, but then his pinky loops around mine.

Careful. Gentle. Out of sight of the camera. The only parts of us touching.

He squeezes once and I squeeze back, my heart tumbling in my chest. The tiny red light flicks on, and Jackson—

Jackson gives the best damned weather broadcast Baltimore has ever seen.

DELILAH STEWART: Hi, Baltimore. We're out in Garrett County at Deep Creek Lake, getting ready to welcome our big winter storm. Light snowfall has started, but no accumulation quite yet. We expect that overnight.

DELILAH STEWART: What do you think, Jackson? Will we wake up to a winter wonderland?

JACKSON CLARK: If the current temperatures hold and that massive cold front pressing in from the north continues to hover, I think we're going to see much more than a wonderland.

DELILAH STEWART: Oh?

JACKSON CLARK: A slower-moving storm means more snow, and plunging temperatures will keep everything in sort of a stasis. And this storm has a wicked back end, with icy precipitation and high winds as a cherry on top.

DELILAH STEWART: A wicked back end, huh?

JACKSON CLARK: Yeah, yeah.

[pause]

JACKSON CLARK: Why are you smiling like that?

DELILAH STEWART: No reason.

DELILAH STEWART: I just like massive cold fronts.

JACKSON CLARK: All right.

JACKSON CLARK: And now, back to you, Baltimore.

DELILAH STEWART: Hey, that's my line.

CHAPTER 16

JACKSON

"Wind is picking up now," Delilah says quietly, a fresh mug of hot chocolate cupped between her hands. She's looking out the window and I'm pretending not to look at her, trying to study my open laptop instead. But my eyes keep drifting back. The tangle of hair pushed over her shoulder. The way her teeth bite down against her bottom lip in thought.

I know what her mouth tastes like now.

She kissed me and every voice in my head went silent. Like someone had yanked a cord from the wall.

I clear my throat and shift my legs, my knee bumping against hers beneath the table. The top of it is currently littered with a collection of notes and half-eaten baked goods. The window we settled next to is almost completely obscured by white.

"Snow is coming in heavier too," I add, digging one fist into my eye. I swear, when I go to sleep tonight, I'm going to be dreaming in barometers and cherry ChapStick.

If I *can* sleep with Delilah curled up in the space next to me.

Delilah turns from the window. "We're in the thick of it."

Yeah. We sure as fuck are.

My phone buzzes on the table.

Send us a picture, Adeline says in our family group chat. *We want to see the snow.*

Penelope follows it up with a series of snowflake emojis.

I can feel Delilah's eyes on me while I fumble with the camera app, her amusement growing as I try to get an angle out the window that doesn't include her or the glare from the giant chandelier in the lobby behind us. She holds out her hand and I wordlessly hand it over.

She snaps a few pictures of the view—limited though it might be—her tongue at the corner of her mouth. Then she flips the camera around and takes a picture of the two of us. Her, smiling so wide her eyes are almost shut. Me, looking like I've just been hit in the head by a falling piano.

It's embarrassing how much a little kiss has me rattled.

She hands the phone back to me and drops one elbow on the table. "You want to talk about it?"

I drag my hand over my mouth, considering. Normal Jackson would want to discuss it at length, laying out repercussions and all the possible avenues in which something like impulsive kisses in hidden alcoves could potentially ruin our professional working relationship. But that version of myself feels like it's shoved in a closet somewhere, and I'm not exactly eager to let him out.

"I don't know," I answer honestly. Maybe Winter Storm Jackson can handle things like spur-of-the-moment kisses without thinking too much about it. Maybe Winter Storm Jackson can be fun.

Delilah's mouth quirks up. "I'm sorry if I made you uncomfortable," she says. "I wasn't exactly thinking."

"Neither was I. I was talking about corn sweat."

Her smile tugs a little wider. "Still. I shouldn't have done it. And I owe you an apology for—"

"You don't," I interrupt, slowly closing my laptop screen.

Delilah's head tips to the side.

"You didn't make me uncomfortable," I clarify. "You figured out a way to knock me out of my own head. I'm grateful, Delilah."

I'm also flustered, slightly smitten, and probably fucked, but I plan to keep that to myself.

She watches me from the other side of the table, looking for the lie. "All right."

"Okay."

"Good."

I nod. "Yeah, great."

She stands, brushing her hands against the front of her skirt. "I'm going to get another scone."

I survey the table. "We have seven scones."

"Technically, we have three and a half scones, if you add all the pieces together. And not one of them is blueberry. So I'm going to get one of those." She collects some of the empty plates and used napkins. "Do you want more tea?"

"No, I'm fi—"

"I'm gonna get you some more tea."

She twirls off to the other side of the lobby where Lottie operates a small café and bakery. I watch as she walks right up to the counter, waving to the young attendant behind the desk reading a book. He immediately sets it to the side to talk to her, a furious blush working up and over his cheeks as he nods with enthusiasm.

I turn back in my seat, sending off the pictures of the snow to my sisters and staring at the selfie of me and Delilah. She's beaming at the camera. I'm looking right at her.

I darken my phone with a tap of my thumb and flip it upside down on the table.

Delilah and I make a good team. I am also begrudgingly attracted to her. I'm not interested in denying either of those things.

If I tried, I'm fairly certain she'd call me on my bullshit. I don't know what that means for the both of us, but I'm trying something new. I'm open to the possibilities instead of trying to map out my options.

"Is that Delilah Stewart?"

I glance up. An older man is standing at the edge of our table. Faded Levi's, tan boots, a well-loved leather cap clutched between weathered hands. He could be either sixty or two hundred and six. It's hard to tell. The lodge has mostly been deserted whenever we've been in the common spaces, and this is the first time I've seen someone who isn't a hotel employee.

"Uh." I glance over my shoulder at Delilah, still chatting away with the charmed café attendant. "Yeah. That's her."

He lets out a deep, rattling breath.

"Is there something you need?" I ask, my voice sharp. I shift sideways, angling my body between him and Delilah.

"Oh, no. No, I don't need anything. I just—" He sighs as he gazes across the room, twisting his hat in his fists. "I'm a—I'm a big fan of Ms. Stewart's work."

My hesitation eases. I recognize that look on his face. It's the same dopey look I have in the picture Delilah took five minutes ago. He's another member of the Delilah Stewart fan club.

I grin, my shoulders relaxing. "Oh yeah?"

He nods. "Saw that segment she did on the Trash Wheel coupl'a weeks ago. She's pretty funny." He clears his throat and looks down at me. He clocks my smile and immediately scowls. "What are you laughing about?"

"I'm not laughing." I tilt my head in the direction of the café. "You should go say hi."

As confident as Delilah is, I don't think she gets to see enough of this part. How much people love her for everything she already is. I've seen the spiderweb cracks that splinter across Delilah's expression when she faces one of the roadblocks Keith tosses up. How badly she wants to be taken seriously. She says she doesn't want to be a joke, but I don't think she understands that to the viewers, she's never been one.

"You should tell her about the Trash Wheel," I encourage.

My temporary tablemate immediately starts shaking his head. "No."

"You could tell her you think she's funny."

He looks at me like I'm insane. "Why would I do that?"

"I don't know. Why are you over here?"

He blinks, confused. "I don't think I know."

"All right." This time I do laugh. "I'll tell her you said hello."

He nods. "Good. That's good." He doesn't move a muscle.

I raise my eyebrows. "What should I say?"

"What?" he barks, jumping slightly.

"What should I say?" I repeat slowly.

"Oh, ah—" He runs his hand over his closely cropped salt-and-pepper hair, still staring in the general direction of the café. He's probably the same height as Delilah. Maybe an inch or two taller. "You could tell her Dustin says hello and, uh, thank you," he stammers. "Tell her thank you for keeping me company on my trips away from home."

With that, he spins on his booted heel and marches off, his shoulders hunched to his ears. Delilah appears with a new tray of snacks approximately twelve seconds later.

"Who was that?" she asks.

I take in the cinnamon bun, pound cake, and three chocolate chip cookies on her tray. "I thought you said you were getting a blueberry scone."

"I did." She points to a baked good at the top-left corner. "But then Tom recommended this other stuff, and I had to try it."

She starts pushing dishes around the table, making room. "Who was your friend?" she asks again.

"Oh." I glance over my shoulder. Dustin is nowhere to be found. "That was a fan of yours."

Her face immediately tumbles into a beaming smile. "Really?"

I nod, struck dumb a little bit by the crinkle in her nose and the way her eyes almost completely shut every time she smiles like that. "Yeah. His name is Dustin. He wanted to thank you for keeping him company on his trips away from home."

"That's so nice." She finishes transferring her bounty to the table, then quickly sweeps the remnants of our first round onto the tray. "I like that I keep him company. Like a little pocket-sized Delilah, whenever he needs it."

I take the cinnamon bun she offers. "Have people always loved you?"

She laughs. "I think you know very well that I'm not universally loved, Jackson." She collapses back into her chair. "Present company included."

"I thought we moved past this."

Her face softens. "Yeah, I know." She reaches for her scone, then changes her mind and plucks the corner off my cinnamon bun instead. "I'm just teasing you."

"You're just—" I nudge the plate closer to her. "Sometimes you feel like a caricature. Something sugary sweet someone whipped up."

She loses her smile. "Is this your way of telling me we *haven't* moved past it?"

"No, no. Listen. I'm—I'm trying to—that didn't come out the way I meant it." I reach for her hand and grab it, needing her to understand. To believe me. "You know I struggle when it's important."

Her face turns back to mine, hesitant but open. "This is important?"

"It is." I flip my hand so our palms are pressed together, the length of her thumb lined up against the length of mine. Her nails are painted a pale lavender. The color of the sky in the middle of the summer, right before the sun melts into the horizon. "This is important, Delilah."

"Okay." She shifts in her seat. "Keep going, then. I can be patient."

I know she can. She always is. I try to find the words that explain this feeling in my chest. The one that winds tighter and tighter every time she laughs or grins or brings up an important discussion point about fast-moving wind systems.

I release an agitated breath.

"You're like a lamp," I finally say.

Her normally expressive face is completely unreadable. "A lamp," she repeats.

I nod. "You—you have this light inside of you that—Delilah, it shines so fucking bright. And I think I've hated that about you because I've never—" I swallow, these words harder than the rest. "It's never been like that for me. My light's gone out, or it's flickering, or maybe it's a faulty bulb, I don't know. I'm getting twisted up in this stupid analogy, but sometimes it feels like there's this brick on the center of my chest. I think I gave everything I had left to the girls."

Delilah shakes her head. "That's not true, Jackson." Her hand squeezes mine. "That's not true at all."

"I've told you my mother is unconventional," I say quietly, trying to find the words for the things I never talk about. "The reason I took on the girls is because—is because—"

"It's okay," she tells me, the look on her face breaking me into absolute pieces. It makes the ache even stronger. "You don't have to talk to me about this."

"I want to," I rasp. "I just need a second, okay? I want to explain why I'm like this. I want you to understand."

Delilah nods. "Okay."

"When it was good, it was really good. But when it was bad, it was—" I flex my fingers in Delilah's grip, feeling all the places we *fit*. "My mom had medication she never wanted to take. Appointments she didn't like going to. She had trouble keeping track of things like that, so I tried to fill in the space for her. I tried to make it easier. I made charts. Got her those little pill containers. But an eight-year-old can't fill prescriptions. She could be passionate and excited one day and sad and lethargic the next. She thought excitement could keep the bad days away. She was always chasing it, something bright and shiny to focus all her enthusiasm on. Sometimes, it was me."

And those were the best days. Cake baking and movies cuddled together on the couch. Surprise visits where she'd pull me out of school early so we could go to a street festival she saw in the paper. Cotton candy for lunch and a balloon tied around my wrist. But that balloon would almost always lose air. I'd find it shoved under my dresser two months later, sad and deflated.

"But most of the time, it wasn't. It was something else. She'd find a new hobby or meet someone who promised a new opportunity, and I'd be left behind."

Delilah's eyes fracture, and I avert mine to the tabletop.

"I'd beg her to stay, but she'd laugh it off. Say I was too old to *need my mommy*. Eventually, I stopped asking and just . . . prepared as best I could instead. It's why I like my routines. I spent a lot of my childhood alone, aware that I was not only unwanted but avoided. I didn't want that for the girls."

I grip Delilah's hand like it's the only thing holding me above water. I haven't said any of this aloud in years. Not since I got drunk at a bar with Aiden during a St. Paddy's Day pub crawl and unloaded on him. Or that first meeting with the therapist Maggie recommended, digging through everything that made me feel itchy and tight.

"You're always smiling, Delilah. You're always positive. You have all this shit you're dealing with, but you find a way to hold it that makes you lighter, you know? I've never been able to do that. It's only ever weighed me down and I think—I've had trouble with that. I've hated how easy it seems for you."

She shifts her hand. For one awful second, I think she's going to pull away. But she just rearranges her grip so our fingers are threaded together.

"You've also hated me for my parking," she says. "It's okay to admit that."

I huff a laugh, tracing my thumb over her knuckles. Her smile fades again, and she's looking at me like she's just lifted up a rock and found a key hidden beneath. Twisted a knot a different way, and the strings came loose. "It's not always like that for me," she says quietly. "Sometimes it's heavy."

"I know. But even when you're hurting, you find a way to glow. You find a way to make everyone else glow too."

"Like a lamp," she says quietly.

"Yeah. Like a lamp."

Her nose wrinkles and she looks down at the table. She sniffles once. Then again.

My hand tightens around hers. "Shit. Delilah. I didn't mean—"

"That's a really nice thing to say, Jackson," she manages, her voice tight. Her eyes find mine, shiny and bright. "That's—thank you."

"I mean it," I whisper.

I let myself hold her hand for another second, then pull away. I busy myself with typing across my laptop, trying not to watch the way she delicately traces the corner of a napkin under one eye and then the other.

She collects herself slowly, fussing with the different baked goods. Shifting plates, rearranging napkins. Drinking out of my mug, and then hers when she realizes she's made a mistake. Watching my face to see if I've noticed. Breaking off a corner and humming under her breath when she tastes something she likes. She's lost in thought until she's not, her face popping up behind my computer screen, her eyes no longer red-rimmed, but just as bright.

"Did you want your scone, or can I have it?" she asks.

"You can have it," I tell her.

I'm pretty sure I'd give Delilah whatever she wants.

DELILAH STEWART: And a special hello and thank you to our friends at Wolf's Lodge, helping us ride out the storm.

DELILAH STEWART: You guys make some of the best blueberry scones I've ever had.

DELILAH STEWART: What did you think of the scones, Jackson?

JACKSON CLARK: I don't know.

DELILAH STEWART: You don't know?

JACKSON CLARK: Every baked good I've received has mysteriously disappeared.

CHAPTER 17

DELILAH

I wake up when the mattress dips.

Sheets rustle and then a pillow falls on top of my head. I push it away, groggy, squinting into the light that filters in from behind the curtains.

My pillow wall is in shambles around us, my arm slung over Jackson's waist. He's half-reclined on the bed, watching me, frozen with one foot planted on the floor.

"Were you trying to sneak out of bed?" I slur, letting the pillow fall back over my face. I'm not used to waking up with someone else. I'm disoriented and still more than seventy-five percent asleep.

I feel his body tense and then relax under my cheek. A gentle tug on my hair. His fingers, maybe.

"Yes," he says quietly. He hesitates. "But you are surprisingly strong."

I rub my cheek back and forth over his T-shirt. I'll probably be humiliated about this in an hour, but right now I feel soft and hazy and warm. Weightless. "And you are surprisingly comfortable. Do you use fabric softener?"

"Of course I do." Another gentle tug at my hair, right behind my ear this time. I peek open one eye and can just barely make out his face. He's staring at the top of my head with a half smile, his glasses slightly crooked.

"I didn't know hair could defy the laws of gravity," he says, his voice hushed.

I snort. "Not true. I looked through your toiletry bag, remember? I saw your hair products."

"Fair point."

He keeps combing gently through my hair and I keep using him as a pillow, the both of us caught in some hazy in-between. It's mundane and magic. Outside this room, cold presses at the windows and a storm settles over the lake, but in here it's just us. The gentle press of his fingers against my scalp. The rise and fall of his chest. The rasp of his breathing and the smell of his shampoo on the pillows. It fills a particular ache I didn't even know I had. It's entirely possible I'm still dreaming. A thought that is disrupted when Metallica starts playing—loudly—from my nightstand.

I groan immediately, loud and petulant, flopping off of Jackson.

"That's an interesting ringtone."

"I didn't choose it." I slap blindly at the nightstand, knocking over the hotel phone and sending the television remote skittering across the floor. "It's Gianna."

His face is open, curious. A pillow line on his cheek. "Gianna?"

"She works in research at the station. Hold on a sec."

I finally manage to grab my phone, answering the call with a slide of my thumb. "Hello?"

A pause. "I forgot what a mess you are early in the morning." A wrapper crinkles in the background. "Weird," she says, mouth half-full. "Considering you've been doing early-morning broadcasts for, like, five years."

Jackson lifts himself from the bed and pads his way over to the window. I watch as he reaches for the drapes, pulling them wide, bathing himself in the light from outside. He immediately presses his face close to the glass, his nose bumping up against it. I grin.

"Delilah? Hello? Are you there?"

"I'm here," I manage. I force myself to stop looking at Jackson. I study my shambolic pillow wall instead. It looks like I burrowed right through the middle of it. That's embarrassing. No wonder Jackson was trying to levitate himself out of the bed this morning. I clear my throat. "I'm here and I'm listening. What's going on?"

"First, an apology. I've consumed all the protein bars in your desk and half of the candy you thought I wouldn't find."

"I put that stuff there so you would eat, Gianna." I sit up in bed and restack the pillows. "Did you find anything with your research?"

After the hotel room incident, I asked her to poke around and see if she could find anything about the person who canceled the reservation.

"I found lots of things." A chair squeaks, papers rustle, and a mouse clicks around. "Keith is definitely up to something with this trip," Gianna says, lowering her voice. "But he was smarter than I anticipated with the hotel cancellation. It doesn't trace back to him."

"Who does it trace back to?"

"You," Gianna answers. "It was sent from your email address to the hotel directly."

"I didn't send any emails, I swear, I—"

"Hush. Relax. I know that. The IP address on it was from the station, and you were already well on your way to Deep Creek when it was sent. I documented it for you and put it in a super-secret folder with the rest of the stuff."

My forehead scrunches. "'Rest of the stuff'?"

At the window, Jackson turns halfway in my direction, then shifts back to gazing out the window. He's listening, but trying not to.

More clicking. Some furious keyboard typing. "There's some other stuff, but I want to follow up on it before I bring it to you. Don't worry your pretty little face about it, okay? Let Momma cook."

I sigh. Gianna never shares anything before she's ready. "Not even a hint?"

"Not a hint." I hear the squeak of her chair as she kicks back. A drawer opening and the rustle of a candy bag. "Now. The important stuff. How's weather boy?"

My cheeks immediately flush hot. I am painfully aware of the silence in this room, and how he might be able to hear everything I'm saying. I watch him carefully, but his face stays blank.

"Fine," I answer.

"Fine?"

I pick at a loose thread on the quilt. "Mm-hmm. Fine."

"Is he being nice?"

I think about waking up with my body on top of his. The way his fingers worked through my hair. How *gentle* he is with me sometimes. "Yes. He's being nice."

That statement makes Jackson turn in my direction, forgetting his attempts to offer me privacy. He leans one shoulder up against the window and gives me a look that I can't quite decipher—heat, hesitation, bone-deep amusement—one side of his mouth curling up into a smile.

"Because if he's not being nice, all you need to do is hand him the phone."

I realize I'm smiling back. "There's no need for violence, Gi."

"Just letting you know your options."

"Oh. Hey. Speaking of options, Mark had an interesting question for me the other day."

"Mark?" she asks. "Is he the tall one with the beard? The one who grunts?"

I laugh. Jackson has moved over to the tiny coffeepot. He places two mugs out, plucking three of the brown sugar packets I prefer from the container.

"You know who Mark is, Gianna."

"Vaguely. What did he ask?"

"He asked if you were single."

Gianna goes silent. No squeaky desk chair. No rustling candy wrappers. I don't even hear her breathing. I have to check the screen of my phone to make sure our call is still connected.

"Want to share what that's all about?"

"I have no idea," she says, sounding guilty as hell.

I laugh out loud. Jackson shifts in front of the coffeepot, hand rubbing at his neck.

"You're such a bad liar," I tell her.

"Yeah? Pot meet kettle."

"I have no idea what you're talking about."

"Sure you don't." She snorts. "He's being *nice*," she grumbles to herself.

I laugh again. Jackson smiles to himself as he pours out the coffee then ambles over to the bed with a mug in each hand. There's something deliciously soft about his bedhead and sleep-rumpled shirt. Jackson, before the rest of the world gets to see him.

"We'll be discussing this at a later date," I promise.

"Not if I can help it. I'm saying goodbye now."

"Goodbye. Eat something that isn't prepackaged," I tell her. "Preferably green."

"*Bah*," she says, and then she's gone. I toss my phone back onto the nightstand and settle against the headboard. Jackson hands me my cup of coffee, our fingertips brushing, then settles on the bed next to me, his long legs stretched out in front of him. It's so simple, so *lovely*. To just sit here quietly with another person. To not have to be anything except myself.

"How's it looking out there?" I ask.

He smiles at me over the rim of his mug. "Like a massive weather system is settling in. By the time we broadcast this morning, we might have some of that *weather people fighting for their lives* content viewers seem to love so much."

I laugh. "I did bring ski goggles, just in case."

"I'd ask if that's a joke, but I saw them in your suitcase."

"Brought a pair for you too."

He snorts, turning halfway, looking back toward the window. His face is cast in grays and blues, his eyes so bright they look like sapphires.

"Lucky me," he says easily. And it doesn't sound like a joke, or sarcasm, or any of the dry intention he usually laces his words with.

It sounds like he means it.

He's right, of course.

Standing out on the patio today is a completely different experience than yesterday. We might as well be standing at the edge of one of the polar ice caps. The wind bites at my cheeks and snow slips through every crevice it can find, burning cold against my skin. We're going to have to figure out something else for the rest of our broadcasts.

I tug my hood tighter and push my snow goggles up my forehead, shivering in my boots. Jackson isn't doing much better. His arms are crossed tight over his chest, his hood pulled up over his head. Snowflakes keep landing against his glasses and he wipes them away impatiently, streaks of moisture obscuring his lenses.

"Do you want your goggles?" I ask.

He shakes his head.

I root around in my pocket and pull out a scone I saved from breakfast. "Food?"

He shakes his head again, looking a little lost. Another sharp gust of wind howls through the trees and I balk, tucking my chin into the collar of my jacket. Jackson finally looks at me, a frown between his brows.

"You're cold," he says.

I laugh. "Yes, well, it's two degrees outside, Jackson."

"It's actually negative seven with the windchill." He lifts his hand, rubbing at the outside of my jacket. It does absolutely nothing to warm my body up, but it does make my heart glow in my chest.

Stupid.

I'm a silly girl with a silly little crush.

"This coat isn't warm enough," he says.

"It's fine."

"What's it filled with? Cotton balls?"

I roll my eyes and try to bite out a response, but my teeth clench down hard around another shiver. We should have waited inside while Mark troubleshooted the livestream. He hasn't had any luck with getting a steady connection to wire our footage back to the station. We knew it would be difficult to connect this morning, and I wanted to be a team player while he tried to set it up in the cold. No man left behind, and all that.

Jackson grips my bicep. "Come with me," he says.

He shouts something to Mark that I can't hear over the wind and then he's towing me across the porch, around the corner, back to our little alcove where I impulsively kissed him yesterday. I immediately flush hot, then cold, then hot again when he drags me in there with him, tucking me up against the wall. He props his hands over my shoulders, filling up the space in front of me as he uses his body to block out the wind.

Dark blond hair. Piercing blue eyes. A little mark on his nose from his glasses.

All I see is Jackson.

"Mark's gonna grab us at the thirty-second warning," he says. He ducks his face down a little bit, closer to mine. I can smell his body wash on his skin. The coffee he had with breakfast. "Okay?"

I nod, my arms curled around myself, still shivering. "Okay."

"Is this better?"

It's less exposed to the elements, for sure, but it's more exposed to my poor decision-making. I watch his face, liquid warmth spilling in my belly at the way we're standing together.

"It's better," I say. My heart picks up. I let myself look at his mouth for one second, two. "How are you feeling?"

He exhales a sharp breath. "I don't know," he mumbles. "It gets worse the closer we get."

"Think you're going to talk about corn sweat again?"

He shifts, the swishy fabric of his jacket brushing up against mine. "I want to say no, but it's a distinct possibility."

I know what I *should* do. I should stand here with Jackson and talk to him about something mundane until Mark taps us for the broadcast. Maybe argue with him a little bit. He seems to like that.

But there's something about the way Jackson is looking at me. He's watchful. Expectant. Like he's waiting for me to take charge, just like last time. The temptation of giving in and calling it a distraction plucks at me the longer we stand tucked together in this tiny alcove. Maybe with one more kiss, I'll satisfy this craving burning a hole through the center of my chest.

It *did* help him before.

"I thought we could maybe start with talking about some of the trees and how they've evolved in this area to bear the brunt of snowfall," he says. "Oak trees, actually, are—" He huffs out a harsh breath, one hand reaching up to anchor against the back of his neck. Physically stopping himself from one of his rambles.

"Delilah," he bites out. "I'm a mess."

I shake my head. "You're not. You're fine."

His thumb catches slightly in my hair. "I need your help," he whispers.

My heart climbs to my throat. "How?"

"You know how."

Behind him on the other side of the porch, Mark shouts my name.

"One second," I yell back, not looking away from Jackson.

I wet my lips. Jackson's gaze lands heavy against my mouth. "Tell me how you want me to help," I say. Jackson shifts closer. "I don't want any misunderstandings. You need to ask me for it, Jackson."

His sigh is low and slow. "I need you to get me out of my head. I'm freaking out over here."

I uncross my arms from my chest and press my palms to his rib cage. Feel the rise and fall of his breathing.

"I need you to distract me," he whispers. His hand slips up my arm and over my shoulder. Around to the top of my spine. He tips my head back. "You still need me to ask for what I want?"

"Yeah," I breathe. "I really do."

I want the words. I want his *choice*.

He ducks his face down to mine with a low hum, and our noses brush together. Every single part of my body swoops, like I've just crested the top of a roller coaster.

"Kiss me, Delilah," he says. "Make it all go away. Please."

My hands are fisted in his jacket before the last syllable is even out of his mouth.

He asked so nicely, I tell myself. *He needs it*.

It's just a kiss.

The justification doesn't feel important as I press up on my toes and slot my mouth against his. I stumble into him and then he urges me back, my shoulders pressed against the scratchy wood siding of the lodge, my hair tangled around his gloved fingers.

Last time, I held myself perfectly still, the kiss over before the action caught up with the rest of me. This time, I am present and aware of everything. My bottom lip, caught between both of his. The harsh pant of his breath against the curve of my cheek. This kiss is not only premeditated, it's indulgent.

I angle my head to the side and Jackson follows, his gloved thumb tracing a firm line in the space below my ear. I let myself soften in his grip, arch my back. Part my lips and breathe out a deep exhale against his. We're still so close that when I wet my lips, my tongue touches the corner of his mouth. He makes a deep, rattling sound that I want to carve into the wall with our names.

It's too much.

It's not enough.

I pull back an inch so I can look up into his face.

I don't expect to see Mark, hovering over his shoulder.

I try to push Jackson away, but he holds me tight, one hand still curved against the back of my neck and the other at my hip.

"No," he says, his voice a low rasp. He's misunderstanding my panic. "Come back."

"Jackson," I whisper-hiss. "Let go. We need to—"

Mark clears his throat and Jackson releases me, his face stricken. Mark doesn't seem surprised to find us tangled in this tiny corner tucked up against the lodge. If anything, he looks grimly resigned.

"Sorry." I force a smile. "We were just going over our notes—"

Mark ignores me, pushing past Jackson and reaching for the collar of my jacket.

"What are you—" I try to pull away. "Mark! What are you doing?"

Jackson tries to wedge his body between us, but Mark is undeterred. This little space could barely fit two people. Now there are three of us ping-ponging off the walls.

I get a good smack to the top of Mark's head. "Stop it, you're going to—"

He finally gets a good grip on my mic and yanks it forcefully from my body. The wire that connected it to the transmission pack at the small of my back tugs loose, and the three of us freeze, staring at it dangling limply between us.

"I was calling you," Mark accuses, defensive. "I called your name three times."

Jackson drags his hand over his mouth. "*Fuck*," he whispers.

Realization is a slow-dawning thing. It rises around me like a tide, licking at my ankles before constricting at my chest. I can't breathe around it. The enormity of the mistake I've just made.

"Your mic was live." Mark confirms my fears. "The broadcast went through. All of Baltimore just heard you two."

SIMONE LEEDS: Well, uh.

[clears throat]

SIMONE LEEDS: Some technical difficulties out in Deep Creek.

SIMONE LEEDS: We'll be back after these messages.

CHAPTER 18

DELILAH

"Which part?" I ask.

Mark looks at me like I'm stupid.

"Which part?" I ask again, slightly hysterical. My phone is buzzing in my pocket and Jackson's is too. I can feel it where he's tucked up against me. I'm so embarrassed I can't bring myself to look at him, locking eyes with a regretful-looking Mark instead.

"I stopped it as soon as I could," he says. His gaze slants toward Jackson. "But I heard you ask her to kiss you."

Jackson tips his head back and closes his eyes. I stand next to him absolutely mortified.

"And did you hear—"

"Yeah," Mark says. He swallows. "I heard everything, which means everyone else heard everything too. The stream has been finicky this morning with the winds. We were jammed and then we . . . weren't." His face softens. "I'm sorry, Delilah."

Jackson whispers another emphatic *fuck* under his breath while I continue to have a full-blown existential crisis next to him.

"What are our options?" he asks.

Mark watches me for another minute. "You have your radio check-in this afternoon, and another broadcast with the evening news. I'll tell production back at the station this was mucked due to technical difficulties, but—" He makes sure I'm looking at him. "You'll need an explanation."

A laugh bubbles out of me. My phone stops buzzing in my pocket only to pick up again. I pull it out and glance at the screen.

KEITH

I silence it.

Jackson grips my arm right above my wrist. My gaze snaps to his, like a key sliding into a lock.

"Mark," he says. "Can you give us a second?"

I've never seen Mark more relieved in my life. "I'm gonna pack up the equipment," he says before high-stepping out of the alcove.

Then it's just me and Jackson and my dangling microphone wire, the repercussions of my carelessness scattered around us like the snowflakes spinning wild from the sky. I wanted to be taken seriously. I wanted to make an impact. And now I've ruined everything.

Hot tears fill my eyes.

Jackson's hands cup my face. He must have taken his gloves off, his thumbs rubbing at my cheeks. He is almost eerily calm, his jaw set in a firm line.

I hiccup a breath. "Why aren't you panicking about this?"

"Because," he says, "I'm with you."

I huff out a laugh. "Well, as current evidence clearly shows, that might not be in your best interest."

I close my eyes, reaching up and looping my fingers around his wrists. I hold on to him while he holds on to me and I try to calm down the heavy *thump, thump, thump* of my heart. I feel like I've been sliced open. A moment that was meant for me and Jackson was just shared with the entire city.

"What do you want to do?" he asks.

I blink open my eyes. Behind his head, snowflakes float lazily from the sky. I wish I was one of them, drifting away.

"What can we do? Everyone heard. I'm going to be—" The words stick in my throat, thick and heavy. The bridge of my nose burns. "Jackson, I took this assignment because I didn't want to be a joke anymore."

And now I'm going to be the weather girl who kissed her partner in the middle of a snowstorm. I'll never outrun the assumptions people make of me. Silly, whimsical, happy-go-lucky Delilah. I've cemented every last one of them into place. Why should anyone ever take me seriously, if I can't even manage it for myself?

Jackson's thumbs rub another circuit under my eyes, over the swells of my cheeks. "You're not going to be a joke. I won't let it happen."

"How?"

Tell me what to do, I want to beg. *Tell me how to fix this.*

Jackson seems to hear everything I don't say, because his face settles into something determined.

"We aren't going to say anything."

"What?" I laugh, thick and disbelieving. "Jackson. The entire city of Baltimore just heard us kissing. Our *bosses*. *God*. Their bosses. No one's going to let us get away with that without an explanation."

"There are no rules that say we can't. We haven't done anything wrong. It's our business."

"We can't just ignore it, Jackson."

"Then we tell them the truth." *And what*, I immediately want to ask, *is that?* He ducks down a little, meeting my eye. "You were helping me work through my on-air anxiety. Distracting me, right? It doesn't need to be more than that."

I bite my lip and stare down at our feet, embarrassed. I don't know what I thought, but I guess—he had sounded so earnest when he asked for my help. Like he *needed* it. Like he needed me, specifically.

Maybe I let myself think it was more than it is.

It doesn't have to be more than that.

"We didn't do anything wrong," Jackson repeats. His fingers press against my cheekbones, urging me to look at him. "Can you repeat it for me?"

"We didn't do anything wrong," I warble.

Logically, I know it's true. A kiss is hardly the end of the world. If anything, we just dangled a giant, scandal-clad carrot in front of our viewers. And if we don't address it—don't explain it—people will be watching our every move, trying to decode the thing between us. We're a piece of the news now. A delicious, enticing question.

I guess I just wish I knew which part of this is the truth and which is the lie.

We decide to do our phone calls separately.

Or it's what I decide, anyway. Jackson clearly has a problem with that plan, lingering in the open door of our shared room, his palm propped against the door.

"I'm telling Maggie it's not up for discussion," he says. "That we'll continue to report the weather, but we won't be discussing anything else."

"Okay," I agree. We've been through these talking points at least twelve times, and every time he repeats those words, it sinks like a stone in my chest. I've got a whole collection of pebbles in there, weighing me down. "What about your sisters?"

Jackson sighs and drags his hand through his hair. "I'm going to call them first."

What will you tell them? What version of the truth will you tell the two people you love most?

But I'm busy sinking deep into a spiral of self-loathing and self-admonishment, so I keep that to myself.

"You sure you don't want to do this together?"

I shake my head. I'm not interested in drawing out my humiliation by having Jackson bear witness to whatever this call with Keith will be. Keith already thinks the worst of me. I can only imagine what he has in store.

I fix a smile on my face that's only eighty-three percent forced. "I can handle a single conversation on my own, Jackson."

"I know you can. I just—"

I stare at him, arching my eyebrow. "You just?"

"I don't want you to apologize," he tells me with another bone-deep sigh, still hovering in the doorway. "You didn't do anything wrong."

"I know that."

Except it feels like I did. Maybe not to Jackson, or Gianna—who has been texting me motivational support memes for the duration of the afternoon—or Mark, even. But it feels like I've done something to let myself down. Made the wrong choice. Or wandered too far down a path that leads nowhere good.

Still, I repeat it to myself like a mantra while the phone rings. *You didn't do anything wrong.* One more with feeling when Keith answers and barks a short, agitated *hello*.

I press my forehead against the glass of the window, letting the cold sink into me.

"Keith," I say. "I'm returning your call."

His silence is loaded. He waits just long enough to have me on edge. Something I'm sure he practiced between all those missed calls.

"Been busy out there, have you?"

Another slice against all my tender parts. My shoulders hike up to my ears. *You don't have to explain*, I remind myself. *You didn't do anything wrong.*

"Mark said there were some technical difficulties with the broadcast earlier. I understand there was a situation with my mic, but I—"

"It's fine," he interrupts.

I stare at my reflection in the window, blinking. "Um . . . what?"

"I said it's fine," he repeats. A loud slurp, likely from whatever frozen Dunkin' drink he sent a poor intern to retrieve. "Can't say I'm shocked, Delilah."

"What do you mean?"

His laugh is like an oil slick. "We can always count on you to be our good-time girl, can't we?"

With one sentence, Keith has diminished my confidence to the size of a thimble. This is exactly what I was afraid of. Keith didn't need to lift a finger to humiliate me. I made myself the butt of the joke, all on my own.

"What you heard," I try to explain, reaching for something that'll make sense, "it isn't what it sounded like. Jackson just—"

"Delilah," Keith interrupts. "Do you think I actually *care*?"

I'm confused, floundering ten feet behind this conversation while Keith breaststrokes ahead.

"No," I answer, my voice faint. "No," I repeat, louder. "There's nothing to care about because it was a mistake, and it won't happen again."

I hate that I sound like I'm about to cry. The last thing I want is for Keith to have any sort of satisfaction that his opinion matters to me. But I've always struggled with buttoning up my own emotions. I'm an open book, a bleeding heart. Usually, I'm proud of that fact.

Just not right now.

"Frankly, Delilah, I don't care what you do or don't do out

there. I was concerned, at first, about your professionalism. But I realized something while I was waiting for you to return my call."

I almost don't want to ask. "What's that?"

"You're a puff piece, at best. The expectations for this series were pretty low across the board. It's no skin off my back if you fail to meet them."

I suck in a sharp breath and close my eyes. "All right," I manage. "If that's everything, I need to go run some reports for the radio spot. Thanks for your feedback."

He huffs some unintelligible string of sounds and then he hangs up. I sit in the window for a long time after, watching the lake and the snow that melts easily against it.

DELILAH STEWART: The storm is picking up in force while slowing down in speed. We expect conditions to deteriorate further in the next twenty-four to forty-eight hours.

JACKSON CLARK: That's the latest on the weather.

DELILAH STEWART: And now, back to you.

CHAPTER 19

DELILAH

My phone alarm goes off at two a.m.

I roll over to my side beneath the thick quilt and silence the buzzing with a tap of my thumb, wedging a yawn in the crook of my elbow. When I crack my eyes open, the room is bathed in a warm orange glow from the fire burning low behind the grate, the pillow wall between Jackson and me still miraculously intact. There's a metaphor in there somewhere, I'm sure.

I lie still for one second, two, waiting to see that my alarm didn't accidentally wake Jackson. Then, when I'm sure Jackson is unaware of my nighttime plans, I slowly slip out of the bed.

Or I try to, anyway. Because as soon as my feet touch the frigid hardwood floor, Jackson's voice says, "Going somewhere?"

I squeak, twisting quickly, my foot getting tangled in the duvet hanging off the edge of the bed.

Jackson is sitting in front of the fireplace in one of the cozy chairs. He's got his left arm slung over the back of it, staring at where I'm trying to untangle myself from the bed. His knees are tipped wide, his long body clad in black joggers and a black thermal sweatshirt. There's a book open against his thigh and a mug at his elbow.

I press my palm to the middle of my chest where it feels like my heart is trying to burst through and fall back into bed, staring blankly up at the ceiling while I try to get control of my breathing. There's a rustle of fabric, the snap of a book being closed, and then Jackson appears above me, concerned.

"Delilah?" he asks. I wheeze in response. "You okay?"

"You scared me," I whisper, still feeling like I want to crawl out of my skin. I wasn't expecting him. The theme of the trip, I'm starting to realize. I wasn't expecting Jackson at all. "What are you doing awake?"

"Couldn't sleep. My mind was running," he murmurs. Amusement quirks the corners of his mouth. "What are *you* doing awake?"

"I don't know. I just woke up."

"You had an alarm, Delilah."

I stay stubbornly silent but he arches an eyebrow, waiting for my explanation. I grunt out a sigh, kicking my feet in agitation. He grips my ankle to keep me from hitting him, and a lightning rod of sensation rockets up the back of my thigh. I immediately still, my breath catching for a different reason altogether. I didn't realize my ankle was the sensual gateway to the rest of my body, but . . . here we are.

"I have my reasons," I say tightly.

His thumb traces over the curve of my ankle, almost absently. "Which are . . ."

I blow out a breath. I can't exactly sneak out with him hovering over me. "I want to go outside."

Jackson stares at me. "Right now?"

I nod.

"At two in the morning," he continues.

I nod again.

"In the middle of a—" He lifts his head and looks in the direction of the balcony as a particularly ferocious gust of wind bucks at the windows. "Delilah," he says, "the winds are hitting forty-eight miles per hour right now. They've gotten substantially worse since our broadcast."

"I know," I defend petulantly. He's not the only one looking at projections.

His grip firms on my ankle, trailing up until his palm is against the back of my calf. "Was our kiss that bad?" he asks. "That you're now sacrificing yourself to the storm gods?"

My stomach flips. "It has nothing to do with our kiss."

It might have a little bit to do with our kiss.

He squeezes gently, fingers spread wide. "Then why in the hell do you want to go *outside*?"

I study his face in the flickering shadows. I can see him better now than when I first woke up. His hair is sticking up at odd angles. There are circles beneath his eyes.

I reach up and trace the edge of one of those purple circles, from the corner of his eye to the middle of his nose. My knuckles brush against the cool metal of his glasses, his breath a warm exhale in the middle of my hand. I touch him the same way he was touching me, when I tried to come up with a reasonable explanation for all the things I'm feeling.

I make another gentle circuit with my fingers and his eyes go half-mast.

I pull my hand away. "Sorry."

"No." He tugs my hand back. "That was nice."

I carefully reach for him and trace another idle path, trying not to read too much into it. It's okay to touch like this, in the hush of the night. When it feels like we're the only two people in the world. It's okay to kiss him too, but only in tucked-away places where no one can see. It's okay to feel something for him, as long as it stays within the boundaries we've constructed for it. None of it has to matter. That's what he said.

But for me, I'm sort of afraid it does.

"I have trouble sleeping," he confesses, his eyes closed, lashes dark gold fans across the tops of his cheeks.

"Always? Or just this trip."

"Always," he whispers.

On my next pass, I trail my fingers back along the temple of his eyeglasses, over the spot where I snapped them ten days ago. I trace over the curve of his ear. To the hidden place below where his skin is so, so warm.

He releases a deep sigh. Some of his hair falls over his forehead. I push it back, then smile up at him when his eyes crack open. I think Jackson might need another distraction. I think I could use one too.

"Want to come outside with me?" I whisper.

We pull on our snow gear in near silence, nothing but the *swish swish swish* of our jackets and the quiet sighs of zippers. Jackson snickers when I start jumping up and down to get my socked feet through the bottom of my cinched snow pants, reaching over and holding me steady with one hand curved against my hip while I wiggle and kick.

"I can't believe you thought you could sneak out of here," he says, his fingers holding me tight. Five distinct pressure points that I could probably map into a constellation later. "How were you going to do all this without waking me up?"

"I assumed you were a deep sleeper," I grunt, blowing my hair out of my face once my feet are through. My socks are mismatched. One of them is bunched at the ankle. In fact, I'm pretty sure one of them is Jackson's.

"What made you assume that?"

"Your overall disposition? I don't know, Jackson."

Twenty minutes later, we're standing in the lobby of the lodge, staring out the window at the wall of pink-tinged white that's waiting for us.

"Just to confirm," he says, "you want to go outside. In that."

Outside the windows, we can barely see across the parking lot. It's a wall of white, the very tops of the trees swaying in the wind.

"You don't have to come." I tug on my hat, pulling it low over my ears. "You can wait in here."

"You invited me," he says, somehow making it sound like an accusation.

"Yes," I say slowly, "but I'm not holding you at gunpoint. You are free to do as you wish, Jackson, and that includes staying inside and watching from the window."

He glances down at his legs. "After I put on these snow pants? I don't think so."

Jackson's snow gear is utilitarian black. Sleek and formfitting. He looks like Jack Reacher's nerdy little brother, snow expedition edition.

I snicker.

His forehead creases. "I really don't understand your fascination with the pants."

"They're just so . . . undercover agent. I didn't realize we were going on a top-secret mission while in Deep Creek."

He rolls his eyes. "And I didn't realize we were making a side trip to Candy Land." He reaches over and pinches the very top of my snow pants. "How does Mark let you on camera with these?"

"The camera hits from the waist up. You, too, could have had hot pink snow pants, if only you dared to dream big enough."

"Maybe next time." In front of us, wind whistles around the door. It's blisteringly cold, and we're still inside. Jackson sighs. "Will you finally tell me why you feel the need to do this?"

I avoided the question the first three times he asked, self-conscious. I tuck the edges of my gloves under the sleeves of my jacket. "Because I want to," I sidestep.

Jackson stares hard at the side of my head. "You want to lose your fingers to frostbite in the middle of the night?"

"Not particularly, no."

I pull the set of keys I stole from Jackson's backpack from my pocket. "I need to get something from the van."

"I brought our bags in."

"You forgot something."

"What did I forget?"

"Something."

Something doughnut-shaped with pink frosting.

Jackson's gaze narrows, turning suspicious. "Delilah," he says, "are you getting your sled out of the van?"

I roll my lips together and refuse to answer.

"Oh my god. You're out here at two in the morning because you want to go *sledding*."

"I checked the projections," I defend. "By the time we wake up tomorrow, the snow will be too deep. I won't be able to sled at all."

He plucks the keys out of my hand. "You're ridiculous."

Fire lights in my belly. I snatch the keys right back. "Yeah, I'm ridiculous. Silly and absurd and a little bit stupid, too, yeah?"

Jackson rears back. "I didn't say that."

"No, but you were thinking it. I'm not an idiot, Jackson. I know what people think about me." That I'm some manic pixie dream girl, hell-bent on toxic positivity and crying over cute little dogs in tiny teacups. That because I wear high-waisted hot pink snow pants, I don't deserve to be taken seriously. "This is what I want to do. For me. The last twelve hours have been—" A shit show. Catastrophic. Completely and totally humiliating. "It's been a lot, and I'd like to have this one thing for myself. I don't care if you think it's silly." I pull my zipper all the way to the base of my throat. "I'm going to do it anyway."

I tip my chin up and attempt to stroll confidently through the door, but Jackson hooks my elbow and tows me right back. He manhandles me until both of his hands are heavy on my shoulders, his face ducking down to mine. He tries to force eye contact, but I stare resolutely at the middle of his nose. At the two small red marks left behind from his glasses.

"I do think it's silly," he says quietly. "But that doesn't mean I don't want to do it with you."

I drag my gaze up. "Yeah?"

He nods. "Someone has to make sure you don't sled yourself into the middle of the lake."

"I was going to sled on the other side of the parking lot." I sulk. "There's a little bunny hill with two bumps at the end."

"Have you been scouting sledding spots?"

"I brought a sled with me, Jackson." I cross my arms over my chest. "It's the practical thing to do."

I get the distinct pleasure of watching his face soften, bit by bit. I might hide behind the costume other people have dressed me in, but I think Jackson wears some masks of his own.

He lifts his hand and fixes some of my hair that's tangled under my hat. "I don't think you're stupid, Delilah."

My nose crinkles. "All right."

"Did you not listen to my lamp speech? I thought I explained it."

"You did."

"Not well enough, apparently." His hands firm over my shoulders and he shakes me a little bit. "Tell me you believe me, or I'll say it again. Weird metaphor and everything."

My stomach hollows out, something warm curling low. I try to fight my smile, but it can't be helped. I grin at him. "Please don't repeat your weird metaphor. Once was enough."

A deep groove forms in his cheek as his smile grows. "You're sure?"

"Yeah." I rub my gloved fingers over my nose. "I may have . . . overreacted just then."

He shakes his head. "You didn't. Like you said, this day has been . . . unexpected. I think we're both trying to recalibrate."

What we're doing is tiptoeing around the issue instead of addressing it. I shared the high-level notes from my Keith call with Jackson as soon as he got back to the room. I told him Keith said it was fine, as long as we focused on the weather. I didn't mention anything about being a *puff piece*.

I scuff my boots against the faded rug in the lobby. "I think I'm carrying around a lot of frustration about how I'm treated."

"Good." He nods. "You deserve better. It's time you start asking for it."

"And now?" I step closer. "Can I ask for this? You sledding with me?"

He looks patiently amused. "I will watch you sled."

I shake my head. "Nope, that's not the deal. If you come outside, you sled." I dig one finger in the middle of his chest. "Those are the rules."

He grabs my finger.

"Ah, how can I resist that?" He folds our hands together, holding my palm over his chest. Right over the steady *thump thump thump* of his heart. He grins at me. "You know how much I love rules."

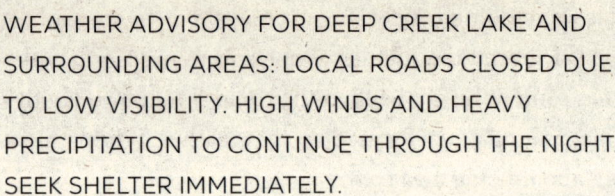

WEATHER ADVISORY FOR DEEP CREEK LAKE AND SURROUNDING AREAS: LOCAL ROADS CLOSED DUE TO LOW VISIBILITY. HIGH WINDS AND HEAVY PRECIPITATION TO CONTINUE THROUGH THE NIGHT. SEEK SHELTER IMMEDIATELY.

CHAPTER 20
DELILAH

Jackson was right about the wind surges. Each gust rolls into the next, making me feel like I'm standing in front of a turbine. I've never felt wind like this before. The kind that burrows in between any crack it can find, stinging at my cheeks and stealing my breath. It whips at us where we're huddled together on my little bunny hill before howling through the trees, a dull roar that builds and builds the longer we're out here. The sky feels alive, heavy clouds hiding the moon and all the stars but holding their light, seeming to glow.

And right next to me is Jackson, his big body wedged in the middle of a doughnut inner tube.

I can't stop laughing long enough to get a good grip on the handle, bent in half behind him as the storm twists around us.

"Pull yourself together," Jackson yells, his head angled back so he can see me. His eyes are unreal out here beneath a sky that's not truly dark. Snowflakes spin wild out of the endless, yawning sky above us, falling in thick clumps.

Jackson's patience is wearing thin.

And I'm having the time of my life.

"Okay, okay." I grip the handle with both hands and take a

bracing breath, snickering at the look on his face. I had to do some coaxing to get him into the sled, but not as much as anticipated. I took three solo trips down the hill before he finally agreed, reluctantly climbing into the center of it with his knees tucked to his chest.

I wish I brought my phone. I want this as my wallpaper.

"Delilah!" Jackson snaps again.

"All right!" I rock back and then use the momentum to push forward, moving him approximately two inches. "Are you ready?"

"I've *been* ready. You're the one back there having a moment."

The wind howls, the snow screams, and I smile so wide my face hurts.

"On the count of three, okay?" Jackson gives a single, sharp nod. "One, two, th—"

I mean to push him over the edge that leads to the shallow slope, but I lose my footing right as I shout "three!" I fall forward with a shriek, my knees digging into the back of the tube, my arms across Jackson's shoulders. He immediately grips both of my forearms as the added weight and sudden momentum move us forward, and together we go rocketing down the hill; me shrieking in delight in Jackson's ear, him holding on for dear life.

With both of us on the sled, we go so much faster. We barrel down the hill on the side of the parking lot and everything blurs around us. Snow, sky, snow, sky. I curl my arms around Jackson's shoulders as we go bumping along and burrow my face in his neck, laughing like a madwoman with every rough bounce of the sled.

With my other attempts, I slowed to an anticlimactic stop at the bottom of the hill. With Jackson's added weight, we skid right past my previous finish line and over the two smaller hills at the bottom. At the crest of the first, I go airborne, landing with another scream directly in Jackson's ear, my knees hugging his sides. At the second, Jackson loses his grip and we both go flying off.

Jackson does his best to take the brunt of it as we hit the ground, but we're going too fast and our position is too awkward. We land and roll, the force of it crushing at my lungs, a dull pain somewhere near my hip. Jackson's *fuck* is low and rough in my ear and then we're still, my body splayed above his in the snow.

We lie there, silent, two victims in a horrible doughnut sled accident.

"Are you okay?" I wheeze, patting at his chest where I can reach, one hand still fisted in the material of his jacket, the other wedged somewhere under his ass. I don't know what it says about me that in a crisis, I immediately reached for his very solid backside.

I suppose subconsciously, I was looking for support.

Jackson's chest trembles under my cheek and I go still. My god, I've killed him. I forced him outside in the middle of a storm, forced him into the sled, forced him down the hill, and now I've killed him.

Or possibly maimed him for life. It's not clear.

I try to leverage myself up on my elbows to get a good look at him, but we're pressed together neck to knee and my legs keep slipping in the snow.

Two hands grip my hips and squeeze.

"Delilah," Jackson grunts, his voice thin. He can barely manage my name. "Stop moving."

"Are you okay?" I ask again, feeling frantic. I don't want him hurt. I don't want to be the reason he hurts. His hands on my hips lift and pull, setting me firmly across his body. He holds me still.

"Delilah," he says again.

Jackson is splayed out in the snow, his hat gone, his blond hair a mess against the fluffy white behind him. There are snowflakes on his coat, across his crooked glasses that I think I might have broken for a second time, and he's—

He's laughing.

Jackson is laughing so hard his eyes are scrunched shut, his body trembling beneath mine.

I stare at him, stupefied.

He lifts his head and cracks one eye open. He sees the look on my face and laughs harder.

My heart turns over in my chest. Like this, he looks so much younger. Happier. Unburdened by all the weight he carries around with him.

I cup his face in my hands, wanting to hold on to this moment. On to *him*. His laughter slows but his smile stays, settling into something heartbreakingly tender while his head drops back in the snow. I rub my thumbs over his cheeks and feel the rush of it. The *magic*. Snow and sky and us smack-dab in the middle of it, cold slipping through the tops of my boots and prickling at my skin. Jackson looking at me like maybe it feels like magic for him too.

Another gust of wind torpedoes around us and I burrow closer. My lips are numb, my fingertips tingling in my gloves. Jackson's gaze slips over my face, settling on my mouth and holding there. That boundless, weightless feeling in my chest amplifies. Like hitting that second hill but wilder. Unrestrained.

The storm, and the snow, and Jackson. *Jackson*. Always looking right at me.

"You feel it, right?" he asks, his eyes searching mine. "Whatever this is. You feel it?"

I need to be careful with this. Jackson wants a vacation from who he is in the real world. He wants to prove to himself that he can let go of all the rigid structures that hold him in place. Nothing good comes from pretending to be someone else for a little while.

But I nod, because I *do* feel it. This boundless, yearning impossible thing. Glowing, glowing, glowing like all the hidden stars behind the clouds.

I can't lie. Not about this. Not to him.

His hand slips to the back of my neck.

"Kiss me," he rasps.

I want to. I want to *so bad*. But I can't.

I shake my head and try to slip off of him.

But Jackson holds me tighter, his other hand rising to tuck against the small of my back. He's a brick of warmth beneath me, watching me patiently, his head haloed in white.

"Tell me," he whispers, his voice cracking down the middle. He looks confused. Worse, he looks hurt. My heart pounds, a zip of awareness up my spine. "If you feel it, too, then tell me why. It's only us here."

"I can't."

"Why not?"

"Because."

"That's not an answer, Delilah."

"It is to me."

His hands tighten. "Don't hide," he says, still with all his impossible patience. Ever since we were caught in that tiny alcove, *he's* been the calm one. He's been the one with the plan. It's infuriating. "Is it because of what happened?"

"No, it's—"

"You said Keith didn't give you a hard time."

"He didn't, but—"

"Are you embarrassed?" His mouth twists down at the corners. "Did I embarrass you?" he asks, softer this time, and *oh*. My breath splinters. A sharp, tingling ache.

I shake my head, throat thick.

"Then what is it?"

The truth rattles out of me. "You need to do it," I blurt. "You need to be the brave one. If that's what you want, then *you* need to kiss *me*. I can't always be the one taking charge, Jackson. I need to know it's—"

His mouth is on mine before I finish my sentence, bruising and certain. He doesn't hesitate. He doesn't go slow. It's an exclamation point at the end of a sentence.

He shifts his hand until he's cupping my face, his thumb under my chin, the rest of his fingers spread wide against my jaw.

We've done this before. Our mouths pressed together, exchanging easy breaths. But Jackson so quickly drags us into something darker, more ferocious, his mouth urging mine to keep up. I asked him to show me he wants it, and he does. With every rough slant of his mouth against mine. With his fingers pressed tight at the base of my skull. He adjusts me just the way he needs to kiss me best, then bites down against my bottom lip with a pained groan.

"Fuck," he whispers. "Delilah."

I kiss him again and settle my weight more firmly against him, letting myself go pliant, my hands inching up to press over his shoulders. We're wearing too many layers. This is a kiss meant for barely lit hotel rooms and fireplaces, not the bottom of a snow-covered hill edging an abandoned parking lot. But I can't stop. I want everything that Jackson keeps buttoned up and tucked away.

I shimmy up his body until my knees are at his hips. He makes another rough sound, scooping me closer, kissing me harder. He licks into my mouth and I meet him there, my hands pushing up to his snow-damp hair, jostling his fogged-up glasses.

"Delilah," he says between our panting mouths, and I hold on to him tighter. "Next time, just tell me."

"Tell you what?"

I'm mindless, selfish. A heavy drumbeat of desire. I want so many things, but I want him most of all. This silly, ridiculous man who kisses me like I'm something precious. Like he's snapped all the strings holding him back.

"What you want from me." He nudges my nose with his. "I'll give you whatever you want."

My stomach twists. "That's not how it's been between us," I whisper.

He stares up at me, his eyes so blue they look black. "That's how it's going to be," he promises.

He kisses me again, ending the argument. Conversation. Whatever this thing we do with each other is. We kiss and kiss and kiss each other, my hands scrabbling for purchase, the most delicious sounds rumbling from his chest to mine.

He drops his head back with a grunt, his cheeks a bright pink, his glasses crooked on his nose. "Inside," he says, chest heaving where I'm spread over the top of it. "I need to get you inside."

I reluctantly peel myself off him and Jackson follows, slower, pressing up to his knees and then his feet while he brushes snow off his coat. I try to help but I only manage three lazy swipes across his torso before he catches my wrist, towing me into him, bending me backward as he kisses me again. I sigh into his mouth, warmth pulsing through my body.

He kisses me so *good*.

It's all so good.

I wrench my mouth away, panting into the warm skin of his neck.

"We need to stop." I laugh a little bit. "I can't feel my nose."

Somewhere above me, he nods, then grabs my hand with his.

Jackson tugs us back through the parking lot and into the lobby, the door slamming shut behind us, making me flinch. He steers me to the corner by the elevator and deposits me there, my body more than content to let him lead.

"Be right back," he says.

I reach for him, hooking one hand in the pocket of his coat. "Where are you going?"

He steps back to me, thumbing gently at my cheek. A reassurance, apparently, that I desperately need.

"Your sled," he says. "We left it outside. I'll be right back."

He leans forward and gives me a quick peck on my nose before striding across the lobby, yanking open the door, and disappearing outside.

The silence is jarring after the roar of the storm, my face and my hands prickling with feeling as the warmth slowly returns. It feels like my brain is doing that too. Sharp, painful bursts of awareness.

You shouldn't have done that, my brain whispers. *You're sinking deeper into a mess you won't be able to find your way out of.*

Professionally. Personally. Emotionally. There's no guarantee that any of this works out in my favor.

And isn't that what I came out here to do? To put myself first, finally. To make the *right* choices.

Oh *god*. What have I done?

Jackson reappears, dusted in snow. Hardly a handful of seconds, but enough to have reality creeping in.

"I put it in the van," he tells me. "Your doughnut is safe."

"Thanks," I mutter, distracted. My head is busy doing the calculations, trying to figure out what this means. Putting together the pieces of the equation and coming up with an answer I don't really like.

He holds out his hand and I slip my palm against his, inexplicably feeling like I want to cry as he tugs us to the elevator. I stare at his shoulders as I walk behind him, then the toes of his boots as we stand awkwardly inside.

I have feelings for Jackson. Real ones.

And Jackson is not an impulsive man. He's rational. A planner. I'm worried our kisses have tumbled into some sort of . . . exposure therapy for him. If this is another distraction for him while he figures out how *fun* he can be in the mountains, I'm not sure I want to be a part of it.

He presses the button for our floor, and we don't say a word to each other. He seems to understand I'm working through something, the only concession the light bump of his thumb over my knuckles. He watches the red numbers slowly tick up and I stare at our blurry reflections in the mirror.

It's the most unbearable three minutes of my life.

The bell dings and I follow numbly after Jackson, my gloved hand in his. Jackson fumbles with the key card to our room and I try to push away the intrusive thoughts that rise like angry bees.

I have a lifetime of being forced into other people's too-small boxes. I have scars and bruises across my heart from every time I've been underestimated, undervalued. And I've made it so easy for Jackson to do the same.

The door clicks quietly shut behind us. Then it's just us, exactly how we started. Standing too close together in a room we're not meant to be sharing.

Jackson hovers in the dark in front of me, his body silhouetted by the fireplace behind him, his face unreadable. Tension rolls off him in waves as I stare hard at the line of his jaw as it clenches then releases.

"You regret it," he sighs.

I shake my head. That's the problem. I don't regret it at all. I want *more*.

I just don't want to be made to look like a fool when I'm the one with my heart in my hands.

"No," I say, just as quiet. "I don't."

He lifts his hand and bites at the middle finger of his glove, yanking it free, impatient, tossing it across the room before repeating the same process with the other. Then his hands are there, *cold*, against the back of my neck. Tangling in all my snowflake-dusted hair, angling my face to his.

"Then what is it? What's got this look on your face?" he murmurs, and I could cry. I almost do. He reads me so well and I'm so scared I'm somewhere he won't let himself be.

"I like you," I whisper, my throat thick.

His thumb finds the curve of my jaw, tracing up to the hollow beneath my ear. "I like you too."

"I just—" I hesitate. Swallow hard. He keeps tracing that gentle circuit, over and over again. I loop my fingers around his wrist and hold on. It feels easier, when I'm touching him like this. "I don't want you to confuse proximity with affection. I don't want— I don't want you to kiss me and not mean it."

Jackson is quiet for a long time. "You think I don't mean it?"

That's what he said, isn't it? *It doesn't have to be more than that.*

He dropped me in the category of *distraction*, and I let myself occupy that space.

He slips his hands from my face and I have to bite my cheek against the words that want to bubble out of me.

No, I want to say. *Come back.*

"I think," I say carefully, looking at the floor by our feet, "today has been an overwhelming day."

His hand lifts and he rubs his thumb over the thick material at the bottom of my coat. Then he drops it with a sigh. "I know there's something here, Delilah."

"Yeah," I agree. "There is." The burning behind my eyes gets more intense, spreading across the bridge of my nose. I sniffle. "But maybe there shouldn't be? I don't know, Jackson. I feel like I'm taking all the wrong steps. I don't want—" I suck in a wobbly breath. "I don't want to ruin anything."

Jackson watches me carefully. He palms the side of his jaw. "I don't know how I can keep myself from kissing you."

"Jackson—"

"I like how I feel when I'm with you," he says, his face earnest. He steps closer, his big body curling over mine. "I don't want to stop."

And that's what I'm worried about. That Jackson likes who he gets to be here. But when we return home to our routines and responsibilities, he'll be the man who glared at me from across a parking lot. I'm not sure I could take it.

"It's just this trip," I explain. "We're on our own up here. I think it's possible we got caught up in the moment."

"So? Why can't we have more moments? As many as we want."

"What are you suggesting?"

In the flickering light of the fireplace, I can just barely make out the curve of his mouth. The way his jaw bunches and then releases. He's frustrated, but so am I.

"I don't want to kiss you as an excuse for something else," he says quietly. "I just want to kiss you."

I look away.

"I don't know," I say slowly. "I just—I don't know, Jackson."

I'm too mixed-up. I'm leading with my heart, and my heart has only ever gotten me in trouble. I need to take some time to decide. Any choice I make tonight won't be a good one.

Jackson seems to realize it at the same moment I do. His face settles into calm resignation. "All right," he agrees softly.

And that makes it harder. A thousand times harder. How well

he seems to realize what I need in this moment. That space is the very best gift he could possibly give me.

"I'm going to get ready for bed now, I think," I say quietly. I tug my hat off and twist it between my fingers. It's damp from the snow. I'm sure my hair is bearing the brunt of the natural forces outside. I smooth it back self-consciously. "We have an early broadcast tomorrow."

Jackson nods, studying his feet. "Yeah."

"I'll just—" I hike my thumb over my shoulder, pointing at . . . something. I really don't know. I feel like I've fallen through the floorboards into an alternate universe. When did I become the person that weighs the consequences?

Maybe we're both different people out here in the mountains.

I move around Jackson and fumble with the zipper of my coat, cursing under my breath when it gets jammed halfway. I yank at it and then yank again, frustrated tears burning behind my eyes when it doesn't budge.

"You stupid piece of—" I grunt and yank again, my hands shaking. "Come *on*."

Hands cover mine.

"Let me," Jackson says quietly.

"You don't have to—"

"Delilah," he says. "Let me."

I let go of the zipper, my arms dangling loose at my sides. He bends his head to get a better look, then plucks the small tab between thumb and forefinger, tinkering. He tugs it one way, then the other, his glasses slipping down as he investigates my jacket. Then he does some sort of twisting motion and it's free, tugging slowly down, the release of each metal clasp loud in the otherwise quiet room. Jackson pushes the material off my shoulders without a word, the jacket landing with a heavy thump at our feet.

He stares at me in the dark, his breathing slow and steady. He's waiting, I realize, for me to stay stop. To push him away. But I don't want to do either of those things.

He slips two fingers into my bulky pink snow pants and tugs at the little elastic cord, loosening them. He goes down to his knees in front of me, urging my snow pants off my legs. I stare hard at the top of his head and suck in a sharp breath. When is the last time someone touched me like this? When has someone ever been this careful with me?

I stumble when he gets to my ankle. His hand reaches up, guiding mine to his shoulder.

"Here," he says, head still bowed. His forehead brushes against my thigh. "Hold on to me while I get your boots."

He works at the laces and tugs them off my feet. One and then the other, my hot pink snow pants following until I'm standing in front of him in my slightly damp sweats. Jackson stays on his knees, his palms coasting up the back of my calves. He squeezes, then sighs and leverages himself back up.

He's reassuring me in the way he knows best.

Not with words, or empty statements that go around and around. But by taking care of me.

My eyes go prickly and hot.

"Thank you," I manage, my voice tight.

He nods, already moving over to his suitcase, discarding his own layers with efficiency. He picks up my jacket and drapes it over the back of the armchair with his, and I stare at the material folded together while I grab dry pajamas to change into.

We're silent as we climb into bed, just the rustle of blankets and the click of the light on the nightstand. It doesn't escape my notice that Jackson waits until I'm settled to flick it off, the room in shadows and warm, golden light from the fireplace. Twenty minutes ago we were standing curled together in the middle of a storm and now we're in bed, a perfectly polite three feet of space between us. I pull the quilt over my shoulder and tuck my face into my pillow.

I'm almost asleep when his rough whisper carries across the space between us.

"Delilah?"

I jolt beneath the blankets and stare blearily across the pillows. He shifts them until I can see his face, then tosses them off the bed. Out of reach. He's curled on his side with one bare arm wedged under his pillow. Smooth, easy lines. A half-moon to match mine.

"Yeah?" I rasp.

He shifts, getting comfortable.

"It was a good kiss," he tells me.

"Yeah," I agree with a smile, a heavy thrum of something good and warm tightening low in my belly. "Yeah, it really was."

PENELOPE CLARK: Should we add Delilah to the family chat?

JACKSON CLARK: No.

ADELINE CLARK: You sure?

JACKSON CLARK: Yes.

JACKSON CLARK: I don't need to expose her to you two.

PENELOPE CLARK: Rude.

ADELINE CLARK: But, like.

ADELINE CLARK: DECKSON is happening, right?

JACKSON CLARK: What is DECKSON?

PENELOPE CLARK: DELILAH + JACKSON. DECKSON. There's a whole thing on Reddit.

PENELOPE CLARK: And since you INSIST on acting like the whole world didn't catch you swapping spit with the cute weather lady, everyone is feral for details.

PENELOPE CLARK: We can see you typing and deleting it, Jackie.

JACKSON CLARK: We're not adding her to the family chat.

JACKSON CLARK: Not yet.

CHAPTER 21

JACKSON

I stop what I'm doing and stare at Delilah, sitting with her legs tucked beneath her on the floor next to her suitcase.

"That is . . . certainly something."

"I think what you meant to say is"—she adjusts her ski goggles so they're over her eyes, tipping her head back to look up at me—"Delilah, baby, you look incredible."

My stomach pulls and then twists. "'Baby,' huh?"

I can't read her expression with the giant opaque goggles, but I can see the way her mouth parts. The pink that spreads over the tops of her cheeks. I have to clear my throat and look away, studying my backpack like Delilah isn't basically on her knees next to me.

I came out of the bathroom to find her in her hot pink snow pants again, fluorescent goggles across her forehead. She looks like a bag of Skittles—and now that I've kissed her, I know that she tastes like them too.

"Sorry," she murmurs. "I'm just being silly."

I stop messing with my zipper. Delilah's head is angled down toward the floorboards. I'm not sure where our boundaries stand after last night, but I go with my gut, reaching for her goggles and lifting them gently. She stares up at me as I rearrange them across her forehead, smoothing her hair carefully out of the way.

"Delilah, *baby*," I say, rolling my voice low to let her know I'm teasing. But she makes a small unconscious sound, and it doesn't feel very much like a joke. "You look incredible."

The color on her cheeks deepens to a furious red, her eyelashes fluttering as she blinks up at me.

"God," she says. "My brain knows you're being sarcastic, but I'm still—" She gestures at her face and sighs. "Really didn't think that one through."

There are lines on the bridge of her nose from where the eyewear was cutting into her skin. I rub at one gently, and then the other, trying to walk myself back from the edge I just tiptoed toward.

After Delilah fell asleep last night, I spent a lot of time lying in the space next to her, thinking. She believes this is some sort of personality experiment. I need to prove to her that's not true.

I can be patient.

I drop my hands from her face. "You look like a cupcake with those pink pants."

"A cupcake?" Her forehead scrunches. "I don't want to look like a cupcake."

"Why not? Cupcakes are sweet." My eyes flick down to her mouth. "Cupcakes are delicious."

She shakes her head, laughing. "You're ridiculous."

"Both can be true."

Delilah, despite her hesitations last night, doesn't seem to be holding it against me this morning. When I woke up she was already in the shower, a cup of coffee waiting for me next to my glasses. A Post-it, right next to it, with a smiley face. I stared at it for a long time while listening to the water run in the bathroom, feeling like a balloon was lodged somewhere in my sternum.

My phone buzzes across the table where our notes are stacked, distracting me from the woman still wrapping herself in winter gear on the floor next to me. I check the ID.

"Maggie is calling," I tell Delilah. "I'm going to take it in the hall while you finish up. We can go down to the lobby when you're ready."

"Oh." Delilah looks up at me from her knees, elbow deep in her suitcase as she searches blindly for something. "That's fine." She holds up a pair of goggles that matches hers. "Do you want me to bring these for you?"

I shake my head. "No, thanks." I keep my attention firmly fixed at a spot just above her head. My dark thoughts are winning. Honestly, the hot pink pants should be more of a deterrent than they are.

"You sure?" she asks. "You might regret it."

I shake my head with a tight smile. I think I'd regret looking like the Terminator even more. We've given the people of Baltimore enough to talk about without adding matching snow gear to the conversation.

"I'm good. I'll see you in a minute."

Eager to be somewhere that isn't a cozy hotel room with Delilah in the middle of it, I make my escape to the hall and swipe at my phone.

"Hey, Maggie."

Silence greets me on the other end of the phone, then, "Why are you breathing like that?"

"Like what?"

"Like a caveman."

I wander down the hall to the window at the end of it, leaning heavily against the frame, my forehead pressed to the thick glass. All I can see is white, the towering evergreens and the sweeping view of the lake hidden behind a blanket of snow. The storm slowed just as we were expecting. Outside the window, Deep Creek is getting absolutely pummeled.

I'm not faring much better.

"I'm breathing the same way I always do." I dot my finger against the glass, drawing a line in the frost clinging to the edges. "What's up?"

"We have a problem," she says.

"Which one?"

"The biggest, most annoying one," Maggie says. "Keith is turning out to be a giant fucking problem."

I drag my hand over my forehead, pressing my thumb and index finger against my temples until I see spots. They're still cold from the window. It's not as soothing as I want it to be.

"Delilah told me her conversation with him went fine. What's he doing?"

"What *isn't* he doing?" she grumbles.

"Maggie."

She heaves a long-suffering sigh from her end of the phone. I bet if I stuck my head out this window, I'd hear it all the way from Baltimore.

"The numbers on your segments with Delilah are good. And after your little mishap"—she clears her throat—"they've skyrocketed. Aiden almost exclusively got calls about the two of you during *Heartstrings* last night and—"

"I told you," I say, voice sharp, "my relationship with Delilah isn't going to be content."

"And I told *you*," Maggie singsongs back, amused, "that I understand. Trust me, Jackson. You were very clear on that point yesterday." She hesitates. "But—"

"No," I immediately say.

"Let me finish." Maggie laughs. "*But* I would like to know what's going on. As your friend."

So would Aiden. So would the girls.

So would I.

I settle on the one thing I know to be true. "I like her," I confess quietly. "I like her a lot."

Maggie hums. "I'll protect you as best I can, but your little slip has made people voracious, Jackson. You're going to have to address it."

"Not if I can help it." Whatever is happening between Delilah and me is for us. No one else. I'm not going to trot it out underneath the harsh glare of everyone else's opinions. "What's going on back home?"

Maggie grumbles under her breath about *coming back to this later*. "Like I said, the broadcast numbers are good. *Really* good. The executive team is paying attention. I think we're making a strong case for keeping us local. And we've certainly scared Orion away for the time being."

"That's good news."

"Great news," Maggie agrees. "Cooper hasn't harassed me in four days."

I frown, trying to place the name. "Is Cooper their acquisitions VP?"

"He's their overlord of corporate greed, yes." Something slams on her side of the phone. "But I believe his reign is coming to an end."

"Are you . . . upset about this?"

"I'm thrilled. Everything is going to plan, but for some unfathomable reason, Keith has become unbearable. You have no idea the barrels I'm dodging over here on your behalf, Jackson."

I think about that hotel across the street. The mysterious stain on the carpet. The . . . *thing* . . . that was living in the closet. "Trust me. I've got an idea."

Halfway down the hallway, Delilah sticks her head out of our room. She's still wearing the goggles across the top of her forehead, but she's added her beanie beneath the band. She gives me a little wave.

I lift my hand back.

"What do you need from me?" I ask.

"Nothing at the moment. I just wanted you to be aware." She pauses. "Yesterday he came into my office and bumbled around for fifteen minutes before he very clumsily asked if I had any concerns about your performance." She scoffs, sounding disgusted. "The man couldn't con his way out of a wet paper bag."

"What's his angle?"

Delilah's face turns interested, the door closing behind her. She moves down the hallway toward me, her snow pants a bright streak of color against the creams and blues of the lodge hallway. She hasn't put on her boots yet and I can see her socks. They're mismatched. One of them has little printed strawberries. The other is a Nike ankle sock, plain black.

I think that one might be mine, actually.

What's going on? she mouths. I shake my head and angle the phone away from my mouth.

"Keith," I whisper back.

She rolls her eyes.

"Is Delilah there with you?" Maggie asks. "Put me on speaker."

I do as she says. Delilah and I tuck our heads together over the phone.

"Hey, Maggie," Delilah says. "Is Keith giving you trouble?"

"It's not me I'm worried about. He seems intent on making your life as difficult as possible," Maggie says. "I think he's planning something."

Delilah's gaze flicks up to mine. She looks tired, defeated.

"Should have known that phone call was too good to be true," Delilah sighs, frustrated.

"I think he hates how much this city loves you. He's looking for any opportunity to minimize your credibility. But we're not going to let that happen. Are we, Jackson?"

I nudge my knuckles under Delilah's chin. A fierce surge of protectiveness settles across my shoulders, pulling tight beneath my breastbone. *This* is how I prove it. *This* is how I show her.

"No," I say. "We're not."

Mark is waiting for us in the lobby, his supplies stacked in a neat pile by the door. Camera. Wires. A large backpack with a transponder inside that will feed our footage back to the station, hundreds of miles away. The one that only works, apparently, when I'm begging Delilah to kiss me.

"I thought you'd be setting up for the shot," Delilah says, reaching for some of the wires. She hoists them over her shoulder. "Do you need help carrying this stuff out?"

"I was just bringing it back inside." Mark rubs his hand over his head. "Our broadcast has been canceled this morning."

"I'm sorry. It sounded like you just said our broadcast is canceled."

"That is what I said."

She snorts. "I'm so glad you finally feel comfortable enough to joke with me after three years but now is not the time." She reaches down and grabs the bag too. "I'm not sure the deck will be a good choice for today's shot. How about we go down the path a little bit. There's a grove of trees that should shelter us from the worst of it."

Mark darts a quick glance at me, then back to Delilah.

"I'm not joking about the broadcast, Delilah."

"You are."

He shakes his head. "I just got a call from the production team.

They won't be tapping us in. We're not broadcasting this morning."

Delilah looks out the window where the snow is falling in earnest. "But this is—" She has to pause to take a deep breath. "It's the whole reason we're here, Mark. The snowstorm. The *historic* snowstorm. The one that is happening. Right outside."

"I know," he says.

"Last night we got almost a foot and a half. There's so much more coming. They're cutting our footage now? It's just getting good."

"I know," he repeats.

"Who made this decision? Who canceled the broadcast?"

Mark just stares steadily at her, his jaw jumping. We both know the answer to that question.

Delilah huffs. "He can't—he can't cancel the fucking news, Mark. What are they going to report on back in Baltimore? The Trash Wheel again? Maybe the goose migration?"

I lightly touch the small of Delilah's back and she exhales a harsh sound. Something that sounds suspiciously like *this motherfucker.*

"What did the production team say?" I ask.

Mark rocks back on his heels, reluctant. He keeps shooting Delilah concerned, apprehensive glances out of the corner of his eye like he expects her to start wielding the aux cords as a weapon. Delilah notices his hesitation and wilts like a flower.

"Don't spare my feelings, Mark." She yanks off her beanie and shoves it into the same pocket she put her snow goggles. "I'm going to find out whether you tell me or not."

Something in his face turns faintly pitying, and my stomach free-falls.

"Delilah," I try, "maybe we should have some coffee over—"

She reaches up and puts her palm over my mouth without looking away from Mark.

"Tell me," she demands.

"They switched the segment to snow preparation. Keith says the city is their main focus, not—" He swallows, cutting a look around the small lobby. Lottie is still placing out the rest of the breakfast items. A few wayward truckers are huddled at the window, staring out at the storm. "Not a bunch of snow in some backward backcountry. He also said he wants someone more professional on the news." He scratches his jaw. "Leon is going to do the report."

Delilah stares. "Leon is going to do the report," she repeats, her voice sounding like she's just done several laps around the perimeter of the lake. She drops her hand from my mouth without looking at me. "Leon is going to do the *weather* report?"

Mark nods.

"Leon is—Leon is going to do the weather report," she says again, a different inflection, sounding out the sentence, picking up speed in some parts and slowing it down in others. "*Leon* is going to do the weather report. Leon is going to do the *weather report*. *Leon*—who I believe has a degree in political science and public communication—is going to do the weather report." She bares her teeth in a snarl. "Leon is more *professional* than me?"

Mark reaches out and offers her a short, awkward pat. "I know, Delilah."

"It's my weather report, Mark."

He pats her again. "I know."

"Can he do that?" I ask. "We have a partnership. Doesn't he have to ask for permission from Maggie?"

He pulls his phone out of his pocket and glances at the screen. "Yeah, Keith can make that decision without consulting your people. The anchors dragged their feet, but ultimately, it's Keith's call. He got full control of content decisions with his last contract negotiations. Production said he used your—ah—moment the other day as justification."

So much for Keith taking it in stride.

Delilah blanches. "Of course he did."

She turns toward the window and scrunches her nose, her teeth working at the corner of her bottom lip. She's trying to compose herself, pack it all away. She does that a lot. Hides behind her smile and her sunshine personality. She uses them to distract from all the bits she thinks will be too ugly for everyone else.

But I don't want her to hide from me.

"What am I supposed to do?" she whispers. "Jackson." She grips the sleeve of my jacket. "What am I going to do?"

I get that heavy twinge in the middle of my chest again. The one that feels like a rope, being pulled taut. The twist of a key in a rusty lock.

"What do you want to do?" I ask.

"I don't know. Half of me is so mad I want to call Keith and give him a piece of my mind. The other half wants to hide." Her eyes dart to Lottie at the breakfast table, to Mark fumbling around in his backpack by the door, and then finally, back to me. "I'm so embarrassed," she whispers.

"Why?" I ask, just as quiet.

"I thought I'd have a real chance with this coverage. I thought I'd get to prove myself. But Keith has been waiting for an excuse to discredit me, and I handed him one on a silver platter." Her voice breaks and that feeling in my chest strains and buckles. She takes a trembling breath. "My grandpa watches every afternoon, Jackson. I don't know how to explain this to him in a way he'll understand." She rubs at her nose. "I don't want to disappoint him," she adds in a whisper.

I finally let myself cup her shoulders, squeezing firmly. "You're not going to disappoint him."

"He's going to look for me and I won't be there." Her chin wobbles until she firms it. I shake her shoulders.

"You're going to be there."

She blinks at me, face crumpling in confusion. "How?"

I glance at Mark evaluating his supplies by the door. The cords, the wires, the backpack. We have everything we need. Delilah and I are already prepped. We have our notes and, for once, my anxiety is nowhere to be found.

"How do you feel about a hostile takeover?"

SIMONE LEEDS: And now for the weather.

SIMONE LEEDS: Leon, I believe you have an update for us?

CHAPTER 22

JACKSON

Delilah stands in the middle of a snowdrift, powdery white up to her hips, her face almost completely obscured by the snow that's falling in heavy, wet clumps.

"If we time it right"—Mark yells—"you'll come in right in the middle of Leon's report. I'm going to patch into the broadcast using the livestream, and Gary in production is going to push us through. He says thanks for remembering his wife's birthday, by the way. She loved the flowers." He unloops another cord, tosses it in my direction, and types furiously into his phone. "Everyone is aware of what's happening. Gianna is running interference with Keith, in case he tries to put a stop to anything."

"How does she plan on doing that?"

Mark's smile is an even split between delighted and diabolical. "She's got a list of options."

"She's not going to get arrested, right?"

"Honestly, it's difficult to know for sure."

Delilah presses her gloved hand to her forehead and mutters something up to the sky.

"I was particularly fond of numbers three through seven," Mark adds conversationally. "On her little list. You know she keeps it on her phone? Says she's been waiting her whole life for this moment."

"That sounds about right."

Delilah had been surprised when Mark offered to help. Then cautious, when he walked us through the rough outline of the plan to get her on the broadcast she'd earned. She didn't want to step on any toes. She didn't want to make a fuss. But then Mark turned his phone around to show her the string of text messages from the station—the production team, Gianna, the anchors, and Leon—all variations on the same theme.

Let's fucking do it.

With a particularly enthusiastic set of knife emojis from Gianna. Apparently, she's been working in the wings on this contingency plan for quite some time.

"We've got about three minutes until we need to go. Remember, you're dropping in during the morning broadcast you were supposed to have. Do everything exactly as you originally planned, and the viewers won't know the difference. You've earned this, Delilah." Mark hefts his camera over his shoulder. "You guys ready?" A smirk curls his mouth. "Or do you need to go disappear to your special place for a minute?"

"Do you want to make sure our mics are off if we do?" Delilah fires back. "It hasn't escaped my notice that you're the one who failed to tell me I was wearing a hot mic."

The smirk drops from his face. "Got it."

"I thought so." Delilah huffs, then looks to me. "You ready?"

"Yeah," I tell her. "I'm ready."

I'm not even nervous. Maybe it's the thrill of our deceit or the unrelenting desire to wipe the fractured, devastated look off Delilah's face, but my stage fright is nonexistent. She told me during our very first broadcast that I should picture my sisters. Pretend I'm talking to them. But now I'm just talking to her. Delilah. The woman standing right next to me with her shoulder pressed to mine.

I pull the matching pair of goggles Delilah brought me out of my pocket and slip them over my head. "What about you? You ready?"

She watches me settle the dumb goggles over my face, her eyes just a shade too wide. A trembling smile tugs at her bottom lip.

"Yeah," she says. "I'm good."

"Good," Mark shouts over the wind. "Because you're live in three, two—" He motions with his hand and the little red light on the camera blinks on. My stomach swoops but Delilah presses closer to my side.

"Hello, Baltimore. I heard we had some technical difficulties this morning, but Jackson and I are happy to give you an update on the winter storm whipping through Western Maryland." A particularly ferocious gust of wind rolls against us and I grab Delilah's arm, holding her steady. "Wind and precipitation are picking up. Jackson, what would you say the wind gusts are up to?"

"Uh, high?" It's not my usual stage fright, but the sheer force of the winds coming at us. I adjust my grip on Delilah, then move fully behind her when she slips again. "The goggles were a good idea."

Delilah barks out a laugh. "Breaking news, Baltimore! Jackson Clark thinks I have good ideas."

I look down at the top of her head, but she's already dropped it back against my shoulder, grinning up at me. I see my own blurry reflection in her goggles. Streaks of gold and blue and white.

"I always think you have good ideas."

"News to me," she says.

"Good thing we're on the actual news, then." She laughs again. "Should we talk some more about the weather?"

All of her is still leaned up against all of me, my arm around her waist as I try to hold her steady. I'm sure we're pouring gasoline all over the rumors that are twisting up around us, but I don't care.

Delilah smiles at me. "Yeah, Jackson. I'd love to talk about the weather with you."

JACKSON CLARK: The version of the storm that will hit Baltimore will be significantly less severe, but the potential for heavy snowfall is still high.

DELILAH STEWART: A combination of factors makes this environment out here in the mountains the perfect storm for, well, a storm. It'll lose steam as it heads east.

JACKSON CLARK: But still plenty of snow for sledding at home.

CHAPTER 23

DELILAH

I burst through the door to our room with the energy of a tiny tornado. If I had any cardiovascular endurance at all, I could probably run up one of the ski slopes. Do a lap around the top of the mountain, then tumble all the way to the bottom. I feel like I could *fly* if I wanted to. I am riding high on the intoxicating cocktail of endorphins, defiance, and exhilaration.

"I feel amazing," I breathe, whipping off my hat, sending it flying with a wet *thwack* against one of the massive windows. I spin on my heel with my arms spread wide. "Don't you feel amazing?"

Jackson chuckles and grabs the edge of the door, keeping it from slamming into the wall. He tugs his own hat off as he closes it, toeing off his boots and shaking off the excess snow. "Yeah, that was pretty amazing."

The broadcast was a success. We patched in directly and Leon did an absolutely beautiful transition, like there was nothing at all out of the ordinary. I bet no one at home even realized that Keith tried to make an ass of me.

But I didn't let him. I stood up for myself. I *won*.

I foiled his stupid plan. I had the station on my side. All of the pieces aligned and for *once*, I came out on top.

I grin wildly and spin around again. "I feel like I could punch a moose right now."

Jackson smiles my favorite smile. "A moose?"

I nod and spin around again, just for the hell of it. I wobble on the dismount and Jackson's hands shoot out, steadying me.

"A moose," I breathe. "I could totally take down a woodland creature right now."

"Luckily, there are no woodland creatures nearby," Jackson murmurs, his eyes drifting over my face before landing heavily on my mouth. "Though I'd love to see it."

The energy buzzing haphazardly around my body settles and sinks, a low, pulsing warmth coiled in my belly. In the palms of my hands. In that secret spot under my ear that only Jackson has ever been able to find.

His hands flex against my hips and he gently tows me closer. I go willingly, my body loose and easy in the hold of his.

Our knees knock together. My hands find his shoulders. He's still looking at my mouth.

"Tell me I was amazing," I breathe.

"You were amazing," he says right away, without any hesitation. "The goggles were a hit. You were charming and funny. So fucking smart."

My heart does a cartwheel in my chest. "Yeah?"

He nods, his tongue dragging across the inside of his cheek. "Yeah. You said *lake-effect* and *changing pressure systems*, then cited the Northeast Snowfall Impact Scale, and I—"

He cuts himself off abruptly, his eyes darting away, finding a vague spot above my head instead of my mouth. I pull at the sides of his open jacket, wanting *so badly* to know the end of that sentence.

"And you, what? What were you going to say?"

He shakes his head. "It's not professional."

Last night Jackson kissed me in the snow and I got scared that he didn't mean it. But right now, in the light of day, he's staring at me like it doesn't matter what pieces of me he gets to have. He'll take whatever I'm willing to give. He'll hold himself perfectly still until I ask him to move, unwilling to compromise my boundaries with his wants.

"It's just us here," I whisper. "Tell me."

He scoops me closer. I make an embarrassing breathy sound when my chest presses to his.

"I thought about kissing you in that snowbank," he breathes. Jackson's expression is tortured. Like he's between two impossible things and doesn't know which to reach for. "I thought about doing more than kissing you."

"Like what?"

"Delilah."

"I want to know."

He shakes his head, dipping his face closer to mine, almost like he can't help himself. Whatever gravitational pull is always dragging me into his orbit works both ways, I guess. His nose brushes my forehead and my eyes slip shut.

"I thought about bringing you back here." His hand drifts up and then down my back. Lower, over my hip to the curve of my ass. A delicious tease, his pinky edging beneath the thick elastic at the top of my pants. "I thought about pulling these ridiculous pants of yours down to your thighs. Making you keep them there while I put my mouth on you. I thought—Delilah," he sighs. "I thought that you probably look so pretty when you come. I've *been* thinking that."

A breath rattles out of me, everything beneath my belly button pulling taut. Like a ribbon, tied in a pretty little bow. I want Jackson to tug on the end of it. To unravel me until I'm a puddle of silk beneath him.

He grunts in frustration and buries his face against my shoulder. "I'm trying to give you space and respect your decision, but it's so fucking hard when you—"

"When I what?"

"When you're *you*," he laughs, a little pained. "You drive me fucking crazy, do you know that?"

"I do, actually." I evaluate the two paths in front of me. I could hold firm to the physical boundary in the name of professionalism, or I could—

I could trust Jackson. I could trust *myself*.

Jackson's right. There are no rules against it.

"I think—" I lick my lips and gather my thoughts. "I think I've changed my mind."

He lets go of me immediately.

"No." I grab his wrists and drag his hands back to me. "I don't want you to give me space, Jackson."

He peers at me through his glasses. "No?"

I shake my head. For a lot of reasons, saying the things I don't want feels immeasurably easier than explaining the things I *do*. "I don't want space," I repeat. "But I also don't want to be used."

Jackson moves closer. "It wouldn't be like that. You set the pace, Delilah. I'm following you."

My heart turns over in my chest. "All of Baltimore is talking about the nature of our relationship."

"I don't care about all of Baltimore." He cups my cheek, his thumb tracing the curve of my jaw.

It's easy for him to say that now, when we're out here in our mountain hideaway. What happens when we get back and he changes his mind? Where will that leave me?

"Can this just be for us?" I whisper. "Not because I'm embarrassed. I just want it to be—"

"Me and you. I get it." He ducks his head down and the corners of our mouths brush and then drift away. I grip the sides of his sweater beneath his jacket, my hands fisted in frustration. Jackson smiles. "That's what I want too."

"Only while we're here," I whisper. "Just for now. I don't want expectations."

I don't want to get my hopes up.

Jackson makes a hum that sounds like a question, low in the back of his throat.

"What?" I ask. "What does that mean?"

"We'll have to see," he says carefully.

"About what that means, or—"

He presses his thumb over my mouth, hushing me. "I won't agree to timelines." He lifts his thumb. Settles it beneath my ear instead, stroking back and forth. "Let's see how it goes."

"Why do you look so unhappy about that?" I ask.

"I don't know. I guess it's because I'm unhappy about it. You know I like my labels, Delilah."

Strangely enough, it's a bit of a comfort. That Jackson isn't willing to toss all his rules and regulations to the side for whatever this is. "You're the one who said it was a distraction," I remind him. "That it doesn't need to be more than that."

He sighs. "I knew that upset you." He leans back to get a good look at me. "I said it *doesn't need to* be, but I never said I didn't want it to be. That first kiss meant something to me, Delilah. All of them did. You just—knocked me on my ass. I wasn't ready for you."

I look at the collar of his sweater instead of at his face. I drag my fingertips back and forth across the stitching. "I don't want to be a pit stop in your quest to push your boundaries. We'll . . . explore this here. No hard feelings at the end, okay?"

He watches me carefully, then reluctantly nods his head.

"And if it starts impacting our work, we stop?"

His eyes crinkle at the corners. He gathers me closer, both hands at the small of my back. "Like, say, if we're caught kissing each other before our broadcast with a hot mic?"

I drop my forehead to the base of his throat. He laughs, that deep, slightly rough sound, his hand cupping the back of my head. It feels so nice to be held like this, my ear pressed to the amusement rumbling in his chest.

Warm. Safe.

"I see your point," I mumble into cozy fabric that smells like aftershave and a coffee with exactly three sugars.

It doesn't escape my notice that this is the most honest I've been with another person. I've shared what I want and what I don't. My hesitations for moving forward and the hope that clings to the very edges. And Jackson has listened, patient and sure, letting me untangle the knots in my head.

His hand slips down my back. "Anything else we need to discuss?"

I rest my chin in the middle of his chest. "I don't think so, no." I smile. "Why? Do you have plans?"

His tongue appears briefly at the corner of his mouth, his eyes tripping a shade darker. "Something like that."

"Want to look at the weather maps?" I whisper.

He cups my jaw with his hand, tilting my face up. "Maybe later."

"You sure? What was it— Oh. The Northeast Snowfall Impact Scale." He makes a low sound and I laugh. "I could talk you through it," I whisper.

"Now that"—his nose bumps against mine—"I'm interested in."

Someone knocks at the door. Three quick raps. Jackson drops his forehead to mine with a groan.

"Delilah," Mark calls through the barrier. "I need you for a sec."

Jackson slips his hand under my hair, squeezing at my neck. "Later," he promises. He steps away from me, keeping his body turned carefully away. "I'll get the door."

Mark's face is torn between exasperation, frustration, and amusement when Jackson swings open the door. He holds out his phone.

"Here," he says.

I stare at his outstretched arm. "What?"

"You're getting calls on my work line."

"Me? From who?"

"Who do you think?"

I tuck my arms against my chest. There's a reason my work phone is still hidden at the bottom of my bag. "Oh. No, thanks."

"Did you hear me asking?" He nudges me with the phone again. "C'mon, Delilah. Don't stop being brave now."

"But I don't wanna," I whine. I'd much rather ride the high of my victory and pretend that Keith doesn't exist. "Tell him I'll call him tomorrow."

Jackson fills the space next to me, propping himself up against the wall with his shoulder. He knocks his boot against the side of mine. A silent show of support.

Mark grunts. "Don't remember becoming your secretary either. The longer you make him wait, the worse it'll be. You know that."

"You have a real gift for motivational speeches," I mutter, staring hard at the phone.

"So I've been told."

The screen lights up with an incoming call. KEITH flashes across the caller ID. It's time to pay the overly greased, Mountain Dew–addicted piper, I guess.

"Fine," I sigh. Mark nods and takes one of the chairs beside the fire. Both he and Jackson stare at me expectantly. "Do you think I could get some privacy for this call?"

"No," they answer in unison.

"Great. That's . . . great." I pace toward the wall of windows, ignoring them both, and raise the phone to my ear. "Hello?"

"Hello, Delilah."

"Hello, Keith."

I don't know what I expected, but it wasn't this polite and cordial greeting. Usually, when Keith is in the throes of a fit, he's inconsolable. Once he hurled a half-full container of caramel macchiato creamer across the newsroom because he *thought* someone else used it. It hit one of the interns in the forehead. Keith tried to sue *them* for workplace harassment.

"Put it on speaker," Jackson orders from somewhere behind me. I wave my hand over my shoulder to shush him.

There's a frustrated sigh and then heavy steps against the carpet behind me. Jackson lifts the phone out of my hand, taps the speaker button, and leans against the window, holding it just out of reach above my head. I kick him in the shin, but he doesn't so much as flinch. We have a silent argument composed of exaggerated facial expressions, rude gestures, and whispered threats. Well, one of us does. Jackson just stands there slouched against the window, his face impassive.

"I enjoyed your reporting today," Keith says, his too-calm voice floating up in the space between us.

Jackson rolls his eyes. I press my entire hand over his face. He swats it away. We have another twenty-second, completely silent argument.

"Um," I manage while Jackson and I twist around each other. His free hand shoots out and loops around my shoulder, holding me tight against his chest. His thumb edges over the base of my throat to hold me steady. A wheezing noise shudders out of me.

Jackson smirks.

"Thank you?" I say into the phone, hoping for the best.

"My favorite part was when you deliberately ignored my direction." Keith keeps that steady, easy tone that inches its way under my skin. "That was nice."

I deflate like a sad little balloon and rip my gloves off, pressing cold fingertips to the middle of my forehead. I can feel the uncomfortable urge to fight rising within me, Jackson plastered against my back. To stand up for myself. To demand something better. Maybe it's someone else finally bearing witness to the bullshit Keith routinely subjects me to or maybe it's just the last snip to a string that's barely holding on, but—

I am so damned tired of being this mediocre man's punching bag.

Jackson lightly touches my hip and I stare up at him. His mouth quirks at the corners.

Give him hell, that look says. *He deserves it.*

I deserve it too.

"*My* favorite part is when you tried to remove me from the broadcast," I snap. "I really enjoyed the lack of communication."

Jackson's eyebrows shoot up. Behind me, Mark lets out a muffled guffaw.

"I wasn't aware I needed to explain myself to you, Delilah."

"You do when you send me out into the middle of the mountains for coverage and then don't let me actually perform that coverage." Some of my patience slips. "What's going on here, Keith?"

"A severe lack of professionalism," he bites out. "Or do I need to remind you about your little *slipup*?"

My face warms. "No, you don't need to—"

"I made a decision this morning to go in a different direction with the broadcast and *somehow*"—Keith continues, infusing his words with a hefty dose of sarcasm—"you're still reporting the weather. How is it that you managed to convince everyone to do as you please, Delilah? Hmm? Did you bat your eyelashes for someone other than the weather boy? Maybe that Neanderthal of a cameraman? Did you flip open that empty little head and—"

"That's enough," Jackson interrupts, his face a thundercloud. His hand grips the phone so tight his knuckles turn white. The arm across the front of my chest tenses. "Don't talk to her like that."

"It's fine," I say faintly, my throat tight. Keith has always been abrasive, but he's not usually so cruel. I guess the takeover really did push him over the edge. He's never handled challenges to his authority well.

Jackson shakes his head, blue eyes flashing. "He doesn't get to talk to you like that, Delilah."

Keith stutters over the rest of whatever his sentence was going to be. He laughs awkwardly and then, "It was a joke, of course," he says.

"I'm not laughing," Jackson says.

All my fight leaves me in a rush, embarrassment filling the space it left behind. I want this conversation over. Reality has popped my soap bubble of empowerment, and I'm back to scraping the floor for crumbs of acknowledgment. I thought this assignment was going to be a fresh start for me, but it's just more of the same in different packaging.

"Take me off speakerphone," Keith orders. "This is a private conversation. I do not consent to recording."

I pluck the phone out of Jackson's hand before he can argue with me about it, ignoring the way his eyebrows knit together.

"No one is recording you," I tell Keith, wedging the phone

between my shoulder and ear. I slip out of Jackson's hold. "And if you want to be mad at someone, be mad at me. I was the one who came up with the idea. I convinced the rest of the team to do it."

If anything, that little lie only makes Keith angrier. "I don't care whose idea it was. They're supposed to follow *my* orders. *My* vision. And that doesn't include you."

My lungs feel itchy and tight. I'm not on top of a mountain. I'm underneath it, an unbearable, unending weight on my chest.

"Will it ever include me?" I manage.

Keith goes silent. I hear the squeak of his chair in the background, the low murmur of the newsroom. I imagine him there at the station, gazing out from behind his glass wall like some untouchable warlord, just the way he likes it.

What did I do? I want to ask. *What did I do to make you hate me so much?*

"Just do your job, Delilah," he says. "And we'll see about the rest."

"That's all I've ever wanted to do," I try to say, but he's already hung up, not interested in my answer.

I sigh and lower the phone, letting it hang limply by my side before I offer it back to Mark. "Thanks for bringing that by."

"I also got an earful, if that makes you feel better."

In an odd way, it does. I always assumed Mark and I were on opposite sides. Or, at the very least, I was on one side and Mark was an apathetic third party floating somewhere in the middle— like Switzerland, or one of those dragon paddleboats out in the harbor. Utterly unbothered. It's a bit of a trip to have him suddenly, very aggressively standing next to me.

Behind me, Jackson's phone starts to buzz. I wonder if Keith is making his way down the roster. I turn to watch him over my shoulder, swiping open his phone and answering with a soft, comfortable hello. He's wearing the smile he reserves for his sisters, and I breathe a sigh of relief.

I turn back to Mark. "I'm sorry you got in trouble."

"Nah, don't worry about it." He gives me an unexpected grin and I find myself smiling back. If nothing else comes of this trip, it's nice to know that I have people standing in my corner now. That I'm not as alone as I thought I was. "It was nice seeing you stand up for yourself, Delilah. You should do it more often, yeah?"

"We'll see," I say. "It kind of sucks."

Mark laughs and heaves himself out of the chair, slipping out the door with a wave over his shoulder. I busy myself with the various odds and ends piled up on the desk, trying to contain my mess to one side while Jackson takes his call with his sisters. I try not to listen but I catch a bit of it, phrases like *Addie, calm down* and *Yeah, I wish I was too* and *Have Aiden make you a milkshake.*

I smile down at the table. A chocolate milkshake sounds really good. Whipped cream and extra sprinkles. I wonder if it would make this hollow feeling go away.

Jackson lightly touches my elbow. I turn to look at him, his phone pressed to his chest and brand-new strain lines at the corners of his eyes. "Adeline needs me. I'm gonna head down to the lobby and talk to her for a bit."

"You don't have to leave." I gesture toward the armchair in front of the fire. "You can take your call here."

"That's all right." He hesitates, eyes searching my face, before he forces a smile that doesn't quite land. "I won't be long."

I nod. "All right, if you're sure. I'll be here."

I wish I knew how to make it easier for him, the way he makes it easier for me. But I'm flying blind, and my usual tendency to rely on sunny optimism and a can-do attitude has gotten me exactly nowhere. I'm bruised and beaten up, and so, so tired.

Still, the idea that he'd rather take his phone call in the lobby is a paper cut that stings. It's a silent confirmation of my worst fears. That he'll turn to me for things that are fun and easy and bright, but keep everything else tucked away. I'll get the version of him he can be here, but not anything else.

Just like the storm, I'm worried we're going to lose momentum by the time we head back home.

I turn back to the table, picking up notepads and shuffling them into neat piles. Rearranging the Post-its I stole from his jacket pocket.

I listen to his boots against the carpet, the whisper of his jacket as he shoulders it back on, and the heavy pause as he hesitates in front of the door. My heart lodges in my throat as I wait, hoping he'll change his mind. Hoping he'll give me something heavy to hold for him. But then the door opens and snicks quietly shut. His voice murmurs on the other side of the heavy wood, and he's gone.

I stay standing at the table for a long time before I finally crawl into bed, thoroughly and entirely exhausted.

I close my eyes and try not to think about anything at all.

AIDEN VALENTINE: I don't think I've ever asked you this before. What's your favorite thing about the weather, Jackson?

JACKSON CLARK: The predictability.

CHAPTER 24

JACKSON

I stare up at the ceiling of the hotel room, tracing the wood grain on one of the exposed beams that runs the length of the room. I sat with Lottie down in reception after I finished up with Adeline, listening to her talk about the history of the lodge while she folded spare linens.

She inherited it from her mother, who inherited it from her mother before her. Over and over, handed down through generations, always to the eldest daughter. *Us oldest daughters,* Lottie had laughed, *we carry enough trauma to be excellent micromanagers, it turns out. Fate has a funny way of shaking out, don't you think?*

Fate. The slip of the word was enough to make me pause, hands frozen over a well-loved cherry red table napkin, mid-fold. But then Lottie had chirped happily on about the recent renovations and the refurbishments that took into consideration the existing structure, and the thought slipped away. I was eager to lose myself in a conversation instead of sitting firmly planted in my own head, and Lottie seemed to know it.

The lodge maintained most of its original pieces. Like the exposed wood beams and the fireplaces in every room. What she could salvage, she meticulously maintained for longevity. That has been important to her. To keep what she could.

"I figured if it's got good bones, why not." Her hands worked easily over the worn red napkins. Folding once and then again. Muscle memory. "It's nice to hold on to some things, hmm?"

I stare at the beam now and imagine what it must feel like. Holding something up for over a century.

"Stupid," I mutter to myself, dragging a hand over my face. These are the asinine thoughts that usually haunt me anywhere between one and four in the morning, twisting with the sharper ones until it's a never-ending stream of chatter in my head.

I roll to my side and grab my phone from beneath the spare pillow with a sigh, careful to keep it tucked under the blanket so the light from the screen doesn't wake Delilah. I didn't come back to the room until I knew she'd be asleep. I don't know why. I think I was afraid to face her. Or maybe I was afraid of what she'd see when she looked at me.

Luckily she was curled into a ball at the very edge of the mattress when I slipped through the door, a wall of pillows between her space and mine.

That damn pillow wall is another thing that's twisting at me. Last night we didn't bother, but tonight Delilah thought she needed it.

I swipe open my phone and scroll to my messages. The latest is from Camille—unanswered, of course.

I know you don't trust me, it says. And for good reason. But I'd like another chance.

Another, right after it. Lighten up, Jackson. If I mess up, you can tell me I told you so.

Like that's what I'm worried about. Being *right*. I want to be *wrong* about her more than anything else, but it's hard to forget the little boy with a hungry stomach, waiting in the kitchen for someone who never showed up.

Adeline had called tonight near tears, wandering around the issue until she finally confessed that all the girls in her friend group were having their mothers attend the midsemester leadership brunch. It's a wound I've never been able to fully patch for them, and my usual assurances felt like dust on my tongue.

I darken the phone, but the words stay illuminated above me. They blink slowly, like a buzzing neon sign on its last breath, flickering brighter and brighter.

Lighten up, Jackson.
Lighten up, Jackson.
Lighten up, Jackson.

I dig the palms of my hands against my eyes until I see spots, trying to push it away. I hate when my brain sticks on a thought, its rusty claws digging in until I *hurt*.

Camille says she wants to be involved in the girls' lives. Adeline and Penelope are old enough to make their own decisions, but I'm having a hard time putting them in a position where they could get hurt.

Like I was. Over and over and over again.

Lighten up, Jackson.

"Jackson?" Delilah's sleepy voice drifts through the dark. The violent swirl of cyclical thoughts eases. Sheets rustle, a pillow shifts, and one brown eye peers at me from her side of the bed. "Are you back?"

After I sat with Lottie, I wandered to the couches at the back windows in front of the fireplaces. I did some random administrative work on my phone. Doomscrolled a bit. I didn't realize how late it was until the sky was inky black on the other side of the wall of windows.

"Yeah." I clear my throat. "I'm here."

She makes a soft sleepy sound. All I can see of her is a lump beneath the blankets. I know she sleeps with her hands tucked under her cheek, curled on her side. She stole the extra quilt from my side of the bed, but I don't mind. I want her to be warm.

She yawns. "Can't sleep?" she asks.

"Yeah," I rasp.

"Okay," she whispers.

She grows silent and I feel myself holding my breath, waiting for her to say something else. Disappointment curls in my gut when her breathing evens out again, her socked feet shifting beneath her stolen blankets. It's nothing but the hiss and pop of the logs burning low in the hearth and the dwindling gusts of wind whistling through the trees outside. The worst of the storm has passed now, over twenty-eight inches of fresh snow in twelve hours.

Everything is still and quiet. Hushed, in the way only snow can do. Sometimes the middle of the night feels like the loneliest time of all, the minutes stretching into hours and the dark pressing in from every side.

Delilah grunts and then shifts, sitting up on her side of the bed. She reaches for the small lamp on the table and slaps at it until the room fills with its soft glow. She squints at me, messy hair and pink cheeks. A yawn cracks her jaw open wide and she digs a fist against her left eye.

It's cute as fuck.

She settles, blinking slow and long, still caught in the webs of sleep.

"Come over here," she says.

"What?"

"Grab my computer from the desk"—she points toward the table stacked with various notepads, candy wrappers, and empty coffee mugs—"and come over here."

I swallow, the sound of it loud in my ears. "Come over . . . where, Delilah?"

She pats at the space next to her.

"I don't know if—"

"Jackson," she sighs, impatient and grumpy and sleepy and soft and so damned beautiful my heart climbs up to my throat. "If you don't come over here, I'm going to come over there. And when I do, I'll take up all your space and steal your blankets." She arches an impertinent eyebrow. *Fuck*. "Make your choice."

"You already steal my blankets."

A smile teases at her mouth. "Yes, well. I'll take *all* of them. And you'll be clinging to the edge of the mattress shivering."

Knowing I'm putting myself in a ridiculously tempting position, but thoroughly unable to resist, I dutifully throw back my blankets and shuffle over to the desk. I grab her laptop, then watch as she tosses the top quilt back and pats at the flannel sheet beneath. The pillow wall goes next and then it's just Delilah in the middle of a cozy-looking king-sized bed, her shirt slipping off one shoulder.

"Sit," she demands. "We're going to watch a movie."

My eyes flick to the clock on the mantel. "It's two in the morning."

"So it is." She yawns again, shimmying down in her blanket nest while she powers up her computer. "I bet I'll last through the opening credits."

"You don't have to be awake," I tell her, still standing at the edge of the bed. "You can go back to sleep. I'll be fine."

"I'm sure you will, but fine isn't good and I want you to be good." She pats the bed again. She's wearing a gray T-shirt with a dancing chicken nugget on it. I didn't see it when I came in earlier, the blankets already tucked high around her neck.

I stiffly slip into the place next to her, my thoughts still tangled up. It's hard for me to let people see me like this. Firmly cemented in the middle of an anxiety spiral I don't know how to battle my way out of. I cross my arms over my chest and my legs at the ankle. It's uncomfortable as fuck, but so is this tight, anxious knot, right at the base of my neck.

"I don't do this on purpose," I say, trying to explain myself. I hate that I've made her worry. That this . . . *thing* I can't change about myself is keeping her up now too. "I'd sleep if I could."

Delilah doesn't look at me, still navigating across her desktop. In a shock to absolutely no one, she has roughly ten thousand icons, arranged in no clear order, spread out across her screen like a handful of stars.

"I know that," she says absently.

I drag my hand through my hair, feeling self-conscious and stupid. I try to joke it off. "I'm just naturally difficult, I guess."

Delilah turns toward me. Soft eyes and soft hair and a soft downward tilt to her mouth that I want to press my mouth to until I soften too.

"You're not difficult," she says quietly. "You just haven't had anyone take care of you."

Then she hands me a pillow, shimmies down in the bed, and plops her computer between us like she didn't just find all my bruised spots with a single statement. Like she didn't just crack me open, reach her hand inside my chest, and *squeeze*.

"Press play when you're ready," she orders.

She chooses *Casablanca*.

"This is a stupid movie," I say somewhere around halfway through, Delilah's shoulder pressed to mine. Any attempt at maintaining space has been demolished by Delilah's wiggly, relentlessly moving leg and her sheer inability to *not* be a blanket hog. I'm fighting for my life on my side of the bed, and she only settles when my thigh is pressed to hers. She keeps drifting off, the crown of her head tipping against my chest before she rouses herself again, trying to pretend like she's engaged in the worst love story of all time.

"I beg your pardon," she says, all cute and indignant. "This movie won the Oscar for Best Picture."

I snort. "*Shakespeare in Love* also won an Oscar for Best Picture. It's hardly a litmus test."

She props herself up on her elbows, looking more awake than I've seen her for the past hour. Her knee jostles the computer.

"Did you just insinuate that the absolute *masterpiece* that is *Shakespeare in Love* is not a good movie?"

I grab the laptop and move it closer to me. "It won against *Saving Private Ryan*."

"Which is a depressing and violent movie."

"A *really excellent* depressing and violent movie."

She huffs and grumbles something under her breath, throwing herself back into her pillows. Her foot kicks my ankle, and I'm not entirely sure it's an accident.

I cover my laugh with a cough. "Did you say something?"

She rockets back up next to me, sending the computer toppling again, and digs one finger into the middle of my chest. "Love stories aren't stupid, Jackson." Another poke. "War movies aren't automatically better and more serious just because people are . . . losing limbs on a beach."

I curl my fingers around her wrist and lower our hands to the bed between us.

"Delilah," I say. "Baby." Her cheeks go pink at the endearment I meant as a tease but that falls out of me like a secret. My ears go hot as I rub my thumb over hers. "I think it's possible you're delirious."

"I'm not." Her mouth turns down. "Why do important things have to be things that hurt us? Why can something only be valued and held in high regard if it's . . . dark and damaging? Why can't we keep the bright things? The lovely things? Why can't those things be special too?"

"We can keep whatever you want, Delilah," I say, trying to ease some of the tension that's settled across the lines of her body. I shift our hands so we're palm to palm. "Soft things are important too. Of course they are."

She studies me, suspicious. "Yeah?"

I nod.

"You haven't always thought so," she accuses.

She's right. About a month ago, I probably would have argued with her until I was blue in the face. That softness has no place in important things. But—

"I think I've learned to appreciate a little color."

Her face splits into a grin that makes my chest hurt. "Like hot pink?"

"Yeah. Like hot pink."

And honey brown and whatever shade Delilah's bottom lip is after I'm through kissing her. A dangerous thought to have at two in the morning, when all of her is tucked up against all of me, blankets piled on top of us.

I straighten the computer and we watch as Humphrey Bogart and Ingrid Bergman meet on a rain-drenched tarmac. Delilah sighs next to me, her head drifting back to my shoulder. Our hands are still clasped together between us and I let my eyes grow heavy.

Like this, night doesn't feel so lonely anymore.

DELILAH STEWART: Behind the snow will be a deep freeze. Plunging temperatures will turn everything to ice, threatening power lines and roadways. We advise you to stay indoors and stay safe.

CHAPTER 25

DELILAH

I wake up pinned to the mattress, Jackson half on top of my body, his face in my neck and both of his arms wrapped around my middle. There's no way his hand isn't numb, wedged under me like that, but he doesn't so much as stir as I shift and yawn beneath him.

We don't have a broadcast until the afternoon radio show, followed by a quick spot on the four o'clock news. Now that the storm is spreading out to other parts of the state, our appearances here at the lodge will become less frequent. As soon as the roads are clear and safe, we'll head back to Baltimore and do a couple of closing segments for the partnership, and that will be that. The official end of Jackson and Delilah, Weather Together.

I reach for my phone on the nightstand, swiping it open and checking my email. It's nothing but discount coupons for the ice-cream shop down the street from my house, a reminder to bring my car in for an oil change, and a collection of spam emails I'm too lazy to unsubscribe from. My thumb hovers over one of the social icons as I mentally debate if I want to open that can of worms. I've been largely avoiding the apps since Jackson and I were caught with our hot mics, but curiosity wins out.

I click in, and my eyes immediately widen.

Bright red notifications ring the bottom of my screen. A frankly terrifying number of them. Gianna did mention the online community was *engaged*, but she failed to mention the sheer volume of people speculating about the nature of my relationship with Jackson.

Jackson grumbles above me, shoving his face more firmly into my neck. I scratch my fingers through his hair absent-mindedly, urging him to settle while I scroll. He's a deep sleeper when he finally falls into it. I don't think he moved once last night, holding me like his favorite teddy bear.

I glance through the topics.

Do we think this Jackson and Delilah thing is a publicity stunt? Or did they actually get caught?

Yesterday's Broadcast—Any clues??

Did you see his HAND around her WAIST?

Matching ski goggles!!! Please I am unhinged!!!!!!!

Aiden won't say anything about it on Heartstrings

Leaked audio remix

I click into the last one, curiosity burning through the center of me. It has the most likes out of any of the posts, a shiny gold star next to the topic title. When I click into it, there is no caption. Just a play button with an embedded audio file.

I raise it to my ear, hoping to listen discreetly, but sound blasts through the speaker instead.

Jackson's voice, low and breathy, "Kiss me, Delilah. Please."

A heavy bass line fills the background as it repeats over and over.

Kiss me, Delilah. Please.
Kiss me, Delilah. Please.
Please, please, please.

Jackson groans into my neck while I fight with my phone, desperately trying to turn it off.

"What are you doing?" he mumbles. He raises his head and blinks blearily. "What the hell is that noise?"

"I don't know!" I cry, trying to close out of the app. But I only turn the volume higher. Whoever made this audio used the hitch in my breath right before I kissed Jackson as some sort of percussion echo. It's creative, if not wildly mortifying. I didn't think anything would be more embarrassing than all of Baltimore hearing me kiss Jackson, but here we are.

Jackson reaches up with a grunt and grabs my phone, muting it. The ensuing silence is the loudest thing I've ever had to endure. My cheeks are on fire.

He drops his face back to my neck.

"Did someone remix our leaked audio into a dance track?" he asks.

I shift, tossing my phone back onto the nightstand. I debate lying. I debate rolling out from under him and locking myself in the bathroom. I debate walking directly into the lake. But he's warm and I'm comfortable and my grandpa always said honesty is the best policy, so—"Yes," I say. I pause. "Do you want to know how many likes it has?"

His sigh is long-suffering. "Am I going to be baffled or humiliated?"

"Probably a combination of both."

"Then, no. I'm good."

He shifts again and his hips slot in between my splayed thighs, his head turning so his cheek is flat against my breasts. His body is deliciously heavy, pressing me down into the mattress. Smooth lines and warm skin. He settles with a little groan, and something thick and hard presses against my inner thigh. My face feels like it's about to melt off.

It's morning, I try to rationalize. *This is normal.*

But I just listened to him panting into a microphone, begging me to kiss him set to a Phil Collins drumbeat, and rationalization has no hope against my desire to jump his bones.

I relax beneath him. His hand shifts, his thumb tracing down the line of my neck. He makes a small, bitten-off sound when I arch slightly. I doubt I'd have heard it if we weren't tucked together.

"Good morning," he slurs, and I laugh, scratching my nails against the back of his neck. It's unfair that I'm enjoying this so much. A handful of lazy seconds in a sleep-warmed bed, thin light filtering in through the window.

I *like* that I get to hear the first words out of his mouth. I *like* the way he's holding me. I *like* the way his hips keep rolling against me, my nipples pebbling beneath my shirt, the space between my legs wanting to shift and roll and grind.

His warm breath tickles the spot beneath my ear. I squirm.

"What time is it?" he asks, his voice like sandpaper.

"Around eight."

I can practically feel the way his brain and body come back online, a tension rippling from the top of his head to the tips of his toes. The easy, soft motion he was moving against me with is replaced by an unnatural stillness, his hips shifting away.

I sigh.

"Why didn't you wake me up?"

"I did."

"I was led to believe that was unintentional." He settles his palm against my hip, squeezing. "How bad is it?" he asks.

"What? The social stuff?"

He nods. "I haven't looked. Aiden has alluded to it and the girls said something about DECKSON, but—"

I laugh. "DECKSON?"

He pinches me gently in admonishment. "Is there a lot?"

I think about that blinking red number in the bottom corner of my phone screen. "Define . . . a lot."

Jackson groans.

Another soft laugh eases out of me. "People are probably just engaged because we're on their television screens twice a day," I assure him. "And on their radios in between. They're fixated, but it'll pass. It always does."

It'll pass for everyone. The guy who made that audio remix. The girls debating Jackson's hand placement. The rest of the city of Baltimore.

Jackson.

I press my lips together. "We don't have anywhere to be this morning. I thought you could use the extra sleep." I pause, still smarting a bit from when he left to take that call. It's silly, and I have no reason to be. He's allowed to keep his private life . . . private. We've made no promises to each other. I hold no expectations.

I keep my hands moving through his hair. "Is everything okay back home?"

Jackson blinks. He's still halfway asleep, by the looks of it. "Yeah," he rasps. He drops his head back into my neck and makes a pleased little sound. "It was my sister, Adeline. But she's okay."

He doesn't say anything else and I tell myself that it's enough. It's enough that he came back last night. It's enough that he let me help him when he couldn't sleep. He doesn't need to unpack his family baggage.

Jackson shifts, his arms tightening around me.

"She's having a hard time at school," he says, still in that rough, slow way.

Hope flares in all my secret, soft places. "Yeah?"

He nods, his nose nudging at the soft skin of my neck. "Yeah. It's hard for her that she doesn't have a mom she can count on. I try to be everything she needs, but—"

He sighs heavily instead of finishing that thought.

"But you can't be her mom," I finish quietly.

"Yeah," he says.

"Yeah."

I know what that feels like. To want something so desperately, while *not* wanting it at the same time. To feel that ache so sharply when everything is changing around you. To have one good parental figure who loves you with his whole heart, but still feeling like you deserve more.

"I could—" I cut myself off quickly, rubbing my lips together. I have a nasty habit of injecting myself into situations where I'm not wanted, and I refuse to do it with Jackson.

Jackson leans up on his elbows above me. "You could?"

"Never mind," I say easily. *Deflect*, my brain screams. *Change the subject*. My fatal flaw is offering too much of myself, too soon, and Jackson is quite literally trapped in a room with me. Now is not the time. I smile. "Do you want room coffee or do you want to wander downstairs?"

"I'd like to finish this conversation." Jackson pulls one of his arms out from behind my back, pushing my hair off my forehead. His hand lingers under the curve of my ear, thumb rubbing. "What were you going to say?"

"It doesn't matter," I whisper.

"It matters to me."

I exhale a harsh sound, feeling stupid. "I was going to say if she needs someone to talk to—someone who gets it—I'd be happy to." I pause. "I've been where she is. Maybe I could help."

Jackson doesn't respond. He remains quiet long enough for me to regret both saying something about it and bringing it up while he's got me flattened against this bed. I want to scurry off to a corner. I want to launch myself into the stratosphere.

"When we get back?" he finally asks. His eyes search mine. "That's when you want to talk to her?"

I don't necessarily see how timing is relevant, but—"Yeah," I say. "I could also talk to her on the phone, while we're here, if you wanted. But sometimes these conversations are better to have in person."

He digs a knuckle into his cheek, then presses his palm into the mattress at my hip. I roll slightly into his arm, but he doesn't move.

"But the first time you said it," he clarifies, "you meant you'd talk to her back in Baltimore."

I nod, feeling my forehead scrunch. "Yes. That is the place we live." I rub my lips together. "But if I'm making you uncomfortable, or crossing a line, I—"

"What about me?" he cuts in, unwilling to let me finish my thought. "Will you see me back in Baltimore?"

"You are her guardian, right?"

"Delilah."

I grin. "You still work at the radio station, right?"

"Delilah."

Something thick lodges in my throat. He's asking for honesty while keeping himself safe. I can still be the brave one, if that's what he needs. "I'd like to," I whisper. "I think we make a pretty good team."

His answering smile is slow. A little bit bashful. "Yeah," he agrees. "I think so too."

"Contrary to what *some* parties initially believed," I add.

Jackson drops his forehead back to my chest with a groan. Then he tilts his head and peeks up at me from one startling blue eye. "Didn't you say I had the personality of a wet paper bag?"

"Wet piece of *cardboard*," I correct. "And hey. You're not wearing your glasses. I just realized."

"Contrary to what *some* parties believe," he snipes, "I do not wear my glasses and a three-piece suit to bed."

I snicker. "You also don't sleep hanging upside down in the closet."

He heaves a sigh. "Everyone always nags me to switch to contacts, but—"

"No." I am immediately, inexplicably defensive. "I like the glasses."

"Yeah?"

I nod. "They make you more *you*, if that makes sense."

"It doesn't, but it feels like a compliment." He grins. "So I'll take it."

"It is a compliment." My heart *ka-thumps* in my chest. I can't believe I ever thought this man was cold and unfeeling. "Can you see without them?" I ask.

He shakes his head, his eyes roving over my face. "Not really, no. Just . . . smudges of color."

"What colors am I?"

He angles my face toward his.

"Pink, gold—" His fingers tangle gently in the ends of my hair and pull. He smiles at me. "Brown." His thumb drags over the curve of my cheek. Lower, down to my mouth. "Red," he whispers, tugging slightly until my lips part.

He keeps his thumb there, across my mouth. My breathing grows shallow. Jackson licks his lips, staring hard at mine.

"You're so beautiful," he tells me. "Sometimes I get mad about it."

I blink at him. "I'm sorry?"

"I'm not."

And then he drops his mouth to mine, kissing me quiet.

It's different from the rest of them. It's not a distraction and it's not impulsive. It's a choice. A decision made. He kisses me slow and careful, the same way the water moves down in the lake. Steady and deep. He keeps his arms bracketed on either side of my head, my hands slipping around his biceps while my thighs hug his sides. I'm surrounded by him. His warm breath and pounding heart and his skin pressed to mine beneath the tangle of blankets.

I arch beneath him but he doesn't stray from my mouth. He doesn't push for more. I toy with the hair at the nape of his neck and I feel his lips twist into a half-moon smile against mine, amused. I make a helpless, happy sound and he echoes it back, deeper and rougher. An ache blooms the longer he kisses me, a sharp want that pulses and spreads.

"This is how it should have been," he says against the curve of my jaw. "From the very start."

"I don't know about all that." I press my head back into the pillows, giving him more room. "I kind of like the way we started."

He leans back. "All that arguing?"

"Mm-hmm. It makes me feel like I know all the shades of you." I reach for his glasses on the nightstand. "Here," I say, unfolding them, taking extra care with the part I accidentally snapped during our run-in at the station. Jackson ducks his face down so I can slide them over his ears. I do it carefully, smiling at him when they're in place. He blinks at me from behind the thick lenses and—this is nice. Being here. With him.

"Delilah," he starts to say, "I think I—"

The rest of his sentence is stolen by the sharp flare of every light in our room. They turn brighter for half a second before they snuff out completely. Even the tiny green lights on our devices go dark, the cheery fire that's been roaring in the fireplace for days sputtering out with a hiss.

We both freeze, staring at each other.

"Was that the power?" I whisper.

"Yeah, I think so." Jackson pushes himself to his knees and looks over his shoulder, then out the window. Beyond the frosted glass is a downward slope to the lake, dotted with strings of golden globe lights. I can see the glow of them when I'm lying in bed, the light fighting from beneath a foot of snow. All of them, like stars caught in the rocks of the cliff.

Those lights are dark now. There's nothing but snow as far as I can see.

"Looks like it might be out for the whole lodge."

r/HEARTSTRINGS RADIO

LEAKED AUDIO REMIX

ORIOLESMAGIC28: Not to be dramatic, but this audio changed the course of my life.

BALTIMORON78: Would it be weird if I made this my ringtone?

CHAPTER 26

JACKSON

The cold sets in quickly.

I tug Delilah out of bed and force my sweatshirt over her head, and then another one on top of that.

"Don't you think this is a little—*Jackson*—" I tug her pale purple beanie over her head, covering her eyes. She pushes it back up, smiling up at me. "I think you're overreacting a little bit."

"I'm not." While I have no doubts that Lottie has a backup plan already in the works, I'm not interested in watching Delilah shiver through her poorly insulated weather gear while the generator gets going. I reach for my jacket and tug it on. "I don't want you to be cold."

"I don't think I'll be cold for the next millennium, Jackson." She lifts her arms. They rise two inches. It's possible I did, in fact, overreact. "How am I going to get out of all this stuff?"

I give her a loaded look.

Her cheeks immediately pinken. "Ah, yes. Nothing says *take me to bed* quite like forcefully tugging a woman out of three layers of sweatshirts, I guess."

I rub my palm against my jaw, hiding my grin. "I think you look cute."

She glares at me from the other side of the bed. "Oh, good. Even better." She forces her feet into her boots, grumbling under her breath the whole time. "It's like the turtle suit all over again."

I round the edge of the bed and grab her hips, holding her steady. "You're always cute."

She pouts. "I liked it better when you said I'm so beautiful it makes you mad."

I can't resist. I lean down and suck a kiss against that full bottom lip. I think I've finally figured out how to crack open the part of me that doesn't have to run through every worst-case scenario before making a decision. I just need to kiss Delilah. She silences all the fuzzy, staticky parts of my brain.

I pull away. She sways with me. I like it so much I curl myself around her, resting my chin on the top of her head.

"You're that too. Everything in between," I whisper. "Let's go downstairs and see if we can help."

Lottie is busy setting up portable, battery-operated space heaters on one of the long tables they use for the breakfast buffet. She smiles when she sees us emerge from the stairwell, a headlight strapped to the middle of her forehead.

"There you are. I was just about to come check in on you two. Everything all right?"

Delilah waves her sweatshirt-clad arms up and down. "I actually think I might die of heatstroke in this thing."

Lottie grins. "I think it's fine to take off at least one of those?" She gestures to the massive fireplace behind her. "We were able to get a manual fire going. Unfortunately, all the in-room fireplaces will be out while we work on the generator. Can I get you anything?"

"We're actually here to help," I say, trying not to watch the way Delilah wiggles and shimmies her way out of her sweatshirt. She finally frees herself and ties the arms around her neck instead. Like a cape. "We don't have a broadcast this morning, so we're all yours."

Lottie looks relieved. "I actually could use some help delivering these to rooms, but I don't want to put you to work."

"We're offering." I need something to keep me out of that room, or else I'm going to tumble directly into that bed with Delilah.

Delilah bounces on her toes next to me. "Yes, absolutely. It's the least we could do after all you've done for us." A tinny version of "Here Comes the Sun" starts playing from the back pocket of her jeans. "Oh. Hold on a second. I'll be right back."

She brings the phone to her ear and quickly walks over to one of the windows. "Hey, Anita. Everything okay?"

I rack my brain for a previous mention of Anita but come up blank. I watch her for another minute, frowning when her shoulders hike up to her ears. She unties the sweatshirt from around her neck and folds it over her arm instead.

Lottie hands me one of the space heaters. "We're placing these in the common areas, then delivering the rest to the rooms. You and Delilah can take as many as you'd like."

"One is fine," I mutter, distracted. Delilah usually talks with her whole body. Flailing arms, excited little shimmies. But right now, she's standing with her arms crossed over her chest, staring out the window. "I'll be right back."

I wander closer to Delilah at the window, taking the wide way around the table so she sees me coming. She catches my eye and gives me a tight smile, nodding as she listens to the person on the other end of the phone.

Okay? I mouth.

She gestures for me to come closer, then reaches out and grabs the string of my hoodie, tugging me the rest of the way. She drops her head against the middle of my chest, still staring out the window, still with her phone to her ear.

"You can put him on," she says quietly. "I can manage it."

A soft, tinny voice warbles on the other end of the phone.

"I know, Anita. But it'll be fine."

I settle my palm at the base of her spine because she seems to need the support. She takes a deep, fortifying breath, then lets it out slowly.

"Yeah, it's me," Delilah says gently. "I'm sorry I missed your call. I was in rehearsal. You know I sometimes get caught up in my music."

Delilah continues talking soft and slow while the pieces knit themselves together. That day in the diner, she said her mother was a musician. That she was raised by her grandfather. But why is she pretending—

"I know I haven't visited in a while, but I'll be there soon." She loops my hoodie string around her fist, thumb rubbing over the frayed end. "Why don't you go with Anita and have some tea? I put some of that lavender kind you like in your cabinet the last time I was there."

A low voice answers and Delilah laughs.

"The shortbread cookies too. Of course I remember." Her smile turns bittersweet. I rub my hand up and down her back. "I love you too. I'll see you soon."

She ends the call and keeps her head against me. I continue the slow and even strokes across her back.

"My grandfather has Alzheimer's," she says quietly. "Sometimes he gets confused." Her throat clicks as she swallows and I tug her closer, wrapping my arms around her. "He's not an angry man, but when he's stuck in a memory it's easier to guide him through it if I go in there with him."

I nod. "You don't have to explain."

She shifts so she's looking up at me. Her eyes are glassy and red-rimmed, the very tip of her nose pink. "I want to."

I rub my thumb across her cheek. "That must be difficult for you."

She shrugs.

"How many different parts are you forced to play, Delilah?"

She stares up at me for another second with a sad little smile, then rests her cheek back against my sweatshirt.

"When I'm here with you? Just the one."

AIDEN VALENTINE: You guys lost power?

JACKSON CLARK: Earlier this morning, yeah.

DELILAH STEWART: The woman who owns the lodge—Lottie—she's been trying to get the generators going, but the ice has everything frozen over. Sorry for the scratchy call-in, but it's the best we could do.

AIDEN VALENTINE: I don't think our listeners mind.

CHAPTER 27

DELILAH

"You need to relax," I say, eyes heavy, shivering despite the four quilts piled on top of me. There's an unrelenting boulder behind me beneath the blankets, his arm like a harness over my waist.

"I am relaxed," Jackson grumbles, right under my ear. He's angry, for some reason, and I'm too tired to deal with it.

"I put on the snow pants. I don't know what you're so mad about."

We spent the rest of the afternoon helping Lottie out around the lodge. Well, Jackson did. He delivered space heaters to rooms and salted the sidewalks while I talked to my new best friend Dustin—Dusty, to his friends—in the café. He had one of those portable coffeemakers that you use when camping. He made me my very own cup of coffee.

I think Jackson is still jealous over that cup of coffee.

"I'm not mad about the snow pants."

"Then what are you mad about?"

Jackson sighs, his knees bumping up against mine. "You're shivering."

I turn to look at him over my shoulder. All I can make out of him is the curve of his jaw and the straight line of his nose. His glasses are folded up on the nightstand next to my emergency Swedish Fish.

Another shiver wracks my body. "I'm not trying to," I whisper. "It's cold, Jackson."

The room quickly descended into cold and uncomfortable as soon as the sun set, the massive window leeching all the warmth from the space. The portable space heater is doing its best, but it's negative fifteen out there.

Jackson makes another low, disgruntled sound. "I know it is, Delilah."

I huff and turn back on my side, trying to ignore that hand that feels like an ice block on my hip. He's not even holding me.

Another furious shiver starts at my shoulders and trips down my spine until I'm shivering into the blankets, both hands curled into fists. I wish I could tuck myself into a shell and hide away until the power comes on. Generate my own warmth.

Jackson sighs behind me and shifts his hand, ice-cold fingertips slipping under the hem of the oversized sweater he forced over my head. I squeak when he touches the bare skin of my belly, kicking my legs wildly when he presses his entire palm right above my belly button.

"What are you doing?" I whisper-hiss.

"Trying not to rupture an organ," he grunts. "Stop *kicking me*." He drags my body into his. "Be *still*," he orders.

My body goes liquid and lax at the demand in his voice. *Okay*, I think faintly. *I guess that's a thing.* I let him arrange me however he pleases, my body tucked tight to his, his arm under my sweater and his face in my neck.

"What are you doing?" I ask again, this time in a whisper.

"I can't stand you being cold."

"I'm not doing it on purpose, I'm—"

"That wasn't a complaint, Delilah." His cold nose presses against the back of my neck.

A knot tightens in my belly, even though I don't really understand what he's saying. Whatever it is, my body seems to get it well enough.

"Want you to be warm," Jackson mumbles, his palm easing up and then down my belly. He settles it low, right at the waistband of my ridiculous snow pants, and everything pulls tight. "Want to be the one who makes you coffee," he adds in a grumble.

I flop backward. Jackson's hand shifts. "I *knew* you were mad about the coffee."

He's silent for the stretch of two heartbeats. "He didn't even make it the way you like it."

"Jackson. It was coffee. I wasn't going to look the gift horse in the mouth."

"Yeah, well, I wanted to kick the gift horse." He grumbles some more. "He flirted with you for the better part of a half hour."

I grin, delighted. "He did not!"

"He did."

"Jackson, I'm pretty sure he's, like, sixty-eight years old. We were talking about his wife. His grandkids."

His shoulders rise and then fall. "I didn't know that."

"Well, now you do." I curl back on my side, the thrill of Jackson's jealousy warming me from the inside out. I settle back into his grip. "You know, I read in a survival pamphlet once that skin-to-skin contact acts like a natural heating blanket."

Jackson's pause is long. "Why were you reading a survival pamphlet?"

His hand drifts back up, knuckles brushing beneath my breasts. I don't know if it's a conscious choice, but I'm acutely aware of everywhere he's *not* touching me. Everywhere I want him to be.

"I like to be prepared for things," I say, distracted, mentally willing his hand two inches higher.

"Like . . . what? What do you need to survive in Baltimore?"

"Apparently, freezing to death in a hotel room," I laugh. I wiggle my hips back into the cradle of his and he grunts. "Take off your shirt, Jackson. It might save our lives."

Jackson snorts. "We're not in danger of dying in here— *Shit*. Delilah."

I toss my sweater across the room, quickly followed by the T-shirt I had on underneath. I keep the snow pants on, because there's no way that won't be a logistical nightmare. But the room is freezing in just my pale pink cotton bra, so I quickly duck back beneath the covers, pulling them to my chin.

"Take off your shirt, Jackson," I order again, my teeth chattering.

He's frozen behind me, not moving an inch.

"Unless you don't want to," I add awkwardly. I try to swallow around the horseshoe of mortification that is lodged at the base of my throat. "In which case it probably would be for the best if we both pretend we've fallen into an immediate and deep sleep. A coma, maybe. Because I plan on dying of embarrassment and would like to be left to my own devices for that."

The bed dips, fabric rustles, and Jackson lets out a bone-deep sigh. A moment later he's back beneath the covers, his chest pressed firmly against my back.

His bare chest. Against my bare back.

"You know exactly how to push me," he rumbles. It's delicious, how he sounds when he's torn between frustrated, amused, and the dark edge of something else. Something I want to peel away like a candy wrapper. Nibble at until it melts in my mouth.

I hide my grin in my pillow. "Sorry."

"No, you're not."

"No," I laugh. "I'm not." I wiggle my body into his. "I feel warmer already."

"Yeah?" Jackson's palm slides over my side, chafing up and down. "How about now?"

"Mm," I hum. "Good."

"And this?" His hand drifts, back to my belly, palm going up, up, up until it's flat between my breasts. Right where my heart is pounding in my chest. He rubs gently with his thumb. "Warmer, now?"

"Yeah," I breathe. He noses my hair away from my neck and presses a soft kiss against the knob of my spine. I am aware of all the places we're tucked neatly together. How my breathing slows only for my heart to beat faster. His hand shifts and his finger edges under the top of my bra, tracing the curve of my breast. My nipples tighten and I arch my back, trying to force his touch lower, but he keeps his hands perfectly, frustratingly polite.

"What's wrong?" he asks, a low murmur right below my ear.

My body feels like it's vibrating, twisted so tight with anticipation I might snap.

But I'm stubborn, and as much as I like pushing Jackson, I don't think I want to push with this. I want it to be his choice. Whatever happens next.

"Delilah," he whispers. "What is it?"

"Nothing."

"You're sure?" he asks. His finger ghosts another light touch, just beneath the strap of my bra this time.

I clench my teeth so tight they click together.

"You're messing with me," I accuse.

I can feel his smile against the back of my neck. "Maybe."

I turn and try to glance at him over my shoulder. All I can see of him is the curve of his ear and some rogue, messy bedhead. The very edge of his shit-eating grin.

"I don't like this version of you," I huff.

He laughs, his arm tightening around my waist. "Which version is that?"

"The one where you don't follow through."

He hums behind me and gently guides my bra strap over my shoulder. "Did you want me to touch you, Delilah?"

"*Please*," I all but beg.

A rough grunt punches out of him and he pushes his hand down, fingers flexing around the heavy curve of my breast. "That's what I wanted," he whispers against the delicate skin at the back of my neck. "For you to ask." His thumb strokes over my nipple, and a tight little whine hitches in my throat.

"Well," I arch back, reaching behind me to thread my fingers through his hair, "maybe mention that next time."

"Noted," he says, still swiping lazily with his thumb. It's a single point of intentional contact, but I swear I've never been more turned on in my life.

"That's how it's going to be with us, isn't it?" he asks. "We'll take care of each other. Better than anyone else."

I nod.

"You're so soft," he tells me, his hips pressing into the curve of my ass. Rocking, once, like he can't quite help himself. He stills with another pained grunt, hand squeezing.

"How much am I allowed to take, Delilah?" His thumb inches up and traces a delicate path along the top of my breast. "How much will you let me get away with before you start to have regrets?"

I shake my head, frantic. Every inch of me is pulsing. I want him *so much*. "No regrets. We promised each other."

He peels the cup of my bra away, tucking it beneath my breast. I try to help, to slip my arm out of the strap, but Jackson stills me with his other hand at my hip.

"No," he says. "Leave it. Like this, you look—" He has his chin hooked over my shoulder, staring down at the shadows of my curves beneath the blanket. I notice the glint of black just above his ear. The only part of him I can see clearly.

"You put your glasses back on."

He nods. "I want to be able to see you."

He repeats the same methodical process on the other side of my bra, my bare breast spilling free, held up by the material underneath. Jackson lets out a slow exhale. Another rock of his hips against my ass.

"Look at you," he says. He cups my breasts with both hands, thumbs rubbing over my nipples. We've hardly done anything and I already feel electric. Like I'm dancing along the edge of a live wire, each spark connected to Jackson's fingertips. He rubs another slow circle. Again and again until I'm making bitten-off noises. He buries his face in my neck, teeth bared against my skin.

"*Fuck*. Delilah. I don't know if—"

"I'm going to need more than this," I beg, body rolling, chasing the maddening friction. It's too slow. Too intentional. There's a hollow heat between my legs and no friction. I need *more*. "You don't have to worry, okay? Whatever it is that's holding you back, stop. You're safe with me, Jackson. I promise, I promise, I pro—"

He rolls me over until I'm pinned with my belly against the mattress, his big body pushing down against my back. One hand sinks into my hair and pulls my head back while the other thrusts into my absolutely ridiculous pants.

"You can't say things like that to me, Delilah."

I wiggle in his hold, trying to spread my legs to give him more room. "Why not?"

He swipes his fingers across the front of my underwear,

groaning when he feels how wet it is. "Because I'll want to keep you," he mutters.

"Good," I groan, my fingers fisting in the sheets. "I want you to keep me."

I don't even feel the cold anymore. Just Jackson at my back and flannel against my front, my nipples rubbing against the material with every shift of my body.

"Stop talking," he grunts as his fingers clumsily tuck my underwear against my thigh, the material of my snow pants making it awkward. But Jackson perseveres, his thumb rubbing short, hard circles at the very top of my clit. "You're driving me crazy."

I bite down on the edge of the pillow with a little whine, hips rocking, chasing the friction he's giving me. I can barely move at all with the way he's holding me down, and that's another rush of liquid heat, right where he's stroking just a shade too rough. His thumb keeps catching against me and my breath hiccups every time, a filthy and indecent soundtrack in the otherwise silent room.

"The way you sound," he grinds out, yanking at my pants, trying to see more of me. He's impatient now. Just as impatient as I am. *Finally.* With his hand pinned between me and the bed, it's the perfect angle for me to work my hips. He lets me rock against his fingers and it's exactly what I need. Messy and delicious. Rough. *Perfect.*

"The way you *look*. Christ, Delilah. You'd let me do whatever I want, wouldn't you?"

I nod into the pillow. "I trust you."

"Good," he breathes, and then he shifts his hand. The pressure, the angle, the slow glide of two fingers inside of me . . . I press one knee up on the bed and chase it. How quickly we went from bare skin to *this*.

Flecks of gold dance at the edge of my vision. My face is half buried in the pillow, half turned toward Jackson, just the line of his shoulder visible, bunched with tension as he works me over. The pleasure is so sharp I almost don't want it. But I lie there and let Jackson take exactly what he wants from my body. I let it build. I take it. I take it and I revel in it.

"So good." He leans more of his weight against me, the hand in my hair planted flat against the bed. I turn my head and sink my teeth into his wrist, grinning when he hisses. "Delilah." A sharp roll of his hand as punishment. "Don't push me."

I laugh, breathy and high. "But look what happens when I do."

His attention between my legs focuses, slows—heavy, thorough thrusts of his hand that shove me over the edge before I can find anything to hold on to. I free-fall into orgasm with my forehead pressed against his wrist, my lips pressed together, a sharp breath through my nose. I feel like a feather in gale-force winds; tossed up, up, up before the winds cut out and I drift lazily down.

I sink into the mattress, a boneless puddle. I am suffused with heat. Sweat at my temples and between my bare breasts. Deliciously warm.

But I want more. I want to see him unravel too.

I prop myself up on my elbows and glance over my shoulder, Jackson still above me with his knees on either side of my hips. I'm caged in, but protected, his body a shelter over mine.

It's the first time I've gotten a good look at everything those button-downs have been teasing at. Jackson's body is lean but strong. A wide chest and narrow hips. Strong arms with solid muscles that flex and release as he twists his hands in the bedsheets.

I reach back and touch his bare hip. Right where his sweatpants are pulled low. He shies away from my touch, chest heaving.

"I don't know if I can—" His head drops back, his face toward the ceiling, eyes pinched closed. I watch the line of his throat flex with his heavy swallow. "I don't know if I can, Delilah."

"It's okay to take something for yourself," I whisper.

His jaw clenches. "I don't know."

"You do." I curl my hand around his hip, tracing the cut of muscle there with my thumbnail. He shivers. "I know you do. And it's okay. You can have it."

I watch his face change in the muted shadows. How his eyes grow heavy with want. The peek of his tongue at the corner of his mouth. His hand rubs at the middle of his bare chest, like he's trying to push away whatever is happening inside of him.

But I want to be the one who does that for him. I want to ease that ache.

"You can have it," I say again. "Whatever it is you want . . . I want it too. I promise."

His hand inches down his chest toward the hem of his sweatpants. I bet he runs every morning. Or swims, maybe. Something that requires dedication and routine. Something where he can keep pace.

"Are you sure?" he asks, and his hand sinks into his pants. He grips himself with a shuddered breath, his head rolling back along his shoulders. His forearm flexes as he moves and he tips his head forward again so he can watch me while he touches himself.

He looks so good like this, on his knees above me. His hair an absolute mess and his glasses slightly crooked.

"Yes," I breathe. I turn beneath him, my hands at his sweatpants, urging them down. "But let me see."

He's gripping himself so hard it looks like it hurts, but his breath comes faster as I inch his pants down his thighs.

"Oh," I whisper.

His eyebrows pull together. "What?" he pants.

"Nothing." I shake my head, then catch my bottom lip between my teeth. "You're just—you look good." The smooth, practiced roll of his hand around his thick cock. How he rubs at himself with the two fingers that are still wet from being inside of me. "What do you want me to do?"

Jackson groans and laughs at the same time. "You don't have to *do* anything, Delilah." His eyes grow serious again, pleasure making his mouth twist. "Just let me look at you," he says.

But I want him to be selfish. I want to make him as mindless as he's made me. So I let myself fall back into the pillows, my arms above my head. My bra is still twisted around my middle, pushing everything up, my breasts spilling obscenely over the material. I drift my fingertips over them, moaning lightly when a soft bloom of warmth unfurls in my belly. I won't come again tonight, but I bet I could. Just from watching Jackson like this.

He lets his body curl over mine with a heavy groan, one hand braced against the headboard over my shoulder. The wood creaks as his other hand picks up speed, his knuckles brushing my stomach with every rough stroke. I lean up and press my mouth to the hollow of his throat.

"On me," I whisper, and he grunts. I drift my fingers between my breasts. Lower, down over the curve of my belly. "It's what you want, isn't it?"

He nods, his temple pressed to mine. He feels feverish. So warm and solid above me.

"Yes," he breathes.

"I want it too." I press my palms to his sides. "Won't you give me what I want, Jackson?"

"*Fuck*," he whispers and his hand slows down. I feel the blunt press of his thick length against my belly and the smooth, easy friction of Jackson moving against me. Fucking me down into the mattress without fucking me at all. He murmurs nonsense as he chases his relief and I sink my hands into his hair, holding him tight.

When he finally comes, it's with his teeth bared against the side of my neck, his release warm against my belly. He falls to my side with a huff, his palm flat against the middle of my chest.

We stay there like that, tangled together, our hearts thundering. It isn't until I shiver again that Jackson leverages himself up on one hand. I watch as he takes careful inventory. My eyes, the curve of my chin. My bare breasts and the mess he's made of me.

His gaze stays there for a while.

"Feel warmer?" I whisper.

"I don't know." Satisfaction hitches one side of his mouth up in a lazy grin. "I can't really feel my legs, to be honest."

A loud laugh bursts out of me. Jackson's grin grows. He pulls his sweatpants back over himself, bashful, but makes no move to clean up the mess across my middle. I bite my lip at the way he keeps staring at it—at *me*.

He walks his fingers over my shoulders, carefully fixing my bra. His hands brush against me while he does and that little kernel of warmth that's heavy in my belly thrums wildly. I make a soft sound and Jackson gives me a chastising look.

"Bedtime, troublemaker."

"Trouble? Me?"

"*We'll be warmer skin to skin*," he mimics, voice feigned in some approximation of mine. It makes me laugh again and he rolls his eyes to the ceiling, slipping from the bed. For a second I'm disappointed, but then I hear the sink in the bathroom. Jackson comes back to me with a wet washcloth, brushing my hands away when I try to take it. He eases it over my belly in gentle swipes, cleaning me off so carefully it makes a lump lodge in my throat. I watch him, curved over me, bare skin and his hair sticking up at odd angles, some pink still clinging to the base of his throat.

Something tender and delicate unfurls beneath my rib cage the longer I watch him touch me—so, so gently.

I shiver, and his eyes find mine.

"Cold?"

I nod, even though that feels like a half-truth.

He bundles me back beneath the quilts with quick, efficient movements. I grab his arm before he can hesitate, dragging him into my little cocoon with me. I lie there like a lump while he rearranges pillows and situates blankets, then hum happily when he curls himself against my back. His arm is a delicious, heavy weight over my hip. Maybe, still, a little bit like a harness. But one that keeps me safe.

"Better?" he asks.

I smile into my pillow that smells like him. "Much."

SIMONE LEEDS: Tonight's broadcast out in the mountains has been canceled due to a power outage.

SIMONE LEEDS: But we'll check back in with Jackson and Delilah soon.

SIMONE LEEDS: If you're anything like us, you're eager for an update.

CHAPTER 28

JACKSON

"I just don't think you can discredit seven seasons of excellent television," Delilah says as she smears more jelly onto her biscuit. She woke up this morning and seamlessly picked up the threads of an argument we were having while we got ready for bed, like there wasn't bare skin, panting breaths, and a pair of incredible orgasms in between.

Meanwhile I'm caught somewhere between *What did last night mean to you* and *When can we do it again*, tongue-tied and stupefied. More than usual.

Delilah sets her knife to the side, pushes up the sleeves of the navy blue sweater I forced her into, and continues, "It's practically a crime that *Buffy* never won any major awards, you know? Like, I feel like it should have won at least one Emmy. *One*."

I can't stop staring at her mouth. At the slight divot under her bottom lip. It's the same exact spot I fixated on while I worked myself to orgasm against her belly last night. That tiny half inch and her teeth clamped against it while she wiggled beneath me.

I clear my throat and continue stirring my coffee. Lottie got one of the generators working late last night. Enough to power the common rooms and the small café where the coffee lives. Dustin and his portable pour-over are no longer needed, *thank you very much*. "I thought we established that entertainment industry awards are meaningless when defining objects of taste."

Delilah narrows her eyes, brandishing her butter knife like a weapon. "I can't tell if you're agreeing with me or not."

"I'll neither confirm nor deny."

I love arguing with Delilah, almost as much as I love everything we did last night.

I keep waiting for the existential dread to rise like acid. Fear that I've made a misstep, or anxiety that I've reached for something that should not belong to me. But all I feel is bone-deep satisfaction, especially when Delilah's collar slips and I catch a glimpse of the mark I bit into her neck.

I guess that's what happens when you have the most intense sexual experience of your life without ever removing your pants.

Delilah's eyes soften. "You look happy," she says quietly.

"I am happy," I answer. I poke at the feeling and examine it, turning it over and looking for cracks. I've always had trouble trusting my own happiness, but Delilah makes it easy to lean into the feeling.

Especially when she's wearing my sweater with pastry crumbs at the corner of her mouth, looking at me like maybe I could make her happy too.

"Good," she says, nodding to herself, glancing down at her plate and then peeking up at me through her lashes. Shy, a little bit. Pleased too. "I liked what happened last night."

Relief crushes my lungs, swift and sweet.

"Me too," I answer, a little too quickly.

Her smile pulls wider. "How long were you going to wait for me to bring it up?"

"A respectable two to four business days." I take a bite of

cinnamon roll. "Then, maybe I would have sent you a notarized letter to discuss it."

A loud snap of laughter tumbles out of Delilah. "Well, I'm glad we discussed it before we made it to formal documentation." She pauses. "It was good, wasn't it?"

Smooth, creamy skin. The tumble of her hair over her bare shoulders. The spill of her breasts over the material of her bra. How for once, she did exactly as I asked. How *delicious* that felt paired with her jagged exhales and sharp whines.

I press out a slow breath, feeling the heat of it against the back of my neck. "Yeah," I rasp. "It was good."

So good it defies logic, actually. So good it's burned through at least eighty percent of my core memories and taken up the headliner role.

"I know we agreed that things could be casual while we're here, but . . ." Delilah pokes around at her pastry. "Maybe we can do that again?"

My wild flare of hope dims. I thought that sentence was going in a different direction. I thought she was going to say she wanted to do this when we're home too.

I think I wanted her to say that.

I clear my throat. "Yeah," I manage, trying to consolidate my hopes and expectations and find the best-case scenario somewhere in between. "Yeah, of course."

Her eyebrows pinch together. "Do you—is that something you want? With me?"

I yank myself out of my own head and reach across the table for her hand. "Of course I want that."

I want it again and again and *again*. I want to see how good we fit together. I want to see what other secrets she's holding on to. I want to be the one to rattle them free. I want my teeth against her neck and her thighs spread wide. I want everything in between.

"Well, good," Delilah says, relief in the curve of her body. She squeezes my hand.

"Yeah. Good," I repeat. Our eyes catch and hold. Hers soften. "Good," I say again.

It's still blistering cold inside the lodge. The worst of it is chased away by the roaring fire in the lobby, but it lingers in the corner of the room we're situated in. Our room this morning felt like stepping directly into a meat freezer, even the carpet cold beneath my socked feet.

Delilah shivers.

"I should have made you put on a hat," I murmur.

"In addition to the two sweaters and scarf you manhandled me into?"

"Should have forced the gloves too."

She rolls her eyes. "I'm fine."

"You're cold."

"It's not so bad down here, and Lottie says they're working on getting another generator from one of the boathouses down at the lake." She finishes the rest of her pastry. She wiggles her eyebrows. "Maybe it can inspire you to warm me up again later."

A tempting thought.

"Does she know why the one here failed?"

I'm not particularly interested in the answer, but Delilah seems to be, because she already has a theory. She also, apparently, has already discussed it at length with Lottie, somewhere in between her two trips to the pastry table.

"Probably something to do with the sheer amount of snow, and the plunging temperatures. The cold wave is well below the averages for this region. It's possible the fuel gelled, preventing it from flowing properly through the lines. Or, more likely, the cold just zapped the battery completely." I make a winded sound. Her forehead wrinkles, a little line right between her brows. "What?"

"Nothing."

She stares at me.

I rub my hand across my jaw. "Something about you talking about fuel lines, I don't know."

What I *do* know is I'm hard as a rock beneath this little breakfast table, and I'm going to have to sit here and think about something—Aiden's karaoke performance, the winter Penelope and Adeline got the stomach flu at the same time, the molting habits of geese—to get control of myself.

Another loud laugh bursts out of Delilah. One of the truck drivers bundled in a parka by the fire turns to give her a curious look. Delilah waves happily, then pushes her chair back from the table.

"Where are you going?"

"To get another one of these powdered doughnut things, and to get you a cronut, since you are seemingly bound to the table for the time being." She grins at me, and another happy and completely foreign swoop twists beneath my sternum. She collects some of our plates, balancing them in her arms. "Lottie made fancy pastries as an apology and I'm not mad about it."

"Wait." I reach out and grip her arm. Rub my thumb along the inside of her wrist, just because I can. Words stick on my tongue. Promises I have no business making. Declarations that aren't suited to half-deserted lodge lobbies. I swallow all of it down, and push it to a place to deal with later. When we're back home, maybe. "Can you get me two cronuts?"

If Delilah notices my deflection, she doesn't comment on it, flitting off in the direction of the pastries but getting sidetracked by the same trucker at the fireplace. He looks flabbergasted by her sudden attention, blinking up at her from beneath his hood like she's a particularly bright and shiny foreign object that's dropped directly out of the sky.

"She making friends again?"

Mark appears at the end of the table with a bag of jerky, a scarf wrapped so many times around his neck that only the top half of his face is visible.

"Yeah," I answer. "I think so."

Mark drags a char from a nearby table to ours. He unwraps some of his scarf. "Once, when we were on assignment in North East, she convinced a bunch of duck farmers to let her hold the babies." He shakes his head. "Almost came back with thirty-two ducklings in the news van."

"I believe it."

On the other side of the lobby, Delilah resumes her quest for pastries, but stops by *another* table, seemingly greeting the two older men there by name. She points to the folded-up newspaper, plucks a pen out of one of their front shirt pockets, and quickly scribbles something on it. I'm tracking her like a weather system, watching as she drifts over to the tables.

"Have you heard anything from Keith?" I ask.

"Nope." Mark takes a gargantuan bite of jerky. "I imagine he's nursing his wounds. He doesn't like being eclipsed in popularity, and Delilah has been doing that since she joined the station."

"Is there a plan for when you get back?" I'm worried that when I'm not around to play buffer, Keith is going to become more antagonizing toward Delilah. "How are you going to—"

Glass shatters somewhere nearby. My head snaps up and Delilah is standing just a few steps from the table she just abandoned, her phone to her ear, the plate she was holding in pieces at her feet. But it's the look on her face that has me pushing out of my chair and striding across the lobby, gripping her elbow as soon as I'm close enough to reach for her.

"What is it?" I ask. "What's happened?"

Her face is pale, her big brown eyes filling with tears. She slips the phone away from her ear, holding it limply at her side.

"It's my grandpa," she manages, voice thick. "He had a fall. They said—" She wets her lips, chin trembling. "The nurse said they don't know how bad it is. That he hit his head and there was a lot of blood and—"

Her breath hitches and she stops. Tries to collect herself. My grip slips up until my fingers are curled around her bicep, tugging her into me. "They're taking him to the emergency room now," she whispers into my chest, nose against the hollow of my throat. "They're taking him to the hospital and I'm *here* and the roads are—I don't even know what the roads are like and, I don't know when I can get there and—"

"Shh, it's all right." I smooth my hand over her hair. "I'm gonna get you back there."

"How?" Her voice wobbles, clouded with tears.

"Trust me," I whisper. "Let me take you home."

It's a relief to slip into problem-solving mode. Like this, my brain and my body work together. *Get Delilah home* pounds through my mind like a war drum. A clear set of stepping stones to walk across until I'm at the other side.

I send Delilah to the room to pack while I track down Lottie. A quick conversation confirms that the roads are still in no state to be driven on, and my stomach sinks.

"How long, do you think?"

Lottie glances out the window. The parking lot is a sea of smooth white, the road beyond sparkling in the midafternoon sun.

"The road crews here work quickly and likely have already started on the main routes in and out of town, but I'm worried about the ice. It could complicate things." Her kind eyes find mine. "The priority in storms are hospitals and other social services, not hotels. I'm sorry, Jackson. But I don't know if I can get you out of here today. Or even tomorrow."

I thread my hands together behind my head. I'm about to grab a shovel and start making a path myself. "What if—"

"Hello, uh. I might be of some assistance."

Dustin, the truck driver with a crush on Delilah, shuffles his way forward, his hat in his hands. He bends the bill of the cap, then smooths it out again.

"I don't mean to overstep, but I was listenin' from the corner."

I wave him off, unconcerned with the semantics of eavesdropping. "Can your truck handle the roads?"

"Lord, no," Dustin laughs, big and booming. "I'm not gonna take an eighteen-wheeler for a joyride after a snow event. Specially not with precious cargo." He gives me a watered-down glare, like I suggested we strap Delilah to the top of a rocket and launch her back to Baltimore. "Drivers who pass through this area are a tight-knit group, though, and I know a few of the private clearing companies. Big business out here, you know, with all the snowfall. With the county folks as busy as they are, it leaves quite the gap for private industries to fill. If you ask me, more of the municipalities should—"

I stretch my neck to the side, impatient. "Dustin."

"Ah, yep. Anyway. I know two guys—Brooks and Brent. Brothers, you know. They owe me a favor from the summer of '82. They've got a real sweet grader that could get you out to the main roads."

Hope blooms, fierce and quick. "Are they available? Can you give them a call? I'm happy to pay."

Dustin waves me off. "Nah. You don't have to pay. It would be my honor to help Miss Delilah." He straightens, his chest puffed out. A loyal soldier, ready to slay any dragons standing in Delilah's path. "I already gave them a call. They'll be here in an hour or so."

I blow out a heavy breath, relief making my head feel buzzy. "Dustin, I could kiss you."

He slips his hat back over his head. "I'd really prefer it if you didn't."

"Noted." I turn toward Lottie. "You think you could pack me up some of those powdered doughnuts to go?"

She smiles. "Of course."

When I finally make it upstairs after coordinating with Mark and Dustin and Brooks and Brent—who finish each other's sentences and prefer to communicate by screaming directly into the phone—Delilah is sitting in the middle of the floor, her suitcase a small explosion around her. The only things she has packed are her emotional support bag of candy and one of my sweaters she must have pulled out of my bag. She looks up at me with big, tear-filled eyes, her mouth trying to twist its way into a smile.

"I'm having trouble," she tells me, her voice thick.

"That's okay," I tell her. This is the Delilah no one else gets to see. The one who feels safe enough to let me see some of her cracks. I put down the bag of doughnuts. "I can help."

She sighs and looks at her suitcase, her cheeks wet. "I'm really sad," she whispers.

"That's okay too." I meet her on the floor and cup her face with my hands, tilting it toward mine, wiping away her tears with my thumbs. She keeps her eyes closed, her forehead scrunched. I press a kiss right there until it eases. Until she's looped her hands around my wrists and tucked her face into my neck. "I'm going to take you home now, okay?"

She doesn't ask any questions. She just nods. Fully and wholly trusting me to do what I said I would.

Take care of her.

WEATHER ADVISORY: ROADWAYS AND BRIDGES MAY BE ICED OVER. USE CAUTION WHEN TRAVELING.

CHAPTER 29

DELILAH

"This feels like the opposite of those tornado chasers," I murmur, my forehead pressed against the glass of the window. "The highest speed we hit was twenty-five, and that's only because we were going down a hill."

Jackson is white-knuckling the steering wheel of the news van, his jaw tight. "I'll take twenty-five over eighty and a ditch."

I snort a laugh I don't really feel.

It makes me nauseous to stare out the windshield when the conditions are so awful, so I close my eyes instead. Except when I close my eyes, all I see is my grandpa alone and bleeding. My grandpa, calling for help and no one coming. *A lot of blood*, the nurse on the phone had said.

"Any updates?" Jackson asks.

I shake my head. "Just that they've taken him to the University of Maryland Medical Center and that he's awake and responsive." But I don't know if he's confused. If he's scared. If he's asking for me. "Do you think you could drop me off there?"

Jackson sneaks a quick look at me, his blue eyes impossibly kind. "Yeah, Delilah. Whatever you need."

Whatever I need. That's more or less been his motto since I dropped that plate in the lobby of the lodge. He's rearranged our work schedules, packed our bags, somehow bribed a snowplow to clear our way out of Western Maryland while I've been . . . utterly useless.

More tears press behind my eyes. "I'm—I'm sorry about all of this. I should be—"

"Delilah," he cuts me off. Somehow gentle and firm, all at once. Exactly what I need. "Let me take care of you. Okay?"

I nod. Whisper *okay*. Wipe a few more pathetic tears off my cheeks.

I spend the rest of the drive in a fog. I keep my legs tucked under me, my forehead against the window, my heart in my throat as we creep closer to Baltimore. By the time Jackson pulls up to the emergency room entrance at the University of Maryland Medical Center, my face feels itchy and swollen, my stomach hollow.

I unbuckle my seat belt. Outside of the covered walkway that leads to the hospital, snow is falling in earnest. We must have moved with the storm as it swept across the state. Or barely beat it into the city, I don't know. The specifics of the drive are lost on me and for once, I don't care about the weather.

"Thanks for the ride," I say to Jackson, distracted. I fight with the strap of my bag to get it over my shoulder. "I can pay you back for the gas, or—"

A big hand untangles the strap and eases it over my arm. Jackson's face is patient.

"I didn't pay for the gas, Delilah. It's the work van, and we had to drive back anyway. We just sped up the timeline a little bit."

What he means is he moved heaven and earth to get me here, just like he promised. He gives me a small, tired smile.

"Thank you for driving me through a snowstorm," I whisper.

The lines by Jackson's eyes deepen. A secret there, somewhere. "There's very little I wouldn't do for you, Delilah."

A single explosive firework twinges somewhere in the middle of me, but there are bigger things shadowing my head and my heart. My anxiety and my sorrow make everything else feel muted, like I'm swimming through Jell-O. Up with the clouds and the snowflakes.

I compartmentalize and tell myself I'll give this the attention it deserves later. When it's fair to the both of us.

A surly-looking security guard with a snowflake blanket wrapped over her uniform makes an impatient gesture at us through the windshield of the van. "You two need to move," she yells. "This is an emergency lane."

Jackson glances pointedly at the empty driveway. The ambulance is parked in the bay, its lights off. There's a guy leaning against the bumper, eating a sub from Wawa.

Her eyes narrow. "This is not a dance hall!" she barks.

"Dance hall," Jackson repeats. He squeezes my arm and leans over my middle, wrenching open the squeaky door of the van. I want to press my face into his neck. I want to run inside. He brushes a kiss across my cheek.

"Go make sure everything is okay," he says. "I've got this."

I nod, then float out of the van and into the lobby. I press the elevator button and watch the glowing numbers change. A collection of people in different color scrubs streams out, more file in, and I'm swept up in the wave.

The last thing I see before the doors close is Jackson pointedly ignoring the security guard, refusing to move until he's sure I got in safely.

"Breaking news," my grandpa says as soon as I wrench back the curtain around his bed. "Old man slips in his favorite slippers. Knocks himself out on a nightstand."

I'm so relieved to see him lucid, I could cry. In fact, I do. Aggressively so. Right into his shoulder. I cry ugly, heart-wrenching sobs that hurt coming out. I snot all over his hospital-issued gown.

He smells like the lemon drops I know he keeps in his pocket and the laundry detergent he used to wash my pajamas in, and he *laughs* while he pats the top of my head.

"Delilah, my sunshine girl," he mutters. "I've really put you through the wringer, haven't I?"

His eyes crinkle when I finally lift my face from his chest. When I was little, it was my favorite place in the world. The place I was safest. The place I was wanted most. He'd wrap me in his arms and sing me some cobbled-together nursery rhyme that never made any sense and we'd stare out my tiny bedroom window at the satellite towers. The ones right outside the news station that stretch all the way up to the clouds, alternating red and white lights. *Wishes on a string*, he used to tell me. *That's where the stars live when they come down here for a bit.*

"What are you doing here? I thought you were covering that big snowstorm," he says. "The one out in the mountains."

"Yes, well." I sniffle and settle back, running a hand under my nose. It's a relief that he remembers where I went this time. After the last two phone calls we had, I wasn't sure what state I'd find him in. "I *was* covering that snowstorm in the mountains. Then Anita called and said you fell."

"I didn't *fall*. I tripped." He gestures at his forehead. "I barely scratched myself. A whole lot of hullabaloo for nothing."

I stare pointedly at the ugly bandage across his forehead and the gauze that circles his entire head. "She said, and I quote, *There is a lot of blood.*"

His eyes crawl back to mine, chagrined. "You know Anita is prone to hysterics."

"Grandpa," I whisper. "Please."

These moments with him are so rare. I don't want to waste them arguing.

He blows out a heavy breath. "Yeah, I know."

My shoulders slump. Now that I know he's okay, I am thoroughly and completely exhausted. I feel like I haven't taken a breath since this morning, in the lobby of a lodge hundreds of miles away from here.

"I was worried about you," I manage, my voice trembling again. Two fat tears spill down my cheeks and I angrily wipe them away.

He reaches for my hand and grips it tight. "I've been doing that a lot lately." When I look at him, he raises two gray brows over sad, tired eyes. "Worrying you."

I nod. His episodes have slowly been getting worse over the past year. The spells of confusion and the loss of time. The horrible anger, and then the meltdowns. The doctors say it will keep progressing until eventually he won't remember much at all.

He heaves a sigh and looks out the window, his thumb rubbing back and forth over my knuckles. "I don't want it to be like this for you. Rushing away from work. Crying." He sniffs, dragging his free hand across his jaw. "Hate it when you cry. Always have. Remember when you were five years old and you'd cry every day at kindergarten drop-off? Tore me to pieces. The guys at the docks used to make fun of me for it."

I snort a watery laugh. "Yeah, I remember. You used to draw me stick figure pictures in my lunch box. You said I could—" I suck in a trembling breath. Let it out slowly. "You said I could hold you in my heart while I was at school. So I wouldn't have to miss you too much."

He gives me a long, searching look, mouth flat at the corners. "You know that's where I stay, right?" He lifts his hand and taps, right in the middle of my chest. "Haven't left. Good luck getting me out of there."

I nod, gripping his hand with both of mine.

"I don't want you running over here for every little bump and scrape."

"Then maybe don't run headfirst into nightstands." A gruff chuckle slips out of him and I lean forward again, resting my head against his shoulder. "Let's save the argument for another day. I'm just glad you're okay. And I'm glad you're here."

He understands what I'm saying. A tired sigh whispers out of him. "Me too, sunshine."

His hand eases over my hair and I close my eyes. I listen to the sounds of the hospital around us. Reassure myself with the steady pound of his heart. It could have been so much worse. I'm glad it wasn't.

"You really aren't gonna tell me?" he asks, an indeterminate amount of time later.

"What?" I am caught in the hazy in-between of relief and exhaustion. My head is spinning.

"You forget, Delilah. I watch every one of your broadcasts," he says, sounding smug as hell. "Want to explain what you're doing kissing that weather boy?" He stares pointedly at my clothing choices. "And why you're presumably wearing his sweater?"

AIDEN VALENTINE: No weather report tonight, folks.

AIDEN VALENTINE: Jackson and Delilah are officially back in Baltimore. We're going to let them get settled before we start asking for updates.

AIDEN VALENTINE: Updates on the weather. Only the weather.

CHAPTER 30

DELILAH

A lovely nurse named Charlene with bright red hair and a booming laugh lets me stay forty-five minutes past visiting hours, until Grandpa Gus is snoring like a runaway train. She hands me a small piece of paper with a few numbers on it and ushers me into the elevator.

"These are the only cab companies that will drive in the snow, sweetheart." She leans in and presses the button for the lobby. "It's getting pretty dicey out there."

She's right. The big windows that line the atrium are walls of white by the time the elevator doors chime open. I rub the sleeve of Jackson's sweater under my nose and sigh forlornly at the list in my hand. I am a collection of tired muscles, wandering thoughts, and a bruised heart. Waiting for a cab is the last thing I want to do.

"Ma'am." The same security guard from earlier is inside now, still wrapped in her snowflake blanket. She's added a lavender scarf and matching gloves. Despite her whimsical choice in accessories, her face is set in stern, unyielding lines. "Please make sure to collect your things before leaving hospital property."

I glance at the bag over my shoulder. "Um. I think I have everything?"

She raises an eyebrow and points to the corner.

The corner, where Jackson is slumped in a chair with his head tipped back, arms crossed over his chest and his long legs splayed out in front of him. For someone who claims to struggle with sleep, he seems to have had no issue falling asleep in the lobby of the University of Maryland Medical Center.

"I believe that belongs to you," the security guard says.

I grin, my heart feeling two sizes too big for my chest. He's still wearing his glasses, and he's using the sweatshirt I left in the car as a makeshift blanket. He's the only one in the lobby.

I wander closer, biting my lip against a smile when his face tips in my direction, still asleep.

"Jackson," I whisper, and he shifts, his head rolling from one shoulder to the other. I reach forward and scratch my fingers through his hair, trying to wake him gently.

He leans into my touch with a low grumble, then jolts forward, half launching himself from the chair.

"I'm not leav— Oh. Hey, Delilah." A massive yawn splinters across his face. His drowsy eyes dart quickly to the security guard behind me, then back again. I get the distinct impression I've wandered into the middle of a feud. "Is everything all right?" He pushes his glasses up and rubs at his eyes. "Is your grandpa okay?"

"Yeah, he's doing well. He's in good hands and he was—he was able to communicate." I pause. Jackson blinks blearily at me from what must be a horribly uncomfortable chair, his hands against his thighs. "You're still here."

He nods. "Yeah. I'm still here."

Except he says it like a question. Like he's not sure where *here* is, but he's happy to see me regardless.

A throat clears behind us and Jackson scowls. "People are

allowed to *wait* in the waiting part of the lobby," he says, his voice carrying.

"Not when it's past visiting hours," the security guard calls back.

Jackson rolls his eyes to the ceiling. I hold out my hands for him to take, a hum of warmth spilling over when he grabs them without hesitation.

He steps into me, gathering me in his arms and lifting, holding me so tight I can barely take a breath. It's exactly what I need. My feet dangle at his shins and I tuck my face into his neck. He smells like snow and spice. The sheets we were tangled in when we woke up this morning.

God. This morning feels like a lifetime ago.

If I had the capacity to think about it before we left the lodge, I would have worried how *this* might go. How it would be for us, back here. So much of our time in the mountains felt like a bubble. Now reality is pressing at the edges, threatening to burst this fragile thing we've found with each other.

"Thank you for waiting," I whisper.

He hums and rocks me a little bit. "Will you let me take you home now?"

"Please."

The walk to the news van is slippery and cold, Jackson's hand firm in mine as we manage the pedestrian bridge that leads to the garage. I don't know why, but the snow almost seems more treacherous here in Baltimore. Something about the ice and the wind and the glow of the streetlights. The shadows of the buildings, towering around us as the wind howls. The city itself, silent and watchful.

Jackson opens my door and helps me in with his hands at my waist, hesitating as I buckle my seat belt.

"What is it?" I ask, shivering at the icy wind that licks through the crack in the door. Jackson shifts his body so he's taking the brunt of it, his forearms braced against the top of the van. He reaches into his pocket, then drops three boxes of off-brand candy fish in my lap.

"Found these in the gift shop while I was waiting." He pushes off the door. "Thought they might make you feel better."

He shuts my door without another word and jogs to his side, jamming the key into the ignition with a muffled curse. I clutch the candy to my chest and try not to cry.

The drive to my house in Hampden takes three times longer than it's supposed to, both of us shivering as the shitty heater creaks and groans and tries to keep up with the plummeting temperatures outside. By the time we pull up in front of my white picket fence, my shoulders are in my ears and I'm daydreaming about the flannel sheets on my bed.

Jackson keeps the engine rumbling.

"I think I'll drive this home," he muses, peering out the windshield at the pink-dappled sky. "I doubt my Honda could make it and I don't want to give Denise another reason to see me again tonight."

"Denise?"

"Our very patient friend from the hospital lobby." His blue eyes are searching from the driver's side of the van. "I think this is where we go our separate ways."

I knit my fingers together in my lap, running my thumb along the edge of one of my candy boxes. "That's right. I guess this is officially the end of us working together. Our assignment is over. We made it."

"Completely intact, no less."

I don't know about all that. It feels like I've carved a piece of myself out and handed it over, trusting him to keep it safe. There are a million questions buzzing around in my brain—*Do you feel it too? Do you want to see what this could be?*—but for once, I silence them. I'm too tired and too soft, my shell cracked open. I'm afraid of the things that might come tumbling out if I let them.

There will be time to discuss the important things. But it's not right now. Right now, I think I just want one more night of ignoring the logistics and the labels.

"I don't want you to take the van."

Jackson's eyes spark in interest before mellowing into a patient sort of caution. "I'm not going to intentionally destroy station property, Delilah. The van is safe with me."

I snicker. "I know that, but—" I glance toward my house. Imagine my flannel sheets with Jackson in between them. My belly gives a happy little swoop. "Come inside. Stay with me."

His hands flex on the wheel. "You're tired."

"So are you." I saw my teeth against my bottom lip and unbuckle my seat belt. "We take care of *each other*," I remind him. "Come inside with me. Get some rest." A thought occurs. "Unless you want to be back with the girls tonight, then—"

He shakes his head. "With how quickly we left this morning, I haven't told them I'm back yet. Besides, they were excited about doing *snow things* with Maya. I'd break their heart if I brought them home early." He reaches across the console and cups my jaw, fingers fanned wide across the side of my face. "You're sure?" he whispers.

I nod. "Very."

The engine cuts out. It feels like I can hear each individual snowflake land against the windshield. I get a glimpse of the clock on the dash. 10:02 p.m. *God.* It feels like it should be two in the morning. A hundred years from now.

Jackson creaks open his door. "Wait there."

"For wha—" I start to ask, but his door is already closed, shaking the cab of the van. I watch through the windshield as he crosses in front of the hood, and then Jackson is in the frame of the passenger-side door, gripping my knees, turning my body, handling me like I'm some precious thing.

"You didn't put on your snow boots before we left," he says in explanation, walking backward over the small patch of grass to the sidewalk while he holds my waist, keeping me levitating two inches off the ground. He reaches back into the van and grabs my bag, easing it over his shoulder, all while he keeps me snug against his body with his other arm. "I don't want you to fall."

"Very efficient." I loop my arms around his neck, punch-drunk. "I should make you carry me like this everywhere."

"I'm sure no one would have questions."

He turns toward my house with one hand braced under my ass to hold me steady, slow as he navigates the stairs. I rest my chin against his shoulder and hold on to him, hanging like—

"What are those fish called?" I rub my nose against his neck. "The ones that dangle off the bellies of sharks and whales?"

"You're delirious, baby," he huffs against my temple, brushing his lips there once. He sounds amused. "And those fish are called remoras. They have a modified dorsal fin that acts like a suction cup."

I grin. "I knew you'd know that."

"Where are your keys?"

"In my pocket."

His hand slides over the curve of my ass, feeling across my back pockets. I snicker into his ear.

"My jacket pocket, Jackson."

He jostles me slightly as he reaches into my jacket pocket instead, pulling out a key ring with a tiny fuzzy bunny on it. He laughs, low and soft, before pressing the key into the lock.

My house is warm and quiet and I feel myself slipping further into exhaustion as familiarity curls around me. Jackson toes off his boots then tugs at mine, leaving both of our jackets in a discarded heap on the floor. He navigates silently through my house while I stay wrapped around him, my nose in his throat and my hands clasped behind his neck.

"Where's your bedroom?"

"Second door," I slur. "Mm, that's the one."

I'm grateful I cleaned before I left, the sheets on my bed soft as Jackson sets me down on the edge. He stays in front of me, his body between my knees, his hands cradling my face in the dark. I close my eyes and lean into his touch as he traces his thumbs under my eyes. The same way I did to him at the lodge.

His thumb catches a tear, and a sigh rattles out of him.

"Baby," he whispers, sounding so impossibly sad. "Don't cry."

"Just a long day, you know?" I sniff, feeling everything like a boulder strapped across my shoulders. "He's okay, I know that, but I'm just—I'm having some trouble with—"

I don't know what's going to happen with my grandpa. I don't know what's going to happen with my job. I don't know what's going to happen with Jackson. All of it twists and braids together until a knot sits heavy over my heart.

Jackson hushes me, his hands pushing through my hair. "You're all right," he says, voice low, and I nod because yes, I am. With him here, everything feels manageable. I don't have to hold it alone. He's here to help. He squeezes my neck and tilts my face back, eyes searching in the dark. "Let's get you to sleep."

I nod and kick my way out of my pants, keeping just the sweater, crawling to the top of the bed and slipping beneath the blankets with a sigh. I hear the clink of a belt buckle, the slip of leather, the click of his glasses against my bedside table, and then Jackson is behind me. Cold skin pressed to cold skin, his hand a delicious weight against my belly. He tugs at me until I'm cocooned by him, our bodies curled together beneath my mountain of blankets.

"Do you think—" Another tear slips from the corner of my

eye. I'm tired and weightless. Already halfway to somewhere else. "Will we still be friends? Now that we're back home?"

Jackson is quiet for a long time. So long, I think he's fallen asleep. So long, I'm almost entirely there when he says, "Yeah, baby. We'll still be friends."

My heart eases. Another tear chases the first one. "Good, cause I think I'd miss you if we went back to glaring at each other across a parking lot."

He sighs, then presses a kiss to the back of my head. "Sleep, Delilah."

I twist my fingers through his, close my eyes, and do exactly as he says.

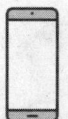

DELILAH STEWART: You stole the news van.

JACKSON CLARK: Borrowed it.

DELILAH STEWART: That's fine. I'm more upset you left without saying goodbye.

JACKSON CLARK: I didn't want to wake you.

DELILAH STEWART: Luckily you did make me coffee before you left.

JACKSON CLARK: Can't let Dustin have all the glory.

DELILAH STEWART: Thank you.

DELILAH STEWART: For everything.

DELILAH STEWART: I don't know what I would have done without you.

JACKSON CLARK: No problem, Delilah.

CHAPTER 31

JACKSON

"Did you get a haircut?"

"No."

"Botox?"

I pinch the bridge of my nose. "Where would I get Botox in the mountai—"

"New glasses?"

"I told you," I say, scraping scrambled eggs out of the pan and onto the three plates lined up on the kitchen island. "I have made no cosmetic changes in the past week."

"Then why do you look like someone shoved a glow stick up your ass?" Adeline says, munching the crust off a piece of toast, eyeballing me from her perch on the barstool directly across from me. She's wearing tie-dye sweatpants and a *Heartstrings* sweatshirt she stole from my closet.

I stare at her. "I left you with Aiden for too long."

Her eyes narrow with her grin. "He does have a very interesting vocabulary."

I woke up in Delilah's bed this morning to her sprawled across my chest, her cheeks still splotchy from her crying. I traced the bridge of her nose with my thumb while the word *friend friend friend* trudged a mad loop along my brain stem, then I slid out from beneath her. I debated collecting my car from the corner of the street, but decided on the news van instead, slowly winding my way through the city to Aiden and Lucie's. I thought the girls might want to stay, but they had both been ecstatic when I knocked on the door.

There had been screaming involved. Hugs. Demands for selfies in the news van.

Now they've launched an inquisition in our kitchen while I make our snow day special of scrambled eggs, toast, and chocolate chip pancakes.

"Something is different about you," Penelope says, eyes narrowed.

"I think it's his hair," Addie insists.

"I think it's his secret kisses with Delilah Stewart." Penelope makes an obnoxious kissy face, pushing her cheeks together with her hands. Adeline immediately descends into bright, cackling laughter.

I turn back to the stove.

"Oh, come on! You wouldn't tell us anything while you were out there. You kept saying you would when you got home."

I shrug. "There's nothing to say. We kissed a couple of times to distract me from my broadcast nerves. We're friends now. That's all."

That is decidedly not all. Not from my perspective anyway.

I pour some pancake batter on the hot pan, watching the edges bubble up.

"So that's something friends do?" Adeline asks. "Kiss each other?"

I turn around so fast, I get a crick in my neck. "No." I point at her with the spatula. "That is *not* a thing friends do."

She blinks at me. "So you're not friends with Delilah?"

"I am."

"Friends who kiss."

"Friends who are . . . just friends," I say. "Friends who kissed once. As a . . . team-building exercise."

"You kissed at least twice, according to the timeline constructed on Reddit."

I rub my knuckles across my forehead. "Timeline," I repeat, equal parts confused and horrified. "On Reddit."

Penelope takes a dainty bite off the end of her bacon, chewing thoughtfully. "She doesn't look at you like she wants to be your friend."

I hate the way my heart leaps to attention. "How does she look at me?"

"Like you have a glow stick shoved up your ass," Adeline deadpans.

I roll my eyes.

Adeline slams her fists down against the countertop. "What are you hiding, Jackson?"

"I'm not hiding anything," I say wearily. But I don't have an explanation either. I drag my hand down my face and peer at my sisters through my fingers. Both of them are watching me with a combination of thinly veiled suspicion and intrigue, a look only two teenagers can perfect.

"Just ask it," I sigh, wanting this part over. "Whatever it is."

They share a brief, conspiratorial look, and then, breathless, Penelope asks:

"Do you have a crush on Delilah Stewart?"

Inexplicably, heat climbs my cheeks. A crush is exactly what I have. A big, stupid, all-encompassing crush on Delilah Stewart and her too-big smiles and the way her nose wrinkles and the way she breathes my name, both of her hands fisted in my hair. Her chaos and her charm. The small, broken bits she hides from everyone else but hands over to me.

My face must answer the question because they both launch off their stools, screaming at the top of their lungs.

"I knew it!" Adeline bellows, pointing at me. "I could tell, you loser!"

"Stop it." I throw a kitchen towel at her face. "That's enough."

She rips it away. "It will never be enough. This is the highlight of my life. This is the best thing that's ever happened to me."

"Okay, that's a little dramatic—"

Penelope launches herself across the room, both of her arms wrapped around my waist. "I'm so happy for you. Your first crush."

I sigh, defeated. "I shouldn't have said anything."

"Technically, you didn't say anything." Penelope tips her chin against my chest, staring up at me with wide, wet eyes. *Christ*. "But that's okay, Jackie. We're gonna get you through this. We're gonna help you get the girl."

Adeline barrels over the kitchen counter, knocking over the box of pancake mix and the bag of chocolate chips. They scatter across the floor, probably sticking to the bottom of her smiley-face slippers as she collides with my side, wrapping her gangly arms around the both of us. I remain squished in the world's most uncomfortable group hug.

"I've been waiting for this moment," Penelope whispers.

Adeline nods. "You finally get to use your spiral notebook," she tells her.

"Do I want to know what's in the spiral notebook?"

"It's a fifteen-step plan to get you a girlfriend." Penelope's voice is muffled, her face buried directly into my shirt. "I've been working on it for a while. The time has come."

"All right. Let's . . . stick a pin in that." I pat both of their heads. "I actually needed to talk to you about something else."

Adeline gasps. "Are you finally asking us for a makeover?"

"What? No." I lift my hand to my hair. "Why?"

"No reason," they answer. Quickly. In unison.

I frown. "Is it the glasses?"

"It's not *not* the glasses," Adeline says, somewhere around my armpit.

Penelope pulls back with a sharp look at her twin. "What did you have to talk to us about?" she asks, deftly changing the subject.

I lean against the counter at my back and pick up my coffee mug. I've been back and forth over it, but I think it's time. They're old enough to make their own decisions.

"Camille insists she wants to come for a visit. She's been texting me for the last week." I watch them carefully for a reaction. Penelope's face blanks. Adeline grows cautiously hopeful. "She says she's eager to have a relationship with the two of you."

They exchange a searching look. "What about you?" Penelope asks. "Does she want a relationship with you too?"

I buy some time by taking a long pull from my mug, considering the question.

"That's not on the table," I finally say. My relationship with Camille is set in stone. I'm not willing to revisit it. But I could be convinced to make an effort . . . for the girls. "This conversation is about the two of you and what you want."

"Will you be mad?" Adeline asks quietly, toying with the mood ring on her thumb. Hers is a burnt orange. The matching one on her sister's ring finger is a pale pink. "If we talk to her?"

I shake my head, feeling her question like a baseball bat to the solar plexus. "Of course not," I tell her.

She glances up at me before her attention skirts away again. Up to the window above the sink. Down to her slipper-clad feet. Reluctantly, back to me. "Do you promise?"

Penelope reaches for her sister's hand. "We don't want you to think we're not Team Jackson," she adds.

I scrub my hand through my hair, then set my coffee mug on the kitchen counter. "There are no teams. Having a relationship with her won't impact your relationship with me." Shame grips me by the back of my neck. I can't believe I ever made them feel like they had to make a choice. That I wouldn't support whatever they needed. *Lighten up, Jackson.* "There's nothing you could do that would change the way I feel about you short of, I don't know, creating a catfishing cult. And even then, I'd probably find some way to defend you."

I grip Adeline's shoulders so she can't look away. "Okay?"

"Yeah, okay." She and Penelope exchange a look. Penelope gives her a small, encouraging nod. "We need to think about it. Do you need an answer today?"

"I don't need an answer at all. Take your time. It's the same deal as usual. You guys let me know what you need and I'll make sure it happens." They nod again and I reclaim my coffee mug with a sigh and a roll of my shoulders. This feels like the right thing to do, but I'm still struggling with it. "Is there anything else we need to discuss?"

"Can we go back to the fifteen-step plan?" Penelope straightens her stool at the kitchen island, climbing back onto it. Her face is way too eager for my comfort. "I think you've progressed past steps one through six, so we'll need to make some adjustments. Maybe start at phase two."

"There are phases?" I ask.

She slams her palm against her forehead. "Wait, what am I doing? I need the notebook. Addie, clear off the dry-erase board on the fridge. We'll need that too."

She scampers off. A second later, I hear her feet pounding up the stairs.

I sigh and drop my head back with a groan. "What are the chances I can wiggle my way out of this?"

"Impossible," Adeline says. "She's been planning it for a while."

She's still staring at her slippers. "Hey." I nudge her shoulder. "You okay?"

She nods, silent. I let her work through whatever it is. She's always been good at coming to me when she needs me. I just need to give her the space to do it.

There's a crash from upstairs, paired with a muffled *I'm okay!*

"What happens in phase two?" I ask, staring at the ceiling. "Do you know?"

"I think it's asking the girl you like to lunch."

I hum. "What if the girl you like just wants to be friends?"

"Then you use lunch to convince her that something more is better," Adeline says, somber and serious. "You'll have to wait for the full presentation. Penelope has a flow she likes to work through."

I try to mentally prepare myself. I'm a strange combination of pleased, proud, and terrified. I know what *I'm* like with a PowerPoint deck and a stack of note cards. I can only imagine the teenage-girl version.

"Jackson?"

Adeline's hand slips against mine. She presses our palms together and squeezes. I stop staring at the hallway and stare at the top of her head instead. Her honey blond hair, darker at the roots, with a cowlick that matches mine.

"Yeah, Addie?"

"I love you."

I shake my hand out of her grip and curl my arm around her shoulder instead, dragging her into me.

"Yeah." I press a kiss to the side of her head and ignore the part of me that wants to take back everything I just offered, hoping I haven't made a mistake. Hoping that for once in her life, Camille will be able to keep her promise. "I love you too."

SIMONE LEEDS: Now over to our very own Delilah Stewart, who is finally back in the studio.

SIMONE LEEDS: Delilah, how was your trip to the mountains?

DELILAH STEWART: It was a great trip, but I'm happy to be home.

DELILAH STEWART: Let's talk snowfall.

CHAPTER 32

DELILAH

I see the Post-it note on my driver's side door as soon as I leave the station. A standard-issue pale yellow, the corner of it lifting in the wind that whips through the parking lot. There's still snow on the ground from the storm, but it's been packed down by cars and boots in the handful of days since we got back.

I peel the note off my window.

Lunch? it says, in Jackson's neat, careful handwriting.

I smile. "Is that a threat or an invitation?"

Jackson hums from behind me, leaning up against the bumper of his Honda with his arms crossed over his chest. "Why is it always one or the other with you?"

I stick the note in my pocket. "Maybe it's both?"

"*Can* it be both?"

I shrug. "I'm not even sure what we're arguing about anymore."

"Oh. Is this arguing?" He pushes off the back of his car and saunters closer. He stops right in front of me, so close I need to tip my head back to watch his face. He has a subdued smile, his eyes tell the truth. He's happy to see me. "Hello, Delilah."

I'm happy to see him too. "Hi, Jackson."

He spares a quick glance at the station, then shoves his hands into his pockets and rocks back on his heels. "How's your grandpa doing?"

"Better. Thanks. He's getting discharged this afternoon. I'm going to go over there and pick him up before the evening report. What about you? How are the girls?"

A smile lifts one edge of his mouth. "They're good. Though I'm not convinced spending so much time with Aiden was in their best interest."

"Oh?"

"Bad influence," he says. "I can tell you about it at lunch." He hooks one finger in the opening of my jacket, using it to pull me closer. I didn't bother zipping it up all the way before I left the station, and his knuckle brushes against the very practical and professional silk blouse I have on underneath. He releases a sigh that sounds like it's come from the very center of his being.

Blue eyes find mine. "We aren't working together anymore," he says.

"No. We are not."

I've felt his absence like a shadow. I keep almost turning during my weather reports, looking for someone who isn't there.

Jackson's face finally loses the tension, his mask slipping. He looks earnest. "Maybe we could—"

"Delilah! Jackson!" Maggie bellows our names across the parking lot, a bucket of ice water over both of our heads. I try to take a step back, but Jackson still has his finger hooked in the front of my jacket.

I arch an eyebrow. He gives me an arch look back and doesn't let me go.

"What?" he yells over my head.

Maggie is shivering in her patent leather boots, her arms

curled around herself. "Can you come inside? I need to talk to both of you."

Jackson mutters an expletive under his breath. "Is it important?"

"No, Jackson. I want to talk about the weather." Maggie's face darkens. "Do I ask you for unimportant things?"

Another expletive, more emphatic this time. He peers down at me, frustration in the lines of his face. "We don't have to go in."

I glance over my shoulder at Maggie, shivering at the entrance of the radio station. "I think we do, actually."

"We could make a run for it," he says, wistful. "Get in my car. Drive to the border. Never come back." He pauses. "Make out."

"A beautiful dream." I pat his chest, already turning and tiptoeing my way across the pockets of ice. "You seem to have a *Thelma and Louise* fixation."

Jackson grips my elbow and gently helps me over the worst of it. "That's not my fixation," he murmurs.

"What?"

"Never mind." He sounds so forlorn it makes me laugh. Like his very favorite toy has been ripped away.

We finally manage to make our way over to Maggie, her palm propping open the door to the station. A wave of warmth curls around me, and I sigh gratefully.

"Come on," she says, angling her head toward the hallway. "Let's talk in my office."

We follow dutifully behind her, Jackson's hand at the small of my back the entire time.

"I'm sorry, what?"

Maggie keeps her face neutral, her hands folded together on top of her exquisitely organized desk. "I'm offering you a job."

"I have a job," I point out. "It's right across the street."

"You do have a job," Maggie agrees. "And it's a shitty one."

I glance at Jackson. He's staring at Maggie with his hand under his chin, his elbow on the arm of the chair. He doesn't look confused, but he does look wary. Hesitant.

"Am I—" He swallows heavily, a quick look cut in my direction. "Am I being fired?"

Maggie is the picture of controlled patience, even though we've been asking the same questions in a roundabout loop for the past seven minutes.

"No," she says. "As I've explained, you're being promoted."

"To what?"

"Production director. But we can discuss specifics in a moment. I want to talk through the Delilah offer first."

Jackson and I speak in unison. "I don't understand."

Maggie's mouth twists. "Yes, that's very clear." She tugs open her top drawer and pulls out a single stick of Big Red gum. "I don't see a reason to put an end to a good thing. The two of you have amazing chemistry. Your broadcast numbers are some of the strongest we've seen since Aiden and Lucie. Delilah, if you come work for us, you'd have your pick of airtime and segments. Jackson could hop on with you to do the weather, then spend the rest of his time in his much-preferred background role."

"I am—" Surprised feels like too small of a word. Gobsmacked, maybe? "How long have you been thinking about this?"

Maggie leans back in her chair, her arms crossed over her chest. "Awhile."

I let that sink in. "I'm not sure what to say. No one's ever tried to poach me before."

Jackson makes a rough sound next to me. When I glance at him, he shrugs.

"Sorry, but that's surprising to me."

"Really? You think people are lining up to hire the girl who face-planted at the horse track?"

Jackson's gaze is steady. "I find it odd that people aren't lining up to hire the girl who laughed after she face-planted at the horse track, then delivered a flawless report on race times and track conditions."

My cheeks warm.

I let myself picture it, for a fraction of a second. Coming to work without anxiety churning in my gut, wondering what clown show I'll be put on next. Hoping for the best, but bracing for the worst. A little desk in a little office. Headphones over my ears and a microphone in front of my face. *Jackson*. Right next to me.

It's a beautiful, *tempting* solution.

But it won't work.

"I'm so sorry, Maggie, but I'm going to have to pass."

The silence is almost a sound. I don't think Maggie is used to people telling her no.

"I can raise your salary," Maggie counters, eyes sharp. "I can double your pay. Easy."

I laugh. I'm not exactly rolling in the Benjamins over at YBAL. "I have no doubt about that."

"You'll get to report on the weather. No goose migration. No . . . reproductive habits of bats."

My smile falters. I forgot about that segment at the Baltimore Zoo. I went immediately home and showered for close to an hour. I swear I still feel their leathery wings flapping in my hair.

Beneath the cover of the desk, Jackson's hand slips over my knee.

"It's not about the nature of the work," I say, feeling like I need to put a stop to this before Maggie starts offering all of the stars in the sky and a lifetime supply of Chaps sandwiches. I'm not sure I'm strong enough to withstand it. "But ultimately, I want my career to be in television. Not radio."

"You'll have the same opportunities here," Maggie counters. "Better, even."

"I know, it's just—" I say slowly, feeling like my heart is on a crank and I'm the one twisting the lever, holding it out and hoping that they're careful with it. "My grandpa set his life around the morning and evening news. I would eat my cereal to the intro music and do my homework to rush-hour traffic. We'd watch the five-day forecast together before he headed down to the docks for his shift." I tuck my hair behind my ears and fold my hands in my lap. "He still watches YBAL. The habit hasn't budged in three decades."

Next to me, Jackson's attention is firmly fixed on the side of my face. His hand flexes on my knee and I shudder out a breath.

"He was diagnosed with Alzheimer's last year and it's—it's progressing faster than we hoped. There are days when he's confused. When he doesn't remember who I am." Where he'll look at me in confusion and forget every moment we've shared together. Every scraped knee. Every bedtime story. Every haircut and half-burned dinner and teenage disappointment. "But he knows Delilah Stewart, his favorite meteorologist at his favorite news station. He knows my face and he knows my voice, even when he forgets everything else."

On his very worst days, when everyone is a stranger, he still has me. The friendly weather reporter with the sunshine smile. The habit that's burrowed so far in his head and in his heart, the disease can't take it.

"So, while I am grateful for the offer, I can't give up television.

Not when it's the only thing that'll keep me connected to my grandfather when things get worse. My hope is that after the success of this partnership, Keith will let me get back to doing what I do best."

Maggie and Jackson exchange a long, searching look.

"I understand your reasoning, and I'm sorry for what you're facing, Delilah. Please know there's no expiration date on this offer. If, in the future, you find yourself looking for new opportunities, I want you to know you'll always have a home here."

"I appreciate that." I bite my lip. "And I hope Jackson still gets the promotion you promised him."

Maggie barks out a laugh. "Yes, those two things were not conditional upon each other." She reaches back into her top desk drawer and pulls out an envelope, tossing it across to Jackson. It hits him in the middle of his chest. "Congratulations. You've been promoted."

Aiden suddenly appears in the doorway, wielding a long, narrow tube. He twists the bottom and confetti explodes in the tiny office. A surprised laugh bursts out of me. Jackson flinches so hard he drops his envelope.

"Aiden," Maggie sighs. "I said no confetti."

"I never received that email," he deadpans, tiny bits of colored paper stuck to his hair. With his sharp features and severe expression, the contrast is striking.

"I didn't send it in an email, I said it to your face. A half hour ago."

Behind me, Jackson is trying to wipe glitter off his glasses. "Were you standing outside the office this whole time?"

"Sure was. Found the confetti canons in Hughie's stash of questionable office supplies and thought they'd come in handy." He reaches behind his back and pulls out another tube. A quick twist of his wrist and more colored paper explodes everywhere. I grin at Jackson as the color swirls around us, hot pink paper stuck in his hair. I am of the firm belief that every meeting should start and end with confetti.

"Well," Maggie says, sounding thoroughly done with everything. "As fun as this has been, I'd like you all to leave my office now."

"Happily." Jackson curls his fingers around my elbow and tries to march me bodily from the room. "Do you still have time for lunch?" he asks, his eyes bordering on desperate.

I grab his hand and twist, glancing at his watch. Disappointment settles like those little flecks of paper. "I have to be in Canton in a half hour."

"And you"—Aiden pokes at Jackson with an empty cardboard tube—"are due in the booth."

Jackson frowns at him over my head. "For what?"

"A meeting."

"Since when?"

Aiden looks like he's having the time of his life. "Since ten minutes ago."

Jackson's sigh is weary. I find his hand and squeeze. "It was easier in the mountains, wasn't it?" I whisper.

Jackson squeezes back. "For so many reasons."

It feels like it's been one obstacle after the other since Jackson crawled into my bed and put his mouth against my skin. I got a taste of him, and now the universe is dangling the promise of it just out of reach.

I'm frustrated. A little bit sad. Confused.

"Walk me out?" I ask, doing my best to pack it away. *We'll have time,* I reassure myself. *He wants to figure it out too.* All of this is still so new. I shouldn't make assumptions when Jackson has proven time and time again that he shows up when it's important.

Jackson nods.

But our escape from the office is delayed by the sudden appearance of an immaculately dressed man in the threshold, one hand curled around the edge of the doorframe. He either doesn't see us trying to leave, or doesn't care much about holding us hostage, his attention fixed firmly on Maggie at her desk, still covered with tiny flecks of gold glitter, yellow and pink paper in her blunt bob.

Her face darkens when she sees him. He grins.

"Hello, Margaret." He glances around the crowded office. "This looks festive."

His dark hair is combed neatly back, his suit tailored within an inch of its life. He doesn't look like he belongs in a moderately run-down but delightfully charming local radio station. He looks like he should be smoking a cigar in a dimly lit room. Maybe tying someone to a bedpost.

Sharp, blue eyes. A devious tilt to his mouth. His grin settles into a smirk, forcing a divot to appear in his cheek.

Je*sus*.

Maggie's eyes narrow. If looks could kill, the stranger would be dust in the hallway, floating merrily to the ground like the paper from one of Aiden's confetti cannons.

"How did you get in here?"

The other three people in this office might as well not exist. Maggie and the stranger are two sharpshooters in a spaghetti western, staring each other down along an abandoned stretch of roadway.

"I walked through the front door," he says, thoroughly amused. "Why? Have you had security installed since the last time I visited your little hovel?" He glances up at the ceiling in distaste. Specifically, at the pieces of confetti that have wedged themselves into one of the air ducts. "Are we celebrating something? Perhaps you received the sponsorship of that fried chicken place your hosts won't stop droning on about." Aiden makes an offended sound. "A new desk chair?"

Maggie's eyes narrow to slits. "Maybe we're celebrating your completely accidental and easily explained demise."

"Woah," Jackson mutters.

But the man just laughs, rapping his knuckles against the doorframe. "Lovely as that sounds, it's not quite time for you to pop the bubbly on that milestone." He beckons her forward with two fingers. "Come, Margaret. We have reservations."

A disbelieving laugh sputters out of her. "I'm not going anywhere with you."

"Of course you are."

"I'm not."

"You are," he says again, voice sharpening. "Unless you'd like to explain to your executive team that keeps the power on in this little shack why you turned down a personal invitation to a *brainstorming session* from Orion. Six times in a row." He levels her with a look. "This is what happens when you stop answering your phone, Margaret. I magically appear."

"Like Beetlejuice," she mutters.

"Please. I'm much better dressed." He pushes off the doorway and strides down the hall. "Let's go," he shouts over his shoulder.

Maggie seethes silently.

Aiden scratches at his jaw. "Is that—"

"Cooper West? Yes."

"The acquisitions guy?"

Maggie squeezes her eyes shut. "Yes, the vice president of acquisitions for Orion," she grinds out. "Fuck my life," she adds in a whisper. She gives herself another second of silent meditation, then grabs her wool coat and tosses it over her arm. "If I'm not back in an hour, one of us has murdered the other."

She brushes past us to the hallway. I can hear the click of her heels against the floor. Cooper's voice, lazily asking—

"Should I drive, or shall we humble ourselves with public transportation?"

"Shut up."

"I could—"

"I said, shut *up*."

A door slams. The walls rattle. Silence descends. Confetti blows across the floor like a multicolored tumbleweed, and the three of us stand unmoving in Maggie's abandoned office.

"Is it . . . always this exciting over here?"

Aiden tosses his confetti canons into the waste bin. "I'd like to say no, but I think that would be a lie." He claps Jackson on the shoulder. "Come on. You have a poorly disguised interrogation to attend."

Jackson gives me a faintly pleading look. I laugh and swipe some of the glitter off his glasses, then abruptly drop my hand. I don't know what he does and doesn't want from me when we're in front of other people.

I tuck my hands behind my back, twist my fingers together, and try not to feel embarrassed.

Jackson frowns.

"I'll see you later?" I ask. But I'm already moving toward the door.

"Yeah, of course you will. But, Delilah, listen—"

I slip out of the office before he can finish that sentence, fixing a smile on my face. I'm not sure I want to hear what he has to say right now. The more I prolong the conversation where he has to let me down gently, the better.

Just keep smiling, I say to myself as I turn and walk away.

You're almost there.

A few more minutes.

Just keep smiling.

AIDEN VALENTINE: Would you like to report on the weather?

JACKSON CLARK: It's not time for me to report on the weather.

AIDEN VALENTINE: Would you like to talk about something else, then?

AIDEN VALENTINE: Maybe a certain brunette weather woman, who was just over here? At our offices?

JACKSON CLARK: That was a work meeting, Aiden.

AIDEN VALENTINE: All work and no play makes Jackson a dull—

JACKSON CLARK: Freezing temperatures will persist for the rest of the week, but chance of snowfall is minimal.

JACKSON CLARK: We've officially made it to the other side of the storm, Baltimore.

CHAPTER 33

JACKSON

It's like the universe doesn't want me to get back to Delilah.

First I have to deal with Aiden's bumbling attempts at emotional connection in the booth, then my programmed weather reports, *and then* a hasty meeting with the corporate HR representative about the promotion Maggie dropped in my lap like a grenade. Any hope of a late lunch after Delilah's Canton report disappears with school pickup, and then I'm living my waking nightmare.

I'm supervising the girl's ice-cream date with our mother. In my kitchen.

Adeline decided she wanted to tentatively establish contact, and I decided I could let go of my own hurt and frustration to give the girls what they needed. I told Camille she could have *one* supervised evening, and we'd go from there.

Letting her in the door had been difficult, though.

"You need to try this time," I warned her. "You need to listen. You need to *be here*."

Her kohl-lined eyes had widened in the yellow glow of the porch light. "Of course I'm going to be here. This was my idea, remember?"

Then she waltzed through my front door and greeted the girls like two long-lost sorority sisters instead of the daughters she willingly signed over custody for. I spent the duration of her visit in the living room, pretending to read the *Farmers' Almanac*, trying not to eavesdrop on their conversation. But I did hear Camille's laugh when she spotted the whiteboard next to the fridge with all of our important dates listed out. Her light and breezy *He still does that, does he?*

When I walked her out an hour later, I stopped her on the sidewalk in front of a cherry red Mercedes that looked like it was held together by optimism and sheer force of will. The bumper had *duct tape*, for god's sake.

"Don't mess this up with them," I told her, nudging my glasses up my nose, ignoring the familiarity in the curve of her chin and the blue of her eyes. I spent so long looking for scraps of affection from this woman. I refuse to do it in adulthood. "This will be your last chance. Do you understand?"

"Always so serious." She smiled and pinched my cheek. "Don't worry so much, Jackson. You'll get wrinkles."

Then she slipped into her car and peeled away.

Now I'm here. Standing at the bottom of the narrow steps that lead up to Delilah's row home, staring at the screen of my phone, wondering if I've made a mistake. But the girls are back at Aiden's for a pre-promised sleepover after their ice-cream date, and I felt the walls of our empty house pressing in on me. I was in my car before I could think too much about it.

Hey, I finally type out. Are you busy?

"Stupid," I grunt. I'm no better than a sixteen-year-old boy. Might as well start throwing pebbles at her window.

But her answer comes through almost immediately. A picture of her in another ridiculous, oversized novelty T-shirt, holding a carton of Chinese next to her face.

Very, she says.

I grin at my phone.

Want some company?

"Hey!" Someone shouts from across the street. "What are you doing over there?"

I turn. An old man in a matching velour jumpsuit is leaning over the railing of his front porch, brandishing a pair of . . . knitting needles. An ancient portable heater sputters at his feet, a lumpy, presumably hand-knit blanket tossed over the aluminum folding chair behind him.

"Yeah, you!" He gestures at me again with the needles. "It's the middle of the night."

I clear my throat. "I'm waiting for—"

"Get out of here!" he interrupts before I can finish. He lifts his weathered fist, scowling. "Go on! Shoo! This is a nice neighborhood, you vagrant!"

A porch light turns on at the house next to Delilah's. Two doors down, a dog begins to bark. I'm not doing anything wrong, but my fight or flight kicks in. I debate making a run for it.

Behind me, a door opens.

"That's enough, Mr. Ribaldi." Delilah's voice floats down. She sounds like she's laughing. "He's not a vagrant."

Mr. Ribaldi frowns, suspicious. "Then why is he loitering?"

"That is an excellent question." Delilah balances her hip against her doorframe, poking around in her carton of Chinese. "Jackson?" she calls. "Why are you loitering?"

Fuck, it's good to see her. All the tension that's steadily been winding tighter at the base of my spine abruptly vanishes at the sight of her in her too-big T-shirt, flannel pajama pants underneath.

"I don't know," I yell back. "I think I'm kind of an idiot. Can I come inside?"

A loud bark of laughter drifts down the steps, curling around me like ribbon.

"Yeah," she laughs. "Come on up."

I can see her T-shirt better when I get to the top of the steps. It's one of those oversized bathing suit cover-ups with the figure of a woman in a hot pink bikini stenciled on. *Delilah* is airbrushed across the bottom in lime green. She spreads her arms wide, kicking out one leg and pointing her toe.

She *still* has my socks, apparently.

"I got it at the Boardwalk in Ocean City. Do you like it?"

"I do." I stop at the top step and gaze up at her in the halo of golden light that spills out from her house. "Hey," I breathe.

Her smile is quietly delighted. "Hello."

"Sorry for just showing up like this."

"Don't be. Come inside before you get cold. Or Mr. Ribaldi shoots you with his BB gun."

"He has a BB gun?" I eat up the space between us with three easy steps, brushing past her. She shuts the door behind me, resting her back against it.

"He's appointed himself as head of the neighborhood security detail. He takes it very seriously."

"While I'm not thrilled with his methods, I'm glad you have someone looking out for you."

Delilah's smile broadens before she looks down at her takeout box, poking at it. "In the very loosest of terms, yes. Mr. Ribaldi looks out for me." Her voice sounds sad. Wistful, almost. Like I've touched a barely healed wound. She pushes off the door. "Come on. I was eating dinner and watching *Jeopardy!*"

Like most homes in this neighborhood, the layout is small but cozy. Family room, dining room, kitchen, all stacked in a straight, narrow line. I didn't notice the last time I was here, but colorful artwork crowds the walls. A combination of photographs and hand-painted canvases, including the patron saint Dolly Parton presiding over the dining room table where Chinese cartons are spread out.

The furniture is simple, but colorful and well loved. A cozy-looking armchair sits next to an overstuffed bookshelf, a thick blanket tossed over one of the arms, a book still open face down in the seat. There are two mugs of something left abandoned. A plate with half a muffin and a scattering of crumbs.

Delilah in every single detail.

"Expecting company?" I ask.

Delilah blinks up at me from where she was rummaging around in one of the bags. "No." She emerges with a fortune cookie, shuffling over to the back of the couch and throwing herself over it. She lands with a huff, her hair wild around her shoulders. "Why do you ask?"

"No reason."

"Is it because I ordered enough Chinese for a family of six?"

"No."

"It's okay. The restaurant gave me four forks. When the DoorDash guy came, he was looking over my shoulder for the party I was having." She pops open the cookie wrapper and grins at me. "Party of one. I couldn't decide what I wanted, so I just got a little of everything. I'll eat the leftovers during the week."

I slip off my jacket and toss it over the back of a velvet green armchair that I'd bet my next paycheck was rescued from Facebook Marketplace.

"Oh!" Delilah leverages herself up, leaning over the back of the couch. She reaches for the bag on the dining-room table, knocking over one of the chairs. I grab the back of her thigh to keep her from falling and she grabs one of the cookies with a small cry of victory. She tosses it at me. "Congratulations on your promotion."

"Thank you." I catch the cookie. "Though I don't think I'll ever understand Maggie's decision-making."

Delilah's face softens. "You deserve that promotion, Jackson. You work hard."

"Debatable," I mumble. I rip open the plastic and crack the cookie. I read the fortune and snort.

"What does it say?"

I look at the tiny scrap of paper. *"A light heart carries you through the hardest of times."*

"That's better than mine. Mine said, *A soft voice may be awfully persuasive.*"

I grin. "Should I start talking in a whisper?"

She laughs. "Depends. What are you trying to persuade me to do?"

"I have a list."

"You and your lists." She tosses the rest of the cookie into her mouth and chews thoughtfully. "Where are the girls tonight?"

I drag my hand through my hair. "Back at Aiden and Lucie's. I think the initial excitement of my early return wore off. There was some show they wanted to watch together, and the promise of peppermint hot chocolate."

Delilah smiles. "It's nice they have that together."

I think of the way the girls ran upstairs when I dropped them off. The happy chatter. Aiden's beleaguered sigh from the living room.

I know more about Olivia Rodrigo's discography than I ever wanted to know, Jackson.

"Yeah, it's good." I let myself collapse onto the couch and turn my face toward her. I've been missing this. Seeing Delilah at the end of the day. Having someone to talk to and share with. Unpacking all the things twisting me into knots and having someone carefully work their fingers through the strands, smoothing and settling until I'm calm again. We only spent one week in the mountains, but it was enough to have me wanting her in all the empty spaces around me.

"I'm sorry about our lunch."

Her smile dims and she readjusts her legs, tucking them close to her chest. "It's fine, Jackson."

I reach out and curl my fingers around her ankle, tugging until her foot is pressed against my thigh. I trace the jut of her ankle bone, then squeeze. "We haven't had much time together since we got back."

"It's all right."

Frustration plucks at me. She's so good at minimizing her own reactions, I sometimes don't know what she's really thinking underneath everything else.

"Do you forgive me?" I ask.

Her smile is half-hearted, her eyes meeting mine for the briefest of seconds before floating away again. "Of course I do." She tucks her chin to her shoulder and looks toward the kitchen. "Do you want some lo—"

"Don't do that," I interrupt.

Her lips quirk. "No? I've got egg rolls too."

"I'm not talking about the egg rolls." I turn so I'm facing her fully, draping one of her legs over my lap, the other trapped between the side of the couch and my hip. My arm stretches out over the back of the couch, fingers reaching. "I want you to tell me the truth. Tell me what you want. I want—I want you to demand more," I say.

She stares up at me, her brown eyes cautious. "I don't understand."

I shift again, closer, the inside of her thigh pressed to my rib cage. I pinch the hem of her ridiculous shirt and rub the material between thumb and forefinger. Affection tangles with desire, so sharp and warm I have to swallow around it.

"Don't smile when you're not happy and don't forgive me if I'm not forgiven. Talk it through with me when I've hurt your feelings." I let go of her shirt. "Ask me to do better. Tell me what you need."

The smile she's holding on to like her life depends on it slips, inch by inch, until there's only Delilah left. More solemn than I've ever seen her.

"I don't know where we stand now that we're home," she confesses quietly. "I don't want to lose all the things we let ourselves have in the mountains just because we're here."

I nod to myself, settling my palms on her thighs. I ease them up her legs until my fingers are braced around her hips, thumbs digging into that dip that drives me insane. The material of her shirt bunches at my wrists. I hold myself perfectly still.

"I don't want to lose that either," I tell her.

She nods, her attention caught somewhere between my eyes and my mouth. "Okay."

I shake my head.

"No, Delilah," I say softly. "You're taking it too easy on me. Do you want to be friends, or do you want to be something else?"

Her eyes are wide as she gazes up at me. Almost afraid. "I want to be your best friend," she whispers.

My throat tightens. I turn and press up on my knees, hovering over her before planting one hand by her head, the other at her hip. She's a perfect fit for me, all her softest parts fitting against my hardest edges. I lean forward and brush my nose against her cheek, my lips ghosting over the corner of her mouth.

"Demand more from me," I rasp. "I promise I'll give it to you."

Relief eases across her face as her eyes search mine. She's starting to understand now. Her hands find the front of my sweater and she pulls my body down to hers. Her chin tips up and she catches my mouth with hers. She does exactly as I requested;

harsh, demanding kisses that punish. I grunt and match her frenzy, working my mouth against hers, sucking in a sharp breath when her teeth clamp down against my bottom lip.

I *missed* this.

"Shit," I mutter.

She soothes the pinch with a swipe of her tongue. Her hands haven't moved from the front of my sweater, like she's afraid I'm going to change my mind and pull away. I sink more of my weight against her, urging her thighs wider with mine to make room for myself.

"Sorry," she mutters.

"Stop apologizing to me."

I cup her jaw and press my thumb against her chin, urging her mouth open, kissing her deeper with another dark sound that punches out of my chest. I hold nothing back, working my apology into her with my tongue and my teeth, hoping she understands how fucking *desperate* I am for her.

"You feel like—" She arches back into the couch, neck exposed. "You feel like you're trying to prove a point," she laughs.

"Good. You're finally getting it."

All the things I'm feeling, all the words I haven't been able to say. I drag my mouth down the line of her throat and work a mark against her pulse point. I hope she has to wear extra makeup tomorrow. That she has to pick something with a high collar when she goes on the air. I hope every time the material chafes against her skin she thinks of *this*. Me, pressing her down into the couch. Her knees inching higher against my sides.

"There's nothing to prove, Jackson," she whispers against my forehead, her hands finally releasing their grip on my sweater. She smooths them over my shoulders, up the back of my head. "Do you want me?"

I have to swallow before I can answer. "So much," I whisper.

She cups my face, forcing my head up, her thumbs tracing over the sides of my glasses hooked over my ears.

"Even the messy parts? The ones that need a little bit of work?" She presses her lips together. "What about the parts that disappoint you? Because I don't know if I—"

I rub my thumb over her bottom lip, quieting her. We've slipped from desperate to achingly still. "Trust me," I whisper.

"I do." She laughs. A short puff of warm air against the hollow of my throat. "That's the problem. I let you in so fast, Jackson."

When I was a kid, I never had the luxury of being greedy. I had to learn how to stretch out the things I wanted; break them into pieces just to make them last.

But with Delilah, I don't want to be patient. I want everything, all at once.

I slip my hand around her back and press my palm to the base of her spine, gathering her close, treating her like the precious thing she is. I was careless before. But I can fix it now. I can show her.

She's made her demands. I'm going to fulfill them.

I reach for the bottom of her shirt. "Can I?"

She nods, lifting her arms above her head. I pull the soft, threadbare material over her, grunting when I see nothing but smooth skin and bare breasts.

"You're not wearing a bra."

"Surprise."

She doesn't hide, doesn't look away. She hooks her thumbs in her pants and slips them down too.

"All of it," she breathes, and I nod, my hands covering hers, taking over, pulling the soft material from her smooth legs and letting it drop by the side of the couch. She stretches out beneath me, completely bare. Heavy curves and creamy skin. She asked me once what colors I saw when I looked at her, and right now it's pinks and golds. Amber eyes that burn hot.

I set my hands on her knees, my thumbs tracing a half circle. I haven't taken off a single thing, but this isn't about me. It's about Delilah and giving her everything she deserves. Reassuring her.

"From that very first kiss," I tell her, "I knew I wanted more from you. I think I tried to convince myself I didn't, but I've always been a bad liar."

I sink down over her, ducking my head to her chest, catching one rosy nipple in my mouth. I lick and I suck and I drag my teeth against her until she's tugging at my hair. Pushing me down. Trying to pull me back up. She's indecisive and bossy, and I love every second of it.

"I want to be your best friend too," I whisper, right above her heart. "I want to keep you safe. I want to hold you steady. I want to—" I drag my mouth back and forth against her skin and laugh. "*Fuck*," I whisper. "I want to go sledding with you in a stupid doughnut. I want to be right here with you."

"Jackson," she gasps, back arched. I press another careful kiss to the curve of her breast, then slip down her body until I'm between her legs, hands caged around her hips, angling her the way I need until—*perfect*, she's *perfect*—one thigh is tossed over my shoulder and my chin is just beneath her belly button.

"Will you let me take care of you, Delilah?"

I drag my mouth back and forth, teasing, savoring every shaky breath in and out. The way her lungs expand and fill beneath me. The way she trembles when I sink lower.

I press my mouth against her in a slow, thorough kiss, gripping the curve of her thigh when she wiggles and whines. I hold her still as I learn what she likes best, then let her go as she leans into it. Her thighs press against my ears. Her hands crawl into my hair.

I reach up and pull off my glasses, tossing them toward the coffee table. They hit the floor with a metallic sound but I'm already working my mouth against her again. Wet and slow and deep, my eyes closed, thumbs rubbing where I'm holding her open for me.

I reach down and frantically yank at my jeans, curling my hand against my hard cock as soon as I can, fingers wet with her, riding the edge of pleasure and pain. It's so good with Delilah it *hurts*. I'm reduced to sensation and action.

When she comes, it's with the bitten-out sound of my name. I have to hold her firmly down while she works through it, her voice whispering my name over and over, a curse and then a praise, her body softening as my mouth lightens. The last time she says it, it twists up at the end, caught around the start of her laugh. I grin into the soft skin of her thigh then wipe my mouth there, crawling back on top of her. I wrap my arms around her and lift until I'm sitting with my back against the couch, Delilah draped over my lap. I want to memorize the feel of her when she's like this, boneless and satisfied, smiling so wide her kiss is messy.

"Do you understand now?" I whisper against her bottom lip. I flex my hands against the curve of her ass. "Do you see?"

All the things I haven't been able to tell her. I'm shit with words when it matters, but I can be good at this.

She laughs, breathless and winded. "Yeah. I get it."

"Do you?"

She nods, nose against my cheek.

She's so warm against me. Bare breasts, bare hips, bare legs. Wild hair, tumbling down her bare back. Her naked body, curled on top of my fully clothed one. I groan and bite at her skin. Sink my mouth against her collarbone and whisper out a quiet, *Fuck, Delilah*.

She rocks her body against mine and I palm the length of her thigh.

"This is how I want it to be with us," I murmur, panting open-mouthed against the hollow of her throat as her hands reach between us, tracing the open fly of my jeans. I'm so hard I'm dizzy. Just the scrape of her fingernail is probably enough to set me off. "Don't settle. Ask for what you need. Let me give it to you."

"Don't let you off easy."

I nod. "Yeah."

She sinks her hand down into my waistband and curls her fingers around me, pushing my jeans over my hips.

"Then give me this," she whispers, so sweet and breathy it makes me ache. "I think I need you, Jackson."

I think I need you too, I almost whisper back.

Instead, I groan. A rough, broken sound. She's rolling her hand against me, and I can barely think, my entire body vibrating. I tuck my forehead to hers and look between us, watching the way her hand works at me. She shifts her body and presses my bare cock against her, right where I've made her warm and wet. She rolls her hips in tight little circles, grinding against me.

My fingers bite into her hips. "Delilah."

A laugh catches in her throat. "Please tell me you have a condom in your wallet."

"I do, but—" I wet my lips. I'm having trouble stringing sentences together. I came here because I missed her. Not because I expected this. "I don't want you to think I do this sort of thing, Delilah."

"Hush," she whispers. "I know who you are."

She's still moving her hips. Getting me wet. Making everything smooth and easy. My cock nudges at her clit with every roll of her body, and her head drops back, the ends of her hair brushing over my still-clothed thighs. "Like this, okay? Just for a second. Then I'll let you get that condom. But I'm—" A deep, satisfied sound rolls out of her. "I'm always careful and I'm protected. You can have me like this, if you want."

I almost laugh. If I *want*. I squeeze her hips so hard I bet she'll have fingertip-sized bruises tomorrow. Ten perfect presses of blue and purple. The shape of my need for her.

"Me too," I grunt. The rest of my explanation eludes me. "I've never missed a physical."

She laughs into the corner of my mouth. "Why am I not surprised?"

"Health is important." I nip at her bottom lip and smile. "You sure?" I whisper.

She nods, fingers curling in my hair. "Very much so."

I black out, a little bit, at that. Gray creeping into the corners of my vision while the desire fists so tight my lungs burn. I urge her off my lap and pull off my clothes, chest heaving, hands shaking. I reach for my wallet, fingers fumbling with the packet, then tearing. Delilah helps, which is no help at all, and then it's my bare skin against hers, my hands smoothing over her hips and turning her until her spine is pressed tight to my chest, my arm hooked around her middle.

"Sit back," I tell her quietly. "Like this." I gently press her legs wide, hooking her thighs over my knees. I angle my cock against her as she reaches down, lightly tracing the length of me. A few tight strokes and then hot, blunt pressure as she eases back. Delilah works herself over me slowly, taking me bit by bit.

Her breath hitches about halfway. It's the most excruciating pleasure of my life. "I don't think I can—"

I bare my teeth against the back of her shoulder, my sanity in pieces somewhere on the floor. "You can," I rasp. I drift my hand down over her belly and swipe my fingers across her clit, trying to ease my way. She whines and I exhale a sharp sound. "That's it. You're perfect. A little more."

She angles her body forward and takes the rest of me with sweet little rocks of her hips, her body shivering once I'm all the way inside her. She wiggles and groans and sighs and makes a thousand other tiny, bitten-off sounds that I want to sink my teeth into.

I hook my chin over her shoulder and stare down the length of her body. I can't make out much, but what I can see makes me groan, my hips rocking under hers. The pink-tipped swell of her breasts as they bounce in time with each smooth roll of my body. My arm, a pale band across her middle as I hold her tight.

All blurry smudges of an indecent picture.

I wish I hadn't thrown my glasses across the room when I put my mouth on her.

"Did you think about this?" I rumble below her ear. "In that hotel room?"

"Yes," she breathes, chasing my hips, grinding down harder. Her hands plant on my thighs, working herself against me, her nails digging half-moons into my skin.

She laughs, breathless. "I thought it might be like this," she says. Her hand finds mine and she tangles our fingers together. "That I would tell you what I want and you would take what you need. That I'd be so, so good to you, Jackson."

I clench my teeth around a moan, then tighten my arm around her waist. I shift forward, kicking at the coffee table, pressing us down on the floor. I've never been like this before. Rough. Demanding. Taking instead of asking. Completely out of control.

"Put your hands—yeah, like that." Delilah grips the edge of the coffee table and I roll back into her. She hiccups a sound that settles like a boulder at the base of my spine. "Fuck," I breathe. "No."

Delilah tosses her head back, looking at me over her shoulder. "No?"

I shake my head. "Want to see you."

She laughs as I pull out of her and roll her over, letting me arrange her body against the carpet. I grab a random pillow and shove it under her hips, then press back inside. The way is easier now. She's soft and warm and so, so wet. She stretches her arms above her head and *yeah*. This is better. This is what I needed.

All of Delilah. Right in front of me.

I slide my palm down her thigh while my hips work and press my thumb between her legs. I draw sloppy circles and her breath hitches.

"Jackson," she breathes, and her body tightens around mine. Her knees ease wider and she says my name again, a sharp whisper that pinches and prods. "You're going to make me come."

"Good."

Her orgasm steals her breath and then it steals mine. More heat, more wet, and that's it. I'm gone. I grip her hips and work myself against her, lightning rocketing down my spine, pulsing through my body in time with her small panting breaths. I come with a deep groan as I collapse against her on the floor, my forehead against her shoulder, my body trembling.

It lasts a long time—the loud panting of my breathing and the tremors that shake free of Delilah's body. I let myself sink further against her and brush soft, gentle kisses over every inch of skin I can reach. Her shoulder. The hollow of her throat. The faint impression of my teeth marks on the curve of her breast. She laughs when I hit a ticklish spot and I groan again, rocking my forehead against the space between her breasts.

Her fingers scratch through my hair. Down my neck. Her knuckles bump against the collar of my sweater and a breathless laugh slips out of her.

"Is your sweater still around your neck?" she laughs, sounding dazed.

I hug her body closer to mine, my arms around her middle. "I think so." I peck a kiss against her shoulder. "I don't know. I'm not really worried about it."

She laughs and tries to wiggle out of my hold. I make a low

sound of annoyance and grip her tighter. She reaches for something I can't see, palm patting at the rug beneath us, shifting some of the pillows that tumbled free while I wrestled her to the floor, arm stretching and body twisting and—

"Here," she says, easing my glasses over my face. Her thumbs rub at the curve of my ears. "Now you can see."

I look at her smile, so wide her eyes crinkle shut. The tousle of her hair and the pink on her cheeks. My heart gives an unsteady *thump*, right in the middle of my chest.

I think I know what this feeling is. This *ache*. This . . . hollow wanting whenever she's not around.

I think I fell in love with Delilah in the middle of a snowstorm.

My mouth opens, then shuts.

"Yeah." I swallow hard. "I can see."

DELILAH STEWART: The birds are singing, the clouds are clearing, and the sun is shining today, Baltimore!

DELILAH STEWART: That big winter storm was more of a blip by the time it made it to us, wasn't it? The snow will continue to melt as temperatures warm, with no other winter events on the horizon.

DELILAH STEWART: A new season is just around the corner.

CHAPTER 34

DELILAH

"Tell me when to start."

"Okay," his low voice rumbles over the line, sleepy and slow. I imagine him tucked into his bed on the other side of the city, just like I'm tucked into mine. We haven't been able to see each other in three days, so we're doing this instead. Calling each other when we can. Waving at each other forlornly through our respective lobby windows. I liked it so much better when we were sharing two hundred square feet. "I'll count down from three. Three, two, one—"

I press play on my remote and wiggle down beneath my blankets. My phone is on speaker, tossed on top of my comforter next to a coffee mug generously filled from the bag of M&M's I found on the hood of my car earlier this week. Unfortunately, that's about as close as Jackson and I have come to seeing each other in the absolute disaster that is our competing schedules. I always seem to be coming when he's going, or vice versa. We're two ships passing in a pothole-laced parking lot, exchanging Post-it notes on cars.

"I don't want to hear any complaints about movie choice from you tonight."

His answer is a chuffed laugh that feels like it's pressed right against my neck. Goose bumps immediately erupt over my skin.

"Who would possibly complain about a film that celebrates the idea of a love triangle?" Jackson muses. He pauses. "Wait. There are three men, right? Love . . . square?"

"It could have been a *Why Choose* film if Hollywood were progressive enough, and I'm choosing to ignore your tone." The opening credits of *The Philadelphia Story* begin to roll. On the other side of the phone, I hear its echo. "You could have picked the movie, you know."

"I did pick the movie. You said, and I quote, 'Over my dead body.'"

I laugh. "I'm not watching *Transformers* before bed! And I don't think Bumblebee would help you fall asleep either."

Jackson hums, and I hear the rustle of sheets. "Hate to break it to you, but it's not the movies that help me fall asleep, Delilah."

I tuck my smile down into the top of my comforter. He slept over after we destroyed my living room, and my sheets still smell like him. If I close my eyes, I can picture him in the space next to me, one arm pushed under the pillow and the other curled over my thigh.

"How did today ago?" I ask, after we've watched Katharine Hepburn drift across the screen with Cary Grant.

Jackson's sigh is weary. "Fine. I think Maggie forgot I'm the one that put together the station's onboarding documents. So I'm basically lecturing myself about the requirements of a job I already do. It's an excellent use of my time."

He's been caught up in promotion stuff while I've been working through a story on the fate of this year's cherry blossom bloom. Keith has been surprisingly quiet since we returned from our trip to the mountains, letting me do my job and actually . . . report on the weather. Needless to say, I'm suspicious.

"That's not what I was asking about, and you know it."

Another forlorn sigh, this one punctuated with a grunt at the end. He's quiet for a long time. I pick at a loose thread at the edge of my duvet while he works through it.

"I don't trust her," he finally says.

"And that's okay," I remind him. "You're doing a good thing. You're giving your sisters a chance at a relationship you never got to have. It's an opportunity for them to explore and find closure with you as their safety net."

"Doesn't feel like a good thing," he grumbles. "Feels like I'm leading the lambs to slaughter."

I rattle my candies around in my mug, searching for the red ones. "Worst-case scenario, what's going to happen?"

"She lets them down," Jackson says immediately. "She breaks their hearts."

The rest of his sentence goes unsaid, but I hear it all the same.
Just like she broke mine.

"She's taking them to that leadership brunch at the school tomorrow," Jackson continues. "Adeline is excited."

"Penelope isn't?"

"Penelope is . . . hesitant," Jackson says slowly. "She's more like me."

I grin at my phone. "Ruthlessly organized with a secret passion for Michael Bay action films?"

Jackson's laugh is tired. "Chronically doubtful," he corrects. "Voted least fun meteorologist three years in a row by *Baltimore* magazine."

"Is that a real recognition?"

"If it were, I'd win it. Every year."

I can hear the sadness that lingers. I hate that the reappearance of his mother has twisted him up and left him doubting his every move.

"Those girls are lucky to have you, Jackson. No matter what

happens with your mom, you've validated their feelings and given them the space to try for themselves. The fact that you're worrying so much about it is proof of how much you care. And boo on *Baltimore* magazine." I pluck a green candy from my mug. "I always have fun when we're together."

"It's different with you."

"Is it?"

"Mm-hmm," he hums, and the sound of it vibrates over my bones. Rattles somewhere beneath my rib cage. "You make it easier."

"What?"

"Everything," he whispers.

I have nothing to say that's not either horribly premature or terrifically embarrassing, so I settle for the comfortable silence instead, letting it stretch and grow between us. I hear him shift on the other end of the phone and my eyes get heavy, even as my heart grows light.

"Jackson?" I whisper.

When he answers, his voice is drawn out and low. Half-asleep. "Yeah, baby?"

I could do it. I could tell him how I feel. Wrapped in sheets that still smell like him with the marks he worked against my throat a tender ache. His easy breathing in my ear.

But there's the unmistakable sound of a door slamming open on the other side of the phone, footsteps against a hardwood floor.

"Hey," he whispers. "It's late. You guys okay?"

A whispered conversation and then a heavy sigh.

"I'm not letting that cat into the house."

I press my face into my pillow to muffle my laughter.

"Addie, what—" There is an increase in the fervor of the other voices in Jackson's bedroom. "Hold on—I said *hold on a second*. Christ. Delilah, I paused the movie. I need a minute to deal with something."

I glance at the clock hanging above the television in my room. "It's late. I can just let you go."

"Don't do that," he says. "I'm going to give this stupid cat some warm milk and then we're going to finish this movie. Just wait here, okay? I'll be right back."

"All right," I laugh.

I pause the movie and sit up in my bed, stretching my arms above my head. I pilfered another one of Jackson's sweaters, though I'm starting to believe he wore the extra-soft forest green one over here on purpose.

Static bursts on the other side of the phone and I stare down at it, dropping my arms with a soft *thump*.

"Delilah?" a voice whispers from the speaker. "Delilah Stewart?"

I blink. "Yes?"

There's a *thud*, a whispered *Ouch, you barbarian*, and then a tussle for the phone.

"Hey, Delilah," another voice whispers. "Thanks for taking our call."

"Um," I scratch at the back of my neck and glance down at the screen, double-checking I'm still connected and this isn't some gas-station-candy-induced dream. "Did I . . . take your call?"

"Thank you for not hanging up," she corrects quickly. "Listen, we don't have long."

I settle back against my pillows with a grin. "Did you con your brother into feeding a stray cat so you could get me alone?"

"To be fair," the other voice says. *Adeline*, I guess. "The cat really does like it when Jackson leaves her milk."

"Yeah, but we also spent, like, twenty-five minutes trying to lure her to our house."

"We're doing a public deed, if you think about it. Feeding the huddled masses."

"It's a *cat*, Addie."

"And it's *cold* out there, Penelope."

I roll my lips together against my smile. "Did you guys have something specific you wanted to talk about?"

"Oh. Yeah. Thanks." They recalibrate, brought back to the task at hand. "We have some questions."

"Okay."

"What's your favorite color?"

"Hmm." I think about it. "Blue."

"And how do you feel about meticulously organized weekly meal calendars?"

Very subtle. That makes me grin. "I appreciate the thought and detail."

"Have you always liked the weather?"

"Always," I answer.

"If you were trapped in your car and you had fifteen seconds to live, what would—"

"How about," I cut in gently, "you ask what you really want to ask."

There's a beat of silence, and then Adeline, I think, in a heated rush, "What are your intentions with our brother?"

"Yeah," Penelope adds. "Because if this is a thing for, like, *views* or *clout* or whatever, we're not going to be happy about it."

The smile slips from my face, pressure blooming across my nose and behind my eyes. A half hour ago, Jackson was worried about protecting his sisters, and now they're protecting *him*.

"I really like your brother," I manage around a throat that feels too tight. I pick up my mug and stare at the candies inside. "I really, *really* like him."

A pause, longer this time. I imagine the silent conversation happening on the other side of the phone and strain my ears for any hint of it.

"Will you be patient with him?" Penelope asks.

"Yeah. I will."

"And you'll help us take care of him?" Adeline adds. "He's not great at accepting help, so you have to be sneaky about it."

"Yeah, I've noticed that." I laugh. "But, yeah. Yes. I'd love to help take care of him."

"Okay," Adeline finally says. "Good. That's what we were hoping for, because Penelope and I are big fans of your work. We didn't want to have to hate you."

A laugh sputters out of me. "I'm glad."

I hear the rustle of sheets as they presumably settle into Jackson's bed. "What are you guys watching, anyway?"

"None of your business," Jackson's voice booms from somewhere in the background. Both girls scream and the sound ricochets around my bedroom.

"You scared us!" Penelope screeches.

"You're in my room!" Jackson laughs back. I hear the muffled thud of a pillow thwacking into something. One voice asking, *Are we going to have snacks with this movie?* Then Jackson's voice, closer to the speaker, We *aren't having snacks.* You *are going to bed.* Some static as the phone returns to its owner.

"Still with me?" Jackson asks. The girls chatter happily in the background and I imagine the three of them tucked together.

I smile. "I'm still with you."

BMORESERIOUS: Do you think Jackson and Delilah would consider covering perfectly normal weather conditions together?

BMORESERIOUS: I miss them.

CHAPTER 35

DELILAH

"Hey." Gianna's face peeks over the edge of my half-crooked cubicle wall. Keith has moved me three times this year, and I'm currently squished between the watercooler with a perpetual leak and the air-conditioning unit that doesn't stop sputtering cold air, even when it's subzero temperatures outside. "I have something to tell you, but I need you to not freak out about it."

"Well, when you put it like that"—I tuck my pen behind my ear—"I am absolutely going to freak out."

Gianna once shared the gruesome details of a major investigative case by blurting out the murderer's MO in the middle of a bagel breakfast, then nonchalantly asked someone to pass her the lox. If she's spooked, then I probably will be too.

"Well," she says, edging around the flimsy wall and collapsing into the chair I stole from the kitchen. "Don't."

I eyeball her jumping knee and the frazzled state of her ponytail. She chews on the corner of her lip and stares at me, eyes a touch too wide.

"How fast can you tell me?" I minimize the programs on my computer and lock the screen. "I have a meeting with Keith in ten minutes."

"Keith," she hisses.

"Yes, that guy who signs all our checks." I swivel in my chair, kicking off the bunny slippers I keep under my desk and trading them for my stilettos instead. "He's actually been fine since I got back. I think maybe this is the start of a truce."

Gianna's lips twist. "I'm not so sure about that."

"What do you mean?"

"I don't trust him." She scratches above her eyebrow. "You know I don't like to share all of my information before I have it."

"Okay, but—"

"*But*," she stresses, "you were right about him trying to sabotage the trip. I did trace that cancellation email back to him. And I also found out that he had the production team tap in early to one of your broadcasts." She stares at me. "You know. The one where the whole city heard you making out with weather boy?"

My cheeks heat. "Keith was trying to embarrass me."

"He's up to something. I just don't know what." Gianna plucks at her bottom lip. "I'm following a couple of leads. I'll report back to you when I untangle it."

"Great. Thank you." I stand and straighten my skirt, only for Gianna to yank me back down to my seat. "Did you have something else to talk to me about?" I ask.

She nods. One sharp, jerky movement.

"Okay." I give her my full attention, waiting. She avoids my gaze, studying her chipped nail polish instead. "What is it?" I prod.

She sucks in a deep breath through her nose and releases it slowly. "I'm just—give me a second."

Alarm has me shuffling forward in my half-broken chair. "Gianna," I whisper. "What's going on?"

"I'm mustering up the courage," she whispers back.

I reach for her hands and grip her fingers tight. She doesn't immediately pull away or try to give me a wet willy, so I know it's serious.

"Are you sick? Do you need money?" I inch closer. "Is it about your sister? Do you need—"

Gianna shakes her head quickly. She squeezes my hands, and with a completely serious and utterly devastated look on her face, she says:

"I'm dating Mark." She exhales a ragged sound. "I have feelings for him," she adds in a rush.

I stare at her. "I'm sorry. Did you just say *Mark*? Cameraman Mark?"

Gianna nods.

"He dates people?"

She bites her thumbnail. "He's a bit of a slut, actually." I blink three times in rapid succession. "All of it happened really fast. You know my moral opposition to dating, right? Because it reenforces—"

"The patriarchal inclinations of our society. Yes, I am aware."

Gianna nods, eyes bright. "Right. You get it. But lately he's just been"—her hands wave wildly between us—"everywhere. Doing things for me. *Nice* things. Did you know he's nice, Delilah?"

"I've never known him to be particularly nice, but—"

"Except sometimes he's mean. He's mean and I like it," she whispers, sounding awed. "He does this thing where he—"

"*No*," I interrupt. "Please don't finish that sentence."

If I know any of the specifics, I'll never be able to look at Mark again. Mark, who is apparently a bit of a slut.

"I just need you to know the sex is unbelievable," Gianna whispers.

"Great." I press my palm to the middle of my forehead and rub furiously, trying to chase away that mental image before it can take root. "I'm so happy for you, but please never speak of it again."

Gianna buttons her lips shut, watching me expectantly.

"I don't understand," I say slowly. "You came over here looking like someone poisoned your cat."

"I don't have a cat."

"You know what I mean. I thought something was wrong," I clarify. Her knee is still jumping up and down. "Is there something wrong? Has he . . . forced you to do something you're not—"

"No! God, no. Nothing like that. I'm just—"

I've never had a conversation in so many whispered half sentences, the both of us curled together in my cubicle. If anyone walks by and pokes their head over my desk, they're going to think we're launching a drug trade.

"You like him," I realize in a moment of sudden, delightful clarity. Only Gianna would be disturbed about something so . . . wholesome. "Gianna." I laugh. "It's okay that you like him."

"It's terrible," she hisses.

"Why?"

"Because I am a strong, independent woman and I don't need a man to make me feel like I'm falling headfirst off the side of a dock."

I grin. "Sometimes that can be a good feeling."

She peeks up at me. "Can it?"

I think of Jackson with his face buried in my neck. The way he curls his arms around me in his sleep, tucking me firmly against him. Sometimes I can't take a deep enough breath and it's—it's perfect, like that.

Headfirst. Over the side of a dock.

"Yeah," I say softly. "It's good."

Gianna's eyebrows bunch together in confusion. It's the start of her research look, and I don't have the time for fifty additional questions and a data set right now. Keith is expecting me in his office—I glance at the clock, *crap*—in three minutes. I squeeze her hands one more time and stand, grabbing for my notepad at the corner of my desk.

"Okay, I've got to run before Keith figures out new and creative means of torturing me. There are protein bars in the bottom drawer for you and—I'm really happy for you, Gianna."

It makes sense, in a weird way. Gianna's complete lack of censorship paired with Mark's reservation. Two opposite ends of a seesaw, balancing each other out.

I'm still mentally sorting through all the information Gianna dropped into my lap when I finally skid into Keith's office.

"Sorry," I apologize quickly, slipping into the seat across from his desk. I have no reason to be, but I'm nervous for this meeting. It's been hanging over my head since we got back. It's not like Keith to let things go or make them easier, and he's been decidedly hands-off. I've been waiting for the other shoe to drop, and I think it might be about to.

Keith doesn't bother turning away from his computer while I wait patiently. He's playing solitaire and losing. Badly. I clear my throat. "I got caught up in a meeting with—"

"I don't particularly care," he cuts me off, sounding bored. He minimizes his game and turns with a sigh. He flicks his hand at the open door. "Shut that, please."

Apprehension prickles along the back of my neck, but I do as he says, standing and slowly walking to the door. On the other side of the newsroom, Gianna is watching me with her arms crossed over her chest. *He's up to something,* she said at my cubicle, *I just don't know what.* Her face is the last thing I see before I quietly shut the door, the noise on the other side immediately muffled.

Keith leans back in his chair, his hands folded over his chest. He eyes me critically and it feels like stepping into an oil slick. His attention clings to me, and not in a good way. "How would you say your time in the mountains went?"

I remain standing. "Fine."

I'm afraid to be too effusive. I don't want to set myself up for whatever trap he's laying.

He hums. "You had a little trouble, didn't you? Following the rules. Listening to my orders."

Him and his orders. It takes every iota of control in my body to not roll my eyes. "I think constructive discourse in the workplace is healthy," I say.

You once had me report from a toilet, I add in my head. *I think your orders are a bunch of shit. Literally.*

"Right, well. The reason I called you in here is because Ava Monroe reached out. She followed along with your weather report, and she had some thoughts."

He pulls a sheet of paper out from beneath his keyboard, flattening it against his desk. My heart leaps to my throat, and I try not to let myself catastrophize. "Good thoughts?" I ask.

Keith makes a noncommittal sound.

"She was happy with the numbers you pulled in and shared that you have a bright future in feature work." He finally looks up at me, tapping his thumb against his desk. "I agreed with her."

I hesitate. "Okay?"

The things he's saying are objectively good things, but Keith has always had trouble with praise that's aimed in my direction. No way he listened to ownership wax poetic about me without a reaction.

He nods. "It's under that feedback and recommendation that, effective today, I'll be moving you to community outreach."

If there were crickets in this office, they'd be chirping.

"Community outreach," I repeat slowly. "What does that mean?"

"After today's broadcast, you'll formally report to Mindy in the features department."

That sentence hits me like a physical blow, one word at a time.

Formally.

Move.

Under.

Features.

Department.

I have to swallow three times before I'm able to pull together a response. "The features team only does their reporting on the Sunday news hour."

Keith leans back in his chair. His mouth twists in a smug grin. "That's right."

I think about my grandpa in his favorite chair, watching his favorite news program. I think about how I won't be on his screen anymore. The one thing I had to hold on to him, and Keith is taking that away.

"But—" My throat tightens, and I order myself not to cry. Not here. Not where Keith can see. "But I'm a meteorologist."

"And both Ava and I believe you'll be better suited reporting on something else." He lifts his hands, his face twisted in mock apology. "Why waste such talent on something as boring as the weather?"

"The weather isn't boring," I say, my voice faint.

Not only is it a demotion and a decrease in airtime, it's a sharp reminder that Keith can do whatever he wants with my career. It never mattered how well I did on this snowstorm coverage. Keith was always going to find a way to use it against me—good or bad.

"And if I don't want to work with the features team? If I want to stay where I am?"

Keith's head tips to the side. "Did you really think there wouldn't be consequences for you, Delilah? You were caught in a compromising position with a coworker. You made a fool of yourself *and* this station. You're lucky you still have a job at all." He glances at the clock. "A job you'll be late for if you don't hustle over to the set. You're due for your noon report." He turns back to his computer screen, clearly dismissing me. "I suggest you enjoy it. One last hurrah for the weather girl."

I want to rage. I want to scream. I want to take the remnants of his Coolatta and hurl it against a wall. If I were braver, maybe I'd have the right words to fight back with. But I'm just a hollow shell, all the things I hold most precious scooped out and dumped on the floor.

"Why?" The loudest I can manage is a whisper. "You've always hated me. Why?"

His eyes harden into flint. "Because," he says, "everyone else loves you."

I float out of his office without another word, trying desperately not to cry. But it claws up the back of my throat. It burns behind my eyes.

The buzz of the set breaks through some of my fog, making me stumble over a cord stretched across the floor. Production assistants rush past one another, updating notes and typing furiously into the teleprompter. Someone shouts my name, but I barely register it. Everything is muffled and muted. Like cotton over my ears or a bandana over my eyes. I move through it silently, weightless and brimming with a violent, trembling frustration. The very tips of my fingers are cold. My breathing is loud. Choppy.

I'm handed an earpiece and my remote for the green screen. I find my mark and I wait patiently for the handover, staring into the camera. Somewhere out there, my grandfather is watching, and it's enough to force another crack in my already bruised heart.

Smile, Delilah.
Just for a second.
Smile, Delilah.
But I can't. I *can't*.

"Now over to Delilah for the forecast," Simone says. She smiles at me from her desk. "Delilah, how's it looking out there?"

The light on the camera in front of me flickers on. I can see my reflection in the curved glass. I am strokes of purple and chestnut brown. Pale and trembling, my hand still curled around my remote.

Will Keith even let me on the set anymore? Or will I be sanctioned off to my corner of the newsroom, never to be heard from again?

I swallow. "There's a—there's a chance of, um, showers on Monday." Tears blur my vision. Somewhere behind the camera, Gianna appears. She whispers something urgent to Mark and he leans away from his camera, looking down at her. I can't be bothered. I'm still underwater. "And, uh, on Tuesday—"

My voice drifts. The studio is completely silent. Gianna tries to gesture me off camera, but I know what I need to do.

Things aren't ever going to change for me here, and I was foolish to think otherwise.

"Breaking news, actually." I pull my earpiece out and let it dangle against my chest. "I quit."

AIDEN VALENTINE: Welcome back to *Heartstrings*, the special afternoon report. Benny is out sick and now you're stuck with me, Baltimore.

AIDEN VALENTINE: Thanks for calling in. What can I do for you?

CALLER: Did you see that Delilah Stewart quit?

AIDEN VALENTINE: What?

AIDEN VALENTINE: When?

CALLER: Right now. She quit in the middle of her report.

CALLER: Does Jackson know? Was it part of a plan?

CALLER: Is it because of the illicit affair they refuse to talk about?

[pause]

AIDEN VALENTINE: We're going to take a break for some music. Hold tight.

CHAPTER 36

JACKSON

I squint at my computer screen, leaning closer. "Who spends $216 on confetti cannons?" I click another tab on Hughie's spreadsheet and scroll. "And why are Doritos a corporate expense?"

The man in question skids to a stop in the doorway of my office, chest heaving. "Did you—" he wheezes out. "Did you see—" He bends in half, pressing his hands to his knees.

"Your Dorito addiction? Yeah, I did. The station isn't paying for these." Hughie plants one hand against the wall, his forehead against his forearm. I frown. "What's wrong with you?"

"Ran here—from the—Dunkin'," he barely manages between deep panting breaths. The closest Dunkin' is almost a mile away, and Hughie has never been much of a runner. "I saw it on my— phone. Delilah—" He makes a sound like a foghorn and slips halfway down the wall. "Delilah—"

"What about Delilah?"

Maggie appears in the hallway behind Hughie, her phone in her hand.

"Did you know?" she asks. Her look is faintly accusatory.

"Did I know *what*?"

"About Delilah."

I feel like my head is about to pop off my shoulders. Tension radiates up my spine, cinching at the very base of my skull. "Someone better start explaining what the hell is going on."

Maggie and Hughie exchange a look. Behind them, Aiden skids to a stop in the middle of the hallway. He still has his headphones around his neck, the cord dangling behind him. His cheeks are flushed, like maybe he ran here from the Dunkin' too.

"Why didn't you tell me Delilah wanted to quit?"

"What?"

"She just quit," Aiden says. "In the middle of her weather broadcast. Our call boards are going insane."

I stand up from my desk so fast my knee hits the underside.

"So you didn't know," Maggie says.

"I had no idea." I grab for my phone, my keys, my jacket hanging on a hook behind my desk. My body is relying on pure muscle memory while my brain runs a mile an hour. "When?"

"Just now."

I glance at the clock. She's supposed to be in the middle of her afternoon report. I've been playing it on the small TV in my office every day this week because I like the way she says *prognosticate*, but I got caught up in my spreadsheets and I missed it.

I force my arms through the sleeves of my coat.

"I'm going to—" I'm already edging out the door of my office, shouldering past Aiden and Hughie. "I need to go."

Thankfully, no one tries to ask me any more questions. I'm on autopilot as I move through the hallways to the front lobby, bursting through the door so hard it swings back and cracks against the side of the entrance.

I scan the parking lot, looking for Delilah's cotton candy–colored car. I breathe a sigh of relief when I see it's exactly where it was when I pulled in this morning, parked half over the line in her usual spot. The Post-it note I left her is still clinging to her window.

And Delilah is at the trunk, trying to force an oversized box inside.

"Delilah," I call. She pauses but doesn't look up, her hair curtaining her face. Her shoulders bunch as she tries to jam the box more forcefully into her car. I am painfully aware of the audience from both sides of the parking lot. Aiden, Maggie, and Hughie pressed to the glass of the radio station. A crowd of reporters doing the same on the television side. I pick out one of the news anchors. Mark, with both of his arms crossed over his chest, a petite woman in an oversized sweater at his side.

I stride across the lot.

"Delilah," I say again when I'm close enough, reaching for her elbow. I hate that everyone is watching, but no one is trying to help. She's on an island out here in the half-frozen parking lot.

My phone buzzes in my pocket, but I ignore it. Delilah shifts the box and tries another angle, a soft grunt that sounds like a sob slipping out of her mouth.

I grip her arm gently, forcing her to stop. "Delilah."

She turns without a word and presses her face in the middle of my chest. I gently cup the back of her head, my fingers threading through her hair.

"Baby," I whisper. "What's going on?"

"I quit my job," she mumbles into the front of my shirt, her voice pitched low. A sigh rattles down her spine. Another sniffle.

I try to urge her backward, try to see her face, but she keeps her body tucked into mine. I smooth my hand over her shoulder and down the line of her back, shifting her slightly so the people with their noses pressed to the glass can't see.

"Just now?"

She nods and gestures at the trunk of her car. "I cleaned out my desk," she whispers.

Her box is filled with various odds and ends. An Orioles foam finger. A small, folded training camp schedule from three seasons ago. A name tag from the Baltimore Zoo and a tiny figurine of a green turtle.

I bite my tongue against the ten thousand questions I immediately want to ask and trace another soft circle between her shoulder blades instead. That's not what she needs from me right now.

"How can I help?" I ask instead.

Her back tenses. It's the smallest fraction of a movement, but I feel it. A second later, she pulls away from me, tucking her hair behind her ears. Her eyes flick to mine and hold my gaze before tripping away again.

"I should go home," she sighs, digging her fist into her cheek. "Sort some stuff out. I'll need to call the insurance company and see how long my coverage will last now that I've—"

"Delilah," I whisper. "Talk to me. What's going on?"

I touch my knuckle under her chin and try to lift her face to mine, but she twists out of my grip. My stomach sinks, and apprehension creeps in.

"Not here," she whispers. Her eyes cut to the windows. "Not where they can see."

My phone starts buzzing in my pocket again. I grind out a curse and reach for it, frowning when I see it's Penelope.

Four missed calls, actually. All from her.

All in the past ten minutes.

I answer with a quick swipe of my thumb. "Pen? You okay?"

"No," she chokes out, her voice thick. "I think I messed up, Jackie."

A spike of fear cuts through the curl of anxiety. "What is it?"

"I got in a fight with Addie." She hiccups a sob. "I said some mean things and she—she left. I can't find her."

"What do you mean you can't find her? I thought you guys were at that brunch thing."

There are supposed to be chaperones there. School staff. *Camille*, I think, with a creeping sense of understanding.

Delilah's hand slips into mine. I squeeze it too hard.

"Penelope," I snap. "Tell me what's going on."

"Mom ghosted," Penelope says. "Addie was waiting out front and she wouldn't come inside. I swear, I didn't mean to lose my temper. But all of this is just so *stupid* and I told her I wanted her to let it go because we don't *need her*. Mom messes everything up and Addie is so convinced she just needs time, but—"

"Pen. Where is your sister?"

Her pause feels like it lasts a lifetime.

"I don't know," she finally whispers, her voice fraying. I can hear the warble of her inhale. The way she needs to brace herself. "She got on a city bus without her phone. I have no idea where she is, Jackson."

JACKSON CLARK: There's one last cold front sweeping through the region. Winter is trying its best to hold on.

JACKSON CLARK: Some cloudy skies ahead while we wait it out.

CHAPTER 37

DELILAH

It's a relief to focus on a problem that isn't of my own making.

Some of my fog clears in the face of Jackson's outright panic, and it's an easy decision to climb into the passenger seat of his car. To take his phone and navigate to his tracker app, clicking on the tiny picture of a blond-haired girl with her tongue sticking out. It's paired with another tiny circle, and I calmly direct him to the museum on the water—the place the girls were supposed to be having their brunch gala.

I break everything down into easy-to-follow steps. I call the school. I call the police nonemergency line. I call Aiden and quickly tell him to be home, in case Adeline goes to Maya. I reduce myself to efficiency, because that's what Jackson needs. And I want *so badly* to be what Jackson needs.

Jackson, who is bending every speed limit between the station and the waterfront, weaving his way in and out of traffic, his hands fisted so tight on the steering wheel his knuckles are white.

Penelope is waiting at the curb with tear tracks on her cheeks, a school official at her side. Jackson barely stops the car before he's launching himself out of it, pulling Penelope into a hug. He doesn't hesitate, doesn't show any anger, and the tightness at the base of my throat pulls tighter. He's so good. He's always doing the right thing, the perfect thing, and I'm—

I'm a disaster.

You made a fool of yourself and this station.

You made a fool of yourself.

The door to the back seat swings open and Penelope clambers inside. Her eyes are swollen and pink and I offer her one of the small, travel-sized tissues I found in the glove compartment. She takes it gratefully, looking up at me shyly through her lashes as she buckles her seat belt.

"Hi, Delilah." She sniffles. "This isn't how I wanted us to meet."

I twist in the passenger seat. "I know, but I am happy to meet you. I'll be happy to meet your sister too. We'll find her, okay?"

She nods, pressing the tissue under her nose. "If Jackson doesn't get arrested first."

Outside the car, Jackson is tearing into the school official. A few words press through the thick glass of the car window: *irresponsible*, *unbelievable*, and my favorite, *fucking idiots*. He turns to climb back into the car, and the official breathes an obvious sigh of relief.

The door slams so hard the entire vehicle shakes. The three of us sit in heavy silence.

Jackson's eyes lift to the rearview mirror. "Where would she go?"

We go to the ice-cream shop, the pagoda in Patterson Park, and the Bond Street Wharf where the geese congregate for stale crusts of bread. I start to get recognized at our second stop, hushed whispers and not-so-hushed whispers behind my back of *That's Delilah Stewart* and *Did you see she quit on air?* and *I wonder what happened*, so I stay in the car for the rest of the stops. I search through the window for Jackson and Penelope, hoping there's a third blond head with them.

But there isn't, and I watch as Jackson slowly slips further into himself. I try to tuck myself into his problem as a distraction while my own mess muddies the water around me. I'm an oil spill hemorrhaging damage, but maybe if I fix this for him, I'll be able to fix everything else too.

"Did you see what bus she got on?" I ask Penelope, pulling up the schedules and maps on my phone. "Maybe if we check the route—"

The car comes to an abrupt stop. We're in the Federal Hill neighborhood, cresting the park. After we checked the girls' favorite spots, Penelope thought Adeline might have headed for Blue Moon Too, a tiny breakfast spot on this side of the city. *The pancakes make her happy*, she had said, voice thick. *And I think she wanted to be happy.*

The seat belt digs in across my chest. I stare at Jackson, but he's staring through the windshield, ducking his head a little to see—

A girl. Sitting alone on one of the benches at the very top of the hill, overlooking the city. Her arms are wrapped around her knees as she shivers in the cold. She's not wearing a coat. Just a pale blue dress, her honey blond hair in loose curls spilling down her back.

Jackson jerks the car into park, uncaring that he's in the middle of the street. A car honks behind us, then another, and he bites out a furious curse under his breath.

"There's no fucking parking in this neighborhood. I don't—" His hand flexes on the wheel. His eyes are panicked, unsure. The driver behind us lays on their horn again. On the bench, Adeline turns to look. Jackson tenses. "I don't want her to leave," he breathes in a rush.

Penelope is already scrambling out of the back seat. Her door slams and she takes off running toward her sister. I quickly unbuckle, rushing to follow.

"I've got them."

I rush across the street, resisting the urge to flick off the small backup of cars behind Jackson's Honda. Despite Jackson's fears, Adeline hasn't rushed off. She's clinging to her sister like a lifeline, both of them shivering in their pretty dresses.

I slip off my jacket and cover them both, offering a smile when Adeline's red-rimmed eyes dart up to mine. They widen slightly in surprise.

"Am I on the news?" she asks.

My smile widens. "No. Though if your brother had it his way, he'd probably have one of the helicopters circling."

She looks down. "Is he mad?"

Penelope pulls back, grabbing her sister's face and squeezing her cheeks. "He's freaked out because you *ran away from me* and we couldn't find you." She wiggles her head back and forth. Affection with a touch of violence, exactly right between siblings. "Why did you do that? What were you thinking? That bus could have taken you anywhere."

Adeline grabs her sister's wrists and lowers her hands. I notice she keeps their fingers knit tightly together. "I don't know. I panicked. The stuff with Mom—" Her chin wobbles. "I know you're right about her, but I don't want you to be," she confesses quietly. "I wanted it to be different. Why can't she be different?"

Penelope scoots closer. My purple jacket slips off her shoulder and I lift it back, tucking it around them both. I bend down to one knee so I can zip the bottom, inching it up.

"Has Jackson told you anything about my mom?" I ask.

Both of the girls shake their heads in unison and I smile. Of course he hasn't. Jackson, who holds on to my secrets and keeps them like promises.

"She's a pretty famous violinist. She signed over custody to my grandfather when I was barely six months so she could pursue an orchestra seat. He was the one who raised me, just like Jackson is the one who is raising you."

Adeline blinks at me, her eyes puffy but bright. Her lashes are a sticky clump around her eyes, some light mascara smudged in circles over the tops of her cheeks. So much about her young face is familiar. I know what the hollow ache in her heart feels like. I know what it's like to chase answers that don't exist.

"When I was thirteen," I continue, my voice soft, the cold, muddy ground seeping through my tights, "I decided to run away from home. I was convinced I needed to know my mother to be able to—I don't know." I laugh. "I guess fill up the parts of me that felt empty."

"Where did you go?" Penelope asks.

I snort. "I stole some cash out of my grandfather's dresser and called a cab. I went to BWI and tried to get a ticket to Amsterdam. That's where my mother played at the time. Her precious orchestra seat. But I didn't have a passport, or enough money for a transatlantic flight." I smile. "I really didn't think the plan through."

The start, maybe, of a string of disasters that led me to exactly right here. But if this one can make these girls feel a little less alone, then maybe it was worth it. Maybe all heartache can lead somewhere better, if I'm just patient enough.

Gravel crunches behind me, but I don't turn my head.

"I sat in baggage claim for a couple of hours, crying my eyes out. I couldn't stop thinking about what must be wrong with me for my mom to put an entire ocean between us. I couldn't understand why she would love music more than me."

Adeline wipes her hand under her nose. "Did you figure it out?"

I shake my head. "No. I stopped thinking about it when my

grandpa showed up." I grin. I can still remember how frazzled he was, wearing his safety vest from the docks. His steel-toed boots clomping across the shiny floors of the airport. "He yelled at me for so long, TSA agents started to wander over. But when he was done, he hugged me tight and—I don't know. I think I got something better than any sort of explanation or answer from my mom."

"What?" they breathe, shivering under my sparkly purple coat.

"I realized how special it is to be loved by someone who chose me. Over and over again." The press of tears makes my voice turn thick. I have to take a deep breath before I say, "And it was enough to make up for all the rest."

Adeline watches me. A tear falls down her cheek and she brushes it away with the back of her hand. Resolve settles across her young face, and her bright, blue eyes melt into something relieved.

Her gaze lifts, over my shoulder. Jackson moves closer, his hand brushing down my arm.

"Yeah," she rasps. "That's enough for me too."

I'm still shivering by the time we make it back to Jackson's house, my arms clinging to my elbows in the small hallway outside of his kitchen. He's upstairs with the girls while I study the tile work that loops in a pattern down the length of the wall. I wonder if he did it himself, or if the girls helped. If they pressed laughter and clay-stained fingertips into the wall together, Jackson working with the same meticulous attention to detail he uses with everything else.

I trace the edge of a tile and wonder why he's never asked me to come here. If maybe, somewhere in the back of his mind, he'd knew I'd fuck it all up.

He finds me like that, staring at the tile on his wall, trying hard not to cry. I don't have any more distractions, and the day is slowly catching up to me.

"They're watching a movie," he says, weary, scrubbing his hand roughly against the back of his head. "*Fuck*," he breathes. "What a shit show of a day."

"Yeah." I laugh, but it sounds hollow and sad. "I can relate."

I'm jittery and uncomfortable, standing in this narrow hallway with Jackson perfectly apart from me. My toes are being pinched by my shoes, my eyes feel gritty and dry from all my almost-crying, and my heart—

My heart squeezes when Jackson slips both of his arms around my waist and curls his body over mine, gathering me close, burying his face in my neck with a bone-deep sigh.

"Thank you," he breathes. He squeezes me so tight my lungs pinch, his arms wrapped over each other across my back, his big palms spanning my rib cage. I am completely enveloped by him, and my composure fractures a little bit more. "Thank you for today. For what you said to the girls. For helping me. I can't—" He swallows, his voice thick. "I don't know what I would have done without you."

The tears are sudden and ferocious. The dam I've been struggling to hold all day breaks, ugly sobs pouring out of me. Jackson scoops me closer, walking me across the small kitchen and into the living room. He tries to deposit me gently on the couch, but I won't let him go, clinging tightly with my arms around his neck.

"Delilah," he whispers. He sits with me draped over his lap, his hands pushing my hair away from my face. I keep my nose against his neck, refusing to look at him. "What's going on? What happened today?"

"Keith wanted to move me to features," I mumble against his skin.

His hands keep moving over my hair. Down my shoulders. Across my back. "He tried to take you off weather?"

I nod.

"So you quit?"

I nod again.

Jackson's sigh makes his chest rise and fall. "I hate that he did that to you. I hate that you felt like you only had one choice."

More tears burn behind my eyes and I'm—I'm so tired of being like this. "It was my fault," I manage. "I messed up."

Jackson urges me backward on his lap. He has dark circles under his eyes. Weariness etched in the set of his shoulders. He drags his hand over his face and guilt hangs like a noose around my neck. He's so tired and I'm making it worse. He has enough to deal with without this layered on. He's always taking care of *me* when he already has so much on his plate.

"How did you mess up?" he asks.

I run a shaky hand under my nose. "In the mountains. I thought I could be different. More professional, maybe. I wanted to show everyone that I can be taken seriously. But I fumbled it, just like I do everything else."

Jackson shakes his head. "That's not true."

"Isn't it?" I slide off his lap and curl into the space next to him, tucking my legs beneath me. "I've always been like this. Maybe I should take some time, you know? Some space to figure things out."

Jackson goes still. "Space from what?"

I lift my hands and drop them. "I don't know. Everything. Is it possible to have a quarter-life crisis?"

He ignores the question. "Am I included in *everything*, Delilah?" He swallows, the line of his throat working. "Will you be taking time and space from me?"

I shake my head, then nod, then shake my head again. *God.* I'm a mess. I keep my gaze on his hand flat against the couch cushion. His rolled sleeves and the glint of his watch. "We said this thing between us would only last for our time in the mountains. We're not in the mountains anymore."

Jackson's knuckles find my chin. He forces the eye contact, because he knows I'm too afraid to do it myself.

"No," he says.

I blink. "No?"

"Yeah, no." He drops his hand and fishes around for something in his back pocket. "I never agreed to *while we were in the mountains*. That was your idea, and it was a stupid one."

"Excuse me?"

He pulls out his wallet and tosses it on the cushion between us, flipping it open and pulling a folded piece of paper from the back.

"You said friends, and I said okay, because I'm going to take you however I can get you. If you wanted to call it casual, I'd take that too. Because I'd still get a corner of you to call mine. But I won't have you call it nothing. I won't have you taking time and space away from me. Not when I know how good it is."

He unfolds the paper he pulled from his wallet, running his thumb along the heavy crease in the middle. It's stained with coffee and has clearly been folded and refolded a thousand times. Jackson extends it to me. "We have a signed agreement, Delilah Stewart."

I stare at our contract Post-it note from that day in the café.

"This agreement was for the duration of the trip."

He extends his arm over the back of the couch, his fingers tangling in the ends of my hair. "Was it?"

I grab the coffee-stained note with shaking hands, bringing it closer to my face. He's struck through one very important sentence.

I, Jackson Clark, promise to be on my best behavior ~~for the duration of this trip~~.* No picking fights, no making fun, and no sad-face notes left on car windows.

*and will allow for mishaps and mistakes, without complaint

"How did you get this?"

"I found it in your coat pocket."

I trace the crooked line through the note. "When did you change it?"

"After that first radio broadcast. Before we left for our trip."

I sniff. "Why?"

"Because I knew I wouldn't be done with you by the end of it." He swallows, knuckles nudging his glasses up his nose. "Our contract says we *will allow for mishaps and mistakes, without complaint.* Why can you help me with my problems, but I can't help you with yours? What happened to us taking care of each other?" He moves closer. "What about . . . getting to be loved by the people who choose us?"

I grip his wrist. "Jackson."

"I'm not done with you," he whispers. "Please don't be done with me."

I press my lips in a firm line so they don't tremble. "I'm a mess," I whisper.

"Then be a mess with me."

"I'm too much."

He laughs. "Yeah, baby. You're too much. You and your hot pink snow pants. Your doughnut snow sled. Your sunshine smile and your ridiculous puns. You laugh too loud at jokes and you talk to every stranger you meet. I don't think we were on time for a single thing in the mountains, because you were busy learning someone's life story. You think candy is a food group and you smile even when you don't mean it and—*Jesus*, Delilah. You drive me insane. You might be too much, baby, but maybe sometimes I'm not enough. Maybe when we're together, we fill each other up the way we—the way we need." His voice cracks and he lifts his hand to my face, the pads of his fingers brushing gently over my cheekbone. "Be too much with me," he whispers.

I want it so badly, but I'm afraid to believe in something else that could be taken away from me. "I don't know how to do this."

"Neither do I." He ducks his face down and brushes a kiss against my mouth. I sway into him.

"I don't want to mess it up."

He smiles against my mouth. "You hit me with your car once. I don't think you can mess it up."

I rear back and stare at him. "Did I?"

He nods, his smile growing wider. "You nudged me in the parking lot." He pecks a kiss on the bridge of my nose. "It's only up from here."

"I'm serious."

"So am I." He trails small, fleeting kisses every place my tears touch. "Things with us have never been simple or easy, but I'd rather be messy with you than have perfect with anyone else." He presses his forehead against mine. "Stay with me. Let's figure it out together."

I nod, more tears cascading down my cheeks. Jackson wipes them away patiently with his thumbs, his eyes impossibly soft.

"Will you let me help?" he asks.

I nod and I feel the weight pressing down on my chest lighten. How easy it is, in the end, to open the door for him. To trust and believe that he'll take care of me.

It's just like he said. We fill in each other's cracks and crevices. Maybe together we can be something whole.

"Yeah," I agree. "Yeah, okay. I don't want space."

"Good," he says, and he punctuates it with another kiss. "I don't want it either."

LEON KENNEDY: And you can expect showers. Later in the week.

LEON KENNEDY: I don't know how to—how does this clicker thing work?

LEON KENNEDY: All right, well. Enjoy this random stock photo of a duckling in a basket, I guess.

LEON KENNEDY: You really want me doing the weather instead of Delilah? Like, for real?

CHAPTER 38

JACKSON

I have immediate concerns about whatever Penelope, Adeline, Gianna, and Maggie are discussing on the couch. There's a lot of whispering, a lot of snickering, and a frankly disturbing number of hand gestures.

Delilah loops her arms around my waist from behind. "Why do you look terrified?"

I lift her hand and brush a kiss across her knuckles. "Because I am."

My house has turned into the interim headquarters for Operation Delilah Gets Her Job Back. Pizza boxes, file folders, and Post-it notes litter every square inch of available space.

Aiden, Lucie, and Maya showed up with the pizza and then Maggie, forty minutes later, with her laptop. The girls brought in the whiteboard from the kitchen, wiping off the week's menu, ignoring my grumbling about having to rewrite it. Then Gianna and Mark arrived, stacks and stacks of file folders in hand.

Penelope and Adeline descend into bright, cackling laughter and Delilah sighs behind me. "Nothing illegal, Gianna," she calls. "I need to convince Ava Monroe I'm capable. She can't catch me egging Keith's car."

"I was going to suggest shaving cream in his exhaust pipe, but whatever." Gianna flops dramatically back across my couch, her head landing in Mark's lap. Mark, who is on his fifth slice of pizza, adding very little to the conversation. He stares down at her like she's hung the moon, tucking a loose piece of hair behind her ear.

She flushes red, and Adeline and Penelope burst into more giggles.

"Fine. Maybe *we* will egg his car," Aiden offers, appearing over my shoulder, his cheek bulging with a slice of pizza he's folded in half, no plate or napkin to be found. He swallows. "While *you* get one-on-one with Ava."

"We won't use eggs," Maya says, rolling her eyes. There are so many people in my house, there is very little space for anyone to move. "We'll use tree sap. It's difficult to remove *and* causes lasting damage."

Aiden gives a nod of approval, offering her his fist. "Nice."

Maya grins and bumps his knuckles with hers.

"Nope." Lucie drifts past, flicking Aiden's ear, then ruffling Maya's hair. "Not nice. No vandalism. No juvenile crimes."

Aiden's laugh is low. "Just some light blackmail instead, hmm?" He trails after Lucie and plucks the top folder off Gianna's precarious stack of files. He flips it open and immediately shuts it again, his face pained. "Where did you even find these?" he asks Gianna.

She beams at him. "I'm a researcher."

Gianna's research is robust. The centerpiece is a very detailed list of every transgression Keith has ever made as the head of the broadcasting department, dating back to 1994. But she also brought statements from members of the broadcast and production teams about his behavior toward Delilah, a history of misappropriating station funds for his campaign to get a city road named after him, data from the last three viewer surveys about Delilah's likability, and the cherry on top—

Maggie reaches forward and peeks at the folder Aiden discarded. Her face blanches and she flings it away.

"*Why* do you have a picture of Keith in a tutu at—is that a *strip club*?"

Gianna laughs, collecting the folder and slipping it into the bottom of the pile. "Like I said, I'm a researcher." She pats her stack. "No stone left unturned."

We currently have a lot of stones, but no clear direction. I tug at Delilah's hands until she's standing in front of me. We've spent most of the past few days together, trying to build a plan while existing on Swedish Fish, but she needs to decide how she wants to handle what happens next.

"What do you want to do?" I ask her.

She glances around the room. My people and hers too. Everyone together. For her.

Delilah stares up at me. She's wearing an oversized hoodie she stole from the back of my closet, the sleeves curled over her fists. Last night she fell asleep at my kitchen table while updating her résumé (*Just in case, okay?*), and I carried her upstairs and deposited her in my bed despite her grumblings that she was fine to drive home. She immediately rolled to my side and burrowed her face into my pillow, muttering something about fancy shampoo.

She wraps her arms around herself. "I don't think I want to blackmail Keith to get my job back."

"Yeah, I would agree," I say, secretly relieved. I think she can get her job back without committing any crimes, but I'd do it. If she wanted me to.

"There's a lot of information," she murmurs. "I guess I just don't know what's expected of me."

I slip my hand under her hair and cup the back of her neck,

rubbing my thumb up and then down. "Would it help if I told you what I expect?"

She nods.

"I expect you to look at the very extensive evidence stacked on that coffee table and realize that *you* are not the one who should have left the station. I expect you to understand that his shit behavior doesn't just impact you, but every person who works at YBAL. You bore the brunt of it, but other people are struggling too. And he doesn't deserve to be in a position of power if he's using that power to do harm to others. This job is your dream. Baltimore is your home. Don't let him take it from you."

A smile quirks the corners of her mouth. "Demand more," she whispers.

"Yeah, baby." I squeeze the back of her neck. "Demand more."

I can see the determination settle across her pretty features. She steps out of my grip and wiggles her way between Penelope and Adeline, taking the marker that's offered. It does something to me, seeing their heads bent together. It's the same feeling I got last night when she curled herself around me in my bed. A tight fist of longing, right at the base of my throat. So heavy I can barely swallow around it.

Delilah peeks up at me, brown eyes shining. She tips her head gently to the side, raising both eyebrows. I nod, scraping my palm along my jaw.

"Hey, Adeline?" I call. My sister glances up. She has some dry-erase marker on her cheek. "Can I borrow you in the kitchen for a minute?"

She hops off the couch and dutifully follows me while I collect rogue paper plates and consolidate pizza slices. In the kitchen, she examines the boxes, plucking some pineapple off one that only Lucie has touched. She hops up onto the counter, her long legs swinging, socked feet drumming against the cabinets.

I toss the plates in the trash bin, then lean up against the refrigerator with my arms crossed over my chest. "We haven't had a chance to talk."

She's been avoiding me for the better part of the week. Every time I try to get her alone, she scampers off with her sister. Or drags Delilah off somewhere to do something with coordinated dance routines and too much laughing. But she can't hide in a house full of people, and I'm determined to hash this out.

Her face falls. "You want to talk about it now?"

"Mm-hmm."

"But—" She looks hopelessly in the direction of the living room. "We're supposed to be coming up with a master plan."

"They won't miss us for a couple of minutes."

I'm not sure they even realize we're gone. Gianna is standing in front of where Delilah sits on the couch, gesturing wildly. Delilah looks concerned, Penelope looks delighted, and Mark looks like he'd like nothing more than to drag Gianna off to the closest dark room. No one's even noticed we've disappeared.

Except Delilah. Her eyes find mine and she winks. That fist tightens. Slips lower to the middle of my chest.

I drag my eyes back to my sister. "We need to talk about it, Addie."

She sucks in a deep breath, then lets it out slowly. "I made a mistake," she finally says, her voice quiet.

I keep my face carefully neutral. "Which part?"

"All of it," she sighs. "Mainly the running away on a bus thing, cause I know that freaked you out, but also the stuff with Mom." I give her the space to find her words. She clears her throat, and when she speaks again her voice wobbles. "I had this idea in my head of how it would be. I thought now that we're older—I thought maybe if I showed her that I'm different, that I need her less, then she'd want to hang around. But I think—" She drags her hand under her nose with a sniff. "I think my expectations were too high."

It's a pinch against my heart. That she'd ever think she needed to change something about herself to be loved.

But didn't I think the same? Didn't I try to clear the overgrown parts of myself so that I could be exactly what they needed?

I cross the room so I'm at her side, leaning until our shoulders are pressed together. "I get it."

Adeline peeks up at me. "Really?"

"I mean, I don't think it's a secret that I'm a little uptight," I say with a laugh. I thought I could be more fun, more forgiving, but if these past few weeks have taught me anything, it's that old habits die hard. "It feels like I'm still holding on to a lot of . . . stuff. I thought if I upset my routine, maybe I could start to let it go. Be someone different."

Her forehead creases.

"But I don't know. Maybe it's not such a bad thing that I'm the way that I am." I have a Rolodex and a whiteboard and Post-it notes in my pocket . . . but the girls doodle on that whiteboard every morning. I caught Aiden flipping through the Rolodex for his favorite pizza restaurant he can never remember the number for. And Delilah loves stealing my Post-it notes.

"I like the way that you are," she confesses quietly.

"I was worried you didn't. I was worried you needed something different from me." I swallow around the knot in my throat. "I was worried you were unhappy."

Adeline shakes her head, hair swinging back and forth. She grabs my hand with both of hers. "Because I wanted to have a relationship with Mom?"

I squeeze her hand. "Because there are times I'm worried I'm not giving you everything you deserve. You and your sister." It's my turn to clear my throat. "Things with Camille weren't always bad. I worry sometimes that I made a decision for the three of us, and my resentment about my experience has kept you from forming the kind of relationship you need. From a mother. There were days with Camille that were really, really good. I want you to have that."

Adeline studies our palms pressed together for a long time.

"We did have good days," she says slowly. "But we also had days when she forgot to make us dinner. And our big brother went out to the closest store and bought us pizza, taking none for himself because he wanted us to eat." She looks up at me. "Penelope and I have never missed a meal with you. You've never missed a doctor's appointment or parent–teacher conference or dance recital. Why do I need a mom when I have a Jackson?"

I have to look away. Tears burn behind my eyes. I thought I needed to shake some part of me loose to give them the things I never had, but I don't. They want me exactly as I am. Lists and routines and all.

I glance at Delilah on the couch, smiling softly at me with her sweatshirt-clad arms wrapped around her knees.

I wrap my arm around Adeline and press a kiss to the side of her head.

"I love you," I tell her.

She sniffs. "I love you too."

"Don't run away again."

She snorts a watery laugh. "I won't."

"We're okay?"

She nods. "We're okay."

"Good." She drops her head against my shoulder and we watch the commotion unfold in the living room. Gianna is drawing frantically across the whiteboard while Delilah nods along. Aiden leans out of the recliner to point at something in the bottom corner and Penelope shrieks in delight, clapping her hands together. There's a focus that wasn't there before, Delilah quietly directing Gianna, determination settling across her face. My pulse picks up and Adeline snickers next to me.

"You got it bad," she whispers.

"So bad," I agree. "The actual worst."

Except it's not the worst at all. It's shared looks and stolen blankets and a weather map open on her computer. It's coffee-stained Post-it notes and candy in my coat pockets. A laugh pressed against my skin and fingertips tracing along my back. I always liked the things I could predict best, but it took the one thing I never saw coming to show me how much I was missing.

Delilah and all her colorful chaos. She gathered the broken pieces of me and put them back together into something beautiful. Something better. Something stronger.

Her eyes find mine across the room.

"You got a plan?" I call.

She grins at me. So wide her eyes squint shut. That tiny gap between her front teeth. "I got a plan."

SIMONE LEEDS: We have a special guest in studio today.

SIMONE LEEDS: Over to the weather for a look at the five-day forecast.

CHAPTER 39

DELILAH

I lean forward in my seat and glance through the windshield of my car. "You're sure she'll be here?"

Gianna tucks her feet under her in the passenger seat, unconcerned. She's reclined the seat all the way back, a bag of Doritos open on her chest. "She's already here."

"What?" My head snaps in her direction so fast, my neck cricks. "What do you mean?"

Gianna pops a chip in her mouth. "Her meeting with Keith started fifteen minutes ago."

"What? I thought we were out here keeping watch."

Gianna shrugs. "I thought you just wanted to have snacks in your car."

"Gianna," I hiss. "This isn't part of the plan."

"What do you mean? This *is* the plan." She holds up one Doritos-crusted finger. "Get Ava Monroe to the office." She flicks up another. "Casually run into her while picking up the rest of your things." She holds up her thumb. "Lure her into a meeting space and speak your truth."

I slap at her hand. "Don't use the word lure. You make me sound like a psychopath."

"Fine. *Encourage* her to find a meeting space with you."

I swat her again. "But she's meeting with Keith."

Gianna slaps me back, then turns her body, clutching her chips to her chest. "She had to have a reason to come to the station, didn't she? I sent her a bogus email from Keith setting it up."

"And how do you expect me to *speak my truth* if Keith is in the room discrediting everything I say?"

She rolls her eyes. "He won't be in the room."

"What? How?"

"Because it is part of the plan." Mark appears in the front window of the news station, executing a series of complicated hand gestures. Gianna huffs and very reluctantly gives him a thumbs-up back. "This man and his need for codes," she grumbles. "He could have just texted me." She reaches down and rockets the seat back up. "All right. Let's go."

I blink. "Go? Right now?"

Gianna is already halfway out of the car. "Yes. Let's go. You have a very limited window of time."

I rush to follow her, anxiety squeezing at my lungs. "What do you mean, limited window of time? This isn't what we talked about."

The original plan was to bump into Ava while she was at the offices for a routine budget meeting, then convince her to give me my job back. I have a file folder full of data points and testimonials, a Post-it note with a small *Demand more* scribbled on top slapped to the front of it.

I follow Gianna across the parking lot, resisting the urge to duck behind the light poles and trash cans like I'm in some budget-friendly spy feature.

"I thought Keith had a dentist appointment today," I whisper-hiss.

It was the only reason I felt comfortable with this plan. I don't want to see him at all.

"His dentist appointment was canceled." She pulls the door of the station open. Mark is waiting for us, silently ushering us in the opposite direction we should be going. Gianna glances at me over her shoulder. "We called an audible."

"Who is *we*?" I whisper-hiss. *When was this decided? Why didn't anyone warn me?*

Gianna's eyes soften as we hustle down a hallway. "Trust me, okay?" Her hand reaches for mine. "We've got it covered."

"Where's Jackson?"

Her mouth twitches. A smile lingers behind her eyes. "He's executing his part of the plan."

"He has a part?"

"It was his idea."

I am flying blind. Not a single thing is going how I thought it would. Mark grips my arm and steers me into an unmarked room. Gianna follows quickly, snapping the door shut behind us.

I glance around, bewildered. "Is that a crab?"

There's a mascot costume discarded in the corner, the head tipped on its side, crab legs protruding from the cheeks like some sort of aquatic Frankenstein's monster. One of the pincers is holding a microphone. I'm honestly sort of surprised Keith has never made me wear this on air.

"Oh. Yeah. There was a short-lived mascot for the television station back in the eighties. This is where he stays now."

I stare at the grotesque, crumpled heap on the floor. "How short-lived?"

"He was on one broadcast, and the viewer outrage was swift and unanimous." She snaps her fingers in front of my face. "Focus. Ava will be here in a minute. Do you feel ready?"

"She's coming to the room with the crab?"

"Delilah."

"I mean, I guess I'm ready." I clutch at my file folder. "You guys are handling Keith?"

Mark doesn't look up from his phone, thumbs moving furiously. "The distraction is in place."

"What distraction?"

"Honestly, Delilah. You're asking so many questions and none of them are the right ones." Gianna grips my shoulders. "There have been some adjustments, but your part of the plan hasn't changed. Do exactly as we practiced. Get your job back. Take Keith down." She shakes me back and forth. "Save the day."

"That seems a little dramatic."

"It's exactly as dramatic as it needs to be."

A knock sounds at the door. Three quick, light raps. Gianna cracks open the door, and Maggie pokes her head through.

"Ava will be walking down the hallway in three minutes," she whispers. "Everyone is in their places." She flashes me a smile. "Good luck, Delilah."

"That's our cue." Gianna grabs Mark by the wrist and starts hauling him out of the room. "Count to thirty, then walk down the hall toward your desk. Make it seem like an accident, okay?"

I nod. This part of the plan I remember. We were supposed to make it look like I was coming to retrieve the rest of my items, then run into Ava in the hall.

Mark, Gianna, and Maggie quickly leave, the door snicking shut behind them. I take a deep breath, hold it in for the count of two, then release it. I squeeze my eyes shut. As much as I love Gianna, I wish it were Jackson who had waited with me in the car. Maybe he could have kissed *me* as a distraction this time.

"Like a lamp," I whisper to myself, starting the slow count to thirty. I hear heels clicking own the hall at twenty-seven, and I slip out, file folder under my arm.

Ava Monroe is the picture of professional elegance. Sleek gray bob. Dark, winged eyeliner. An evergreen sweater and a smart pencil skirt. A flicker of surprise flashes across her face before she schools her expression.

"Delilah," she says, her low voice melodic in the otherwise empty hallway. "This is certainly a surprise."

"Hello, Ava." I clutch my file folder so hard the thick paper crinkles under my grip. "I was hoping for a minute of your time."

"I was wondering why I was summoned for an emergency budget meeting Keith seemingly had no idea about." A rare smile breaks across Ava's severe features. "Though I will say, I did enjoy watching him hustle around his office looking for something to present to me."

I roll my lips against my grin. "I'm sorry there was so much... subterfuge, but I wanted to have a chance to speak with you. Uninterrupted."

"I can see that." She gestures at the file folder that's beneath my hands. "All right, Ms. Stewart. What do you have for me?"

I glance down at the file folder holding the evidence we compiled against Keith. Gianna and I practiced my talking points. The order in which I'd reveal all my facts. I know exactly what I'm supposed to say, but I flatten my palms against it instead, keeping it closed. I'm so tired of the scheming and the plotting. I've been twisting myself into knots for weeks trying to be a version of myself that's damned near perfect to make up for all the mistakes I've made. But I don't need to be perfect.

I've just got to try.

"Do you know why I wanted to be a meteorologist?"

Ava settles back in the busted-up chair that's missing an arm, looking like a queen on her throne. "Why?"

I blow out a breath and summon my courage.

"When I was a kid, my grandpa used to turn on the weather report while I was getting ready for school. The five-day forecast was the soundtrack to every half-soggy bowl of cereal I had between the ages of five and eighteen. My whole day was shaped by those forecasts. What to wear. What to expect. But do you know what my favorite part was?"

Ava shakes her head, still with that unreadable look on her face. It's easy to see how she became the head of a multimedia powerhouse. She radiates calm, competent energy.

I try to channel some of it.

"I loved that the reporter knew the city. He knew what streets were prone to flooding. He knew which neighborhoods had outdoor festivals and when they were. He knew the best tailgating spots, and when people would start lining up at the lots. He knew Baltimore, and he made sure the rest of us did too."

I twist my fingers together. "All I've ever wanted to do is be a part of that, but Keith has made it impossible to do my job well. Last week I quit because I thought it was my only option, but I know my value." *Finally.* I know my value. "You might look at me and think the way I behave on camera is silly or juvenile or—I don't know—some sort of a gag. I know I've made my fair share of mistakes. But it makes our viewers feel like they're a part of my community. Because they are. And I'm a part of theirs too." I squeeze my hands together beneath the table. Gather my courage and *try*. "The real mistake I made was when I quit a week ago. This is where I deserve to be. I would like my job back. And I'd like for some changes to be made."

Ava watches me with sharp, contemplative eyes. I try not to fidget, but the silence is unbearable.

Finally, she says, "I agree."

"You do?"

Ava's smile is faint, but there. "Was that not the whole point of your speech? To convince me?"

"It was, but—" I decide now is probably a great time to stop talking. "It was," I say.

She nods, then leans forward with her elbows on the table. "Some things are starting to become clear," she says wearily. Her pointer fingers taps against the back of her hand as she studies me. "I'm assuming that you were *not* the one who made the request to move to features?"

I shake my head. My heart feels like it's about to flutter out of my chest, and not entirely in a good way. I'm not built to withstand high-stress situations.

"Keith has been my only line of communication into this news station for quite some time. I can see now that somewhere along the way, he began to shape the narrative to suit himself. I apologize for the oversight, Delilah. It won't happen again."

I'm almost afraid to ask, but I force myself to. I won't come back to this office if things don't change for me. It will hurt to walk away again, but at least I'll do it with the knowledge that I've tried everything I could. "And Keith?"

"I believe Keith will find it's time for him to retire." She stands, smoothing down her skirt. I do the same, rising slowly. I can't believe it was truly that easy. It's both an incredible relief and unbearably frustrating. That I could have ended Keith's reign of terror years ago, if only I was brave enough to stand up for myself. Ava collects her things. "I'll give him the news before I leave, assuming he's done with that man in the turtle suit."

The words float around me like alphabet soup, arranging and rearranging.

"Turtle suit?"

This time there's no mistaking Ava's grin. "There's a man in a turtle suit currently rambling his way through a weather report." She grips the door handle and pulls, eyes sparkling. "It's a very good distraction."

JACKSON CLARK: Temperatures at this time of the year average between thirty-four and fifty-two. This morning, we saw temperatures around forty-two. That's about eight degrees higher than the average low, which, of course you know. You can do math.

JACKSON CLARK: I mean. I hope you can do math. I hope you can do that sort of math.

[pause]

JACKSON CLARK: I'm trying really hard not to tell you about the history of the Fahrenheit temperature scale, but it's difficult.

[pause]

JACKSON CLARK: All right, so the United States' insistence to use the Fahrenheit model is deeply antiquated. It was useful in the eighteenth century, back before thermometers existed, but those exist now, so—

CHAPTER 40

JACKSON

The turtle suit is trying to kill me.

It's at least two sizes too small and there's no air flow. I'm roasting alive under the bright lights of the studio with Delilah's remote in the palm of my hand. The decision to wear the turtle suit was a last-minute one and I'm sort of regretting it now, but here we are.

Standing in front of a weather map with a turtle shell on my back, staring into the fathomless depths of Mark's camera while Keith paces the length of the studio like a wild animal. He can't interrupt me when I'm live on the air without looking like an ass, so all I need to do is stay live on the air. I've had better ideas, but I've also certainly had worse. All I care about is that Delilah gets the time she needs to talk to Ava.

Easy enough.

Or it would be, if I'd had any sort of script when I stepped onto this set. Instead, I've been following every errant thought that crosses my mind, including the history of ancient scientists. For once I'm not trying to fight the weather rambles. I'm leaning in.

"Daniel Gabriel Fahrenheit was, uh—" Next to the camera, Keith gestures wildly as he attempts to force me off, his face beet red and fuming. I covertly flick him the middle finger. Delilah did say the camera hits from the waist up, right? Well, I guess it doesn't matter now. "Fahrenheit was a German scientist. Born in 1686. And while most of the world adopted the Celsius system in the mid-twentieth century—"

"Jackson," Simone interrupts from the news desk, her chin in her hand and a laugh in her voice. "Do you think you could tell us what to expect with this afternoon's rain showers, and not about old German scientists?"

I'm grateful for the redirect.

"Oh, yeah. Sure. Thanks, Simone." I squint at the reference screen to the right of the camera, nudging my glasses up my nose. The strap for the turtle shell digs into my neck. This is a sensory nightmare. "Looks like there's about a thirty percent chance of showers. That means there's a thirty percent statistical probability that at least 0.01 inches of rain will fall at any given point within the forecast area during the specified time period. It's not about how much of the area will get rain, but rather the likelihood of rain at that specific location. That's, uh, that's a common misconception about forecasts."

Keith shifts his body so he's standing fully in front of the screen I'm supposed to be reading from, blocking it. We make eye contact. I don't look away. When we first started this thing, Delilah told me to pretend I'm talking to my sisters. But I'm not thinking about Penelope and Adeline right now. I'm thinking about Delilah, and her doughnut sled and her pale pink car with the dinged-up bumper. I'm thinking of the way she looks curled in my sheets and the way her breath hitches when she's excited. The microphone in her hand. That overflowing box of things she couldn't fit in her trunk.

"It's no secret that I'm not the one who is supposed to be reporting the weather right now." I drag my attention away from Keith and look into the camera. "Delilah should be here."

The set is almost eerily silent. I can hear my blood rushing in my ears. The heavy *whomp whomp whomp* of my heart.

"It also shouldn't surprise you that I haven't gotten much better at this over the last couple weeks. I think I'm always going to be a bit of a mess when it comes to broadcasting." I lift my arms and drop them. "But I wanted to try. For Delilah. Because she always tries, even when it's hard."

Behind the camera, a door quietly eases open and shut. Delilah stands at the very edge of the too-bright light that spills from the television set, blinking at me in shock. I see her mouth move, but I can't hear what she says.

"I've made a lot of mistakes," I tell the camera. I tell *her*, watching as her face softens. "But I think underestimating Delilah Stewart might be the worst of them. But I can promise you, I won't make that mistake again." She twists her hands together and I forget for a second that I'm live on the air. Until Simone clears her throat from the other side of the stage, and I forcibly drag my attention back to the camera. "We don't deserve her, Baltimore, but we're going to do our best. Okay?" I clap my hands together. "Okay. Here we go. Partly sunny skies. Maybe. I don't know, guys. Read the *Farmers' Almanac*."

I toss the weather-clicker-thing over my shoulder and step off the set, heading straight for Delilah. I grab her wrist and tow her after me, ignoring the press of people around us. It looks like the whole station made it to the studio for that report, and a late rush of nerves has me feeling jittery. Keith bellows Delilah's name, but I don't look back. I urge her along faster, encouraging her in front of me, blocking her body with mine.

Gianna can handle Keith. I'm sure Mark would love to watch.

I finally stop in between a stack of old speakers and an unmarked door, the space narrow but secluded. It's quiet back here. As private as a television studio in the middle of a broadcast can be.

Delilah stares up at me, her body pressed to mine.

"You're wearing the turtle suit," she whispers.

I nod.

A wet, choked laugh sputters out of her. "Why are you wearing the turtle suit?"

I curl my fingers around her wrists, rubbing my thumbs over the butterfly wings of her pulse. We've shared so much with each other, but this feels different. This feels like cracking open a door to a hallway I've never been brave enough to explore. I pull in a deep breath, then let it out slowly.

"Because I wanted you to know you don't have to be alone anymore." Her fingers twitch and I slide my hands up so we're palm to palm. I tangle our fingers together. "I wanted you to know that if you have to dress up as a turtle, then I'm going to dress up as a turtle too."

Her pretty eyes are wet, luminous. "Don't make any promises. Turtle suits might very well be in my future again."

"You got your job back?"

Delilah nods, pride flashing across her face in the dim light of this too-narrow back-set hallway. "Ava offered it to me. She said she'll take care of Keith. Early retirement." She huffs. "It's more than he deserves, honestly, but I'll take it. Turns out I can be assertive when I want to be."

I snort. "Of course you can. You got several weeks of practice giving me all sorts of trouble."

Her face softens. "You like my trouble," she whispers.

She says it like a secret, like a confession, and I hear all the words that fill the space in between. *How long are you going to want my trouble?*

Delilah has been the brave one, the strong one, the resilient one this entire time. Maybe now it's my turn.

"Yeah," I say. "I do." I make sure she's looking at me when I say, "I will. Always."

She shifts closer, resting her chin in the middle of my chest. One tear glances down her cheek, and then another. "Always," she whispers back.

I let go of her hands so I can cup her face instead, wanting so badly to feel the shape of her beneath my palms. My thumbs rub at those damned tears. "This morning, when I was getting in the turtle suit, I was thinking about that thing you always say," I tell her. "At the end of every broadcast. *And now, back to you*."

"I know it's silly, but—"

I shake my head. "It's not silly. It's yours." I have to swallow around the heavy press of it. The realization that this is true. This is right. This is exactly where I'm supposed to be.

"But I was thinking about it and thinking about all those run-ins we've had with each other over the years. The pudding incident. The car parking. That time you broke off my rearview mirror with a hockey stick."

"Did I?"

I nod, tucking some of her hair behind her ears. "You did. It's almost like—it's almost like the universe kept bringing me back to you. Or, I don't know, throwing you directly in my path. And now," I say with a grin, "back to you. Every mishap, every accident, every—" I laugh. "Every hallway collision and spilled coffee. It's always been me coming right back to you. You're the end of every sentence, Delilah. I've just been too stubborn to see it."

Her lower lip trembles before she catches it with her teeth. "You said you don't believe in fate."

"But I believe in you," I rasp. "God, Delilah. Do I believe in you."

Her face crumples and her nose scrunches, the cutest little divot between her eyebrows.

"Don't cry," I laugh.

"Then don't say things like that to me." She sniffles, composing herself with a shuddering inhale. "Does that mean you could love me?" she asks. "Someday? Because the way I feel about you, Jackson, I—"

I cut her off with my mouth against hers. I angle her chin up with a press of my thumb and I'm—I'm too rough, a little desperate, but it feels like my whole body is humming.

I pull back and Delilah sways after me. Our noses brush and I dip down to drag another kiss against her mouth. Two, just because I can.

"Yeah," I whisper and she sighs out something sweet. "I can love you in the mountains and I can love you back home. Watch and see how good I'm going to be at it."

She laughs, then peppers kisses all over my face. My cheeks, my chin, the tip of my nose and the bridge of my glasses.

"And now?" she asks, holding on to me tight.

"Back to you," I reply, curling my arms around her. I pull her closer until I can feel her heart tucked to mine. "Always right back to you."

AIDEN VALENTINE: So how did you two meet?

JACKSON CLARK: You know how we met.

AIDEN VALENTINE: For the sake of the show you are currently on, Jackson. How did you meet?

JACKSON CLARK: But the listeners know we met through that weather report.

JACKSON CLARK: We are both meteorologists.

AIDEN VALENTINE: But you're not here as a meteorologist.

AIDEN VALENTINE: You are here as a person who is dating another person.

AIDEN VALENTINE: On the romance hotline.

JACKSON CLARK: But—

DELILAH STEWART: I heard his voice on the radio.

DELILAH STEWART: Before I knew you were the guy leaving me Post-it notes on my window, I heard your voice.

JACKSON CLARK: Really?

DELILAH STEWART: Yup. You were talking about atmospheric instability.

DELILAH STEWART: I thought you had a nice voice.

DELILAH STEWART: Do you remember when you saw me? For the first time?

JACKSON CLARK: Yeah, uh–

DELILAH STEWART: You can say it.

JACKSON CLARK: You were dressed like a chicken in the parking lot.

DELILAH STEWART: [laughs] Of course I was.

JACKSON CLARK: And you were laughing at something someone said.

JACKSON CLARK: I thought you were cute.

DELILAH STEWART: Even as a chicken?

JACKSON CLARK: Yeah. Even as a chicken.

EPILOGUE

DELILAH

"It's a little muggy out here today as the humidity settles in, which means storms might be on the horizon." I glance down at the notepad in my hands—a new addition, courtesy of Jackson. The sparkly stickers decorating the front of it were my idea, of course, and the glitter pen shoved through the spiral is part of a set from the girls.

But the Post-it note smooshed in between the cover and my notes is all Jackson, and I smile as I read it quickly. Then I remember I'm live on television and I have a broadcast to finish. "Storm chances are hovering around forty-five percent, but I expect that to increase as the afternoon wears on. Stay cool out there, Baltimore." I snap the notebook shut. "And now, back to you."

The little red light on Mark's camera goes out and he straightens, giving me a thumbs-up. To the left, Jackson continues eating his ice-cream cone, his long legs stretched out in front of him on the park bench. The girls are practicing their cartwheels on the grass behind him and something warm and fuzzy settles in my chest.

This is how our Sundays go.

Sheets that smell like Jackson's shampoo, and a coffee on the nightstand, kept warm by one of those fancy electric coasters. Voices and laughter drifting up through the floorboards. Pancakes on the counter. A kiss brushed against my temple and more, later. Indecent ones stolen up against his closed bedroom door when I go upstairs to change. Weather broadcasts live from the park, Jackson waiting—always waiting—to the left of the camera.

Post-it notes stuck in notepads.

While Mark packs up the equipment, I wander over to Jackson, his blue eyes shining at me from behind his glasses. I settle myself on the bench next to him, leaning against his shoulder heavily until he relents with a sigh, holding the ice-cream cone in front of my face.

Plain vanilla custard. Nothing extravagant for Jackson. The occasional swirl of chocolate, if he's feeling daring. "One of these days," I tell him, around a mouthful of stolen ice cream, "you're going to get me in trouble with your little notes."

Jackson smiles at me, pleased. "I told you. I like your sort of trouble."

My heart does a happy little flip-flop in my chest.

I was so worried that I'd be a phase for Jackson. A test to himself to prove that he could deal with my chaos on a daily basis. That he could be *fun*. But he's shown me—with every cup of coffee, with every pack of candy hidden in my jacket pocket, with every note taped to the window of my car—he's shown me that I'm not a novelty.

I glance at the note in my hand. A simple *I love you* written in his neat, slanting handwriting. A frankly disturbing-looking smiley face right underneath.

I like these notes so much more than the ones he used to leave me.

Though he still corrects my parking. And grumbles about the

half-empty coffee mugs I leave all over the house. That hasn't changed.

I pat his knee. "Ready to go?"

He nods and stands, letting me have the rest of the ice cream cone. We'll go to Skullduggery after this for a box of pastries, then spend the afternoon with Grandpa Gus. He's been teaching the girls how to play chess, and they've been teaching him how to do various TikTok dances. More and more of his days are becoming fuzzy, but at least they're filled with laughter instead of frustration.

Jackson pulls a stack of napkins from his pocket and busies himself with cleaning off his hands, quick, efficient movements that I'm far too focused on. He calls the girls and they go running to the car, dark blond hair streaming behind them.

Then he looks at me and smiles, his hand sneaking its way back to his pocket. He fumbles with something in there and my flip-flopping heart turns to a free fall. He's been doing that a lot lately. Toying with the small piece of rose gold I found buried in his sock drawer three weeks ago. He likes to carry it around with him, I know. Probably waiting for the perfect moment. For all the details to come together exactly right.

But I've never been one to worry about the details. The big picture suits me just fine. And I know that with Jackson, I'll always be coming right back to him.

So I can be patient.

I can also sneak a peek in the sock drawer every couple of weeks.

His face softens the longer he looks at me and he holds out his hands. I launch myself into his arms instead, laughing when he grunts. He urges me closer, both arms wrapped around my middle, the look on his face so damned earnest I want to stay in this moment forever. On a hill that overlooks all of Baltimore, sun on my skin and Jackson's adoration warming me from the inside out.

"Jackson and Delillaaaaahhhh!" someone yells from far off in the park. "Weather togetherrrrrr!"

Jackson rolls his eyes, but I laugh.

"I knew it would stick!"

"Like a staple to the head," Jackson grumbles, but he's smiling.

"You really don't miss being on TV with me? Not even a little?"

He shakes his head. "Absolutely not."

"But you got so good at it!"

His eyebrows arch up. "I think you're biased."

"Actually, I think I'm the expert." I wiggle my way out of his arms and twist my fingers through his, towing him toward the car. "I can't believe you won't report the weather with me anymore."

"Why would I restrict myself to three times a day when I can have you whenever I want?" He steers me toward the passenger side of his car, opens the door, and guides me in so I don't smack my head against the top. He rests his forearms against the frame, smiling down at me while I situate myself. "I got everything I wanted, Delilah."

"A promotion? A newfound confidence in the European model?"

"No, baby." His blue eyes shine bright in the afternoon sun. "You."

ACKNOWLEDGMENTS

When I started thinking about who Delilah would be, I knew I wanted to create a character who was unapologetically whimsical. So often in media, we see the sunshine girl portrayed as a manic pixie fever dream. No one takes her seriously. She's not allowed to be strong. She's a bit of comic relief and a bit of a joke. I knew with Delilah that I wanted her softness to be a source of strength. I didn't want her to change a single thing about herself to be worthy of love. I wanted Jackson to see all her bright spots and love those pieces of her just as much as the rest.

I have a Delilah in my life. Her name is Adri, and her great big heart is her strength too. She's colorful and kind, and even when things at her work become very heavy, she makes sure to bring a little sunshine to the people around her. She wears her heart on her sleeve unapologetically. So my biggest thank-you goes to you, Adri. For your bunny key chains and your softness. You have shown me in a million different ways that leading with empathy is the bravest thing we can do. I love you and your pink pants.

Writing this book came at a very turbulent time for me. I had just had my son and postpartum left me feeling like I was drifting outside of my body. I'd like to thank everyone who was patient with me—in particular, my editor Kristine and my agent, Kim.

Unfortunately for you, Kristine, I think now you'll always have to deal with a first draft that is in absolute shambles.

Thank you to the rest of the Berkley team for making me look good, particularly Mary, Kristin, Anika, and Katie. And thank you to the always delightful Pan Mac team, especially Kinza, Carol-Anne, and Chloe.

Thank you to all the incredible, brilliant women in meteorology who patiently walked me through the ins and outs of weather broadcasting. Thank you in particular to Megan at the National Weather Service. Your insight on weather models is positively unmatched.

I always say every book starts and ends with Annie, and this book is no exception to that rule. Sharing this with you remains one of my greatest joys. I'm so grateful for all that you do.

I'd also like to thank my husband, who brought me tea and listened to me whine and gently encouraged me to go up to the office and take some time for myself (and Jackson and Delilah). It's always me coming right back to you.

And last but never least, a very heartfelt thank-you to every reader who picks up this book. You changed my life with Lovelight, and you changed it again with *First-Time Caller*. There are no words to express to you how grateful I am. You have given me my dream, and I will hold on to that always.

Keep reading for a preview of

LOVELIGHT FARMS

the first book in B.K. Borison's Lovelight series, available now!

There's this bar in the city that Luka and I like to go to. The beer is cheap, the floors are sticky, and when I kick the jukebox in the bottom right corner, it'll play Ella Fitzgerald thirteen times in a row exactly. It's perfect.

But sometimes on a Saturday night when the bar gets crowded and bodies press close, I have trouble holding my space. Emboldened by whiskey, it's always inevitable that a hand lands on my ass or some pretty, dumb thing who thinks he's a gift and a delight leers down my shirt. And always, Luka slips his hand over my shoulder, under my hair, and presses it to the nape of my neck. He pulls me close and tucks his chin on top of my head. I fit perfectly there, folded in close to his body. I find my space.

I've thought about that a time or two in the stillness of night. How his hand feels against my skin, his palm gently cupping the back of my head, the move both possessive and reverent. I've thought about what it might feel like for his fingers to tighten, to sift up into my hair, to pull and angle me until his mouth finds mine.

I've thought about a lot of things when it comes to Luka. Things you shouldn't think about your best friend.

We met when I was twenty-one years old. I ran smack into him as I was leaving the hardware store, lost in a shadow of grief I couldn't shake. It clung to me like an uncomfortable blanket, relentless since the passing of my mom just three months earlier. I remember standing in one of the aisles, holding a mismatched set of nuts and bolts, determined to do something with all my listless energy. Build a birdhouse. A new shelf for the hallway. I stumbled into Luka on the front steps when I was leaving, and he cupped his hands around my elbows to hold me steady. I remember staring at his caramel brown hair just starting to curl from beneath his baseball hat, the way his smile pulled at one side of his mouth before the other. It felt like the first time in a long time I noticed anything. Luka had cleared his throat, steadied my arms, and asked if I wanted grilled cheese. No "Hello." No "How are you?" Just "Wanna go get a grilled cheese?"

I don't know what made me say yes. I'd barely been talking to people I had known for years at that point. I was existing at best. Floundering at worst. But I went with Luka and ate grilled cheese at the little café in town. It turned out his mom had just moved to Inglewild, and he was helping her get settled. I offered him the array of hardware I picked up, and he had stuttered a surprised laugh. I can still remember the rasp of his fingers against my palm as he took the stupid wing knob I had aimlessly purchased.

Luka called it kismet. He had been on the way to the store for that exact piece of hardware.

From there, we fell into a routine. Whenever he was in town, he managed to find me, and we got grilled cheese. Grilled cheese turned into afternoon walks through the park and early-morning farmers markets. Afternoon happy hours and trivia nights. His trips to Inglewild became more frequent, and he invited me to stop by if I ever found myself in New York. I got brave and tried, booking a bus ticket on a whim.

Luka filled the empty places in my life slowly, carefully, with his easy smile and stupid jokes. He brought me back to myself.

And it's been that way ever since.

Frustratingly, perfectly platonic.

This wouldn't be any different, I try to tell myself. Asking Luka to pretend for five days would just be . . . a friend helping a friend. I'd do the same for him or Beckett or Layla. It doesn't have to—it doesn't have to mean whatever my mind seems fixated on having it mean.

Layla's suggestion isn't the first I've thought of it. Of course I've thought of it. I've been trying to ask him all week. He's the reason I wrote it down in the first place. Call it wishful thinking or living a fantasy, but I know when I typed those words who I was thinking of.

But it does feel a little like crossing a line we've both been careful to hold. A line I have been absolutely meticulous in my desire to hold. Luka is the very first person in my life who hasn't disappeared. He's more than my best friend—he's tradition and familiarity. He is homemade Pop-Tarts on the first Saturday of the month. He is late-night viewings of *Die Hard* in the sticky summer heat, both of our phones propped up on our respective coffee tables. He is pizza with extra mushrooms and light sauce, a crust that has to be perfect.

The relationship I have with him is the closest thing I have to family. I can't—I wouldn't—risk that for a chance to see what we could be.

Even if I wonder. Even if the reason I haven't been with anyone in seventeen months is because I always inevitably compare every man against Luka, and I'm always left disappointed.

But maybe this idea—this pretending to be together—maybe this is the solution. After a week of pretending, I can get it out of my system. Get *him* out of my system. I can stop with the wondering and the comparing and just move on.

After all, if something were supposed to have happened with Luka, wouldn't it have happened already?

The thought aches like an old bruise, one I press my thumb in from time to time just to feel the dull hurt of it. Because the truth is, there have been times when I thought he might want something different too. Sometimes after a night of drinking, I'll catch his gaze lingering on the curve of my shoulder or the swell of my bottom lip. His touches become freer. A hand on my hip as he swings me around the tiny dance floor. His forehead pressed against mine. Moments frozen in time throughout the years, always just for a second or two. But it has always been enough to make me feel like maybe he might want me the same way I've always wanted him. More than a friend.

More than anything.

But then I press that bruise and tell myself it's better this way. Because this is the way I get to keep him.

"I'm not sure he's in town that week," I respond to Layla after a lengthy retreat down memory lane, very aware it's a thin excuse at best.

She gives me an unimpressed look. "He lives three hours away. Plus, haven't I seen him like twice this month already?"

Beckett decides this is a fine time to chime in. "And didn't you ask him to come home for the strawberry jam cook-off in April?"

I sink farther into my chair. "He loves strawberry jam."

Beckett heaves himself out of the tiny leather chair and wipes his palms on his thighs. He has officially removed himself from this conversation. Mentally, he's somewhere amongst the balsams humming a merry little tune, a fresh loaf of zucchini bread cradled gently in his hands.

"I'm leaving," he announces and turns on his heel.

Layla hops up to join him and curls her hand around his elbow before he can get too far. She points a threatening finger in my direction. "Ask Luka, or I'll ask for you."

I don't even want to know what that would involve. A PowerPoint deck, probably. My total and utter humiliation, likely.

As if on cue, my phone skitters across my desk. It gives one long violent buzz and then comes to a standstill. I turn it over carefully and stare at my notifications, a perfect storm of anxiety pulling in my gut and creeping over my shoulders.

7 MESSAGES
Luka

3 MESSAGES
Charlie

1 MESSAGE
Charlie, Brian, Elle

Ah, crap. Not many people have their dad in their address book with their first name, but that about sums up my relationship with my father. I decide to tackle that one first.

> BRIAN: We'll be having our Thanksgiving dinner the first weekend in November. Estelle, you may bring a pumpkin pie.

I may bring a pumpkin pie. Awesome. I bet if I were the type of person to save text messages, I'd have this exact same message on this exact day at this exact time from last year. In fact, I'm not sure my father has ever sent me a text message beyond this little nugget. That explains the three text messages from Charlie, then. I delete the group chat with my dad, his wife, and my half brother and move straight to the next.

> CHARLIE: He sure has a way with words, doesn't he?
>
> CHARLIE: Don't let him get to you.
>
> CHARLIE: Dare you to bring pecan.

I huff a laugh and send a stupid GIF—something with a dog and flames that sums up my overall feelings at being summoned like a petulant child. My dad and his family do not celebrate Thanksgiving on the first weekend of November, but it is the one I am invited to so my dad can check off his yearly holiday box. Maybe it assuages his guilt for the way he left me and my mom high and dry, or maybe Elle makes him do it. Whatever the reason, it is always a painfully awkward dinner broken up only by Charlie's well-meaning attempts at making conversation and my dad's sullen mumbling under his breath.

I'm definitely bringing pecan pie.

I pull up Luka's messages next, the stress of the day catching up to me. I think tonight will be a boxed-wine-*Sleepless-in-Seattle*-pizza-in-bed kind of night.

LUKA: How was your vendor call?

LUKA: You're cute when you're lying to me, by the way.

LUKA: Also, why are there three episodes of Naked and Afraid downloaded on my TV? Do I even know you anymore?

I sometimes forget we share streaming services. Thank god I watched those porny Netflix movies at Layla's place.

LUKA: Charlie is texting me about pecan pie.

LUKA: Dear god.

LUKA: Is Layla making pie now?

I shouldn't feel a stab of jealousy over pecan pie, but there it is, all the same. This is what Luka reduces me to.

LUKA: Sleepless in Seattle is on HBO again.

I close my eyes and press my phone against my forehead. I tap it there twice and make a decision. I'm going to do it. I'm going to ask him. I'm going to ask him and it's going to be fine.

STELLA: Can we FaceTime tonight? I need a favor.

My phone rings almost immediately, a picture of Luka from five years ago stretched across the screen. It's from when I made him try seven different pizza places in one day because I couldn't find a sauce I liked. In the picture, he's wearing a stupid hat that looks like a giant slice of pizza. He looks ridiculous.

I love it.

I let it ring a few more times and try to channel a more resilient version of myself. A version of myself that maybe doesn't have maple syrup from this morning's stress waffles still on her shirt.

I can do this. I can ask Luka for this simple thing, and nothing has to change.

"Hey!"

It's overly perky and forced, and I'm immediately met with a ringing silence. There's muffled shuffling, a door closing, and then a huff.

"Can you please just tell me what's going on?"

I fiddle with one of the pine cone air fresheners I didn't throw in my bottom drawer, twisting the string forward and back over my thumb. "What do you mean?"

I'm officially a pathological liar.

"You've been weird all week."

"I have . . . not."

"You're being weird right now," he says. He sighs again, and I hear a flop like he's just thrown his body down on his bed. I imagine the way his long legs starfish out, ankles hooked over the edge. "Come on, Stella. What's going on with you? I can't remember the last time you asked me for a favor."

I frown and turn in my chair, peering out the large bay window that looks out over the trees. We're pretty isolated all the way out here. But if you travel down the narrow dirt road that leads to our farm, you'll find the tiny town of Inglewild. About twenty years ago, someone tried to brand Inglewild as Little Florence, likening us to the stunningly beautiful city in Italy. It was an effort, I think, to pull in more tourists passing through to DC or Baltimore. Unfortunately for that marketing campaign, there are exactly no similarities between Inglewild and Florence. It didn't stick.

"About a month and a half ago," I tell him. "I made you bring me back three gallons of chocolate ice cream from that shop on the corner by your apartment. You had to buy a special cooler and everything."

His laugh rumbles over the line, and it tucks itself right between my ribs. "Okay, that's true. But you're being weird. What's up?"

My stomach grumbles and I shoot a glance at the clock. There's ramen waiting for me in my pantry. And I don't especially want to get into this here where anyone could walk in. I'd much rather have a glass of wine in hand.

"Could I call you back when I get home?" I stall for time, tossing the air freshener down on my desk. I have a bright red mark across my thumb from the string. Apparently, I want to draw this anxiety out some more. "I'm about to head out."

"Well, funny story," he drawls, "I'm actually in town visiting my mom. I can be at your place in twenty?"

Crap.

"Yeah, sure," I say faintly, panicking. Leave it to Luka. I remind myself that he is my best friend, and I have done far more embarrassing things in our long relationship than ask him to be my fake boyfriend. Like the time I threw up on his welcome mat after betting someone I could consume an entire jug of mystery wine. Or the time I cut my bangs and I wore a bucket hat everywhere we went together for eighteen weeks. I swallow the nerves.

"That sounds good."

Photo by Marlayna Demond

B.K. BORISON is the author of cosy contemporary romances featuring emotionally vulnerable characters and swoon-worthy settings. When she's not daydreaming about fictional characters doing fictional things, she's at home with her family, more than likely buying books she doesn't have room for.

VISIT B.K. BORISON ONLINE

BKBorison.com
AuthorBKBorison
AuthorBKBorison